THE PARALLEL SOCIETY COLLECTION

VOLUME 1

STUART JAFFE

The Parallel Society: Volume 1 is a work of fiction. Names, characters, places, and incidents either are the product of the author's imagination or are used fictitiously, and any resemblance to any persons, living or dead, business establishments, events, or locales is entirely coincidental.

THE PARALLEL SOCIETY: VOLUME 1

All rights reserved.

Copyright © 2024 by Stuart Jaffe
Cover art by Deranged Doctor Design

ISBN: 978-1-963517-10-1

First Edition: April, 2024
First Hardcover Edition: April, 2024

This compilation includes the following three novels:

THE INFINITY CAVERNS
All rights reserved.
Copyright © 2017 by Stuart Jaffe
Cover art by Deranged Doctor Design

BOOK ON THE ISLE
All rights reserved.
Copyright © 2018 by Stuart Jaffe
Cover art by Deranged Doctor Design

RIFT ANGEL
All rights reserved.
Copyright © 2018 by Stuart Jaffe
Cover art by Deranged Doctor Design

For Glory and Gabe,
of course

ALSO BY STUART JAFFE

Max Porter Paranormal Mysteries

Southern Bound
Southern Charm
Southern Belle
Southern Gothic
Southern Haunts
Southern Curses
Southern Rites
Southern Craft
Southern Spirit
Southern Flames
Southern Fury
Southern Souls
Southern Blood
Southern Graves
Southern Dead
Southern Hexes
Southern Hart

Nathan K Thrillers

Immortal Killers
Killing Machine
The Cardinal
Yukon Massacre
The First Battle
Immortal Darkness
A Spy for Eternity
Prisoner
Desert Takedown
Lone Star Standoff
The Puppeteer
Blowback
Prime

The Ridnight Mysteries

The Water Blade
The Waters of Taladoro
Waterfire

The Parallel Society

The Infinity Caverns
Book on the Isle
Rift Angel
Lost Time
Pages of Glass
The Bold Warrior
City of Infinity

The Malja Chronicles

The Way of the Black Beast
The Way of the Sword and Gun
The Way of the Brother Gods
The Way of the Blade
The Way of the Power
The Way of the Soul

Gillian Boone novels

A Glimpse of Her Soul
Pathway to Spirit

Stand Alone Novels

After The Crash
Real Magic
Founders

Short Story Collection

10 Bits of My Brain
10 More Bits of My Brain
The Bluesman
The Marshall Drummond Case Files: Cabinet 1
The Marshall Drummond Case Files: Cabinet 2
The Marshall Drummond Case Files: Cabinet 3

Non-Fiction

How to Write Magical Words: A Writer's Companion
For more information, please visit ***www.stuartjaffe.com***

CONTENTS

INTRODUCTION

Stories come from all sorts of strange and wonderful places, and the creation of The Parallel Society was no different. It began with a simple enough idea. I had noticed that fantasy stories featuring elderly heroes did not really exist. You might come across the odd short story or novel, but those were noteworthy because they were rare occurrences. Since I happened to be looking to start a new series at the time, this seemed like fertile ground to dig into.

Now, most writers I know agree that the real problem with new stories is not coming up with ideas, but rather sifting through the onslaught of endless ideas that plague our brains. With The Parallel Society, that problem kept me bouncing around from one crazy concept to another. Most were easily discarded. After writing nearly sixty books, I've developed a sense for this kind of thing. Not an infallible sense, but better than I had decades ago. And really, it's safe to say that elderly transformers that can only shift during the full moon, have a penchant for racecars, and speak only in ancient dialects that I don't actually know is probably a bad idea. Though, I have no doubt some of you reading this would argue.

And so, after a few weeks of trying out several of the less insane ideas, I found three pieces that appeared to fit nicely together. The first piece — heroic elderly folks. The second piece — a magic bookstore. This is a weird, little subset of fantasy novels and one that I thoroughly love. There are many books about bookstores with secret floors, secret doors, secret secrets. Magic libraries, too. Basically, any repository for special books grabs my interest, and I figured that I'm not alone. The third piece — a female lead different from what we regularly see in urban fantasy.

This turned out to be a bit controversial. See, in most urban fantasy series, a female lead is a kick-ass, super-competent warrior — often clad in leather — going around killing vampires and other beasties. She'll have a single problem that hounds her, maybe an emotional issue or a physical issue, and it is there to ground her, make her seem more human and less superhero. Nothing wrong with that. A lot of us love that kind of thing.

But I wanted to see the journey that gets us to that woman. I wanted a character that didn't have a clue about the secret world and had no real desire to be a hero. She's had her traumas, plus she's grown up in our real world. She's been taught to doubt herself, to control how she shows herself, to not be the hero of the story. But now she must.

That's how I created Roni.

For some readers, this hits too close to the bone. Roni appears to frustrate them because they want her to do the right thing, stop doubting, stop whining about it all, care more about others, and essentially, not be a normal person. They want a superhero. And while this is not that kind of series, Roni does, sort of, get there. Eventually. But not fast enough for these readers, and that's okay. Every book is not for every reader.

For the rest of you, Roni is seen exactly as I wanted her to be. A woman unprepared to take on a monumental task, but somehow (over the course of seven books) she finds the strength within to accept her role in life, to be the leader, and to kick ass.
I hope you enjoy her journey as much as I enjoyed writing it.

— North Carolina, 2024

THE INFINITY CAVERNS

THE PARALLEL SOCIETY BOOK 1

STUART JAFFE

CHAPTER 1

Veronica Rider, "Roni" to her friends, unlocked the door to the *In The Bind* bookshop and entered with a tipsy giggle. It had been a long time since she went on a date and even longer since she had bothered to drink alcohol. Two glasses of Riesling had gone to her head.

The Old Gang sat at a large square table that dominated the center reading area of the store. Gram, Elliot, and Sully all raised their heads from the store's ledgers to smile at her. Roni thought of them as the Old Gang mostly because they had been running the store since before she had been born. But also, the youngest of the group, Elliot, had recently celebrated his sixty-seventh birthday.

"How'd the date go?" Gram asked. Lillian Donaugh, aka Gram, was a rotund woman who had owned *In The Bind* from age twenty-two. The business had been in Roni's family for five generations.

"Fine," she said.

Elliot laughed. He was a large, shiny-bald black man with a larger voice. Born in Kenya, he moved to England in his twenties and then to America at forty-two, and as a result, he spoke in an exact manner as if he feared being misunderstood. "Lillian, you cannot attack the kids with those kinds of questions. Roni does not want to discuss her sexual life with her grandmother."

"Who's talking sex?" Gram said. "I just wanted to know if the date went well."

Sully, a small man with white tufts of hair ringing his head, pushed his glasses up his nose as he looked up from the ledger. "Asking if a date *went well* is the same as asking if she ended up in bed."

Gram scoffed. "Oh, poo on that. You two are the dirtiest old men I know."

"We're the only old men you know. The rest are dead."

Elliot laughed again. "Roni, you must ignore your Gram. We are happy you had a good time. You deserve it after that unfortunate man you were dating. Bob? Billy?"

"Brian," Roni said. "Thanks."

"Bastard was more like it." Gram finished writing in a few numbers and closed the ledgers. "All done for tonight. Roni, hon, will you be a dear and put these back under the register?"

"You know, I've heard there's a new-fangled contraption called a computer. It could make all that bookkeeping a ton easier."

The Old Gang stood and stretched their weary bones. Sully had a slight stoop but he appeared to straighten a bit as he said, "Sometimes, the old ways are the best ways. Never forget the power of writing words to paper. It'll amaze you."

Elliot grabbed his cane, a gnarled oak limb that he had shellacked years ago. "Ignore these old fools. When you take over, you should go ahead and modernize this place."

Roni had no intention of letting the business go under, but she also had no intention of taking over. She wanted something different for her life. Though, at thirty-two, she had hoped to have figured out what that different thing was by now.

She stepped down to the sunken reading area and collected the ledgers. "Good night, everyone."

A quick round of hugs followed. Gram grabbed her big bag — an oversized purse that she never went without — and the Old Gang meandered toward the back. An elevator would take them to the fifth floor of the bookshop where they lived.

Roni took a moment to embrace the quiet of the store at night. With only a few dim lights on, the place closed in like a warm blanket. She had grown up here — played hide 'n' seek amongst the tall aisles of endless books, hurried over after school for a snack with Gram at the big, square table, had her first kiss in the Romance section, and her first breakup near the Mysteries. If she hadn't gone away to college, she probably would have lost her virginity in the Erotica section.

A knock at the door startled her. She peered out the window to find Darin, her date, waving like a fool. Perhaps it was his dimpled grin or the rich flock of dark hair on his head, or perhaps she had been taken in by his deep voice or the fact that she had not been out in the seven months since Brian had left — whatever the reason, she felt a satisfied warmth about Darin. She chuckled at his goofiness as she let him inside the store.

A shy voice in her head reminded her that she had only just met this man a few days ago. He had walked into the bookshop one morning, spent over an hour searching the aisles, and when he finally brought a few books to the counter to purchase, he asked Roni to dinner. The question took her so off-guard that she stammered a polite refusal.

But he flashed a friendly smile and said, "I understand. These days you can't be too careful. It's a shame, though, that a man can't ask a woman on a date anymore without having known her for several weeks first. I mean, the whole point of a date — well, an initial date anyway — is to get to know each other. Right? To see if there's any chemistry. I looked over at you from that aisle and I could feel my heart beating faster. I just had to try. I really want to know if the woman on the inside is as beautiful as the woman on the outside. I'm sorry. I hope I didn't embarrass you."

"Yes."

"I truly didn't mean to. I'll get out of here and —"

"I meant that yes, I'll go out with you."

If pressed, Roni would never be able to answer why she had changed her mind. She guessed it was a combination of thoughts and feelings mixed with the simple desire to break free from her mundane life. Being single and unemployed did not fill her with joy too often. Why not go on a date and be treated with some attention?

As Darin entered the bookshop that night, he inhaled deeply. "I love the smell of an old bookstore."

"I never notice it anymore." Roni flicked off the back row of lights. She didn't want Gram to find out she had brought somebody in after hours.

"Oh, that's a shame. That old paper, the glue, the dust — it all blends into this special aroma that you can only find in a place like this." He walked along the main aisle, his footsteps making dull thumps on the wood floor, and his fingers trailed along the stacks. "You said this place belongs to your grandmother?"

"That's right. I guess one day it'll belong to me."

"Won't it go to your parents first?"

Roni hesitated. Darin looked back and she could see the worry on his face. "It's okay," she said. "My mother died when I was little."

"I'm sorry."

"You didn't know. And that's the point of a first date, right? Getting to know each other."

He grinned, but it didn't ease her much. "The first date ended an hour ago. I really enjoyed it, and well, I couldn't wait for a second date. So, here I am."

She couldn't help the warmth that reddened her face. "Okay. Date number two."

"Okay, then. Tell me about your mother."

Roni leaned against the cash register. "Not much to tell. She was a wild one. She liked cars, men, and hard booze. One night, she went out and picked up all three. Ended up dead in a ditch with a steering wheel around her neck. My father couldn't handle it. I used to think it was the cheating that got him, but as I get older, I think he just loved her so much that he couldn't function in a world without her. But he's a religious man. Suicide was not an option for him. So, he buried himself in his Bible, and that's where he'll be until age takes its toll."

She had not intended to say so much, and thankfully, stopped before divulging the rest — especially that her father lived as an inpatient at Belmont Behavioral Hospital in West Philadelphia. The dark mood that followed her words threatened to destroy the start of their impromptu second date, but Darin must have sensed the same and quickly changed the tone. "You know," he said, "from the outside, I thought this place was going to be huge."

Hiding a sniffle, she said, "It is big. Five floors. But the top floor is broken up into two apartments — Gram's apartment and one for her two business partners. The third and fourth floors are for our highly collectibles — things we can't put on display for various reasons. Sometimes it's liability. Sometimes the books are so frail, they need to be in a specially-designed climate controlled area — which we had built on the fourth floor over a decade ago."

"And the second floor?"

"More books. There's a staircase in the back and an elevator off to the side. You want to go up there?"

"No need. I was just curious."

He watched her for a short time. He had done so several times over the course of their earlier dinner, and each time, she felt an odd mixture of emotions — her body flushed with warmth at the attention even as her skin crawled under the scrutiny. Maybe she had been stupid to agree to any of this. She had the sudden urge to be done with him — at least for the night — yet she didn't want to offend him by asking him to leave.

Instead of returning his deep gaze, she stepped behind the counter.

"Oh, no. I forgot all about the day's records. Gram won't be happy when she sees I didn't update the ledgers. I was so excited about the date, I simply closed up without finishing the job."

"Go ahead and finish it up. I'll tell you about my parents while you work — if that won't be too much of a distraction," he said.

Unsure of how to make it any clearer that she was done for the night, and unsure of how he might take a more direct approach, she flashed a smile. "Sure. Okay," she said, and opened up her laptop. Tapping away on her computer, she pretended to finish up her work.

"My parents were decent folks." He rested his back against the end of one aisle. "I owe them a lot. They taught me to think for myself and to think critically — two things most kids don't learn anymore. My mother showered me with affection. A little smothering at times, but she always made sure I knew how proud she was of me. Above everything I could mention, though, the greatest gift they ever gave me was a love for reading. Going to the bookstore or the library or even getting to spend an hour browsing through Amazon — those were events for me. They wanted me to adore the written word, so they made sure each book I purchased, each book I read, each book I casually glanced at meant something."

"Sounds like good people."

"They were. My father worked in construction and my mother taught high school English. Not very high-brow professions but honest ones. They were the kind of people that never thought twice about helping out a neighbor. Real quality folks." He let his eyes wander around the bookstore. "It's because of them that I love places like this. I'm also rather fond of the people who work at places like this."

Roni forced herself to yawn. "That's sweet, but I'm really tired. I wasn't expecting a second date so soon, and I do have to work tomorrow."

"I thought you were unemployed."

"I am, but I work here a few times a week. I don't get paid, but I like to help out." She made a cheering motion with her fist. "Gotta get out there and find a job, too."

Darin paused, and Roni could not read the look on his face. She braced herself for any possibility. "Sure," he finally said, and headed toward the front door.

She wanted to smack herself. This poor guy clearly hadn't meant any harm, and now he would be leaving feeling rejected. And she liked him. Their dinner date had gone well.

"I'm sorry," she said, inwardly cringing at the meek sound of her voice. "I really don't mean to be rude. I told you at dinner that I haven't dated in a long time. This all feels a bit new."

"It's okay. You should never have to apologize for being truthful. You're tired and you've got to finish the bookkeeping. I understand."

Roni closed her laptop in case he saw that she had been playing Candy Crush. "Maybe we can go out again another night."

"Sure." He put his hand on the door. "You want to know what I always loved most about a bookstore like this? It's the little hidden places. There's always some extra special room where the really cool stuff is kept. I mean, you mentioned the third and fourth floors, but I bet you've got a basement level, too. Right?"

Roni frowned. "We do. But it's mostly old magazines and stuff that needs to be sorted through."

He snapped his fingers. "That's what I'm talking about. That's the kind of space that thrilled me when I was a kid. You never knew what you were going to find down there." He lowered his chin and lifted his brow. "I don't suppose, maybe, you'd let me see it real quick. I promise I'll go after that. It's like a nostalgia thing for me."

"I don't know. It's late."

"Please?"

She figured she had already been rude enough. Plus, if she played along, she would be done with this faster. With as much levity as she could summon, she said, "Okay. But only five minutes. Then I've got to call it a night."

As she led the way, she could feel his eager energy like a hot lamp shining on her back. She walked down the stairs and flicked on the basement light. The large area had a low ceiling and a musty odor. Many of the boxes had been sitting around for years. An old dining room table had been placed underneath one of the four bare bulbs that lit the basement.

"That's where the magic happens," she said with a slight chuckle. "We sort through boxes and decide what stays and what goes."

Darin approached the table with a bit of reverence. A crate sat to the side with a crowbar resting nearby. Books had been piled in the crate. Stacks of old LIFE and TIME magazines formed miniature towers against the table legs. He stepped in close and brushed his fingertips along the top of the table. "I could spend hours down here. Just give me a good book and I'd sit here and read away the day. You're so lucky to have this place whenever you want it."

"I never really thought of it that way."

"You should. Books are too important to take for granted." His eyes lifted to a door on the wall opposite the table. A large padlock like something from a medieval dungeon prevented the door from opening. "What's that all about?"

"Gram's private collection. And before you even ask, the answer is *No*. Nobody gets to go in there. I mean it. I grew up in this bookstore and I've never even seen it."

He shrugged. "We all have our secrets. I guess your grandmother likes to have hers a little more clearly marked than most."

Roni flickered the lights. "Okay. Your five minutes is up. Time to go."

"It went fast, but I thank you."

Darin went back upstairs and stopped at the register. He reached out and took hold of Roni's hand. She let her hand hang limp but he clamped down tight.

"I guess this is good night again." He raised her hand to his lips. "A bit shorter than I had hoped for but a pleasant second date anyway."

"I suppose we should —"

He yanked her closely and pressed his mouth against hers. She pushed him back, pulling her hands free, and made two fists.

Raising his hands as his face dropped in shock, he said, "I'm so sorry. I thought you wanted me to kiss you."

"You need to go."

"I'm sorry. I don't know why —"

"Please, go now."

"I know. I'm so sorry. I'll go. Could you just — and I'm real sorry to ask — but could I have a glass of water or something? I feel faint. This isn't like me, and I think I'm panicking here."

She looked him over. He had broken out into a sweat and his skin looked pasty. "Stay here," she said and hurried to the side room that had a refrigerator, a sink, and some cupboards.

As she grabbed a coffee mug and filled it with water, she had to marvel at how strange the evening had become. Why did Darin have to go ruin everything? Their dinner had been light, fun, and friendly. Why the pressure for this crappy attempt at a second date romancing? If he only had shown some patience, she probably would have ended up sleeping with him. A normal second date a few nights later. And on the third, she would have been itching to take him. But now — there would not be another date. She didn't even want to see him again once he left the store.

When she returned with the mug of water, Darin was no longer at the register. The front door was locked, so he could not have left the building. Setting the mug on the counter, she walked up and down the main section of the floor, glancing across from aisle to aisle.

Her heart hammered in her chest. She knew a few self-defense moves from a class she took at the Havertown YMCA a few years ago, but her racing thoughts made it difficult to focus. When she reached the back of the store, her stomach twisted — the stairs. She knew it. He had gone down into the basement.

"Darin?" she called, but not too loudly.

No answer.

"Darin?"

A loud thump came from below.

She put a tentative foot on the top step. Another thump. But before she went further, her mind woke up — she had a small container of pepper spray in her purse. Hustling across the bookshop, she tried to ease the tightness in her chest. No good.

She rummaged through her purse but couldn't find it. At length, she upended the contents onto the counter. The pepper spray fell out last. Snatching it up, she rushed back to the stairs.

Listening intently, she tried to make out what he might be doing. A metal clang followed a wooden creak.

"Oh, crap," she whispered.

Despite the sense of urgency surrounding her, Roni could only manage to take one step every few seconds. The closer she came to the basement floor, the harder each step felt. Her legs thickened like cement, fighting her from moving forward.

In a desperate desire for normalcy to reassert itself, she wanted to call out again, to have Darin call back and assure her that all was fine. She wanted to step onto the floor and find him sitting at that table, thumbing through an old magazine. He would have a sheepish look and would profusely apologize. He would leave and all would be right once more.

Except none of that happened.

When she reached the bottom of the stairs, she found the lights on but no Darin. He did not sit at the table. He did not thumb through a magazine. He did not offer his apologies.

Instead, she saw what she feared she would see. The crowbar was missing, and the padlock to Gram's private room had been pried open.

It lay in pieces on the floor.

The door stood ajar.

CHAPTER 2

Roni's teeth chattered together. Part of her wanted to race upstairs and ring for Gram. This was her room, after all. She should know that somebody had broken in. But another part of Roni feared what Gram might think.

Would she assume Roni had taken this man downstairs for a private fling? Of course, she would. Gram had many great qualities, but she also rushed to judgment, and her judgment could be harsh.

Once when she was eight, Roni wanted to help shelve the latest acquisitions. She didn't know one book from the other, so she picked up the first to catch her eye — a first edition of *Tropic of Cancer*. She never bothered to open the book, but merely started looking for a place to shelve it. When Gram saw her walking off with the book, she assumed her granddaughter wanted to read some dirty words. Gram snatched the book away and punished Roni with three weeks of cleaning the restrooms.

Standing at that open door in the basement, Roni wondered what Gram would do to her this time. After all, this room had been marked *off limits* all of Roni's life. But if she could get Darin out of there without disturbing anything, maybe Gram would never know.

In her quietest voice yet, Roni said, "Darin?"

No answer. Of course.

With small steps, she entered the room. At first, it appeared to be a bunker for books — a metal box of a room with metal shelves lined with numerous old leather-bound volumes. Fluorescent lights hung from the tiled ceiling.

As Roni walked deeper into the room, she noticed that the air grew colder with each step. The only sound — the tentative click of her heels. She stopped twice to listen for Darin but heard nothing. When she reached the back end of the room, she understood why.

A large hole in the wall opened into a cavern. A cavern? But that was the only word for it that Roni could think of. Stone walls carved out by millions of years of underground rivers and lakes. Dirt and rock stubbled the uneven ground. Stalactites hung from the ceiling, and a twisty path led downward and away.

Cool air wafted over her as she gazed out with her mouth agape. The steady trickle of water echoed off the curving walls. And in the walls, somebody had wired lights and carved bookshelves.

But as Roni followed the maze of turns further into the cavern, she noticed that the books were even stranger than their location. They were all extremely old, hardbacked, many bound in leather and a few in metal. For a while, none of them had titles — merely colored diamond shapes as if that were information enough. However, after a few minutes of walking, she came upon a new section of books unlike the others.

The cavern walls had narrowed to the width of a typical library aisle. On one side, she saw books with strange symbols on the spines and covers. Not occult symbols or New Age symbols or anything she had encountered before. Rather, these looked like symbols of a unfamiliar language, like Tolkien's elvish, one created by a single mind and not a system evolved over centuries of a civilization. On the other side, she saw similar books, except these had chains attached to the spines that stretched to rings embedded into the stone walls as if the books were held prisoner with no hope of escape.

Roni's curiosity could not stop her churning stomach. Coupling Gram's desire to keep this place secret with the chained books spelled danger in bold red letters. Roni backed up several steps. She should hurry up to Gram's apartment, wake the old lady, and get her down here. Gram would know the fastest way to find Darin and she would know which books to stay away from.

Before Roni could head up toward the bookshop, however, a loud *whoosh* came from further below followed by the unmistakable sound of a man groaning.

"Darin?" she called out. No response. "Darin, let me know you're okay. I'm not mad at you. I just want to make sure you aren't hurt."

The groan returned — drawn out and muddy.

She hastened her pace downward. Gram would have to wait. Darin's groans suggested he had fallen and needed help. Plus — and

Roni felt a twinge of guilt for this thought — there was still the possibility of finding Darin and getting him out of the basement before Gram ever found out.

As she rounded a wide bend, she saw tall stone pillars reaching into the darkness of the high ceiling. Books spiraled up along the pillars, some so high nobody could ever reach them without a fireman's ladder or sturdy scaffolding. Other books were higher still.

The groans continued and their echoes brought back a ghostly sound. She continued on, the periodic sconces her only light source. As the ground leveled out, she came upon a door nestled into the stone. It stood open.

She entered a reading room with two long tables for research and study as well as four overstuffed chairs for more casual reading. Next to each chair stood a tall reading lamp and two smaller desk lamps provided light for those at the tables. Darin sat at the furthest table, a thick volume placed right in front of him.

"Darin? Are you okay?"

With his eyes closed, he said, "Better than okay. After all the searching, after the countless times I doubted this place even existed, I'm finally here."

"I don't understand what any of this is, but we need to go back upstairs."

"Let me show you."

He lifted the cover of the book before him and it slammed out of his hands and flattened, fully open, on the table. A bright blue light burst from the pages. The whooshing sound from earlier filled the room. As if a door on a jet plane opened at twenty thousand feet, the room depressurized and the book sucked everything towards it.

The big chairs slid towards the book. The desk lamps sparked as the cords wrenched free from their power source and then tumbled into the book. Straight into the pages — through them — as if the book was a deep pit.

Roni stumbled forward a few steps. The wind grew stronger. She leaned away, reaching for the door as if caught in a sudden squall.

Darin's satisfied smile dropped into horror. He gripped the edge of the table and leaned away from the open vacuum of the book.

Roni clung to the door jamb. She yelped as her legs lifted off the ground. She heard Darin scream and his head went in first. As his shoulders sunk into the pages, his white knuckled hands kept their lock on the table — the only thing saving him.

With Darin's body blocking much of the book, Roni's legs settled onto the floor. The wind was still strong, but she could stand on her own. Part of her screamed to run, get safe, and ignore everything else. But she searched for some way to help Darin. Except if she moved in close to that book and freed him, the hurricane would resume and she would be swept into those pages.

Maybe she could use a rock to dislodge the cover and force it closed. The idea seemed far-fetched, but nothing else came to mind. Tears welled in her eyes. If he died, she would be partly to blame. Straining towards the door, she tried to recall what rocks she had seen on her walk to this bizarre room.

Everything changed when she reached the door — Gram, Elliot, and Sully stood in the way.

"Gram, I'm so sorry," Roni cried out, but Gram did not pay her any attention. The old woman's eyes locked onto Darin.

She stepped forward and opened one hand. A long chain dropped loose from her sleeve. As she twirled the chain at her side, Sully scooted over to Roni.

He pushed her towards the wall and pressed an arm on either side of her. "It'll be okay," he said and lowered his head as if he tried to move the wall.

Looking over his shoulder, Roni watched as Gram whipped the chain across the room. It latched onto the spine of the book like a giant magnet. Jerking the chain, she pulled it clear off the table, leaving Darin behind. The massive winds returned.

Roni fell forward and would have toppled over into the book if not for Sully blocking the way. He remained motionless like a stone statue, his feet firmly planted in the floor. Gram did not slide toward the open pages either. Instead, she leaned back as if in a tug-o-war with the book. Elliot held onto the chain with one hand and his cane with the other. He wore a tall-collared cape that fluttered and snapped in the harsh winds.

Darin did not fare so well. He shrieked as his grip on the table's edge slipped. The howling air continued to pull him in. Tears streamed out of his eyes and into the book, never getting the chance to touch his cheeks.

Yelling above the cacophony of wind, Elliot said, "Hold on, young man! Do not give up!"

With stuttering steps, Elliot worked his way along the chain. Once he reached as close as he dared, he locked his arm around the chain and with his free arm, he stretched toward the book with his cane. The end of the cane bumped the cover. Elliot tried to work the cane underneath to close the book, but he needed to get closer.

"Forget it," Gram yelled, the strain in her voice matching that of her entire body as she leaned further back. "Get the boy."

Elliot shifted his body toward Darin. He pressed his feet into the floor and reached out with the cane. "Grab hold," he said.

Darin stared at the cane, a lifeline dangling before him. But Roni could see the way his arms trembled. To reach for the cane meant letting go. If he missed ...

"You can do it," Elliot said.

Darin shook his head and buried his face into the table.

"Come on, now. Grab the cane."

Roni shouted, "Darin, do it!"

He gazed up at her. His eyes glistened. Everything she saw in his face screamed of his doubt. Even before he made his half-hearted attempt, she knew he had given up. Fumbling his hands free, he flapped his arms about, bumped the cane, but had no control.

Elliot lunged along the chain. But when he reached the book, Darin had already fallen in. Elliot had only time enough to pry his cane beneath the book and slam the cover closed. Any longer, and he would have joined Darin.

The wind died instantly. Sully straightened, as much as he could, and placed his hands on Roni's shoulders. "All over now."

Gram rushed forward. She stepped by Elliot without any notice of him and grabbed the book. With furious energy, she wrapped the chain around the book seven times before tucking the end underneath. Only then did she look at the others.

"Everybody okay?"

Elliot said, "I think so. Though my arthritis is going to flare up in the morning."

"You think you've got it bad? You can take a pill for your pain," Sully said. "I had finally gotten to sleep right when all this went off. Fat chance I'll be getting back to sleep tonight."

"There are pills for that, as well. Besides which, a little insomnia is nothing compared to my aches."

Gram set the book on the table and sighed. "Enough bickering. You both did a good job. Thank you. What about you, Roni? Are you okay?"

Roni stared at Gram, then Elliot, then Sully. Everything that had transpired bubbled up her throat and in a booming voice, she said, "What the fuck just happened?"

CHAPTER 3

Sully and Elliot's open-faced shock did nothing to ease Roni's swelling panic. Gram, however, snagged Roni by the ear and pulled her down into one of the chairs.

"Sit and calm down."

"How can I —"

"And watch your language, young lady. You're in enough trouble as it is."

That quieted Roni. With all that she had witnessed, she forgot that she wasn't supposed to be down there in the first place. However, being quiet and being calm were two supremely different states at the moment. Especially when Roni could see the book bumping on the table of its own accord.

Gram placed a firm hand on the cover. "Roni, look at me."

Roni lifted her eyes.

"Are you injured?"

Both men watched her carefully, and she thought all three of them held their breath waiting for an answer. She couldn't trust herself to speak. If she opened her mouth, she thought she might start babbling or screaming or something. But she managed to shake her head.

"Good," Gram said. The book bounced under her hand once more. "Sully, lock this thing down and then fix my padlock alarm on the door. Elliot, when he's done, please refile this book where it belongs."

The two old men gave quick nods and got to work. Gram put her hands on her hips and looked at the mess in the room. Shaking her head, she started pushing the chairs back where they belonged.

Sully hunched over the book. Roni watched him closely but couldn't see what he was doing. When he backed away, the book no longer moved and he had unraveled the chain around it.

Clearing his throat, he said, "All done here. Do you want to chain the spine?"

Gram gave it a moment of thought before snatching up the book. She took the chain from Sully and made a fast motion along the book's spine. As she returned to tidying up the room, Roni saw that the chain was now embedded into the middle of the spine. She leaned forward to get a better look, but Elliot swiped the book away.

As both men left the room, Gram picked up one of the tall reading lamps and reset its shade. "I'm surprised this thing survived," she said. "Never underestimate the power of dumb luck. Although, in my experience, that kind of luck usually doesn't work in your favor. This time, though, I'm glad it did — I like this lamp." She faced Roni, and her mouth tightened into a thin line. "Now, we have to deal with you."

Shrinking under her grandmother's glower, Roni glanced away. Her mind swirled in a clutter of images as fast moving as the hurricane winds from that book. Bad enough to try understanding that Darin had been sucked into a book, but trying to rectify Gram and the Old Gang with these new persona gave Roni a headache.

Gram stepped closer, looming over, and said, "This was your first date with Darin, yes?"

"What?"

With a sharp bite to her voice, Gram said, "Pay attention. You can be worried or confused or upset later. I need to know how many times you've dated Darin."

"J-Just tonight. This was our first — though, he called it our second."

"Did he threaten you? Did he threaten me?"

"No. He was fine. A little pushy. A little strange. I was uncomfortable and wanted him to leave, but he never threatened anybody."

"Then how did he get you to open the door?"

Roni looked up. "I'm fine, by the way. I wasn't hurt."

"Don't get sassy with me. I know you're fine. We already asked you that. Are you suffering memory loss?"

"No. I don't think so."

"You remember we asked if you were injured?"

With an impatient sigh that made her feel ten years old, she said, "Yes, I remember. I'm a little shaken up, that's all."

"We may not have time for you to get feeling all perfect. So, pull yourself together and answer the damn question. How did Darin get you to open the door?"

Roni flinched at Gram swearing. "I didn't open the door. He had me go for some water and when I got back, he had gone down here and smashed it open."

"I see. That's why my alarm went off. One more question — before he distracted you with the water, at any time before that, did he make a call, try to contact somebody, anything like that?"

"I don't think so."

"I need you to be sure. Did he contact anybody?"

The insanity of the evening finally flooded Roni. "I don't know! I don't know! What the hell is going on around here? How come there are caverns under our bookstore? Why is there a book that swallowed my date? And who the hell are you people?"

Breathing heavy and dabbing at her tears, Roni barely noticed Gram's hand on her shoulder. "It's going to be okay," Gram said. "Come with me."

The old woman led Roni back up into the basement and then further up to the main floor of the bookstore. She gestured to the big table and Roni sat. Gram then headed to the front counter, reached under, and produced a bottle of vodka and two shot glasses.

Despite Roni's trembling fingers, she managed to cover her mouth in surprise. "How long has that been under there?"

Gram grinned as she shuffled over to the table. "I've always kept it there — behind a sliding panel. As you're discovering tonight, this place is full of secrets." She settled in a chair next to Roni and poured two shots. "I'm sorry this happened tonight. I truly wish this all could have waited a few more years but it is what it is. I'm afraid the shocks aren't over. You need to know some more of the truth."

Roni knocked back the vodka. "I'll settle for any of the truth. None of this makes sense to me."

"I know." Gram eyed her shot glass but left it untouched. "Now, where to begin?"

"How about at the beginning?"

"That's too far back. Long before my life. Perhaps before any life began."

"Well tell me something because if you keep talking cryptically, I'm going to start screaming again."

Lacing her fingers together, Gram bumped her hands against her chin. "The world, the universe, is more complex than most people know. It is made up of many worlds, many universes, and they are meant to be kept separate from each other. Sometimes mistakes happen. Sometimes the thin veil between worlds tears open. Elliot, Sully, and I are the repairmen."

Roni poured another shot and downed it fast. "What does any of that mean?"

"You're not listening. You're trying to find some simple explanation that will dismiss what you experienced. But that's not reality. Pay attention and understand. These rips between worlds are dangerous, and as long as humans have existed, we've had individuals who could fight back, repair the damage, and protect us all."

"And that's you and Elliot and Sully?"

"Exactly."

"Just you, or are their elderly mystic superheroes all over the world?"

"Thankfully, the world only needs the three of us. These problems don't arise too often. But when they do, we're ready. But of course, as you've pointed out, we're getting old. It's time for some new blood to learn the ropes and be ready to take over."

Roni rubbed her temples. "How is any of this possible? How could you be this person and I never knew it? And what about Darin? Is he ... is he dead?"

"I don't know yet. If he's dead, he's dead and there's nothing to do. If he's alive, he should be okay for now. Us old folks aren't mystic superheroes. At least, we don't bounce like superheroes. I'm sure those boys are every bit as exhausted as I am from this evening, and you look like you could use some sleep, too."

"Sleep? But if Darin is alive, don't we have to do something?"

"We will. But we'll be no good to him if we're too tired and weak to perform our duties."

"But —"

Gram put her palm up. "You've only learned a smidge of the real world. Don't start thinking you understand what needs to be done. Now, I've explained enough for tonight. You go home and get some sleep. I promise that if Darin is alive, we'll do everything possible to get him back. In the meantime, you have big decisions to make."

"About what?"

"For starters, whether you want to know anything more. There's a lot I can share with you, but only if you're willing to take that path where it will lead. Otherwise, I'm afraid I can't tell you anything more.

You'll have to stop visiting here. I can't have you tempted to go into that room again. And, of course, you absolutely cannot tell anybody what you've learned."

"Are you going to magically wipe my brain?"

Gram chuckled. "I wish such a thing existed. That would have made my life a lot easier over the years. No, honey, nothing will stop you from telling the world except that you know the world won't believe you. In fact, they'll end up locking you away, studying you, writing papers about your mental aberrations, and in the end, you'll die stuffed in a straitjacket with your mind clouded by drugs."

"Drugs sound pretty good right now."

Placing her hand over Roni's, Gram said, "I know this a lot to take in. That's why you need to listen to your old Gram. Go home, get some rest, and decide if you really want to know all that I know, all that the world truly is. If you do want that, then you come in here tomorrow morning, and we'll show you everything. If you don't, then don't come in." She patted Roni's hand. "Now, I'm tired."

Roni knew that when Gram patted her hand after a talk, that was the polite way of saying to get out. Still feeling wobbly — and the vodka didn't help — she walked over to the counter to gather her things together. She glanced back at the table. Gram stared at the full shot glass and did not move.

"Good night," Roni said out of habit. She left the bookstore and wondered how long Gram would stay in that chair before she finally drank the vodka.

Walking to her apartment three blocks down, Roni never saw the cars, the people, or the town. Her mind juggled everything from the terror on Darin's face to the powerful strength Gram displayed as she pulled on that chain to the way Sully protected her and never budged to Elliot's brave attempt to save Darin. She thought about the idea that there were ruptures between worlds — heck, that there was more than one world, one universe. Gram promised to save Darin, but from what? Killer books? Magic chains? How could Roni be sure that any of this was true? Three old people being the protectors of the universe? That was crazier than anything she had witnessed. And now Gram wanted her to come back and hear more. Worst of all — Roni knew that no matter how late she stayed up thinking it all over, no matter how many times her brain would toss around all she had learned, no matter if she rejected it all or accepted it as gospel, she knew she would have to go back in the morning. She had to hear the rest. No matter what it meant.

Passing a narrow alley, she leaned in and threw up.

CHAPTER 4

As the morning sun warmed Roni's face, she winced and offered a slow moan that echoed in her head. Hangovers were something she thought had ended years ago in college. It took her twelve minutes to overcome the pain and get out of bed. She spent another five minutes navigating her way around the plates on the floor she had meant to get into the overflowing sink, discarding last night's clothes onto the floor, and stumbling into the shower. After washing up, fifteen minutes passed as she rummaged through piles of dirty clothes searching for something semi-clean to wear.

Exhausted from the effort, she plopped down on the side of her bed and concentrated on breathing. To her right, she had a short bookcase with all her prized hardcovers neatly arranged alphabetically. No matter what chaos arose in her life, she could always look at that bookcase and it calmed her.

She lowered her head into her hands and closed her eyes. A full minute went by in which she held her mouth shut tight for fear of throwing up on the floor. When the feeling passed, she took a deep breath and opened her eyes.

On the floor, under a bra, she spotted the photo album — the blue one with thin lines of gold swirls painted on the front, the only one she owned. It contained the only photographs she had of her mother and father. The only memories she had of them. Most of her memories from the time of her mother's death through her teens were a fuzzy mess, but whenever she wanted a clear image of them, she had her photo album.

Gram called it Roni's "Lost Time". Doctors had looked her over, tested her, and found nothing neurologically wrong. Psychiatrists went to work and said that the trauma of her loss had created a mental block into forming new memories as clearly. They suspected that once Roni had fully come to accept all that had happened, she would be fine and the block would lift.

That sort of happened, but not exactly. As high school came around, Roni had a short but intense phase in which she delved into the world of alien conspiracies. Though her experiences with Lost Time were drastically different than alien abductees, her sense of knowing others out there suffered similar things made her feel better. By the end of her freshman year, her new experiences locked into her memory in full color, texture, and sound. Her memory worked again.

But the period of Lost Time remained. She did not get back those memories, and the ones she clung to remained faint sketches of moments.

Back on her feet, with more pep but still a headache, she dressed, picked up the album and walked into her tiny living room. She managed to drink a glass of water. She considered ditching the day and wallowing in the few memories she had of her mother. No. She had to report to the bookstore.

By the time she wrestled her hair into an acceptable appearance and locked up the apartment, she had begun to feel close to human. Walking up toward *In The Bind*, she checked her phone for the time — another hour had gone by.

Why had Gram given her that vodka? Why had she accepted it?

Images of the cavern of weird beneath the bookstore rumbled around her head. Oh, yeah. There was that.

She inhaled the fresh morning air. If nothing else, Pennsylvania had some good, fresh air. Even living in Olburg, a small town of little note other than being within thirty minutes of Philadelphia — except now Roni would have to revise that statement. There was something of note about Olburg. Something big.

Walking along the brick sidewalk, a minefield with missing bricks and tree roots creating sudden swells in the path, Roni looked at the town as if she had never seen it before. She trudged uphill and while the neighborhood appeared pleasant enough — narrow homes lined with trees, a decent downtown within walking distance, a thriving community of artists, musicians, bankers, doctors, everything a town needed to function — yet it all seemed off.

How could all of what she had seen exist right underneath everyone's feet?

She pressed the heel of her hand against the side of her head. She could barely describe what she had seen let alone comprehend how it mixed with a town like Olburg. Gram had promised answers but as Roni walked closer to the bookstore, she wondered if she really wanted to know.

When she reached *In The Bind,* Elliot waited on the sidewalk. He leaned on his cane and offered a light wave as she approached.

"Good morning," he said. "Are you feeling okay?"

Roni smirked. "I'm a bit hungover. Gram's vodka packed a helluva punch."

He laughed. "That it does. Come walk with me. I'm going to fill you in on things."

Gesturing to the front door, she said, "Did Gram ask you to do this?"

"Your grandmother rarely asks; she orders. And yes, this is the way she wants it to be."

"She won't see me? I thought she wasn't still mad at me."

"Do not worry about that right now. You've got a big day ahead of you. Trust me on this. You need to walk with me."

Roni followed Elliot as he shambled his way further downtown. "Where are we going?"

"A quiet place that I really like."

He led her toward First Street, turned right, and kept going. Most of the shops had yet to open for the day. Roni thought that was odd considering nine o'clock had come and gone, but then she remembered her date with Darin was on Saturday night. For a Sunday morning, she was surprised to see anybody awake yet.

After two blocks, Elliot stopped at the locked door of the Ol' Olburg Gallery — a local art gallery that never opened on a Sunday. Mrs. Esther Simon owned the three-story building, renting the top two floors as apartments and running the gallery from the bottom, and she believed that Sunday was meant for prayer and nothing more.

Elliot glanced up and down the street before he leaned over the lock. He brought his hands up, closed his eyes, and murmured to himself. If he knelt on a prayer rug, Roni would have assumed he had taken up with his Muslim roots.

A soft click, and Elliot smiled. He turned the knob. The door opened, a bell jingled from above, and he walked in.

"How did you do that?" Roni asked.

"One of my specialties. Where Sully is good at locking things, I am good at unlocking them."

"But how? You didn't use lockpicks or a credit card or anything. All I could see was you whispering to it."

"Patience. I will explain as much as I can. I promise."

He waited for Roni to enter the gallery, then he closed the door, making sure to mute the bell. A desk had been situated off to the side of the entrance. Elliot slid open one of the drawers and pulled out a key. He used this to unlock another door which led to the main hall of the gallery.

This open area had several walls of paintings and four sculptures placed at different sections of the floor. Most of the work came from local artists of varying skill levels — paintings of farmland, family pets, and even an old galleon at sea. All of it had heart. Even the least among them showed a passion to create and express through paint or sculpture.

Elliot escorted Roni to a wall filled with color swirls in a series of abstracts. "Did you understand what your grandmother told you last night? Or were you too much in shock to take any of it in?"

"A little of both. I barely slept because I couldn't stop thinking about it all."

"Perhaps this will help. Take a look at these paintings. Imagine each one as an entire universe upon itself filled with stars and planets and life. The edge of the painting is the limit of the universe. To those inside, it may seem infinite but the truth is that it does have boundaries."

"I'm not up-to-date on my physics but I'm pretty sure Einstein or Hawking or one of those guys showed that the universe curved around like a ball. You'd never reach an edge."

"I asked for you to imagine. This is not an exact replication of reality. Besides, after everything you saw last night, are you really going to fall back on Einstein?"

"You've got a point there."

Using his cane to underscore his words, Elliot continued. "Now, each one of these paintings is a universe — a place with its own physical laws, its own chemical makeup, its own everything. Sully, Lillian, and I each have been given a special gift to aid in keeping order within our universe. We are the frame around the painting. Our job is to keep our painting within its frame and make sure the others don't come into ours. Usually that is not difficult, but on occasion it happens — sometimes by accident, sometimes by a person like your Darin."

"*Special gifts?*"

"Oh, yes. You have already seen how your grandmother controls the books and the chains that bind them."

Roni nodded. "And Sully stood like a boulder."

"That is but an offshoot of his true power. You will see what he can do later today."

"And you?"

"I can touch the life essence of a soul. I can locate and heal all sorts of things. I'm also the fittest of us three, so I am often called upon to be our muscle. The older we get, the tougher our job becomes."

"You are getting older, though, right? You're not immortal or something?"

Elliot chuckled. "No. And I wouldn't want to be. When we die, there will be others to take our place. That is the way it has always been. It is not always instantaneous, but eventually a full complement will reform. I imagine there must be similar groups in the other universes as well."

"It's just you three here?"

"That is right."

Roni covered her mouth and laughed. "I always wondered how the three of you ended up together. You always seemed like the start of a bad joke — a Christian, a Muslim, and a Jew walk into a bookstore."

"You should not assume anything about us simply by those titles."

"But the Priests and the Rabbis and the Imams, they are the ones who call on you from all over the world, right? I'm thinking about all those trips you three would take. You told me that you had religious scholars and other friends around the world who would tell you about rare books they found, but that wasn't true, was it? You were going off to fight whatever had slipped through from another universe. Right?"

"The fact that you see it that way tells me you are starting to accept the truth. To answer your question — yes and no. Most of the time, yes, we were doing our jobs to protect our world. But sometimes we actually did find rare books. Sometimes both things happened. And it is not always religious leaders who contact us. It is anybody in a unique position to know the truth and be able to respond."

A moment of silence descended upon them as they observed the paintings. Roni wanted to speak or make a noise but something told her to stay quiet. From the corner of her eye, she watched Elliot. He seemed at complete peace, content to look upon the paintings and be still.

"I'm sorry," she said. "I can't act like this is all normal."

"But it is normal. What you believed to be normal before was the crazy part."

Her head throbbed waves of pain from the bottom of her skull up into the backs of her eyes. "I really shouldn't have drunk so much. I don't usually get such a bad hangover, though."

Elliot frowned. "Did your grandmother use the bottle under the register?"

"Yeah. Why?"

"I think she was trying to help you acclimate. That bottle is a Relic with a capital R. Sometimes when we close off a tear from another universe, items fall into ours."

"Wait. Are you saying she gave me vodka from another universe?"

"I suspect so."

Roni didn't know whether to be amazed or pissed off. The latter won out. "Are we going to stand here all day or can I go back to the bookstore?"

"Not yet. You have to understand. You have to make a choice."

"I understand fine. There are countless universes out there and like these paintings, they are meant to stay separate. But that doesn't always happen. So, you three are the stopgap. You go out there, catch whatever came through and send it all back, then you plug up the hole. Right? Now, what's this about a choice?"

Elliot wagged his finger. "Not exactly right. You see, we cannot close the holes. We don't know how. That is why we have your grandmother. She creates the books. We stop the gaps by containing them into the books."

"What?" Roni had lost count of how many times her heart had skipped a beat. "Are you saying that all those breaches into our world still exist? That they're all sitting underneath the bookstore, locked away in some kind of magic books?"

"Good," he said with a broad smile. "That is correct. The cavern, the books, the chains — all of it is designed to house the tears between universes."

She tried to digest this, but then recalled the question he had yet to answer. "What about this choice? What is it you want me to do?"

All the brightness on his face faded. "This group of ours — well, we are old. When Darin broke in, it set off an alarm that Sully had placed on the padlock. We knew at that moment that somebody had gone into the caverns. Yet ..."

"It took you guys a long time to get down there."

"Yes. We were slow to hear the alarm, slow to get out of bed, slow to dress for a fight, and slow to actually reach the caverns. That is not to say that we do not have some good years still in us, but simply that we are not young people anymore. Protecting the universe tends more to the youthful side."

Roni put her arm around Elliot's waist and gave him a loving shake. "I'm sure the three of you have plenty of strength to spare."

"You know, we originally were four. My wife, Janwan, passed away."

"Because of all this?"

"No. Pancreatic cancer. Excuse my language, but fuck cancer." He leaned on his cane so that his face came in close to her. "When Janwan died, your grandmother wanted your mother, Maria, to take over. But then, unfortunately, your mother had her accident. So, we decided to keep it just us three until the time would come that we found a good match for a fourth. That time is now."

Elliot said nothing more. He stood there, staring at her. Addled by the overwhelming volume of shocks coming her way, Roni stood there staring back for a while before her eyes finally widened. "Oh. You want me?" She backed away. "No, no, no. That's not ... that doesn't make sense. Why would you want me? I don't have magic powers. I'm not ready for this kind of thing. Besides, I'm an atheist."

"Perfect! It is our respect for each other's differing opinions that we hold as one of our greatest strengths."

"I mean, everything you've said is amazing, and if I hadn't been down there and seen it all, I would have thought you were nuts, but I did see it, I did experience it all, and it is amazing. How could I turn down a chance to be part of that?"

"Exactly."

"But my life is in turmoil enough. I don't even have a job."

"The Society provides a healthy income, so you won't have to worry about that. And, best of all, you can't be fired. This is an appointment for life. Like the US Supreme Court."

"What's the Society?"

Rolling his eyes, Elliot said, "Unfortunately, this sort of universes ripping apart in each other doesn't stay hidden and secret forever. A few centuries back, the Society was formed as an oversight committee to make sure we are accountable for what we do. Mostly, it exists as a method for those in power to feel like they have some control over us.

They do not. You will learn all about it when you join us."

"Hold on there." Roni glanced down the hall, part of her thinking that a good sprint away from all of this would be a smart start. "I haven't agreed to anything. This is a lot to accept."

"I do apologize for throwing it onto you this way, but Lillian insisted. After all, we do have some urgent business to get working on, and your grandmother leads our trio."

"Business? You mean saving Darin?"

"Exactly."

Roni headed toward the door. "Great. Let's put this decision of mine on the back burner and we'll go help Darin. I'm sure by the time we're done with that, I'll be able to make a choice."

Elliot did not move.

She looked back at him and crossed her arms. "Really? After everything I've seen and all that you've told me, you're going to make me choose now?"

"You should never have seen the things you did, and the only reason we decided to tell you what we have is because we feel strongly that you will join us. But the rest of the secrets we still hold will remain secrets unless you do." She started to answer but he raised a hand to shush her — too much like Gram. "I will go wait outside. Stay here a moment. Look at the paintings. Let your mind relax and open your heart to your thoughts. Only then will you know the true answer of what you want."

He walked out and Roni resisted the urge to follow. Instead, she did as he had asked. She stood there, staring at the swirls of color on the canvases, and she tried to relax. But how could she relax when the last twelve hours had been overflowing with insanity? How could she go back to her mundane existence knowing what reality truly was?

Her pulse pounded in her chest. The decision had to be based on more than a gut feeling. After all, there was a massive chasm between dreams and reality. It could be fun to dream of living the life of an international spy like James Bond — the action, the adventure, the gadgets, and the close calls — but the reality of that life would be quite different.

She thought about the Old Gang. She had known them her whole life. They never appeared to be enjoying martinis while gambling in Morocco as an undercover agent. They were quiet people, living quiet lives. She saw now that wasn't by mistake or happenstance. They had to maintain a low profile, an unassuming life, in order to keep their job a secret.

Any dreams Roni harbored of a future would disappear. No chance for fame or fortune or maybe even happiness. Once she accepted the job, she would be in it for life. That would be it. No change of career.

And what of love? Family? How could she build a relationship with someone when she had this enormous secret to hold?

Worst of all — while there would probably be times of great excitement, her one experience already had been more terrifying than exciting. This wouldn't be fun-filled action like a movie. This would be a case of make a mistake and die.

Elliot walked up behind her. "I'm sorry to interrupt, but you've been standing here for almost an hour. If you're going to join us, we've got to get working."

An hour? Roni glanced up at Elliot, tears wetting her cheeks.

"It's okay," he said. "This life is not for most people. No need to cry. You won't be disappointing any of us."

She shook her head. "It's not that. I think I'm mourning the life I thought I would live."

"Oh?" Elliot put out his hand. "Then you'll join us?"

She nodded and shook his hand. "Let's go save Darin."

But Elliot pulled his hand back. "No, dear. I did not offer to shake hands. I need you for a little balance. I left my cane in the hall."

"Sorry," she said and set his hand on her shoulder.

Together they ambled back, picked up his cane, and left the gallery. A few people meandered outside, but nobody bothered them. Walking side by side, heading toward the bookstore, Roni's chest swelled. She couldn't help it. As much as she looked forward to helping others and protecting the universe, she kept wondering what special power they would gift to her. She kept thinking — *I'm going to have magic.*

CHAPTER 5

"You don't get a power." Gram never even glanced up from the books spread out on the main table at the bookstore.

"But all of you have powers."

Gram glared at Elliot. "How much did you tell her?"

Elliot offered a sheepish smile. "She is your family. I figured she could be trusted to know a little more than most."

"Then why does she think she gets a power?"

"I may not have mentioned all the finer details of that point."

That got Gram's attention. "Then she's here under a false assumption. Her decision to join us must be pure."

"Hey!" Roni said. "I'm standing right here."

Gram slammed her book closed and shifted in her chair to face Roni and Elliot. She rested her hands on her belly, absentmindedly fiddling with the long, beaded necklace she wore. Moving her index finger only, she pointed at Elliot. "Will you kindly go downstairs and get an update on Darin, please? We need to keep an eye on how that man is faring."

Bowing slightly, Elliot made his way toward the basement. Gram then cocked her head towards Roni. Her eyes roved up and down as if appraising a meager painting from an unknown artist.

This was hardly the first time Roni had endured that disapproving appraisal look. Most every important milestone of her life had been met with those harsh eyes — straight As, making a new friend, first period, first love, first college acceptance, and on and on. Gram meant well — Roni told herself that many times — yet she lacked the ability to show it. Roni had always assumed it had something to do with herself, but now she wondered if the difficulties of leading a double-life or the great strains of meeting her job requirements had contributed to her hard parenting style.

At length, Gram said, "Powers are not handed out like invitations to the school dance. Everybody doesn't get one. In fact, nobody gets one handed to them. You have to earn the right to see if you are capable of gaining a power. If you pass that point, we'll discuss it further."

"How do I earn that right?"

"You spend the next several years, perhaps even decades, working with us. You do a good job, show yourself to be responsible with our secrets, and never talk back to me."

Roni squinted. "You made that last part up."

"Maybe. Are you going to risk losing a chance at a power to find out?"

Roni closed her mouth and said nothing. Then Gram laughed.

"Okay, okay," she said. "I made up that last part. But you'd be smart to listen to what I have to say. I've been doing this a long time. And before you speak up, you still have to make your choice. Now that you know you won't be given a power, at least not yet, do you wish to remain here and learn all we have to share?"

"I do. I can do this. Even without a magic power."

"We'll see."

With that Gram rocked forward and onto her feet. Brushing her backside, she headed for the elevators. "My legs are a bit achy today. You can take the elevator with me or meet me on the third floor."

Roni hustled to Gram's side and helped her into the elevator. They rode up in silence. When they reached the third floor, Gram led the way through the old room.

The cool air — always maintained at a low 64 degrees Fahrenheit — prickled Roni's arms. Four light tables dominated the center of the room for working on restoration and preservation while metal shelves held brittle, decomposing books waiting their turn. Gram ignored all of this and walked straight to the back.

Roni's skin prickled again — this time from the fear that she would see another hole in the wall leading to another hidden cavern. The fact that they were on the third floor did nothing to alter her unease. At the back wall lined with full bookshelves, Gram paused to face Roni.

"This is your last chance. I'm sure you feel like your whole world has flipped, but you know nothing compared to what I'll show in the years to come if you join us."

"I'm not turning back on this. How could I?"

Gram's head wobbled as she seemed to weigh possible answers. Finally, she pushed the spines of three books on two different shelves. An entire section of the wall slid open.

Roni grinned as she shook her head. "How many secret rooms are in this building?"

"Maybe more than I know about. Come on. Time to see Sully's workshop."

They entered a room easily as big as the one they had left. Roni marveled that she had never noticed the third floor wasn't big enough to cover the entire size of the building, that there had to be more space beyond what she thought of as the back wall. To be fair, she rarely went to the third floor. In fact, as she thought about it, there were numerous times that one of the Old Gang went out of their way to prevent her from going to that floor — usually with the excuse of a new book in such bad condition they had to limit the number of people on the floor at any one time. Body heat, body oils, even the human breath could all be damaging to something so fragile.

Sully's workshop proved to be a marvel of its own. One giant room, ten-foot ceiling, filled with lights and all manner of equipment lining the walls. The center of the room had a grid painted on the floor and remained mostly clear except for whatever project Sully worked upon.

At the moment, this consisted of a seven-foot tall block of clay. Sully stood on an A-frame ladder as he carved away large, reddish chunks. It looked like a block head sitting atop a block body.

"What's he doing?" Roni asked.

"Didn't you pay attention to Elliot? He explained all this already."

"He didn't say anything about this."

"Sully makes Golems."

"Is that what this is?"

"It will be when he's done. Most of last night was spent getting all this clay up here. Not so easy anymore. In a few hours, he'll have enough shape carved out that we can proceed."

Sully pushed his glasses with the back of his clay-stained hands. "It won't be pretty, and it'll probably move a bit stiff, too, but it'll do the job."

Roni waved. "Do you need any help up there?"

"Not today. Thanks. Besides, we all have our assignments. This thing only works when we do our part. Now, let me get back to work or we won't be saving anybody at all."

Gram ushered Roni further across the floor until they reached the far windows. She sat on the deep ledge and scooted over to make room for Roni. "Something about these windows makes me want to smoke a cigarette."

"You smoke?"

"Not for years. But a spot like this one that's almost like a window bench, well, that gets the craving going for a bit."

Roni chuckled. "I have to say it again. This is all amazing. I still can't believe you were able to hide this from me all these years."

With a dismissive wave, Gram said, "You were more interested in your own life than mine. That's normal. You'll see it for yourself once you start having to hide this from others you know or care about. It's not too hard. Usually."

"I guess I've got a lot to learn."

The edge of Gram's lip curled upward. "That's one of the first sensible things you've said since last night. But don't worry. Elliot, in particular, is a good teacher. Sully and I will do our best, too. For now, though, you're going to have to accept a lot without question or else we'll run out of time for Darin."

Roni wanted to ask why? Did books have a time limit on them? What would happen to Darin if they passed the limit? What would happen to the book?

She opened her mouth but snapped it shut. Then, after a short breath, she said, "Tell me what I have to do."

"Your main job will be information retrieval."

"You want me to be your librarian?"

"Librarian and researcher, yes. This building houses numerous important volumes filled with lore and history and wisdom from ages upon ages. We even have some very unique works, ones that you will never find anywhere else. On the occasions that our little group comes across something we've not encountered before — and considering what it is we do, that happens quite often — you will be required to find out whatever we need to know. Then you report it to us so that we can handle the situation properly."

Roni let it all sink in. "Oh Lord. I'm Giles."

"Who's Giles?"

"Television reference. Forget it."

"See, that is one of the reasons we need you. The world has changed around us so fast, but you are of a younger generation. You understand it better than we do. We're not idiots, mind you. I know how to use my phone for a lot more than calls, but there are plenty of ins and outs to the digital world that we've never learned. You'll be a great asset with your knowledge. Plus, you've worked around this bookstore for long enough. You know it better than you realize."

"Just to be clear — when trouble comes, you three will have me do all the legwork and then I'm supposed to sit back and let you get in on all the action."

"Nobody said saving the universe would be glamorous." Gram squeezed Roni's knee. "Baby steps, dear. Someday I'll pass on, as will Elliot and Sully. You need to learn the ropes so that you can take over and train others."

"I understand. I do. I guess after last night, I was thinking things would be more eventful right away."

"Trust me on this — you'll find plenty of excitement."

"I only meant —"

"I know what you meant," she said, her familiar bite returning. "But as usual, you never listen to everything that's told to you. I said your job was information retrieval. Yes, librarian and researcher are two aspects of that, but they are hardly the entire job. You have to get us the information we require, even when that information is not available in this building."

Roni perked up. "Oh?"

"Those books I was reading when you came in detail the precise things we need to attempt a rescue of your boyfriend."

"He's not my boyfriend."

"Good. I don't care for him. Though we should talk a little about men and how you'll have to deal with such things in the future."

Before they could sidetrack into a conversation Roni knew she never wanted to have, she said, "The books downstairs — what am I supposed to do with them?"

"Nothing. I've already done that part of the research — in case you failed to join us. What I need you to do is acquire something of great personal value to Darin."

"Like what?"

"I don't know the boy, so I don't know what he values. That's some of the research you'll have to do."

"Okay." She grinned. "This is like voodoo or witchcraft or something."

Gram's face paled. "Don't ever say such a thing again."

"I didn't mean you were a witch or that, well, I just, I didn't mean —"

"Be quiet, dear."

"Yes, ma'am."

"Find something meaningful to Darin. Something that will touch him deeply no matter what state his mind is in when we locate him. Something that will lure him away."

"Away? From what?"

Gram huffed as she stood. With her mouth tight and thoughtful, she looked at the giant clay statue Sully worked on. She took four small steps before glancing back at Roni.

"Pray we never find out."

CHAPTER 6

Roni left the bookstore. She walked downhill toward her apartment building where her car was parked. Part of her watched her feet moving, shocked that she could even stand after all that she had learned. Her head felt as numb and confused as if she had gone three rounds with a champion boxer. Though she knew she would do as asked, her mind still debated her new reality.

On the one hand, she had all that the Old Gang had told and shown her, plus she had her direct experience from the previous night. On the other hand, maybe she had gone batty and needed to commit herself. Maybe she was still in her apartment, passed out, dreaming all of this.

No. She could feel the sun on her face and hear her steps on the sidewalk. She smelled the air and saw the world around her as it always appeared. Not a dream.

"That's it," she scolded herself. "No more doubting. This is the way things are now."

She got into her car — a black Ford Focus that looked reasonable on the exterior and like the city dump on the interior. Old fast food wrappers, torn seats, and clumps of mud were only the start. It had once been her prize possession when she bought it used as a high school graduation gift. Almost fifteen years and two hundred twenty thousand miles later, it was little more than her mode of transportation — one she crossed her fingers would start each morning.

When the engine kicked in, a short whining sound wound up before disappearing. "That's new," she said as she leaned over to the glove compartment. Inside, she had an old bottle of aspirin. Popping two in her mouth, she dry swallowed, coughed, and buckled her seatbelt. "Okay, let's go information retrieving." She pulled onto the road.

On their date, Darin had taken her to an Italian restaurant near Philly called Mariano's Grove. He had implied it was his favorite place to eat, and without any other hint of where to start, she figured that would be her best chance to find out anything.

As she drove, her brain threatened to argue more on what reality had thrown her in the last twenty-four hours. But she pushed it away. Denying the strangeness would do nothing to change it. She had to keep moving forward. Dwelling on this would only drive her crazy whereas simply living her life would settle the bizarre world around her into a new state of normal.

At least, she hoped that was what would happen.

Besides, doing things the way Gram suggested meant that Roni would have a job, an income, a chance at a life. And maybe it would be fun. She never thought she would get to be a detective, yet that was exactly her duty this morning. Retracing the steps of a victim in order to help save him.

That sounded good to her ears. She could work with that.

Mariano's Grove was in the town of Exton just off of Route 30. The building had once been a chain restaurant that went out of business. Mariano bought it, refurbished it to give the place a warmer feel, and starting plating recipes from his family that reached all the way back to a little town in Italy. All of which created a fantastic atmosphere for that first date.

But under the Sunday afternoon sun, without the candlelight or wine, Roni saw the flaws more than anything — the threadbare carpet, the constant clatter in the kitchen, the bored waiters, and the inattentive hostess. In fact, Roni waited at the front counter for ten minutes before being helped. When the hostess realized Roni wasn't a customer, she plastered on a fake smile and said she had to go on break.

"Don't mind her," one of the waiters said. "It's not personal. She's always bitchy."

Roni winked. "I thought maybe I smelled bad or something."

The waiter, a tall black man with a dazzling smile, said, "You seem fine to me."

"Maybe you can help me out. I was here last night on a date, and I want to do something nice for the guy. He told me this was his favorite restaurant, that he came here a lot, so I thought maybe you guys might know a little something about him. What he likes. That kind of thing."

"I wasn't here last night. Didn't see you."

"His name's Darin Lander."

"Oh, sure. Everybody knows Darin. Comes in here every week, sometimes twice. Good tipper, too."

She faked a bit of embarrassment. "It was just our first date, and we didn't talk a lot about him. I tried, but he was very tight-lipped." As she realized her "lie" actually was true, her face reddened for real. How had she managed to go through an entire date and only talk about herself?

"What is it you want to know? I won't give you his address or credit card info or anything like that."

"No, no. I'm going to see him tomorrow night for our second date. This time it's my turn to plan the thing, but I don't even know what he does for a living. If he's a pastry chef, I don't want to take him to a bakery."

"He's a lawyer."

"Really?"

"Oh, yeah. Works with Page Brothers. You know them, right? They've always got those commercials on TV with the guy in a full-body cast."

"Yeah, I know the one." So, Darin was a low-level ambulance chaser. "Thanks. You've helped me out so much."

"No problem." He paused, then rested his arm on the wall to show off his muscular frame. "You know, if it doesn't work out, I'd be happy to give you my number."

Roni smiled. "I'll keep that in mind." As she left, the smile drifted away. She had no interest in a man who asked her out knowing that she was dating another man. But she had to admit that her chest filled with flattered pride. Getting asked out like that never happened to her. She didn't have the classic beauty features that drove men to do crazy things. Perhaps, in part, she exuded more confidence because she now had a job, had a purpose. *Or perhaps he was hard up and thought I'd be easy.*

She got back in her car and pulled out her phone. Page Brothers' offices were in Paoli, only a few minutes from Exton and quite close to Olburg.

When she arrived at the law offices, two men in business suits hustled from office to office. They fluttered papers at each other, made phone calls, and grumbled. The receptionist gazed up from her bulky computer — a leftover from seven years ago — and asked, "What do you need, honey?"

"I'm here about Darin Lander."

The two men in the back froze. One, a pudgy fellow with a waxy mustache, rushed over. "You've seen Darin? Where is he? He never showed up. What do you know about it? Is he hurt? He better be hurt or we'll kill him."

The other man, slightly older with deep wrinkles around his eyes, approached. "Forgive my brother. We're floundering a bit by Darin's unexpected absence. It all just happened a few hours ago and we've had to reschedule a lot. You can imagine the courts will not be too cooperative with us tomorrow if we are unprepared."

"So," the first brother said, "do you know where he is or don't you?"

"That's a bit complicated," Roni said. As the words left her mouth, she wondered why she hadn't simply answered *No*.

"Complicated? What's complicated about it? Is he in some trouble? I knew he had been chatting it up with some odd people lately, but I didn't get the sense that they were trouble. I mean, he's not dealing drugs or doing anything stupid like that. Is he?"

"No, no. Nothing like that. He's, um," she said, and decided she might as well go all-in, "he's working a side project. One that might bring you all quite a bit of money."

That got the older brother's full attention. "Are you the client?"

"I'm only the messenger. A private firm needed somebody with his skills to handle a sensitive matter. The people I work for are quite secretive and they didn't give Mr. Lander a chance to contact you. I apologize I wasn't here sooner this day, but it took me a while to find you."

"Why didn't Darin tell you where we are?"

"Like I said, I'm only the messenger. I've never even seen Mr. Lander, and I was given nothing more than a name."

The first brother huffed. "You couldn't find our address online with his name?"

Roni wanted to smack herself. She was so spun around by recent events, she forgot to do the most basic thing possible. She didn't even google the guy. "The people I work for are finicky about their privacy. They shun employee internet usage."

"Doesn't seem a sensible way to run a business. What business are your bosses in, anyway?"

She raised her palms out. "I'm not at liberty to say anything more."

"I'd say you're done there then. You've delivered the message. At least, we don't have to worry about Darin's well-being now. But that doesn't make the day any easier. Excuse us. We have a lot of cleaning up to do because of this mess."

"Of course." Roni snapped her fingers. "One more thing, though. If you don't mind, I was told to fetch a few items from his office."

The older brother said, "Fine, fine. Don't take any case files out of here, though. We need those."

With nothing more, the Page Brothers returned to their bustling. Roni quietly entered Darin's office — wood panel walls, a beaten couch, and a fake fern. She couldn't believe it had been so easy to get in there. Of course, the brothers were in a state because of Darin's unplanned absence, but the way they accepted her story flummoxed her. Then again, greed could motivate a lot of poor choices, and she had seen it on both men's faces — they hoped that Darin's side project would reward the firm with plenty of high paying business. After all, who else but rich people had sensitive, secret jobs for lawyers?

Despite the gullibility of the Page brothers, Roni did not want to push her luck. She needed to be quick. Eventually, one of the lawyers would get an idea in his head that she might be lying.

She scanned over Darin's desk — stapler, laptop, stacks of files and papers, a fancy pen in a fancy stand, nothing that suggested an item of personal importance. She checked the drawers — nothing but files, office supplies, and a bottle of brandy. Roni's stomach churned at the thought of alcohol.

Gazing at the walls, she noted the bland paintings — the kind of thing found in hotel rooms. In fact, everything about Darin's office suggested he was a bland human being without any defining characteristics. It felt strange and invasive to be combing through his life this way — especially after having been on a date with the man — but the Old Gang needed this object. Darin needed it.

Except I've got nothing.

Great. Her first assignment would end in failure. She could already see Gram's disappointed expression.

Roni's eyes shifted downward. On the desk, she saw a large calendar planner that doubled as a large blotter. Sliding the laptop to the side, her finger traced the daily notes Darin had made. Client names, times, and phone numbers had been meticulously written into the correct boxes for the days of the month. And one week away, circled and given an exclamation point, were the words *Mom's Birthday!* Whether out of habit, a touch of OCD, or because he truly needed to be reminded, he had written the phone number next to the entry.

Roni stored the number into her phone and extricated herself from the offices as quietly as possible. The Page Brothers never bothered to acknowledge her as she walked by, and even the receptionist simply nodded without looking up from her computer.

Once she had safely returned to her car, Roni brought up the number on her phone. She thought about calling but it would be too easy for Darin's mother to get suspicious and hang up. It would be far more difficult in person. Not wanting to make the same mistake twice, Roni brought up her browser and with a few searches on some basic phone directories, aided by the benefit that Darin's mother used a landline, Roni had an address in Lancaster.

"Of course," Roni said to the phone. "You couldn't bother to live nearby."

Ninety minutes later, Roni drove into a seasoned development off of Lititz Pike. She parked in front of a gray house with brick trim, walked up to the door, and rang the bell. When an elderly woman with more wrinkles on her face than teeth in her mouth answered, Roni said the first thing that came to mind. "Hi. I'm Darin's girlfriend."

CHAPTER 7

The woman's eyes sparkled as she opened the door wider and waved Roni in. Waddling like a penguin, she rushed off down a hall and returned with teeth in her mouth. "Oh my, I'm so embarrassed. I didn't know you were coming. Darin didn't say a thing. That rascal is forever letting things surprise me."

The house was immaculate — not a speck of dust on the coffee table, not a mismatched pillow on the couch, not a single picture askew on the walls. The carpet still bore lines from recent vacuuming. Even the plants looked vibrant as if freshly watered.

"Come, come," Darin's mother said. "Have a seat."

Roni settled on the edge of a couch cushion. She feared sitting fully into the couch and messing up the perfectly smooth cushions.

"Mrs. Lander —"

"Please, call me Jane."

"It's a pleasure to meet you, Jane."

Jane eased next to Roni. She was a hefty, small woman with a confident swagger behind her words. Not at all like Darin had described her. "Are we having dinner tonight? Darin hasn't bothered to call me in a few days. He can be so forgetful."

Roni coughed to stall an answer. She had forgotten to plan a lie again, and this time there would be no business or money distraction like with the Page Brothers law firm. "I don't think so," she said. "At least, he didn't mention it to me."

"Get comfortable with that. He's very spur of the moment."

Roni glanced around the room for something that might lead her to the item she sought, but everything she spotted belonged to an old woman, not a young man. On the fireplace mantle, she saw framed photos lined up. Most were of Jane Lander as a young woman or a middle-aged mom and most had a taller black man standing with her.

"Is that Darin's father?"

Jane smiled as she gazed at the photos. "Patrick. He was a great man. Died too young, though. Only fifty-seven. Heart attack."

"He's handsome."

"Did you lose somebody early, too?"

Roni's hand went to her chest. "My mother. How did you know that?"

"Because when I told you Patrick was dead, you didn't say you were sorry. People who have lost somebody early in life learn that there's no need to say that. It doesn't help." With a gentle tap on Roni's knee, Jane said, "How rude of me. I didn't offer you anything. Can I get you a cup of coffee? Are you hungry?"

"No, thank you. I'm fine."

"Are you sure? I don't mind. It's not often that Darin brings home a girlfriend. Where is he anyway?"

"I guess he's still at work. You know how it is with lawyers."

Jane turned her head to the side and peeked back at Roni. "I wouldn't really call him a lawyer. I mean, he's not arguing difficult cases or anything. He won't be in front of the Supreme Court."

"He's got to start somewhere." Roni didn't want to think about how she found herself in the position of defending Darin. She tried to stay focused on the goal — a deeply personal item. "Do you know where we'll be eating? It seems food is kind of important to him."

With a worn expression, Jane lowered her head. "Please, don't try to fool an old lady."

"Pardon me?"

"You know, when I was younger, I could play this game all night long. I'd lie to myself and to the girl sitting where you are, and I'd promise that he surely just got caught in traffic or perhaps an emergency happened at work. If I really liked the girl, I'd even take her out to dinner. Sometimes they were so naïve, they really thought Darin would call soon to apologize. But as you get old, you get to a point where you're done with all the nonsense of life — the so-called courtesies that really are nothing more than lies we tell to avoid being honest with each other. So, why don't you tell me why you're really here? You afraid Darin is cheating on you?"

"Um ... I ..."

"Too blunt for you?"

"No. It's actually refreshing."

"Take some advice. Go find another man. I love my son. I truly do. But there's something not right with him. He doesn't handle relationships well. I'm telling you this because you look about his age, and I know thoughts of marriage are coming up in his head more and more lately. I think he thinks I need grandkids. What do I want with a bunch of dirty little tykes messing up my house? But he thinks it, and once he gets something in his head, it's hard to get him to change course. Thing is — he's not the marrying type. He won't do well with that kind of responsibility. It breaks my heart to say all this. I want him to be happy, but I have to be honest. If you're thinking he's the one — and at your age, I understand the pressure to settle down — well, go find another. He's not the one."

As Jane went on exposing the flaws of her son, Roni could see the future painted before her. A full, normal life complete with marriage and children that, apparently with Darin, also included infidelity, heartbreak, and eventually divorce. On the previous night, while dining with Darin, she had an ideal future vision running through her head. Either one could have happened. If it hadn't happened, she figured she would have been headed to plenty of lonely nights and a lot of cats.

But then the world changed. And as Roni sat there listening to Darin's mother, she could only think about how happy she had been all afternoon. Once her hangover had cleared, she found the day exhilarating. Even if she never got a special power, even if all she ever did for the Old Gang was look up information in books and go on the occasional excursion to find an object or two, the whole experience thrilled her. The drab world she had lived in had been flipped on end, and she found herself feeling an odd sensation deep inside — gratitude.

An idea sparked, and she put out her hand to clasp Jane's. "I appreciate everything you've said. But I'm afraid I'm in love with him. I can't turn back. I think about him all the time, and well, like you suspected, I came here because I think I might be losing him." It scared Roni a little at how easily the lies came. "Please, Jane, please. I've heard what you're saying, but I also know what's in my heart. I think I need to — no, I know it — I've got to try to win him back. If it's meant to be, then it'll happen. If I fail, I'll listen to your warning. But I've got to try."

Jane covered their entwined hands with her other hand. "Well, I must say that I like you a lot. You've got what we used to call grit. If you're determined to be miserable with my son, then at least I'll get to have you as a daughter-in-law. That much I think I'll enjoy."

"There won't be a wedding if I don't get him back on my side."

"You came here for advice on that?"

"I was thinking that I'd do something special for him. I want to take something that he cherishes, something personal to him that would fill him with feelings of love and connection, and I'll make it special, and then give it as a present. I want to show him that I really understand him."

Jane's face brightened. "I know the perfect thing." She crossed the room to a low bookshelf and lifted out a heavy photo album. Beaming as she returned to the couch, she said, "You know I think you're a bit crazy to stay with him, but the idea that I will have you in my life is wonderful. Before you say anything — I know we've only met, but I've seen enough of Darin's girlfriends. I can tell. You're something special. Your honesty alone is a significant improvement."

Roni tried to hide her discomfort. "I'm sure you'll find my flaws eventually. That's even if I can get him to stay with me."

"Oh, he will. He's an idiot but he's not that much of an idiot. Oh, you wouldn't believe how many lying little tramps I've met. And for what? They think because he's a lawyer that he's rich. But you — you don't strike me as a gold digger."

"He made it clear to me from the start that he wasn't rich."

"Did he?"

Roni cleared her throat. She tried to recall the things Darin had talked about on their only date. Maybe he hadn't said anything so bold. Well, since Jane appreciated straight talk, Roni figured that would be the best approach. "I don't remember now. I could have sworn he said something like that, but then maybe it was more of an impression."

"Probably. While I wouldn't expect him to brag about money he doesn't have, I don't think he'd go out of his way to diminish himself either."

Roni let a short silence slip between them and kept her eyes on the photo album. Jane took the hint well. She flipped through several pages until she reached one that had a photo of Darin in his twenties sitting with his father courtside at a 76ers game. Two tickets stubs were next to the photo.

"It was a gift for graduating law school," Jane said, peeling back the plastic and removing one of the ticket stubs. "Patrick and I were so proud. We wanted to do something special, but we could only afford two tickets. So, we went out to dinner as a family and then the boys went to watch basketball. The two of them talked about that game for a week after it happened. I think it was the closest they ever felt together. It was also the last big thing they ever did. Three months later, Patrick died."

When Roni took the ticket stub, she swore she could feel energy coming off it. However, she also knew that her pulse quickened under the pressure of her lies. She wanted to grab hold of Jane's shoulders, look her deep in the soul, and tell her that Darin was in trouble, that his life was threatened, but not to worry. A great team had assembled to save him.

Great team. Sure. Three geriatrics and an unemployed slacker.

"Thank you," she said. "I'll make sure to take good care of this."

"Please do. I have a strong feeling that he's going to love whatever you do."

"You've been very kind to me, Jane."

"No, no. Let's be perfectly positive about this. You call me Mom."

Roni blushed. "I'll try."

Jane laughed. "Good luck now."

After a few more pleasantries, Roni hurried back to her car and headed for Olburg. During the first half of the drive, she periodically burst into triumphant shouts followed by giddy laughter. She had succeeded. First day on the job and she had succeeded. She had started with nothing more than a name and a restaurant, and by the end, she had retrieved the ticket stub, met Darin's mother, learned a lot of possibly valuable information about Darin, and been invited to join the family.

As the sun lowered and sent annoying orange rays glaring in her rearview mirror, Roni exited the highway. A few minutes later, she parked out front of the bookshop. Eager to see Gram's face when she handed over the ticket stub, Roni almost forgot to lock her car — even a monstrous piece of junk could get stolen.

When she entered the store, her proud smile vanished. Gram slumped on the floor with her back against the endcap of a bookshelf — her eyes wide, her face pale, and her hand clutching her chest.

CHAPTER 8

Roni shot across the room and slammed onto her knees beside Gram. "Hold on. I'm here now. I'm going to call for help. Just hold on."

She fumbled out her phone. Under trembling fingers, she dialed 9-1-1. This couldn't be happening. After all she had learned in the last day, after her world had been upended, it would be the cruelest joke to rip apart her family again. Salty tears flowed into her mouth.

"Why aren't they answering?" she yelled.

She looked at the phone and saw that she had forgotten to press SEND. Before she could raise her thumb toward the green icon, Gram's hand batted at the phone.

"No," Gram said.

"You need an ambulance and the paramedics. I don't know any first aid to help you."

"They can't help me." Straining through her pain, she added, "Get ... Elliot."

"But —"

"Get Elliot!"

The urgency of Gram's voice cut straight through Roni's brain. Nodding like a bobble-head, she pressed the phone into Gram's hand and dashed to the stairwell. The elevator would be too slow.

She bolted up flight after flight until she reached the top floor. Both the stairs and the elevator opened into a tiny lobby big enough for the doors to the two apartments and two chairs to sit while waiting for the elevator. Roni went to the right — Elliot and Sully's apartment — and banged on the door.

"Elliot! Elliot!" Why wasn't he answering? He always spent the early evening in prayer and almost always in his apartment. At least, she always thought he was praying. But then, she never saw him being observant of the Muslim traditions. Still, he should have been in his apartment. Did something different happen today or was he asleep? She slammed her fist against the door over and over. "Wake up! Elliot! Gram needs you!"

She heard a muffled sound from inside followed by the locks on the doors clicking. Elliot opened the door looking confused. "What are you doing making all this fuss when I'm trying —"

"Gram's having a heart attack!"

She had never seen Elliot move so fast. He dashed back into his apartment and returned seconds later with his cane — though he never let it touch the ground. He rushed down the stairs faster than Roni could keep up, pivoting on the landings like a youthful athlete, and sometimes skipping a stair.

At the bottom, he soared to Gram's side. When Roni caught up, she saw that perspiration covered his face. He had pushed himself harder than he should have, and Roni worried he might have a heart attack as well.

He held his cane parallel over Gram's body, closed his eyes, and murmured words Roni could not identify. His free hand caressed the air between Gram and the cane. Roni watched — unable to breathe, unable to move. Elliot continued to pass his hand back and forth at a steady pace.

A golden light appeared in the air around Elliot's moving hand. At first, it looked like sunshine cutting in on a summer day — light, breezy, and warm. But then Roni spotted pinpoints of light that moved within the general glow. Fireflies of energy that swarmed around Elliot's hand.

Elliot shifted his side-to-side motion to an up-and-down one as if fanning the air. The energy descended like glowing ash. When it touched Gram's skin, it disappeared within her, absorbed like water droplets on a dry cloth. As fast as it happened, Gram's color returned to her skin, her breathing eased, and all impressions of pain left her face.

Sitting back, Elliot sighed. "She's going to be okay."

Roni stared at these two people like they were aliens. "How?"

"I heal people. That is my main gift. I thought I told you that."

"Maybe you did. But there's a big difference between hearing something like that and seeing it actually happen."

Dabbing at his forehead with his sleeve, he said, "I'm surprised you look so astounded — after what you saw last night."

"Me, too. But I am." She crouched next to Elliot and wrapped her arms around him. "Thank you." He had a comforting, smoky aroma as if he had a wood-burning stove in his apartment. "Thank you for saving her."

Gram sat up and rolled her shoulders. "It isn't the first time."

Roni tried to ease Gram back down. "Lord woman, lay down. You've got to rest."

"I've lived more decades than you. I think I know what my body needs and doesn't need." Gram shoved Roni's arms away. "Elliot's been bringing me back from near-death more times than I care to remember. So, if you want to be a help, then quit pushing me and start helping up to my feet."

Elliot took one arm and Roni the other. Together, they lifted Gram up and placed her in a seat at the big table. "She will be fine," Elliot said.

"It goes with the territory," Gram said. "After you put in a few dozen years or so on the job, you'll have been exposed to all sorts of stuff."

"Exposed?" Roni didn't like the sound of that. "Like radiation?"

"Sure. Maybe. I don't know. Each one of those books in the cavern contains a rip into another universe. You think that's benign? Every single universe is going to have its own unique bacteria, unique air mixture, unique properties of everything. There's no way you can do this work and not inhale a bit of another universe. That has lasting consequences."

"You're saying you had a heart attack because of germs from another universe."

Gram drummed her fingers on the table. "Now you're starting to see. Except in this case, no. I had a heart attack because I'm in my seventies and I've had a bad ticker for a long time. Partly old age. Mostly bad genes. If it weren't for Elliot, I'd have died ten, maybe twenty years ago. He's also saved Sully's life a few times."

Roni kissed the side of Elliot's head. "Thank you."

He leaned on his cane, wincing but trying to hide it. "Nothing to thank me for. Keeping us healthy and running is part of my job. But there are limits to what I can do." He leveled his eyes on Gram. "And how often."

Gram waved him off. "I know, I know. He's implying that soon he won't be able to stop the natural order of things. Nobody gets to cheat

Death, after all. Elliot can stop me from croaking to a heart attack, but he can't stop old age. Eventually, my body's going to have had enough."

"My body, too." He shifted on his feet, once more tightening his face with the movements. To Roni, he said, "I can summon a lot of energy from the air to give myself a boost, but as I get older, it takes more and more from me."

Roni said, "Is that how you ran down the stairs like a twenty year old?"

"That's right. But my body doesn't like it. If I die before I have a successor, this group will be in serious trouble for a while. Eventually, you'll find somebody, but that doesn't mean you won't suffer in the meantime."

"Are you suggesting that I —"

Both Elliot and Gram laughed. "Not at all," he said. "You've gotten your job. But this team of four needs more youth than just you. Eventually, that is."

"That's right." Gram used the table to prop herself up to a standing position. "Eventually means later — much later. Let's deal with right now. We've got work to do. Roni? Did you get what you were assigned to find?"

Without intending to do so, Roni stepped forward with her chest puffed up. She lifted her head like a Greek warrior returning from battle under the cheers of the people, and she pulled the ticket stub from her pocket. Adding a final flick to the stub, she presented it with a reverent nod.

Gram picked it up and checked over both sides. "It's rather small."

"You never said anything about the object having to be large."

Elliot snickered. "Come on, give the girl a break. You know very well size doesn't matter. Not for this."

"Don't get saucy," Gram said without any mirth. "Particularly in front of my granddaughter."

Roni didn't know whether to laugh or scream. She opted for a third choice. She snatched the ticket stub back and asked in a firm voice, "Will it do or won't it?"

"As long as it is a deeply personal object to Darin, it'll do fine."

"Then this will be perfect."

Gram weighed Roni's confident words. "I hope you're right."

Apparently almost dying did nothing to quell Gram's rough side. As Roni pocketed the stub, she said, "Is there anything else you need from me?"

"Oh, yes." Gram's eyes blazed and her voice uttered words with dark intent. "Endless things." Then she rubbed her back like an accountant stretching from a long day pouring over financial statements, and in a pleasant tone, she said, "But for tonight's work, this will do. Sully should be ready. Elliot and I will go downstairs to prepare. Please be a dear and help Sully. He sometimes needs a hand."

Threading her arm around Elliot's arm, Gram rested her head on his shoulder. She hoisted her big bag, and the two ambled off toward the elevator with all the warmth and closeness decades of friendship could create. For a fleeting moment, Roni's tension evaporated under that warmth.

Until Gram circled her finger in the air. "Hup, hup. I don't want to be awake all night waiting for you and Sully to get downstairs."

As Roni trudged up the stairs, she muttered, "Almost dying sure has made you cranky." Thankfully, Gram did not respond.

On the third floor, Roni walked back into Sully's workshop. The Golem stood in the center of the room. It appeared like a giant figure made of simple shapes — a square block head, a cylinder body, cylinder arms, and thick rectangular legs. The head had two divots for eyes and a carved outline for a mouth. Sully ate a turkey sandwich at one of his desks.

"Are we ready?" he asked as Roni entered.

"Gram and Elliot are preparing things downstairs. She asked that I come help you."

"Not much left to do. I have to wake him up, and then we'll all go down together."

She gazed up at the clay thing. "Are they always so plain looking? I'm sorry. I didn't mean that to sound like an insult."

Wiping his hands on his shirt, Sully said, "You're wondering why, if I've been working all day on this, doesn't it look better."

"That's horrible of me. I'm so sorry."

"It's a valid question." Sipping from a straw stuck in a soda can, he pulled over a thin strip of white paper and a pen. After stifling a soda belch, he started to write in Hebrew. "It all has to do with the purpose of the Golem. Some purposes require more time than others. This one needs to be able to withstand some powerful forces. It doesn't need to look pretty. So, I put my efforts into the things you can't really see on the outside."

He adjusted his glasses, looked over what he had written, and seemed satisfied with the result. He then rolled the paper into a tight tube about the length of his fingernail. Scooting off a metal stool, he walked toward the ladder beside the Golem.

"Can I help you?" Roni asked.

"Wait there," he said and climbed the ladder. At the top, standing next to the Golem's head, he leaned out, holding onto the ladder with one hand.

Roni rushed over and steadied the ladder with her body. She arched her head back to watch, ready to attempt to catch Sully if he fell. Of course, if he fell, she figured they would both end up in the ER getting stitches, but what else could she do?

Sully placed the rolled up paper with Hebrew writing into the Golem's mouth. Then he swung over to the side and whispered into the thing's ear — not that he had made an ear, but that was the position where an ear should have been. When he finished, he climbed down.

"Don't dawdle now," he said, taking Roni's arm and guiding her toward the entrance.

As she walked away, she chanced a glance back and froze. The Golem moved. The giant, barely-sculpted chunk of clay stepped forward and thudded toward them.

Sully gave a short wave. "Good evening, there. You should take the elevator down. Much easier than the stairs. We'll meet you in the Specials Room. Did I write that part down for you?" The Golem's head nodded in an exaggerated up-and-down motion. "Good. We'll see you there."

"That's amazing," Roni managed.

"Far from my best work," Sully whispered. "But don't let him hear that. He's going to do a great service for us."

"W-What's he going to do?"

"Help us with Darin, of course. Come on. Time to save your boyfriend."

As Roni followed Sully toward the stairs, his words sunk in. "He's not my boyfriend!"

CHAPTER 9

Roni paused at the door to the caverns. The last time — the only time — she had gone through that door, her entire world had changed. After seeing all that the Old Gang could do, after learning the truth about reality from them, and after watching a slab of clay move on its own, she could not be sure that another massive change to her life did not wait beyond that entrance.

"Come, now," Sully said, but then he met her eyes. He pulled over a chair, sat, and crossed his legs. Clutching his knee, he said, "I understand."

"You do? I don't."

"I was exactly the same when I learned the truth. I'd think I had it straight in my head, I'd think I had arrived at acceptance, and then poof! All the doubts, all the fears, all the confusion threatened to drown me. It would take all my will and some kind words from those who knew, and I'd overcome the feeling, reassured that I understood the truth, the reality around me, and that I could handle it. A few days later, sometimes only a few hours later, poof! Here comes that tidal wave of worry once again. Took me about a week to fully adjust."

"A week?"

"But after that I was perfectly fine."

Out of frustration, and with a touch of defiance, Roni threw open the door and marched into the caverns. The temperature dropped. Sully's scuffling feet echoed from behind her.

"You ought to let me lead the way," he grumbled. "Too many bad directions to go in if you don't know where you're headed."

Roni waited for Sully to catch up. She wanted to storm off and decide for herself where things should happen, but Sully was right.

Besides, already nothing looked familiar. Getting lost would not be an ideal way to finish her first full day at work.

Sully led her around one rock wall, then another. Each one had books chained into their shelves. This time, however, Roni understood that each book contained a tear in reality, an opening into another universe.

"There are so many," she said.

Sully's head made a short turn as he scanned across the walls. "People have been doing this for a long time. Sometimes I think we're no better than the old Dutch boy with his finger in the dam. But I suppose we should consider ourselves lucky."

"How so?"

"The dam hasn't burst yet. Some generation down the road will have to deal with that problem. But if we can hold it off another few decades, I'll be dead. Won't be my problem anymore."

"Isn't that a bit morbid?"

"Not at my age. Nobody likes to talk about dying, but when you get into your seventies, your eighties, and Lord-willing, your nineties, well you can't really deny what's coming your way. All my friends are gone except for Elliot and Lillian. The only reason we're still here is because of Elliot. You know about what he can do, yes?"

"Yeah, I know." Had Elliot really saved Gram's life less than a half-hour ago? It felt like years.

"That's that, then. Not much else I can say. We're old people and we won't live forever." He stopped, looked back, and winked. "But we're gonna cause a helluva ruckus on our way out."

After a few more passageways, Sully brought them to a metal door. They stepped inside to an entirely empty room save for a podium near the center. Carved from a stalagmite that spread into the ground, the podium had two thick chains locked into its side. No furniture or lamps or anything loose could be seen. Two lights embedded in the walls provided illumination.

A long strip of metal ran around the room at shoulder-height. Elliot and Gram stood at one wall facing the strip. Gram hefted her big bag as she adjusted her robe — a long sleeved piece like something out of an old martial arts movie.

With a flick of her hand, a thin chain dropped from the sleeve. Elliot took hold of it and connected it to rings welded into the metal strip. Three more chains had already been attached. Gram looked up as Sully and Roni entered.

Before Gram could speak, the heavy footsteps of the Golem thumped in the air. She smiled. "Sounds like you made a good one for this job."

"Of course I did," Sully said, straightening his collar.

"Make sure everyone is set. I'll get the book."

With barely a glance at Roni, Gram left the room. The thumping grew louder, and in a few seconds, the Golem ducked its head as it entered.

"Wait there." Sully pointed toward the podium, and the Golem walked over and stood at its side.

Roni had a dozen questions in her head — a number which could easily grow into a million — but she kept silent and observed. That seemed to work better with this group. Sure enough, Sully waved her over toward the wall.

"Do like me," he said.

He picked up one of the chains. Roni did the same. He took the free end and wrapped it around his waist like a belt. She did the same. He pinched the tip of the chain and it snapped open like a snake's mouth. She did, too.

"This is called the dead end." With his free hand, he pulled on the part of the chain secured to the wall. "This is the live end. Got it?"

Roni nodded. He then clamped the dead end onto the live end. It cinched along his waist, and he let out a light huff. Roni followed suit. Her chain tightened fast but stopped short of being uncomfortable.

Sully walked over to Elliot and whispered something. Roni ignored them. She had enough to digest without worrying about things they wanted to keep secret.

She tugged on the thin chain. For such a small thing, it sure appeared to hold well. But anything built to handle weight or stress was only as strong as its weakest point. The chain might be stronger than it looked, but what about the metal strip? She searched along the strip to locate how it fastened to the wall, but before she could find an answer, Gram returned.

Sully and Elliot grew still as Gram walked with solemn steps to the podium. As she set the book on the podium and undid the chains around the book, she moved with reverential grace. Roni half-expected organ music to start playing. Gram took the open chains and attached them to those chains embedded into the stone podium. She then walked to the wall and went through the same procedure Sully had instructed Roni in. When finished, all four of them had secured themselves to chains connected with the metal strip in the wall.

With a nod from Gram, Elliot stepped in front of Roni. He adjusted the chain around his belt so that it did not get tangled with Sully's. Easing Roni with a smile, Elliot said, "The ticket stub, please."

She pulled it out, and he turned her hand over, setting the stub on her palm. He then inhaled slow and deep, exhaling with a satisfied and audible sigh. "Ready?" he asked.

"No," Roni said. "But you might as well do whatever you're going to do anyway."

He held his cane at the middle and raised it to the same height as the ticket stub. With his other hand held straight upward, he drew a circle in the air, going completely around Roni's hands. First one direction, then the other. Back and forth. Clockwise and counter-clockwise. Over and over.

She first noticed the aroma. Similar to Elliot's wood fire smell, she gave it little thought, but as he continued to encircle her hands, the smell grew stronger. A rich, musky scent like a humble cabin in the mountains. Then she felt the air warm around her fingers as if she held them over a campfire. Finally, the light surrounding her hands altered — shifted into a pleasant amber.

Elliot touched the top of his cane to the light and stopped making circles with his hand. The light held to the cane like a balloon statically stuck to a sleeve. He plucked the ticket stub from Roni's hand, and placed it in the light. Floating like a gliding butterfly, it hovered in that light with majestic grace. Roni's heart leaped. It was beautiful. Elliot made a graceful bow of his head and gently stepped toward the Golem.

But a few steps short, he stopped. With an incredulous look, he turned toward Sully. "You didn't give it any hands."

"There wasn't time, and it was more important that he have the structural build to —"

"Without hands, it cannot hold the ticket stub."

Speaking in a slow growl, Sully said, "He doesn't need hands. The ticket only has to be on his body."

Elliot glanced at the Golem. "It doesn't have anything to put the stub on."

"Oh, for crying out loud," Gram said. "Sully, fix it."

Grumbling as he crossed over, Sully gave Elliot a slight push out of the way. He snapped his chain aside and approached the Golem. "Sorry about this," he said. He jabbed his hand into the Golem's side — right where the appendix would be, if it were human — and scooped out some clay. Making a grand bow, he said, "Will that suffice, your Highness?"

Elliot did not take the bait. He simply strode forward and used the cane to set the ball of light with the ticket stub into the hole Sully had created. "How do we keep the ticket from falling out?"

As if staring at an incompetent student, Sully slapped the clay he held back over the hole. "Your ticket doesn't need to be visible." He scurried back to his spot on the wall with a smirk on his lips.

Elliot scowled but did not provoke the situation further — probably because of the sharp look Gram sent his way. Instead, he took up his position and paused to make eye contact with each person. Each time, with Gram and then Sully, they nodded back at him. When he looked to Roni, she nodded, too — a bit vigorous, but she did nod.

"Let's get on with this. Darin can't wait forever." Sully said. To Roni, he added, "This guy can be so dramatic."

"Very well." Elliot reached out toward the book with his cane and flipped the cover open.

As had happened before, the room depressurized. Air sucked into the book at typhoon speeds. If not for the chains around their waists, the whole team would have fallen in.

Gram cupped her mouth and yelled each word slowly. "We only have about ten minutes before these chains give way. Get that thing moving."

Sully gave her a thumbs-up. He then made a series of gestures at the Golem which Roni could not follow. The Golem stomped across the room. Its size and weight kept it anchored to the floor despite the winds whipping around it. When it reached the podium, the Golem raised its leg high and stepped into the book like one might step into a bathtub with a tall side.

For several seconds the gale died down as the Golem blocked much of the path for the air to enter the book. A high-pitch whined while the Golem lowered itself deeper. Roni opened her mouth to ask how long the Golem could handle such strong winds, but it disappeared from sight and the winds picked right back up.

Lightning flashes flickered from within the stormy book, creating monstrous shadows upon the cavern walls. Several seconds later, thunder cracked — miles away in the distance of the book. Roni watched her three teammates for some clue as to what might come next. All three remained stoic as they watched the book. Only the occasional strain against the chains registered on their faces.

Thinking about the chains made Roni aware of the biting sting on her hip. The wind howled as it pulled and pulled. She needed to readjust her chain or soon it would cut into her skin.

With one hand, she slid her fingers along the spine of the chain, seeking the point where it had connected with itself. Hopefully, she could ease it up so she had some room to maneuver. But when she brushed across the connecting end, the clamp sprung open.

She screamed as the wind grabbed hold of her, wrenched her off her feet, and reeled her in toward the book. Her fingers stubbed into the edge of the podium. Panicked, she scrabbled for a grip.

Her legs rose higher, and she heard a shout. "I've got you!" Over her shoulder, she saw Elliot standing with his legs angled and his arm locked around her foot.

She attempted to bend at the waist, to reach out and pull herself closer to Elliot. No good. Her stomach muscles were not strong enough. Something to work on — if she survived this.

A hurricane roar poured out of the book along with a hot, foul odor like a decomposing animal in the worst of summer. With her hands finding holds on the podium, she dared to gaze into the book.

She saw a tunnel of blood-soaked flesh — red and undulating. Like an internal organ exposed to the air, she could see the small veins and arteries along the tunnel walls. Things moved from behind the thin membrane. Some of the things looked like they had faces.

But the tunnel wasn't everything. Roni also saw an opening at the end. Bright light shined and strong winds blew across as if she were in a balloon with miles of sky below. A dark cloud passed by, crackling with lightning, only to be followed by a darker, more violent storm cloud.

As she watched, she felt as if something watched her back. A glance to the side — she saw a human face with jagged teeth and sunken eyes staring at her from behind the membrane. But it vanished, leaving her to question if she had seen it at all.

"Hold on!" Gram yelled.

Roni saw her grandmother whip out a new chain from her sleeves. This one looked thicker than the others as it flapped in the wind like a streamer. Elliot tried three times to snag it, and on the fourth attempt, he succeeded. He wrapped the chain around Roni's ankle, secured it, and then carefully walked back to the wall, pulling himself along his own chain but never letting go of Roni's chain.

Sully waved his arm in the air and pointed at his watch. "Two minutes left!"

Lowering her head so she wouldn't have to see that horrific tunnel, Roni thought to ask what they would do in two minutes. The thin chains would give way, and she had the distinct impression that the thicker chain keeping her tethered to this world had been an emergency situation. Gram would not be able to create enough of those in time to save the whole team. Making them in the first place must have taken a lot out of her, otherwise, she would have made them all thicker at the start.

Or not. Perhaps she purposely made them thin so that they acted like a timer. Gram had said these other universes brought with them strange bacteria and such. She would want to limit everyone's exposure.

Which meant that if the Golem did not return in time, they would close the book. Darin would be lost forever.

Roni's head snapped towards Gram. She could see it clearly on the old woman's wrinkled face. Gram's lips rolled in as she nodded back. There would be a hard choice coming in less than two minutes. No, not a choice — a duty.

"One minute," Sully called out.

Roni adjusted her grip on the podium and gazed into the book. "Darin!"

"Close the book," Gram said above the harsh winds. "Close it now."

"There's still a minute."

"We can't wait for the chains to snap. Close the book."

Roni strained to see any sign of the Golem or Darin — only sky and the foul tunnel that turned her stomach. She put her hand on the book cover and felt her body pulled closer in. The thick chain on her ankle kept her from spiraling into that blood-drenched abyss.

She saw her hand on the cover. Darin had fallen in there, had seen those faces, and confronted those storms. They couldn't leave him in there. But then they couldn't leave the book open for too much longer. The whole point was to close these rips to protect everyone in the world — not simply one man who lied in order to get to these books.

Gram pointed to Elliot. "Help her."

"I can do it," Roni yelled back.

She tried to lift the cover but the strong winds kept it flat on the podium. Changing her grip, she tried again. Half-an-inch maybe. Putting more muscle into it, she worked to pry the cover loose. A little further. If she could get it to the point that enough air shot underneath, it would snap shut on its own.

But she stopped. A flash of lightning revealed a dark spot in the clouds below. It grew fast as it bulleted toward her.

The Golem!

When it reached the tunnel, its body blocked most of the airway. The winds died and Roni flopped to the ground. She scrambled back to the wall, her heart hammering, her lungs burning.

The chains around her never snapped apart. Instead, they fell to the ground and fractured into hundreds of tiny pieces. Before Roni's astonished eyes, those pieces then broke apart into bits of dust.

Elliot sped across the room with his cane at the ready. The Golem stepped out of the book and the terrible winds returned. But Elliot wedged his cane under the book cover and put his body weight down on the other end. It levered the cover up and over. Before the book had slammed shut, Gram had fresh chains, thick chains wrapping around it.

Roni's shoulders dropped. The Golem had returned empty-handed. "We failed," she said.

"Not at all," Sully said, his eyes on his watch. "4 ... 3 ... 2 ... 1 ..."

The Golem lost all appearance of life. It stood like nothing more than a block of clay. Pieces of it crumbled off. Then more. In seconds, the entire creature disintegrated into a pile of clay pebbles. Standing in the middle of the pile was a naked man. He had stark white hair and his eyes blazed wide open, but Roni knew right away — this was Darin.

CHAPTER 10

For Roni, the next several hours blurred by in a rush of activity. The moment Darin appeared, Elliot jumped into action. Using his cane and hand motions, he checked that Darin was unharmed — physically at least. Sweat poured down Elliot's face as he worked, but when he finally gave Gram an affirmative nod, she said he could rest. Elliot then collapsed.

In a calm yet authoritative voice, Gram instructed Roni to go further into the caverns until she found the door marked with the number 2. Inside, Roni found two wheelchairs. She brought one back and assisted Gram in helping lug Elliot into the chair.

"Get the other one," Gram said.

Roni hustled back to the storage room and wheeled the second chair to the group. She brought it straight to Gram.

"Not for me," Gram said.

Roni looked over at Sully. He had been leaning against the wall ever since the book had been closed. Roni had not given it any thought, but now she saw the pasty look in his face and the stark concentration in his eyes. Sully used all his will to keep standing.

As she helped the man settle in the wheelchair, she thought how frail these people really were. They could summon tremendous strength in short bursts but nothing could change the fact that their bodies had been around a long time. Sixties and seventies were not ages for most people to be fighting off other universes.

"They'll be fine," Gram said, as if she could read Roni's mind. "A good night's sleep and they'll be back up as if nothing ever happened."

Roni imagined a porcupine in a tutu and then stared hard at Gram. After a moment, Gram raised her eyebrows. "What?"

"Nothing," Roni said, hiding her relief. "Just testing something."

"I can't read minds."

"How do you know that's what I —"

"I've known you for your entire life. I can read your face easy."

Roni decided to accept the explanation. "Are you sure you don't need help, too?" she asked.

"Elliot healed me right before we started this. I'm fine. Another time might be different."

Following more orders, Roni wheeled each man to the elevator and took them to their apartment while Gram kept on eye on Darin. For his part, Darin never moved. He barely blinked. He stared straight ahead, and never even flinched when Gram placed a robe from the storage room around his body. Even though it appeared that Darin would be no trouble, Roni hurried to situate Elliot and Sully so that she could return to the caverns as fast as possible.

When she finally rejoined Gram, part of her wished she had stayed with Sully. She had heard of the soldier's thousand yard stare, and she had seen the glazed look of dementia patients. Put the two together and it came close to what she saw in Darin's eyes — close but not enough.

"What do we do now?" Roni asked.

Gram looked him over. "He's alive, and Elliot said he's in good enough health. We'll cut him loose. Let him decide for himself what he does now."

"We can't do that."

"What do you think we should do? Hold him prisoner against his will?"

"First off, look at him. He looks out of his mind. And after what he just saw, he probably is lucky for that. Don't we have a responsibility to him?"

"We didn't ask him to break into our private rooms and attempt to steal from us. He did this to himself."

"But what if he talks to people? He's seen what you can do."

Gram rubbed the back of her hands as she flexed her fingers. "I swear, these old hands get worse every day."

"Gram!"

"Stop worrying. You think this has never happened before? That in centuries of these books being in existence, you think nobody has ever discovered the secret we hold? Nothing will happen. We let him go, and he'll return to his life. Or he won't. That's his business. If he tells anybody what he saw, where he was, any of it at all, you know what will happen?"

Roni knew right away. "They'll think he's crazy."

"If he's lucky, they'll think he's joking or having a bad day or something like that. If he's unlucky, he'll be institutionalized in a psychiatric facility, possibly for the rest of his life. Which, I'll point out, is not always the worst outcome. Considering what happened to him, a shrink could be exactly what he'll need."

Crossing her arms, Roni bumped her back against the wall. She swallowed down the bubble of emotion riding up her throat. Her voice shook as she said, "Dad is institutionalized."

"Exactly. You know that he gets good care. If Darin's mind can't handle what he saw, he can get good care, too."

"I-Is that what happened to Dad? Did he see into another universe?"

Gram's face shifted as she put out her arms. "Honey, no. Your father never knew about this side of our life. He simply loved your mother — more than most ever love another. When she died, he couldn't take it. That's all. I promise."

She hugged Roni, and for a few seconds, being smothered by Gram's large bosom felt safe. But then Roni lifted her head and saw Darin.

"Doesn't this trouble you?"

Following Roni's gaze, Gram stepped back and straightened her robe. "I'm too old to worry about things that don't matter. He'll fall into whatever he falls into. Serves him right for meddling where he doesn't belong."

"That part, though. That's what I mean. Shouldn't we be concerned about the fact that he must be working for somebody. He obviously used a date with me as a way to gain access to the caverns. That means he targeted me specifically. I saw where he works, and I met his mother. Trust me. This man is not a criminal mastermind, and I didn't see anything to indicate that he would be taking the time to watch me, learn my habits, confirm that I'd be able to get him into the basement, and then try to charm me into a date so he could steal a book all on his own. Not this man."

"I'll think on it, but you need to get used to it. A secret as big as ours is never really a secret. He wouldn't be the first to attempt to steal a book for somebody else. As long as there have been people like us fighting to protect our universe, there also have been those who want access to these other worlds. For greed, for power, for curiosity, in some cases for religious confirmation — whatever the reason, you'll learn that sometimes our worst fights are with other people, not the creatures living in these universes."

"I suppose," Roni said. Then her head caught up. "Did you say creatures?"

Gram smirked. "We'll deal with that another time. Please escort Darin out onto the street. He's not to be our problem anymore."

Roni knew Gram's tones well — the conversation was over. Without another word, Roni took Darin by the hand and walked back up through the cavern. He followed simply and quietly. Even his footsteps were quiet.

In the elevator, she watched his immobile face. Nothing. He stared blankly at the wall. More than anything, his white hair spoke volumes of the horror he had witnessed. And not just the hair on his head. His eyebrows, his whiskers, even the hair on his arms — all of it had gone stark white.

On the main floor, she led him out the front door. The sun rose to start a new day. How could that be possible? Roni had no idea so many hours had gone by. She felt tired but not the *up all night* tired she knew from her college days. In that cavern, there were no natural indicators of the passage of time, and so much had happened that she never bothered to check her phone. But an entire night?

She would have to ask Gram or the boys about that. For now, though, she had to deal with Darin. He stood on the sidewalk, his eyes roving up and down the street. That seemed like an improvement.

"Darin? Can you hear me?"

He turned his head towards her.

"Hi," she said. "You're safe now. We got you back."

He said nothing. He only gazed upon her face with an inscrutable expression.

"That's okay," she said. "I'm guessing it'll take a while for you to readjust."

She thought about what Gram had said — that she should let Darin loose to find his own way, that he would probably end up committed to a mental hospital of some kind, and that he would be better off there because professionals could look after him. Except she couldn't do that. Maybe an institution was where he would end up, but she had to give him a chance for something better, at least.

"Come on with me," she said. Leading him by the hand, she walked to her car. They got in — she had to buckle his seatbelt for him — and she headed west for Lancaster. “I’m taking you home.”

CHAPTER 11

As she drove west on Route 30, Roni discovered that some lies are easier than others. For the entire length of the trip, she struggled to come up with any story that would be plausible. One look at Darin, and his mother would know something serious had happened. On top of which, Roni had to maintain the fiction that she was Darin's girlfriend.

She texted Jane to let her know she was coming and that she had Darin. Roni figured this would put Jane in a joyous mood, and that might ease down whatever lie she could concoct. When she pulled up to the house, Jane rushed across the front lawn, tears streaming, arms open.

After kisses upon kisses, shock at his appearance and tears at his arrival, Darin's mother helped him into the house. Roni followed, still unsure of what to say, but Jane didn't ask. She focused entirely on her son. With a hug, a kiss, a hand always on him as if afraid he might vanish, Jane brought him upstairs to his childhood bedroom, now a plain guest room.

From the doorway, Roni watched as Jane clucked about the room. She chatted to Darin about her worries and fears and the neighborhood gossip and anything else that came to mind. All the while, she wiped down the dresser, fluffed the pillows, and cleared away some toys for a cat Roni had yet to see.

Darin stood in the center of the room, staring out the window. At one point, Jane halted her manic preparations and put her hand on his cheek. He tilted his head towards her — just a bit — and his lips formed a hint of a smile.

"You probably need a little rest. We'll let you be. Okay? We can talk at dinner." She kissed him again and shooed Roni downstairs.

When they entered the living room, Roni headed for the couch, but Jane pointed down the hall. She followed Darin's mother through the kitchen and into a back room. It was small and lacked all the charm the rest of the house held. An ironing board stood against one wall. Two folding chairs had been placed next to a window, and an ashtray sat on one chair next to a pack of cigarettes.

Jane lifted the window open and set the ashtray on the ledge. She sat in one chair, pulled out a lighter from her pocket, and grabbed the cigarettes. As she lit up, she indicated the now empty chair for Roni. Though Roni did not smoke, she noticed that Jane never offered her a cigarette.

Puffing away, Jane stared out the window. Roni started to speak, but Jane put out her hand. They remained quiet until she had smoked half of her cigarette.

"I'm sure you have quite a story to tell me, but I don't want to hear it."

"I know you think —"

"Don't embarrass yourself. Be smart and shut up."

Roni didn't know whether to be happy or concerned — especially because she never did come up with a good explanation.

Jane went on, "I really thought we had hit it off. I suppose on some level you were being honest with me. But I don't want to listen to you lie about Darin. It's obvious that you knew where he was and what he was up to when you came here. You must have at least had an idea of where he could be. Otherwise, you never would have been able to bring him back so soon. Then again, you didn't really bring him back, did you? You brought me a ghost of my son. So, if you ever gave a crap about him, if anything you told me was true, then please answer me directly. Is he a drug addict now? Did you get him hooked on something that made him this way?"

"No. Never." Roni did not have to pretend her shock.

"Do you know what's wrong with him?"

She hesitated, and Jane picked up on it right away.

"You won't tell me, will you?"

"I'm sorry," Roni said. "I really can't. It wouldn't matter anyway."

"How can you say that? You've seen him. He looks older than me. What did you do to him that would cause that?"

"I didn't do anything. I swear. He did it to himself."

"What?"

"He ... well, it's like he stuck his hand in a raging fire and then was surprised that he got burned."

Jane stubbed out her cigarette with more force than necessary. "You're blaming him for this?"

"It's not like that. It's hard to explain. I mean, I can't explain it. I'm not allowed to." Roni dropped her head into her hands. "I'm messing this whole thing up."

"That's evident. Why don't you stop tiptoeing around the things you can't tell me, and start with the things you can tell me? How about that?"

Roni thought it over a moment. Crafting her words carefully, she said, "Your son asked me out on a date because he needed access to where I work. I didn't know that at the time. I thought he liked me. But he didn't care about me at all. He used me to get into a private collection of items and exposed himself to highly dangerous, um, things. It was contact with those things that changed him."

"And I take it you won't ever tell me what those things are."

"I can't. I don't even know for sure what he saw or exactly how it all happened for him. But I do know that you shouldn't treat him like he's crazy. You'd be better off approaching him as if he were a war veteran or something — a person with PTSD. That might get you the best results."

Jane digested this information before leveling her coldest glare at Roni. "I want you to leave my house and never come back. I don't ever want to see you again. If, someday years from now, you walk into a store or a restaurant or anywhere, and you see me, please have the decency to leave so that I don't have to endure the pain of being reminded you exist."

Roni wanted to say something that would repair the damage, but those cold eyes stopped her. Unlike Darin's lifeless eyes, Jane's spewed an icy venom that threatened violence along with the hatred behind them. Roni lowered her gaze as she stood.

"I am sorry," she said. "I had no idea that Darin had intended —"

"Get out!" Jane's body quaked as she yelled.

Roni left. She got back in her car and turned the key. Nothing happened. She tried again and heard a slight whine. She could feel Darin's mother watching from the living room window. Trying again, she almost had it. Ten more excruciating seconds went by before the engine finally turned over.

She floored the gas and screeched her tires as she roared onto the street. As fast as the road would allow her, she got onto the highway and made for home. But in Lancaster, Route 30 had sections which could slow down to a baby crawl — especially around the shopping outlets. After twenty minutes and four lights — miles of store after store after store — she needed a break.

When she hit the small village of Ronks, she knew she had finally gone through the last major section of shopping outlets. On her left, she saw Miller's Smorgasbord — a Pennsylvania Dutch all-you-can-eat buffet that had been in Lancaster for decades. That sounded perfect.

In minutes, she had parked, entered, grabbed a plate, and piled on the food. Mashed potatoes, macaroni and cheese, and dried corn. A chef standing by a slab of roast beef cut her three lovely slices to which she added a thick gravy. She set the plate at her table and returned to make a second plate with a baked potato, creamed spinach, and popcorn shrimp. On her way back, she saw a slice of shoofly pie which she nabbed with her free hand.

Sitting in the back corner, she stared at her gluttonous banquet and felt all desire to eat drain from her gut. All the food slapped together on her plates reminded her of the twisted mess she had seen within that book. A tunnel of evil stretching down to a tumultuous sky. But at times it became a pleasant sky. It could not have been too pleasant — it destroyed Darin's mind.

All for what? Even if he had succeeded, what then? After such an experience, would he simply hand the book over to whomever had hired him? Just take the money and forget about it?

No. He would never be able to do that. Unless they were paying an enormous sum. Which, considering the value of a book like that, they just might.

Since Darin would not be delivering the book, the buyers would most likely be sending others to steal it. The more she thought about it, the more she understood why Darin chose to go through her. Gram was too old to play at a date, and all three of the Old Gang had been defending their turf for so long that they would have recognized Darin for what he was right away. Which meant that the others who might come looking for the books would also attempt to get it through Roni.

I'm never going to be to able date again, she thought with a chuckle. But the humor faded fast. Not only would she forever have to doubt the motivations of those she came into contact with, but she could never warn them either. After all, she would not know who was an authentic person and who was a liar attempting to steal a book until that person took action. After that point, it would be too late — as it was too late to save Darin.

She hated the thought that crept beneath the surface, the thought that she knew she had been circling for too long, the thought she feared giving voice to — but the time had arrived. Staring at all her untouched food, she said, "I can't be a part of this."

Usually, when she voiced a decision that troubled her, she felt better. Not this time. Because voicing it did not put it into action nor did it make the next step any easier. She had to tell Gram.

The lengthy drive back to Olburg mounted the dread for her. She envisioned the arguments Gram would make, the anger and fierce words Gram might throw at her, and she prepared her counter-arguments. But in the end, she knew how it would stand — she had agreed to join the group, and only a day or so later, she was backing out. It didn't help that Gram, Elliot, and Sully were approaching the ends of their lives. At least, that was what Gram would say. The fact that they had at least a decade each to go meant nothing to them — especially considering the dangerous lifestyle they lived.

Back and forth the debate raged in Roni's head until she blared rock music to drown out her thoughts. It worked for a short time. Nothing, however, could stop the inevitable. Roni reached the bookstore.

The front door was locked. Gram had mentioned that she would not open the store for the day — Elliot and Sully needed rest. Roni used her key to get in, locked the door behind her, and rode the elevator to the top floor. She knocked on Gram's door.

"Come in," Gram called from her kitchen.

Roni entered the comfortable apartment. Decorated with the right balance of furniture, rugs, books, and paintings to create a cozy, lived-in feel, the rooms never bordered on cluttered or dirty. In the kitchen, Roni found Gram sitting at a small, round table eating her lunch — a tuna sandwich with a dill pickle on the side.

Gram's welcoming smile faded when she saw Roni. "What's wrong?"

Standing in the doorway, Roni picked at her nails, keeping her eyes down, and figured barreling through would be her best option. "No easy way to say any of this, but after looking into that book and seeing what it did to Darin and then I thought about the years ahead, well —"

"It's not usually like this. If it was, we never would have lived this long."

"Still, I don't think this is right for me."

"I see." Gram returned to her sandwich.

"I want to help you, but I don't see how I can go through what you all do. Especially because you have powers. I'm just a regular person."

"Sure. We'll find somebody else to take your place." She gazed out the window near the kitchen table.

Roni's fingers clenched. "Don't be like that."

"What now?" Gram said, still remaining calm. "You said you don't want to be in this, and I said that was fine. What's the matter? You want out, you got out."

"Don't you even care? Or am I just another employee?"

"I learned long ago that I can't force you to do the right thing. I never could."

"And there it is," Roni said like a lawyer who caught a witness in a lie. "You think what I'm doing is wrong. You always think I make the wrong choice."

"No, Roni. You are the one who thinks you make the wrong choice. But then you do it anyway. The fact is that I told you to walk away from all of this before you learned too much. Now that you know, you regret getting involved. Well, I'm sorry that reality isn't filled with all the easy-living dreams you wanted, but that's reality no matter what universe you're in. Running away from your commitments won't change that. I would have thought you'd have figured that out by now."

"Are you saying that I run from commitment?"

Gram set her sandwich down and wiped her mouth with a napkin. "You clearly want to have a fight, so I'll ask you to leave. I'd like to eat in peace. Also, please leave your key to the store by the register."

Roni's face dropped. "You're kicking me out? Firing me?"

"You were never hired, so I can't really fire you."

"But I'm no longer welcome here — is that it?"

Gram leaned back in her chair. As she played with the beads on her necklace, her stern face grew dark. "We shared with you our greatest secrets, and we did so because you made a commitment to us. These secrets take precedence over all else in our lives — even family. I love you, Roni. I truly do. I don't regret all the years spent raising you after your mother died. I don't want you thinking that. But if you are not part of this group, then you cannot be in this building ever again. The secrets we hold here are too important, too powerful, for us to risk another Darin situation."

Roni wanted to scream. But she wanted to break down crying, too.

Before her body or mind could decide which reaction to have, her cellphone rang. Out of habit, she glanced at the screen — Jane Lander.

Roni accepted the call. "Jane?"

"You have to come back here right now. You just have to. I don't know what to do. What's going on with him? I need your help."

"Calm down. What's happened?"

"It's Darin. He's gone."

CHAPTER 12

Roni ignored the sickening roil in her stomach as she drove yet again to Lancaster. Part of her felt ill over what might have happened to Darin. But mostly, she felt ill over Gram.

Their argument — and no matter how pleasant a face Gram put on it, Roni knew it was an argument — had not ended with Jane Lander's phone call. If anything, it grew worse.

"I'm on my way," Roni had said to Jane.

But after ending the call, Gram said, "You most certainly are not. This is a situation that no longer has anything to do with you."

"How can you say that?"

"I didn't. You're the one who wanted to quit all of this. Well then, quit. Elliot, Sully, and I have been dealing with jokers like Darin for ages. We'll find him, and we'll take care of it."

"And what's that mean? You'll lock him away in a mental hospital? Or maybe you'll drive him out to Philly or Baltimore and let him loose to live out his life as another homeless person talking to himself on the street corner. Is that your idea of taking care of it?"

"You think I would do that after —"

"You told me to do that very thing. Why wouldn't I expect you to do it, too?"

"Because, young lady," Gram said, her glower silencing Roni, "things changed when you brought him to his mother's house. You've involved other people, extra variables, and so the simple option, the one I suggested for you, no longer applies."

"But —"

"You can argue all day long but it won't change the truth. And while you're waffling on where you actually stand in these matters, remember that Darin is out there, walking around. The longer we wait to find him, the more likely our chance that something bad will happen. So, make up your mind. Are you part of this team or not?"

Roni's eyes narrowed. She felt her pulse beating along her neck and up the side of her head. "I'm going out to find him."

Gram's mouth raised into an annoying *knowing* smile. "Then we're glad to have you stay with us."

"Only for this job. Once all of this with Darin is sorted out, I'm done."

Roni didn't wait to hear or see Gram's reaction. She stormed out of the apartment and took the stairs down to her car. That was over an hour ago.

As she neared Lancaster, Roni cleared her mind of her personal problems and focused on finding Darin. Thankfully, Darin's mother had the sense to keep this private. Had she called the police, and if they found him, he would certainly be held for psychiatric assessment. This way, at least, they could bring Darin back to Jane's house.

But was that even the best thing to do for him? Roni had no idea how to gauge such a determination when dealing with other universes, hellish tunnels, and magic warriors. She let free a short laugh at the idea of Gram and her boys as magic warriors.

In the town of Gap, there was one intersection with a traffic light at the bottom of a steep hill. Slowing down for the red light, Roni's jaw dropped. There he was. Walking on the side of the road and headed her way. She pulled into the parking lot for a local chain of pizza shops called Two Cousins and got out.

"Darin! Are you okay?"

Approaching him with caution, she marveled at her luck in stumbling upon him. But then she decided it hadn't been luck at all. Route 30 was the main road connecting Lancaster with Philadelphia. Presumably, Darin wanted to get back to his own home or perhaps his office at Page Brothers. It wasn't strange at all, then, that he would take this route. But walking? That was strange.

She stepped in front of him and he stopped. "Hi, there. Remember me? Roni?"

"I need to get to the zoo."

"The Philadelphia Zoo? That's a long way from here." She pointed toward the pizza shop. "You'll need your energy, and I'm starving. Missed out on lunch. Let's go sit and have a bite. We'll figure out how to get you to the zoo. Sound good?"

She didn't wait for an answer. Taking him by the arm, she led him into the restaurant. He did not resist.

The savory aroma of cheesesteaks and pizza caused her stomach to growl. At the counter, she ordered two cheesesteaks — one with mushrooms and one with sweet peppers. On their date the night before, Darin had mentioned liking sweet peppers. At least, she thought he did.

They sat in a booth — the place was empty — and while they waited for the food, she rifled off a text to Jane telling her that Darin was safe and would be home soon. She also texted Gram saying much the same. Then she set the phone down and took hold of his hands.

"You in there? Remember this? You and me out on a date? This is how it all started. I know you used me to get to the books, but maybe you actually enjoyed our date a little. See, I'm thinking that you're like a coma patient, and if I keep connecting you with the real world, if you keep hearing my voice and remembering our date, then maybe you'll come back."

"I'm here," he said in a monotone. "I need to go to the zoo."

A man walked out with their food. He set down two plates and two plastic, red baskets that each had a cheesesteak. After he returned to the kitchen, Roni jumped right in, taking a big bite of her sandwich.

"I need to go to the zoo."

"I know," she said around a mouthful of food. "I'll figure out how to get you there, but right now, you should eat. You've got to understand that your mother is worried about you. And there are others, too. People who want to make sure you don't cause any trouble about the books. So, let's eat up, and I'll take you home. Then we can work on getting you to the zoo, if that's what you want."

She nudged his plate closer. He glanced down, and something must have clicked in his head because he picked up his food and took a bite. And another. He pushed the food in fast, chewing hard, as he tried to inhale the whole thing.

"Slow down. You'll choke."

But he continued to wolf down each bite. "Good," he grunted.

"Darin, I want you to listen to me. Can you do that?"

He stopped eating and raised his head.

"I want to help you," she said, putting her hand on the table, palm up. "I forgive you for using our date to get to the caverns. I don't know why you did it or if somebody hired you or what, but I forgive you. Nobody deserves what happened to you. But in order for me to help, I have to understand what exactly happened. What did you see in there that scared you so much?"

Darin scanned the room, but Roni could not tell if he searched for an attack or an escape. "I need to get to the zoo."

"Why the zoo? What's there? What's so important?"

He reached across the table and clasped both hands to her face. "You want to help me? Zoo." Before she could answer, he leaned closer and kissed her on the lips.

When he returned to his seat, he tucked into the remainder of his meal. Roni watched him, the taste of him lingering on her lips — sweet and clean. He peeked up at her like a schoolboy afraid he had scared off the girl. But then a mature look crossed his face, one filled with masculine confidence.

He leaned back and grinned. "Don't take me back to Lancaster. I love my mother, but she can't handle this right now. I'll be better off at my apartment. Can we go there?"

Roni could not move. She could not speak. Her brain kept trying to process that this man who had been like a zombie suddenly spoke free and fluent while flirting with her in a casual manner. She had no idea what to make of any of it, but she agreed with one thing — taking him back to his mother's place would be a bad idea.

"Sure," she finally said. "Let's go to your apartment. We'll figure things out from there."

After clearing their trash and placing the red baskets on the counter, they got in Roni's car and drove toward the Philly area. Darin moved like a normal person — strolling to the car, settling in the passenger seat, buckling up. It was as if some loose wires had reconnected and his brain now worked properly.

Except Roni did not feel comfortable. A voice deep within urged her to drop Darin off at his apartment, get the heck out of there, go to the bookstore, and report everything to Gram.

No. That was her nerves talking. Too many cop shows and horror movies had warped her sense of human behavior. Not to mention the fact that Darin's behavior could not be predicted upon anything she had ever experienced. She had no base for measuring how a man would react to being pulled into a book and seeing insane things only to be rescued by a clay statue come to life.

Darin lived about ten minutes from his law office. His apartment building stood two blocks off the main drag next to a small park that consisted mostly of a basketball court and a thin patch of grass. Roni parked on the street, and they walked up together.

He lived on the third floor, and from what Roni could see, the place desperately needed to be remodeled. Probably hadn't had any major work since the 1960s.

The apartment itself looked much better. When it came to cleanliness and organization, Darin had followed in his mother's footsteps. Even after a few days of neglect, the place sparkled. Not a fleck of dust had dared to settle on the carefully positioned furniture.

"Damn," Roni said. "This place even smells perfect."

"Wait here." Darin set his keys on a silver plate by the door and disappeared down the single hallway that led to a bathroom and a bedroom.

"Sure. No problem." She pulled out her phone and rang up Jane. "I found him."

Jane cried for a moment and reduced it to a few sniffles. "Thank goodness," she said. "Tell me where you are and I'll come pick him up."

"That's not necessary. He asked me to take him back to his apartment. I don't know what happened to him, but he's starting to sound normal again."

"Don't be foolish. He obviously needs my care right now. Unless you're planning on spending the next few days with him until we know for sure that he's okay. I take it by your silence that you won't be doing that. So, please, get in your car and drive him back."

"I can't. He specifically asked to be here, and I'm inclined to —"

"I don't care about your inclinations. I want my son home, in my house, by the end of the day."

Back in her high school days, Roni had crossed swords with more than her share of overprotective parents. The psychologist Gram had her seeing once said that losing her parents at such a young age had created a void, and she sought to fill that void with boyfriends. Maybe. But maybe it had more to do with the type of boyfriend she chose rather than choosing any boy. As an adult, however, Roni had no intention of letting another parent walk all over her — even if she wasn't really Darin's girlfriend to begin with.

"No," Roni said. "I am not driving between Philly and Lancaster again. Not tonight. Darin told me he wanted to be in his own place and that's where he is. You want to dote on him? Be my guest. Come on by tomorrow at any time, and he's all yours."

"Now you listen to me."

"Jane. I called you so that you wouldn't worry about your son, not so that you could yell at me. Good night." Before Jane could say another word, Roni ended the call.

"Thank you," Darin said from the hallway. He walked out of the shadows wearing his pajama bottoms and a t-shirt. "I love her. I do. But I have important things to do, and she would only get in my way."

Roni plopped down on the couch. "You don't have to do anything tonight. Come here. Sit."

Darin obliged, settling in next to her. She put her arm around his shoulders as he nestled his head on her chest. "I have to get to a zoo."

"Tomorrow. You can explain it all to me then. I'm just glad you're okay. You are, right?"

He peeked up at her. "I don't know what I am."

Stroking his hair, she said, "Of course. You've been through a lot. We all have."

"The zoo," he said, but his words drifted off.

Roni let her head fall to the back of the couch. She closed her eyes. Nothing felt right in this apartment, but she was too tired to do anything about it. Besides, she needed to stay for Darin. Tomorrow, Jane would come and Roni could be done with it. Until then, she would have to take care of him.

Darin's soft snoring drifted up to her ears. "Well," she whispered, "at least one of us can get some rest. I don't think I'll be sleeping for a long time. How'd I even get here? Not your apartment but here — this moment. I'll tell you, the last forty-eight hours have been so insane — just one thing after another that took all I knew and turned it into mush. I don't know what to make of it. I haven't had time. Now that I'm here, all I want to do is sleep and my brain won't shut up.

"I mean, take yourself. Here you are, lying to me from the beginning — I should be so angry at you. I shouldn't care at all what happens to you. Yet all I want to do is heal you, fix you. And not in some childish, schoolgirl way of 'Oh, my. He's a broken man, and I'm the only one who can fix him.' No. I feel responsible. Like maybe if I had refused to let you go down in that basement, if I had not simply shown it to you. I know you probably would have found some other way down there, but at least then, it wouldn't be weighing on my shoulders.

"And then — pay attention here because this is something that I keep dwelling on — if I hadn't brought you straight to that basement, if you had been forced to find a different way in, then I wouldn't have had to be part of saving you. I wouldn't have learned anything about any of it. You would have been nothing more to me than some guy who dated me once and never called me again. That would have been much easier.

"Now, what do I do? I can't really go back to a normal life after all of this. I don't see how I could ever pretend none of this has happened. But I've screwed everything up with Gram. She's been so good to me over the years. Yes, she lied to me, too — I haven't forgotten. But I get it. She couldn't tell me the truth. Look how I'm handling it now. I can't imagine how I would have handled it any earlier in my life.

"I just wish there was some way I could get all this set right. Some way to not have you screwed up in the head and not have Gram mad at me."

Roni chuckled. "Strangest thing. I think even if I could fix everything else, I wouldn't want to go back to not knowing the truth. I mean, it sucks knowing — not being able to tell anybody. It sucks thinking how twisted and bizarre the universe is and how at any moment, if the Old Gang fails at their job, all of our existence might get ruined forever. But at the same time, I kind of like knowing. I like that our world is truly magic. I mean there's real magic out there. It gives me a perspective that feels right."

Crossing her feet on the glass coffee table, knowing she would leave behind a smudge, she said, "Who am I kidding? It's all screwed up. It'll always be screwed up. That's the way life is. We keep thinking we can control it, fix it, bring order to it, but chaos is the natural state of things." She glanced down at the snowy hair. "At least tomorrow I can put you right. I know it can't go back exactly the way it was — hair color ain't changing for one thing — but we'll get you some help. Maybe a psychiatrist. Something. Then this job will be done, and I guess I'll have to find a new job somewhere."

Roni rambled on for a few more minutes and never realized when she fell asleep.

CHAPTER 13

Roni's eyes did not want to open. She could have used another hour of sleep — maybe two — but as she rubbed an itch out of her nose, she knew sleep would not return for the day. The stiffness in her back and the crick in her neck attested that she had fallen asleep sitting up. But she felt no weight on her chest. Her eyes snapped open.

Where was Darin?

She zipped down the hall and poked her head in his bedroom. Empty. The bed looked like a model display at a linen store. Nobody had slept here.

"Dar —" she tried to call out but her voice cracked under the strain. She tended to hold tension in her neck, so whenever she held a lot of tension for too long — such as sleeping tense for a few hours — losing her voice often followed. Though inconvenient, she had been through it many times before. If she took care not to talk too much, her voice would return later in the day. Of course, getting rid of the tension would be most helpful, but she did not see that happening anytime soon — especially if she couldn't find Darin.

She walked back up the hall and stopped to check in the bathroom. Empty. And clean and well-appointed.

Back in the living room, she glimpsed the balcony. A terrible thought jumped into her head and she darted to the railing. Gazing over the ledge, she searched the sidewalk below — no blood, no corpse, nothing. Thank goodness. She would rather have been waterboarded than have to tell Jane Lander that her son had committed suicide.

Inside, she crossed the living room and entered the kitchen. Bingo. Darin stood in the center of the functional but minuscule kitchen.

Slack-jawed and leaning over like a man determined to spend his later years hunched over with pain in his back, Darin faced a framed, artistic print of lions walking across an open plain. She guessed the Serengeti. He did not appear to notice anything around him.

Careful not to jar him or make any sudden loud noises, Roni stepped over to the refrigerator and poured herself a glass of orange juice. Then she inched into Darin's field of vision, closed her eyes against the expectation of pain, and said, "Darin? Can you hear me?"

The words scratched her throat, but they came out clear and audible. She opened her eyes. Darin showed no reaction.

In the living room, Roni dug through her purse until she found her cellphone. She brought up Gram's number, but her thumb hovered over the call button. Things were bad enough. Roni didn't want to make it all worse and give Gram even more reasons to be against her.

Instead, she called Sully. He had made the Golem statue and Darin acted like a statue. Granted, the tenuous connection offered nothing to be hopeful about, but when she listened to the phone ring, hope sparked in her nonetheless. But Sully did not answer.

Perhaps Elliot's healing ability would solve the problem. She called him, though no hope grew within her. After all, if Elliot had the power to heal whatever problem Darin had, surely he would have done so the moment Darin had returned from the book. The call went straight to voicemail.

Roni bumped the heel of her hand against the side of her head. Foolish. Sully and Elliot still recuperated from their ordeal. They wouldn't be answering phone calls. She would have to drive out there and see them in person.

Gathering her things together, she wondered if Darin would be safe alone. Probably. In all likelihood, he would remain in the kitchen staring at the wall. Plus, she could be at *In The Bind* within twenty minutes, if she hit the traffic lights right. Thirty minutes, otherwise. A few words with Sully, and they would return. Less than an hour gone.

Convinced Darin would be fine, Roni sped down the stairwell, out onto the street, and into her car. Luck graced her with no traffic, no police, and all green lights. Seventeen minutes and twelve seconds later, she parked and walked up to the bookstore.

The front door had been set open which meant, at the least, Gram minded the store. It also meant that the electronic bell would be turned on. It rang a simple two-tone chime whenever somebody crossed the entranceway to alert Gram of a customer. If Roni intended to get to

Sully and Elliot without encountering Gram — which she very much did — she had to wait.

Luck stayed with her — a young couple with a baby in a stroller approached the store. Roni didn't want to consider how much good luck she had wasted on this trip already, and instead, she hoped it would last a bit longer. Staying close behind the couple, she walked into the store, letting the electronic bell ring out. Right away, she spotted Gram with another customer off to the left. Roni headed to the right and behind the first aisle of books.

"Welcome to *In The Bind*," Gram said. "Browsing or can I help you find something?"

"We're looking for a gift for a friend. He's big into old histories and that kind of thing."

"Come with me. I'll show you what we have."

The History section put Gram's trajectory directly in Roni's path. No problem, though. Roni grew up in this bookstore. Years of playing hide-n-seek would finally pay off — though, Roni had to admit that this particular round brought with it no sense of fun or play.

As Gram led the couple deeper into the store, Roni crouched behind a short shelf, and crossed to the left. She scurried to the end of the aisle and swiftly maneuvered her way to the back wall. Here she had to wait until Gram finished with the couple — the stairs and the elevator were both within easy sight lines of the History section.

Sitting on the floor, waiting, she remembered those years when playing like this would have been the height of fun. A miserable cloud followed her actions now — not just this day, with all the pressures of her recent awakening to reality, but most days. As a child, despite the tragedy of losing her parents, she had mostly happy memories.

Those that lasted. She had only a few.

At length, Roni heard Gram say what she had waited for — "I'll take this up front and when you're ready, it'll be waiting for you." She counted to ten, giving Gram enough time to walk away but not enough time to reach the counter. With Gram's back to the stairs, Roni had a clear shot and she took it.

As fast and as silent as possible, she slipped across the aisles and up the stairs to the second floor. From there, she could relax as she traversed flight after flight until she reached the fifth floor. Elliot's door had been propped open — he claimed to prefer the air circulation but Roni always suspected Elliot preferred being able to see who came and went.

She entered the apartment, rapping her knuckles on the door. "Hello? Elliot? Sully?"

"Back here," Elliot called out.

Roni found both men sitting at the small kitchen table, each one concentrating hard on the cards fanned in their hands. "Good morning."

"Uh-oh," Sully said. "Your voice is all broken up. Rough night?"

Elliot tapped Sully's arm. "Do you recall the time when she went on one of her first dates. A boy she really liked a lot and after waiting all day, she could barely talk."

"Or the time she had to get up in front of the school and —"

"Okay, enough," Roni said. "We all know that this happens to me. Not as often as it did, though. Keep that in mind."

"Always," Elliot said with a smirk.

"What are you playing?"

"Just some Gin," Sully said. "And I'm not doing so well."

Elliot pushed out a chair. "Care to join us?"

Both men wore their bedclothes beneath full-length robes. A glance downward revealed slippers on their feet. Sully caught her gaze. "Don't worry about us. We're feeling a million times better."

"You've got Elliot here to take care of you, right?"

"As much as possible," Elliot said.

Sully coughed — a hard, phlegm-filled sound that did not encourage the image of health. "What brings you up here?"

Elliot laid down his cards. "Gin."

"Damn." Sully tossed his cards on the table and pushed his glasses up his nose. "Not that we aren't happy to see you for just a visit. Frankly, after your spat with your grandmother, I was afraid we might not get to see you for a long time. But here you are."

"Here I am," she said as she sat. "I doubt Gram would greet me with half the joy you fellows show me."

Elliot shuffled the cards. "Oh, don't look at it like that. Your grandmother is rough, you know that, but she's good-hearted, too."

"I know, but —"

"Let an old man speak. You might learn something. She has been through a lot."

Sully snorted. "We all have."

"Yeah, but she was doing this job long before us. She's seen more. And fighting with you is not what she wants. But she loves this job. She loves it, respects it, and values it above all else. It's not personal."

"Of course, it is." Roni crossed her arms. She caught her reflection in the glass of a photograph on the wall and saw a young version of Gram. Snapping her arms to her sides, she said, "I know you two have worked with her a long time, but remember that I'm no stranger here. I've known her my whole life. For her, everything is personal."

With a begrudging nod, Elliot said, "All I'm trying to say is that when you agreed to join us and then changed your mind so fast, you sort of bruised the thing she holds most important. Understand?"

Sully said, "And I'm old, but not a fool. You're not here on a social visit and you didn't come for family relationship advice. What do you need?"

Roni checked her watch. She already had spent too much time trying to get up to the apartment and now wished she had taken the time and effort to have brought Darin along. But then Darin would be outside, sitting in a hot car — she couldn't very well bring him inside with Gram running the store — and the chances of things getting worse would have grown exponentially. No, she had made the right choice. But getting back to him fast also needed to happen.

She launched into an abbreviated version of events culminating in Darin's current state and her lack of solutions. When she finished, she said, "I thought that maybe you'd be willing to come out to Darin's place and take a look at him. Maybe you could help."

The men shared a mischievous twinkle. Sully then said, "I assume you don't want your grandmother to know about this."

"That might be best for now."

Elliot chuckled. "We'll absolutely help you."

From a sideways glance, Roni said, "Why are you happy to do this behind Gram's back?"

"Number one — we want to help you. Truly. Number two — it's fun to do stuff in secret. That's part of the allure of this job."

Tapping his nose and pointing, Sully said, "Plus, at our age, any secretive fun that's new is extra fun, and we want as much of that as we can get. We never know when our last day is coming, and I can't expect Elliot to save me all the time."

Checking her watch again, Roni said, "Fine, fine. But we need to go now. You boys take the elevator down and meet me out by my car. I'll take the stairs and go out the back. If you run into Gram, stall her a little, please."

Elliot rubbed his hands and laughed. "This is getting better every minute. Let's go."

CHAPTER 14

When they approached the door to Darin's apartment, Roni's heart sank. It stood halfway ajar. Her lips rolled in as she fought back the urge to scream.

Like a newfound mantra, she said, "No, no, no, no, no."

She bolted into the apartment, racing down the hall to check the bedroom, slamming open the bathroom door, and ending with the room she knew she would not find him — the kitchen.

"He's gone." Her voice was a mouse peep almost drowned out by the rattling air conditioner.

"Don't worry about it," Sully said. "Do you know how many times we've botched up a job? Goes with the territory. I mean, the learning curve with this position is enough to kill you."

"I'll never know." Roni could not take her eyes away from the empty space in the kitchen where Darin had stood. "Gram will kill me first. Especially if she finds out about this." That thought jolted her back. She glared and pointed her finger at both men. "Not a word to her. You understand me? Not a single word. Promise me."

"You think we want to tell her any of this?" Elliot said. "We are here with you. As far as she's concerned, we are accomplices."

Roni's cellphone rang, and before she looked, she knew the name that would be on the screen — Jane Lander. "You two search this place. See if you can find anything useful." She took a deep breath and accepted the call. "Hi, Jane."

"I want to speak with my son."

She expected that — hoped it wouldn't happen, but the day's luck clearly had been used up. "I thought you were going to drive over here to see him." Stalling seemed about the only good approach.

"Never you mind about what I'm doing. Now put my son on the phone this instant."

"I'm sorry, I can't. I'm not inside the apartment."

"You left him there alone?"

"I'm downstairs on the street getting something from my car. I'll be back up there in a minute. He's a big boy, and he's doing a lot better."

Sully and Elliot's idea of "searching the apartment" leaned more towards the idea of "tossing the apartment." They rifled through drawers, sifted paperwork, and threw cushions aside with such abandon, Roni wondered if they had ever gone through police training when they were younger.

"I'll wait," Jane said. "Put him on the phone."

Gesturing to the phone, Roni mouthed a plea for help, but Sully and Elliot shrugged. Without a good option, Roni chose a classic form of evasion. "I'm sorry, Jane, what was that? You're breaking up. I think my phone is dying. I'll try to call you soon." She ended the call.

"Nothing is here," Sully said.

Pocketing her phone, Roni went back to the kitchen — the last place she had seen Darin. She surveyed the room for any sign of what he had been thinking or where he might ... she smacked her forehead. "I'm such an idiot. I know where he's going — the zoo."

"Lots of zoos," Sully said.

"The Philadelphia Zoo."

Elliot pulled a laptop from underneath the couch. "Not quite," he said and he displayed the screen to the others. "Looks like he signed up for an Uber account. And he has Google Maps focused on the Baltimore Zoo."

"Baltimore? Why go there when the Philly Zoo is so much closer?"

"You said he was thinking clearer for a time. Perhaps he started thinking clearly again. If I needed to get to a zoo, any zoo, and I had already expressed to you that desire —"

"Then you wouldn't go where you know I'll end up searching for you."

"Precisely." Elliot checked the website again. "He has had about a forty-five minute lead on us. We should be moving now."

"Paper," Sully said, snapping his fingers at a notepad on the kitchen counter. "And a pen."

Roni swiped the pad and a pen, handed them over, and the three went to her car. As she sped down the highway toward Baltimore, she kept one eye on her rearview mirror — not watching the cars, but rather watching Sully. He sat in the backseat with his pad and pen.

Starting at the right of the page and working left, he wrote several words in Hebrew. When he finished, he removed the page from the pad and folded it. Sometimes in half, sometimes unfolding and refolding from a different start point, sometimes only crossing a small portion of the page. After a few moments, he had produced an origami crane.

He opened the car window and lifted the crane. Though Roni knew what would come next, she still found it astonishing. Sully brought the crane's head close in and whispered to it. Seconds later, the paper bird flapped its wings and soared out the window. With barely a pause, Sully picked up the pen and started over. By the time they spotted signs announcing The Baltimore Zoo, Sully had made and released ten cranes.

After nothing but silence, Elliot cleared his throat. "Are you doing okay?"

"Me?" Roni said. "Yeah, I'm fine."

"I meant with all that you have learned and with Lillian. The last time we talked you had a big decision to make. Now, it seems you have come to regret that decision."

"I don't know. I mean I don't regret it — I'm glad I know the truth — but at the same time, I don't know. It's like Santa Claus."

Elliot had the polite grace not to laugh. "How is that?"

"When you're a kid — well, not you and not Sully, but when you're a Christian kid — parents will tell you the whole Santa Claus story. Then one day, somewhere along the line, you learn the truth, and so far as that goes, usually you're okay. The world existed in one way before and now it's become something altogether different, but it's okay. In fact, you might even be grateful to know the reality of the world. That's how I felt learning all about you guys and the books and the universes and all."

"Are you going to say that some kids regret learning about Santa Claus?"

"No. But some kids, once they do learn the truth, realize a larger, more horrible truth. They understand that for years, their parents lied to them. Sure, it was all in fun and playfulness and giving presents and all, but they lied. The two people that child expected nothing but truth from lied about something so inconsequential and kept that lie going for years. What, then, would those same people do when a serious problem arose? Does that make sense?"

"I think so."

"It's not just being lied to, either. What really screws up those kids — the ones who see the full truth — is that they are then expected to be complicit in continuing the lie. I figured out on my own that Santa was a myth and when I told Gram, she asked that I don't tell any of the other kids. She said that they might not know yet and that I shouldn't spoil it for them."

"Ah," Elliot said. "And here we are telling you to keep all of this secret. But, of course, this is not a holiday game resulting in presents. Our secret is dangerous information."

"Don't you think if Darin had known that information, it might have saved him from ever going near that book? He would have known to be careful around such things, known the consequences of opening the book, maybe he even would have turned down the job because of it."

"It's good that you question these things. It's good that you think this way. That is one reason it is always necessary to bring in young minds. But old minds know a lot, too. We have experience. The dilemma that you describe is not new. It has been argued out for centuries. Sadly, I have to tell you that nobody has come up with a satisfactory solution."

"What then? Am I supposed to roll over and accept that it sucks and that's it?"

"Not at all. In fact, you should do quite the opposite."

"Huh?"

"I told you that this has been argued for a long time. That is because there have always been people like yourself, passionate people, caring and empathetic people, who are willing to argue, to debate, to fight. Without that, those who wish to impose their will on others win."

Roni's face scrunched up. "How did we suddenly get to fighting the establishment? Is there an establishment? I thought it was just you three."

"Did you already forget that we are called in by religious groups to investigate? There are others, too. Governments, sometimes. Private groups. I would not go so far as to suggest that there is an actual establishment, but there are people out there thinking, discussing, and debating the bigger questions of what we do — including how much to keep a secret."

"Great. How does any of that help me?"

Elliot gave a knowing grin. "Because, you see, your decision is not as Earth-shattering as you fear. Make a choice. Be part of this, wholeheartedly, or do not. It is easy. Most decisions are. They only feel difficult when you waffle between your choices."

Pointing to their exit, Roni said, "Saved by the zoo."

"The decision will not go away."

"I know." She followed the winding road into the parking area and picked a spot under the shade of a tall tree. "But right now, we have to figure out where to find Darin in this place. I've been here before. It's big. We better get started or we might be here all night."

Sully snickered. "Wait a moment, please."

"We've already lost most of the day. Let's go."

"Such impatience. Only a little longer. A short wait. I promise. Please."

Roni looked to Elliot for support but he closed his eyes with a calm demeanor as if waiting for a few days in this car was well within his ability. "Is this how you usually run an operation?"

Keeping his eyes closed, Elliot said, "There is no *usually* in this business. We have learned that the only thing we can trust is each other. If Sully tells me that we need to wait, then we wait. I trust him."

Though every muscle in her body itched to get moving, Roni eased back in her seat. "Okay. We wait."

True to his word, the wait did not take long. Only a few minutes had passed before Sully opened his hand at the window. One of his paper cranes flew in and perched on his palm. He stroked its head before whispering to it. In the next breath, the crane stopped moving — it had become nothing but paper once more.

Working with deliberate motions, Sully unfolded the paper. Roni studied the care he put into each step of his process — it was more than a magic gift to him. He treated his work with reverence and love. She guessed that when he had faced the decision to join or not, he had no problems — because Sully knew himself, understood his own heart. Then again, he projected that surety now. Back when he was her age or younger, he may have been more conflicted. After all, he had admitted that it took him a while to accept the shift in reality, so perhaps he had trouble with the bigger questions, too.

Did that mean that eventually she would discover the self-assured confidence Sully and Elliot now displayed? And did they only acquire that through this kind of work?

"Here we are," Sully said.

On the paper, flattened out on his lap, Roni saw the Hebrew words.

However, these were not the same as the ones that Sully had written. Though she could not read Hebrew, she could see easily enough that the handwriting and the number of words had changed.

Elliot shifted in his seat so that he could look directly at Sully. "Okay, friend. You have had your moment. Now tell us what the birdie said."

Sully winked. "I thought you had the patience and the trust for me."

"I do. I also know that when the spotlight is on you, there are times when you like to linger in its shine. However, as our dear Roni has made clear, we should consider our limited time. Therefore, I ask you again with the greatest of respect, what did the birdie say?"

"Very well. Mr. Lander is at the wolf exhibit. He went right there from the start and sits there still. That is where we go."

Roni rested her chin on the back of her seat as she looked at the paper. "That's weird."

"All of this is weird," Elliot said. "If you stick with it, you get used to weird."

"I mean it's weird that he picked the wolf exhibit to go catatonic again. When he was like that in the kitchen, he focused on the animal picture on the wall, but it was of lions. I sort of expected him to go to the lion exhibit."

Elliot shook his head as he pondered Roni's words.

Sully shrugged. "I only tell you what the crane told me. Wolf, lion — does it really matter? Each world we touch is unique in some way. Some more than others. Who's to say what we should expect?"

"I guess," Roni said. "But how do you prepare for any of this, then? How do we know what to do with Darin?"

"We don't," Elliot said. "We know how the books work. And the cavern."

"And our gifts," Sully added.

"Yes, our gifts, too. The things that exist in our universe are the things that we do understand. But when we must deal with another universe — by that, I mean more than locking it away into a book. Rather I mean something like we are dealing with now, with Darin — well, when we must handle these kinds of situations, we rely on the things we do know and improvise the rest."

Roni drummed her hands on her seat as she opened the door. "Anybody ever tell you that you use a lot of words to say the simplest things?"

"Our friend in the backseat often tells me so."

Sully rubbed the back of his hand against the loose skin under his neck. "Ignore him. We have work to do. Eyes open. This could be dangerous."

The playfulness in their banter had lulled Roni into forgetting the seriousness of the situation. Only for a second or two, but it left her with a sense of being unprepared. As they exited the car and headed toward the main gate, she tried to convince herself that entering with two seasoned veterans ready to face anything would be enough — no matter how old they were. Watching Sully shuffling along the way and seeing how Elliot leaned heavier on his cane than before did not inspire her with confidence.

Chapter 15

When they bought tickets to enter the zoo, the cashier raised an eyebrow. "The zoo is going to close in about an hour."

"That's okay," Roni said. "We won't be long. Just looking to get some exercise in these old bones."

"Who you calling old?" Sully said.

The cashier chuckled and handed over the tickets. As they walked in, droves of haggard parents and sugar-high kids meandered out through the exit turnstiles. They wore baseball caps with flamingos attached to the visor, sported new t-shirts displaying the zoo logo, and carried bags full of toys and games — all zoo themed, of course.

The welcome area had a large fountain as the centerpiece of an open air section. Roni walked over to a large map of the zoo and pointed off to the right. The two men followed her.

Elliot gazed ahead as they walked by gibbons on one side and eagles on the other. He chuckled — a soft rumble deep in his throat — and said, "I do not know if you will recall this, but when you were a girl, maybe six or seven, your grandmother and I brought you here for a day."

Shaking her head, Roni said, "I don't remember a lot from those years."

"I know. It is hard to hold onto memories when you have suffered the loss of a parent. I wish you could remember that day, though. It is a happy memory. You were like a bee, buzzing along, hopping from one flower to the next — except these flowers were the exhibits. You loved it. And down at the bottom of the hill — I do not know if it is still there — they had a mini-train to take the children around part of the zoo. When your grandmother mentioned this, you were enthralled.

Choo-choo. You said it over and over in every possible variation of pitches. *Choo-choo.* We laughed about that for a long time."

They moved at a steady albeit slow pace. Roni did not mind. The extra time gave the stragglers a chance to exit the zoo. That meant less people around when they confronted Darin. Should he not leave with them willingly, should he lash out or behave aggressively, there would be less people to get in the way.

After about seven minutes of walking, they reached the wolf enclosure. Darin sat on a wooden bench facing the wolves. Tall trees shaded the brick path and a trashcan decorated with wood slats stood a few feet away. A sign above the trashcan read: *Don't be an animal. Throw away your trash.*

If not for Darin's harrowing experience and his unstable state of mind, Roni would have thought she looked upon a man's serene moment of quiet contemplation. Perhaps she had. Though she felt dread and danger around her, that only existed because the Old Gang told her this would be dangerous. Not exactly true, though. She still shivered when she thought of all she saw within that book. So, even if Darin meant no harm, she knew the Old Gang was right to be cautious. She just didn't want it to be that way.

Nudging her shoulder, Elliot said, "Go talk with him."

"Are you serious? Isn't that like walking into the lion's den?"

"Sully and I need to clear the area before we can make a move." He indicated a couple walking hand-in-hand and an old woman with her dog. "As well, you clearly have some connection with him."

"Maybe. But —"

"Did he harm you when you took him to his mother's place?"

"No."

"Did he harm you when you found him walking on the road?"

"No."

"Did he harm you at his apartment? Or while you slept?"

"No. I get it. I'll go talk to him. What am I trying to do? Just distract him?"

"Distraction is a good start. Keep him calm. From what you have described, he goes in and out of lucidity. Right now, I would guess that he is not aware of much. Perhaps hearing your voice will bring him back to consciousness. If so, then try to talk him into leaving with us. That would be the ideal. Otherwise, stick with distraction, and we will handle it from there."

Elliot snapped his fingers at Sully and the two men walked ahead.

Elliot approached the woman with the dog while Sully smiled at the couple. Roni tried to stay focused on Darin.

When she stepped in front of him, she first noticed that he did not appear to be in contemplative meditation. Instead, he looked like a couch potato too lazy to change the channel from a nature show to something more lively. She wiggled her fingers in an attempt at a cute *hello* wave but saw no reaction.

A strange, sharp flicker of light — amber and orange — crossed his skin. She turned her head toward the sky but the sun had begun to set. It could not have caused that bright flicker. She waited to see if it happened again, but nothing changed.

As if he had woken from an afternoon nap, Darin took in his surroundings as he stretched his arms. "Hi, there. Have a seat."

Roni settled on the bench but kept her feet ready to spring away. "How are you feeling?"

"Better and better. It's taken me longer than I expected to get comfortable with this reality."

"Tell me about it. You spend your whole life thinking up is up and down is down, and by doing nothing more than opening a book, it's all different. I can't begin to imagine what you must think since you actually went in there."

"Book? I mean the reality around us, not some story."

Did he not remember? "Of course. This is quite different from inside the ... that is, from where you were."

"Beautiful creatures, aren't they?" He watched the wolves as they watched him. "Working in concert together, following a hierarchy that keeps them safe and functional. That's a reality which makes sense."

"It's certainly less complicated than what we deal with. I don't even know where to start with you. I want to assure you that we can help you, but I don't even know if we can help me. I don't mean that in a self-centered way. I only meant — oh, forget it. I'm screwing this all up."

"You're fine. I should apologize to you. I'm sure my earlier behavior was disturbing."

"I guess." She found his current behavior more disturbing but kept quiet.

"It was difficult, at first, to function in a new reality. Difficult to get my new way of thinking to respond to my old understanding of the way the world worked."

"I've been going through it, too. It's like there's this battle going on inside my head. I look around and it all seems like it was but then there's this other layer of knowing what else is out there, things most people will never see, but I've seen them and I can't forget them and I think I'm babbling." She giggled. "I'm sorry."

"You know, Darin really liked you."

"What?"

"On your date the other night. Even though he used you to gain access to the basement, he really liked you. I thought you might like to know that."

Roni's mouth went dry. She inched further to the edge of the bench, ready to bolt. "Darin told you that?"

"Oh, yes."

"Does that mean you're not Darin?"

The amber-orange light flickered again, only this time Roni saw it clearly — coming from under Darin's skin. He grinned. "I am so much more."

In the distance, Roni spotted Elliot taking up a position that both flanked Darin and cut off one of the exit paths from this section of the zoo. She suspected Sully did the same behind her.

Attempting to maintain her composure, she said, "You know, when people start talking about themselves in the third person, often it means they're a bit crazy. But I don't think that's the case with you."

"I appreciate that."

"In fact, I think you're being absolutely sincere. I mean you honestly are not Darin anymore. So, I'm guessing you came from that other world. Right? You saw Darin in there, and you did something to him, jumped inside of him somehow, and then came out here like a stowaway."

"Not quite." His skin flickered again — more intensely this time. "I did not jump inside the man. I copied him. As much as I could in the time given. Once I arrived here, it took me more time to figure out how his mind functioned — language skills, in particular, are difficult. But here I am."

Roni frowned. "You're a copy of Darin?"

"I am."

"Then what happened to Darin?"

"I left him. Locked away in my world, just as I am locked away here. Though I certainly ended up with the better situation."

Swallowing against her dry throat, she asked, "What now? You planning to live your life as one of us?"

"Don't be disgusting." Again the light beneath his skin flickered. Shadows of his bone structure appeared in the stronger light. "I can do so much better."

Roni called upon all her will power to remain seated. She feared any sudden action — like running for her life — might startle this creature, perhaps trigger a predator/prey instinct. "Maybe you should relax a little. You don't look too well."

Darin jerked to his feet. "I feel better than I have since I was born." He faced Roni — his eyes manic, his gestures broad, his skin flickering like an orange strobe light. "I spent my whole life in that ooze. Fighting to eat. Fighting to breathe. Fighting to mate. That world is nothing like this. This is superior in every way."

The wolves rushed to the edge of their cage. Some growled. Others barked. Their attention solely on Darin. He watched them again, his fascination unending.

Something tugged on Roni's arm. She looked over to see Sully. Even as she wondered how he had managed to sneak up so close without being detected, she found her legs unwilling to move.

Darin snapped his focus onto Sully. With a vicious bark of his own, Darin lashed out. He moved fast, his fingers locking on Sully's thin wrist and twisting hard. Sully groaned as he bent further over in pain.

"Run," he managed, but Roni could only watch.

Darin squeezed tighter, his eyes blazing with anger and curiosity as if he wondered how long it would take to break Sully's wrist. He never got to find out.

A blinding sun burst before him — Elliot stood in the way, his cane a glowing mass of light. He pressed forward, and Darin had no choice but to back off. Freed from Darin's vice grip, Sully scurried off toward the exit, nursing his wounded hand.

"Come on, Roni," Elliot yelled as he pushed his cane at Darin.

"I-I can't move."

To Darin, Elliot said, "Release her!"

But no magic constrained Roni. Fear kept her frozen. Fear and a bizarre sensation — kinship? No. That seemed too strong. But something inside her refused to let her move.

Elliot tried to yank her to her feet, but he couldn't get her to budge. The wolves howled from their cage. Elliot glanced over, and Roni knew the animals had created a diversion. Darin lunged forward, gnarling his teeth as he bowled into Elliot. The two rolled on the ground until Darin popped up, straddling the old man. Two strong punches, and Elliot went limp.

Darin glared at Sully until it became clear that the fight had ended. He then walked toward the wolf cage. "Where I'm from, these men would be dead, but I want to show you that I can adapt."

Elliot rolled on his side. The days of Sully and Elliot punching their way through problems had ended long ago, but they did not want to admit it. Roni wondered if she acted similar — that Darin presented a new reality and she did not want to admit it.

"Adaptation is the most important skill in my world." Darin unbuttoned his shirt revealing a smooth chest with sparse definition. "I want you to see. I can adapt to your world, I will adapt, better than any living thing you have here."

"What are you saying?" Roni asked.

"Watch and see."

With one hand, he squeezed his fingers together and compressed them against his stomach. As if his skin has been made of gelatin, his hand slipped through. Roni's eyes dried from not blinking, but she could not force a change. She had to watch.

He dug around within his body for a moment, grunted as he gripped something, and pulled his hand free. The skin around his stomach sealed, leaving behind no scar. In his palm, he held a bright amber-orange goo. It glowed and snapped out light at odd times. It undulated.

Roni's brain shrieked at her, pleaded with her, demanded that she move. She had to get up, turn around, and run. Sprint. Get the hell out of there.

She stayed motionless.

"Is that you?" she asked.

It flickered faster. Roni looked to Darin, but his face had gone slack, his eyes empty. But his body moved.

He stepped toward the wolves. They stood on their hind legs, whining and scratching like domesticated dogs begging to be let outside.

Roni's body numbed as her brain attempted to place this image into her concept of reality — new or old. But even in her new reality, human beings could not do what she had witnessed.

She reminded herself that this thing before her looked like Darin but could not be called human. The real Darin still suffered within the universe in the book. This impostor could not be counted upon to follow the behavior and physical attributes of a human being. The glowing puddle in his hand proved as much. If she doubted any of her thoughts, he made it undeniable in the next seconds.

Darin leaned over the railing, stretching his arm as close to the wolf cage as possible. One wolf, a gray and black hulking animal — the Alpha — shoved its snout between the bars. Whimpering, it pushed harder in an attempt to reach Darin. Like a lightning bolt, arcing and twisting, the puddle of muck in Darin's hand shot out and latched upon the wolf's nose.

Without a sound, the rest of the pack sat on their haunches like obedient, well-trained police canines. The gray and black Alpha tried to retreat, but the glowing goo kept the animal locked in place. The wolf snarled as it foamed at the mouth. Its breathing shortened as if the animal struggled underwater until finally succumbing to the inevitable. The muck stretching between Darin and the wolf detached and languidly returned to its puddle form in Darin's hand.

With casual grace, Darin slipped the undulating goo back into his abdomen. Arching back, he dangled his hands at his side. Roni swore the man's face had changed. His mouth thrust forward as he inhaled deeply and let loose a long, wailing howl. The pack of wolves lifted their heads and sang notes of their own as his personal chorus.

When he straightened and looked upon Roni, her fears had been confirmed. His face had transformed. He had taken on many wolf-like qualities — his mouth and nose pushed forward, whiskers poked out from the sides, hair grew along his jawline, his teeth had lengthened and sharpened.

He put out his hand. "I have no intention of being alone here. You were the first, the only one of this world to show me kindness. I shall reciprocate. Come with me, and I will make you better than you are. Better than anybody from this world."

Recoiling, Roni found the strength to say, "I like being human just fine."

Darin growled, and the pack barked and growled in concert. They jumped over each other. They scratched and gnawed at the bars in an endless attempt to break through.

"You will come with me, or you will suffer."

"Not a good line to win me over."

He furrowed his brow in thought. "Ah, *suffer* is the wrong word. I meant that if you do not come with me, you will be my victim."

"Not really any better."

"Then you will die."

The threat of death finally broke the mixture of fear and amazement that had kept Roni rooted to the bench. She leaped to her feet and sprinted for the exit behind her. The snorting snarls chased after her along with Darin. Ahead, Sully and Elliot stood like two action heroes past their prime. Not the most comforting image, but better than nothing.

To her surprise, Sully stepped forward. He gestured toward Darin as Elliot hunched like a linebacker ready to catch Roni. Peeking around Elliot's arm, Roni watched as all of Sully's paper cranes soared in. They circled Darin's head, dive-bombed his body, and pecked at his skin. Pricks of blood dotted his arms and face.

"Go! Go!" Sully said.

The three hurried back up the path, leaving Darin swatting at the nerveless attackers.

"No way will that stop him for long," Roni said.

"True," Elliot said. "But he will not follow us further." Proving his point, Elliot slowed his pace.

"He wants to kill me."

"We have seen this before. There is a madness that strikes some when they travel between worlds. He sees our home, and it is more beautiful, more bountiful, more innocent than whatever existence he endured before. In his madness, he desires all of it."

"Including me."

"Perhaps. But desiring an entire world outweighs chasing down one woman."

Sully wiped his glasses with the bottom of his shirt. "Usually."

Elliot nodded. "Usually. The birds stopped him long enough to get some distance, and since he has not attacked us yet, I suspect my interpretation of his mental state and attitudes is correct."

Fluttering her shirt to cool down, Roni said, "Can we get the heck out of here?"

"Certainly. We must soon return to the bookshop and report to your grandmother."

Roni stopped. "We don't need to tell her any of this."

"I am afraid we can no longer keep this secret. We must have her help."

Roni slumped as they trudged uphill toward the parking lot. "Great."

CHAPTER 16

The big table in the middle of the bookstore's main floor had always been a joyful place for Roni. As a girl, she would bring her stack of books to the table and let the day drift by between their pages. As a teen, she would sneak a boy underneath the table for a stolen kiss, and in later years, for more. But as an adult, sitting on one side along Sully and Elliot, the table made her feel small and foolish. Gram's beady-eyed rage probably had something to do with that, too.

"Of all the stupid, idiotic, addled-brained things to do!" Gram paced the length of the table as she blasted her sternest looks at each of the men. "I can comprehend on some ridiculously childish level why Roni would think that going off to face this creature without any sort of plan or forethought might be a good idea, but you two? You should have known better. Haven't you had enough bad experiences to know that your little foray into stupidity would end badly?"

Sully's top lip lifted. "You would rather we left your granddaughter to face all of that alone?"

"Don't you dare try to pretend that this was all in her best interest. If that were true, you would have come to me, told me what was going on, and we could have dealt with it together — as a team. You remember that concept? We're supposed to act like a team instead of going behind my back."

"Teammates don't give ultimatums."

Gram's face reddened even as her eyes blazed. "You're going to lecture me now on the choices I give my granddaughter?"

Elliot splayed his fingers wide on the tabletop. In a thoughtful delivery, he said, "I believe you know that Sully did not mean that. Rather, he is trying to point out to you, in his own way, that you should be less upset that we did this *behind your back* and more concerned with what circumstances existed in which Roni felt it necessary to enlist our aid without you."

"Oh? Is that right? I see. After all these years raising her into a bright and capable woman, I'm suddenly no longer a good judge of her best interests. She's facing a shift in how she will perceive the world from this point to the end of her life, a shift I myself made decades ago, but I don't have the skill to guide her through it. Is that what you're trying to say?"

Though he continued to speak calmly, the mounted tension could not be missed. If not in his voice, then certainly in his fingers. They clawed into the table as he spoke. "I always have said the words I mean to say. Your inability to understand them or willfully misinterpret them is something I have no control over."

"Enough," Roni said. She tried to stand but Gram's cold glare kept her seated. "You all can argue about me when I'm not around."

"Young lady," Gram said, thumping the table with a meaty fist, "I don't think you are in a position to —"

"You're wrong. I'm in the perfect position because I am the one at risk here. Darin isn't interested in coming after you or Sully or Elliot. He wants me — either to love or kill, he may not even know, but he wants me."

"Then why did he let you go?"

"Maybe he believes in the old *set it free and see if it comes back* kind of love."

"Perhaps," Elliot said, "we should focus on steps forward."

"I would love to do that," Gram said, "but unfortunately, my granddaughter and my two imbecilic friends decided to challenge a creature from another universe before knowing the first thing about it and what it can do."

"I only meant that —"

"I know, I know. I'm not done yelling yet. Can I have that? Is that okay with you? Or if I don't shut up and follow your lead on this, do it exactly how you think it should be done, are you going to go off and take Roni and Sully behind my back again?"

Breathing hard, Gram glowered at them. Nobody said a word.

She looked off to the side, her face going through several awkward motions as if she had a conversation with herself. "Well, I guess I'm done." She sat at the table. "Now, if I can trust that you've all learned your lesson here and that you'll be more open, more forthcoming, in the future, let's get moving forward on this. Do we know where Darin is right now?"

"No," Roni said. "I would hazard a guess that he's either back at his apartment or at his mother's house. Those were the places he went before."

"He also went to the zoo. And those places were part of Darin, not this creature. He only went there to bide time while he adjusted to our world."

Sully pushed his chair back as he stood. "I'll get to work on it."

Gram wagged her hand at him. "We can't afford to waste your time on that. You need to get in your workshop and build us something to handle this. Or did you boys not get beat enough to know that you're not young anymore? The days of you knocking out a threat in one punch left us long ago."

With a bashful grimace, Sully said, "You will mock us with that for years, won't you?"

"If I'm lucky." As Sully left for the elevator, Gram turned her attention to Elliot. "I want you to track down Darin."

Elliot's mouth dropped as if he had been slapped. "Shouldn't that be Roni's job?"

"Roni has shown us that she is not ready to handle jobs on her own. Look at how she botched up this one." She raised both hands to stop anybody from talking. "She's made it clear that her only interest in helping us goes to the end of this current job, so let's not get dependent on her aid. Of course, if you don't agree with me, we have procedures for challenging the leader of the group — procedures you should have followed instead of running off to the zoo. Do you want to do that now, or can I trust that you'll follow my orders?"

Elliot grabbed his cane. "I will find this creature. When you are ready to make a move, I will have his location for you."

After Elliot left, Gram laced her fingers on the table and looked at Roni. For her part, though she felt bad for how things went down, she pulled her shoulders back and met Gram's eyes straight on. For three solid minutes, no words passed between them.

At length, Gram got to her feet and stepped toward the elevators. "Come with me."

Roni obeyed. They climbed into the elevator and Gram pressed the wall beneath the floor selector buttons. A hidden panel slid open with several more buttons on it. She pressed one button and the elevator descended. They came to the basement level but kept going until the digital display above the door read B2.

"A second basement?" Roni said.

Flashing a mischievous smile, Gram gestured to the opening elevator doors. Roni stepped into a cinderblock hallway with lamps hung periodically from the ceiling. The air reminded her of the caverns — uniformly cool with a taste both fresh and old.

Gram led the way down the hall until they reached a metal door. "This is the last time I'm going to show you any of what we have and do. You understand? There won't be another chance after this." Before Roni could protest or explain, Gram stopped her with that powerful hand in the air. "I know. You keep forgetting that I raised you. This wouldn't be the first time you've made a decision without getting all the information."

"You didn't really offer much."

She rested her hand on the door handle. "That was an unfortunate decision on my part. I know you've only seen the three of us — we are all there is now, but not all that ever was. Others came before us, and others before them. No organized group lasts as long as this one has without some bit of ceremony or tradition growing up along the way. When it came to initiating you into our fold, I had a choice to make. I could go with tradition or go with my gut. Now, my gut told me that you are impulsive and would have to make a choice and live with it for a little before you would know whether or not it was the right choice. That's how you've always been. But the tradition was to withhold most of the information and make you choose based on whatever you had experienced. I ignored my gut feeling because my brain hoped you would be different."

"Gee, thanks."

"I don't mean it like that and you know it. I only mean that I hoped there was some magic, I guess, magic in the tradition. Somehow, talking with Elliot in the morning and facing the decision to stay with us or forever give up all of this, I thought maybe it would light a fire within you that had been dormant. Like it was for me."

Roni's stomach knotted. "And I messed up for you."

"I miscalculated a little, that's all. I should have listened to my gut and known that you are who you are. I could have made this easier. But better late than never, right? You made your decision to leave us after this Darin business is over, and you've had to live with that decision for a bit of time. You may even think you know what your final decision will be."

"Gram, I'm sorry, but after all that happened, what makes you think I'll change my mind?"

"I want you to see one more of our secrets." Pushing the handle, Gram opened the door. "If you're going to turn your back on your legacy, you should know exactly what you are turning away."

They stepped into a beautiful library room decorated as if it belonged to an aristocrat in the nineteenth century. High-ceiling, Turkish rugs, handcrafted tables and chairs, wood walls with original oil paintings hanging in gold frames — each one a portrait, Gram explained, of former members in the Parallel Society.

"That's our official name," she said.

Off to the left, Roni saw a wine rack filled with dusty bottles. Though there were two computers humming away on the tables, an old card catalog had been placed off to the right. And, of course, there were books. Hundreds of them. They overflowed the shelves, stacked up on the floor, lined the tops of every surface. Some were leatherbound, some with metal covers, and a few had no cover at all but were scrolls tied with strips of cloth.

Gram eased into one of the chairs. "Everything that's vital to us is in here. Books on every subject we've ever found important. Many of the books are the only copies in existence. But more importantly, we have all the diaries and journals of our former members. That's a key part of our job. We document everything. Hundreds of years of information can be found in this library."

Roni found herself both amazed and appalled. "How do you find anything in here?"

"It was better organized long ago. We haven't had a good librarian for ages."

"I see. You thought I would do this work."

"I remember how you were with your school books. You'd have them lined on your shelf, sometimes based on size, sometimes alphabetically, sometimes I don't know what. But you were always keeping good order to things."

Roni shook her head and laughed. "Have you seen my apartment? It's a sty." Except for her bookshelf, but Roni didn't want to give Gram any extra ammunition.

"There's often a difference between the way one lives and the way one works. I've seen you work in the bookstore. I know that you would love taking care of this place."

She had to admit Gram's words held some truth. "I don't know."

"Don't decide yet. We're doing things for you the right way this time. Experience it. Let it sit. Give it time. Besides, I didn't bring you down here just to show off the library. We've still got the Darin business to deal with. This library is chock full of information. If there's anything that can help us handle Darin, we'll find it in here."

Leaning forward, Gram cleared some yellowed papers off of another chair. Part of Roni resisted the idea of taking that seat. She had a sudden fear that if she sat down, she might never leave this room again. She might look up and discover she had aged forty years, her life had become nothing but dealing with these books and papers, that all the excitement of the last few days would be nothing but a memory.

But Gram had one thing right — Roni made better decisions when she dove in and experienced a thing. She sat, clapped her hands against her knees, and grinned. "Let's get to work."

CHAPTER 17

When Roni got involved with a book, the rest of the world slipped away. She absorbed the words, internalized them, and made them real — in some cases, more real than the outside world. Even with non-fiction, she could delve in between the letters and words and punctuation to find the world beneath the words.

As the hours drifted by, Roni and Gram combed over book after book, and throughout it all, Roni relished each treasured word like a connoisseur of fine wines. Most of these books had never been read by anyone other than those few souls who were brought to this special room. In some cases, the books had never been read at all. The robust aroma of the old paper, the crinkling of it as she turned the pages, the weight of each volume in her lap — it combined to make an experience she knew she would never have again. Even as she sought vital information, part of her brain tried to savor the moment itself, tried to record it within its firing neurons. This was something to remember until her final breath.

After another hour, Gram stretched her legs. She mumbled about a coffee machine, and a few minutes later uncovered the relic sitting behind a rolling cart full of books. A few minutes of fiddling and a quick trip upstairs for ground coffee beans, and Gram served up two hot mugs of caffeine.

Once Gram got back to reading, Roni took a lap around the library to get the blood flowing through to her legs. In the back corner, she found two tall shelving units that had been set up in an L-shape, closing off the area. They looked odd, and it took Roni a moment to figure out why — something was behind them.

The tall ceiling meant that none of the shelving units went all the way to the top. Roni could see clearly that the room continued beyond these shelves. Peeking over a few books, she could make a dark shape, perhaps a table, and little else.

Picking the smaller of the two shelves, she removed every book in it — making sure to check the titles in case anything might be useful for the Darin situation. She stacked them in order so they could be refiled with ease. Once emptied, she reached in, grabbed hold of the shelf, and lifted one side of the unit.

Though heavy enough to elicit a hearty grunt, the shelving unit pivoted inward close to a foot. Holding her stomach in, Roni slipped through the opening and discovered a table with rolls of paper. She spread them open, one after the other. Maps. Each one depicted part of the caverns. In many instances, numerical codes designated the various books chained to the walls. In some cases, entire areas had a marking with names like *Painted Worlds, Unbreathable,* and *Carlson's Journey.*

"Ah, the maps," Gram said, leaning her back against the shelving unit while she sipped her coffee. "There are more somewhere around here."

"More? How big is this cavern?"

"Don't know for sure. I have no doubt you could fit entire cities in here."

Roni's fingers traced one path after the other. Near the bottom of each map, she saw the cartographer's name along with the words *The Parallel Society.* "Why do you call yourselves that when these aren't parallel universes? Are they?"

"Not in the sense of another Roni, another Sully and Elliot, another me running around. And you won't find another Earth where Hitler won the war or the Industrial Revolution never happened or anything like that. As far as I can tell from what I've read in here, these worlds are not alternates to our own, but rather co-existing universes, each unique unto itself."

"Then why *The Parallel Society?* That seems wrong."

"I didn't name it. Perhaps back in the 1400s, that was the best way they could understand what was going on. Who knows? But for whatever reason, that was the name the original founders of the Society chose, and it's stayed with us."

"The 1400s? This thing goes back that far?"

"Maybe further. I suppose the answer is somewhere in this library, but we haven't had a dedicated librarian down here for a long time. So, things get hard to know."

"I can see that."

Roni opened another map, and near the center, she noticed a roughly circular area. Usually that sort of section marked a manmade pool that gathered water from natural, underground streams — she had seen quite a few on the other maps — but this time the words *Lost Memories* had been written in, along with several numerical notations near the symbol for books.

"What does this mean?" she asked.

Gram craned her neck to see without moving. "Oh, nothing. There are a ton of fanciful names the mapmakers used. Most are mere flourishes more evocative than meaningful."

"There's no way you can read what I'm pointing out from over there."

Gram's mouth thinned. "I can see the type of thing you're pointing at, even if I can't read the specific words. Grab any map and you'll see many similar labels."

"But this one says *Lost Memories.* What kind of worlds can that mean? Or is something else there?"

"Right now, it doesn't matter. We need to stay focused."

Roni read those words again. "I have lost memories. Lost time — that's what you've always called them."

"Look at those maps long enough and you'll see infinite answers to infinite questions. It's like tarot cards or astrology. You can interpret those writings to mean whatever you want them to mean — none of which will help Darin."

"Maybe."

"Even if you found some proof that the labels meant something real, you'd still have to go find the place. Map or no map, these caverns are not easy to navigate. More than one Society member went in there looking for some answer and never returned."

Roni brushed the words *Lost Memories* before rolling the paper back up. Gram was right. The maps were disorganized, and Roni had no idea how they connected. She had no way to know what route to take in order to find that area nor what to do should she actually locate this specific pool.

Together, they returned to their books. Roni delved into the daily journal of Nigel Cuthbert, a Londoner who came to America in 1807 at the request of his Aunt Millicent. Three years later, he learned of and joined the Society.

Roni had picked out this journal because earlier in the day, she had read a short chapbook entitled, *A Discussion Regarding Doppelgangers and Their Multitudinous Primal Forms*. The chapbook read more like wishful thinking or creative interpretation, but considering the strange, new reality Roni found herself in, she could not discount anything outright. Still, Mr. Cuthbert's writing on the subject had numerous open-ended questions and winding paths that lead to no conclusion. Roni hoped that she would come across mention of glowing puddles of ooze, but when it came to primal forms, Mr. Cuthbert had to admit he never encountered such a thing. Worse, in his final paragraph, he admitted that he never encountered a doppelganger and that the entire book contained his best estimation of the possibilities.

That had been a waste of time earlier, but she needed something humorous to clear her head. She hoped Mr. Cuthbert's daily journal would provide the levity she sought. It did.

He wrote often of a young widow who lived several blocks over. His infatuation with her grew stronger each day, and he invented reasons to visit that area as much as possible. While amusing enough to read about, Roni could not help but chuckle at his failed attempts to woo the young lady.

He brought her flowers which caused a sharp allergic reaction. He bought her a chicken and as he delivered his gift, a rabid dog chased him down, taking the food for itself. He even attempted to write her a poem but stymied himself with the word *orange*, and refused to change it no matter how long he would have to search for the perfect rhyme.

But then Roni read a sentence that caused her to bolt upright. Gram raised an eyebrow as Roni went over the passage again.

"Well?" Gram finally said when it appeared Roni would get lost in thought.

Roni's knitted brow loosened. "I think I have an idea. This fellow here is trying to win the heart of a woman, writes a poem, and gets hung up on the word *orange*. I know, but here's the thing — he writes in his journal that the word must be in the poem because, *'it was over that rare fruit in which I first saw her. It is no more or less than a talisman to call her heart to mine.'* A talisman. That's our answer."

"How so?"

"You had me get a deeply personal item of Darin's — the ticket stub — and we used it to lure him back to the Golem so he could come back to our world."

"Except that isn't him."

"Really? What proof do we have? None. The only thing suggesting that Darin is not Darin is, well, Darin."

Gram sipped her coffee and crossed her legs. "I'm fairly certain that the Darin you went on a date with did not have the ability to turn partly into a wolf."

"I'm not saying Darin is one hundred percent the human being that went into that book. I'm saying that he did come out and that this creature inside him is a parasite. Who else but Darin would be lured by that ticket stub?"

"Okay. Let's say you're right. Where does that get us?"

"To the next logical question — if Darin is really here, then why did he lie about it? I mean, why did his parasite force him to lie? I think that parasite is controlling him. It couldn't at first, it needed time to take over, but once it did, then Darin was more of a traveler in the backseat of his own body."

"I hear a lot of supposition and see nothing in the way of evidence."

"Isn't that why I'm here, though? To read these books, put ideas together, and come up with possible answers. I mean, you know we're not going to find a book that says the answer is X. If that answer existed, we could have stopped all of this a long time ago."

Gram gestured to the disorganized heaps of books. "Are you not seeing the mess here?"

"I do. But Darin — the real Darin — snuck into the caverns and picked out a specific book. It had to be a specific book because otherwise he could have grabbed much closer and easier to reach books. So, whoever hired him knew about that book. All of that means the answer is not hidden away down here where nobody can get to it or everybody forgot about it — clearly somebody knows about this particular book and what can be found in it."

Gram set her coffee down and leaned forward. "Are you suggesting that somebody wanted Darin to have this parasite in him?"

"To bring it back here."

"It's a chilling thought. And you might be right. All the more reason we have to stop Darin before he has a chance to do whatever he intends. Him or whoever hired him — which is a bigger question for another time."

Roni bounced on the edge of her seat as she pointed in the journal. "If I'm right about Darin, then I'm pretty sure the answer is in the talisman. It was his personal connection to that ticket stub which gave him the strength or the will power to find his way back."

"And you think he can do it again. Only this time instead of clawing his way to a Golem and out of that book, he'd be clawing his way back into commanding his own body."

"I think so."

Gram leaned closer to read the passage from Cuthbert's journal. "Perhaps. But we have a problem. The ticket stub doesn't exist anymore. It was destroyed with the Golem."

"Lucky for us, he didn't go to that game alonc. There's a second stub. But you'll have to come with me to get it. No way will Darin's mother hand over that other stub to me."

Gram's eyes widened. She stood and stepped behind Roni. Patting her granddaughter on the shoulder, she said, "I think we can work that out."

CHAPTER 18

Halfway to Lancaster, Roni's nerves fired off. Her fingers tap-tap-tapped against the steering wheel while her heart tap-tap-tapped against her chest. "Are you sure you're okay with this?" she asked Gram.

"Dear, I hate to spoil your image of me, but this isn't my first time doing this kind of thing. Not even my tenth. If you're uncomfortable, that's perfectly fine. We can switch roles. I've done both parts, so it doesn't matter to me."

Roni shook her head. "Better not. If Darin's mother sees me, she'll probably call the police."

"That wouldn't do. Best to keep the plan as is."

Though it would be a solid thirty minutes before they turned into the housing development, to Roni it felt like three. The pale moon cast a dim light across the dark, and the night felt thick. Despite the streetlights and a few houses with signs of life, the shadows encroached upon every surface like hands reaching out. Roni tried to clear her mind of such ominous thoughts, but she could not stop — every shadow bore monsters to her eyes.

"Park here," Gram said. "We don't want to get so close that she recognizes your car."

Roni pulled up behind an oversized SUV. Gram unbuckled, gave Roni a reassuring squeeze on the arm, and got out. Before closing the door, she leaned in. "Give me a few minutes but please don't take too long. I hate small talk."

As she left, Roni wanted to laugh. Gram could talk for hours about anything — the more banal, the better. Either she had a false self-image or she did not understand the meaning of the phrase *small talk*.

Watching Gram waddle along the sidewalk toward Jane Lander's house, her big bag like an extra appendage at her side, Roni had an image flash in her mind. She saw how Gram must have been in her younger years — walking into danger with that same hefty confidence. That image connected to a slim memory from many years back. Gramps had yet to be ravaged by cancer, and Roni sat on his knee at a park in the summer. She asked him how had he fallen in love with Gram.

"Oh, that's quite a story," he said, his rough whiskers white against his brown skin. "A long story, too. Maybe someday, when you're much older, I can tell you all about it. Now don't get all huffy with me. I can see that stubbornness in your eye like you're planning on causing me trouble tonight — won't eat your vegetables or some kind of fuss. Calm down. I'm going to tell you what I can." He scooted her closer so that he could whisper his answer. He had warm breath. Warm breath and rough whiskers. "One of the first things I ever noticed about your Gram was the way she walked. She's a big woman, but she never thuds around. She's got style and grace and a whole mess of confidence. She knows she's worth something, always has. Back when we were young, she wasn't taking sass from nobody. Would hardly accept a date because she was waiting."

"For you?"

"I hoped so. Don't think she had me in mind, though. Naw, she was waiting for the right guy, whoever he was, the first one who would see her for the beauty she was — still is. I happen to be the lucky one — met her at the right time."

Roni remembered that moment so clearly because it changed the way she saw Gram. But it also was the only memory of Gramps that stayed with her. The rest had been lost along with so much else.

Gram turned up onto the walkway leading to the house. Almost time. Roni crossed her fingers and tried to control her breathing. She would need some of Gram's confidence tonight — any bit would do.

She checked her phone — 10:07 pm. She would have to wait at least five minutes before moving. Hopefully that would be long enough for Gram to do her part but not so long that Gram would be pissed off at having to endure small talk for any significant length. She checked her phone again — still 10:07 pm.

Five minutes — if she could get her mind thinking on something, it would go quick. But her mind blanked. She stared at the street, clenched and unclenched her fingers, and waited. Five minutes. It snailed along, giving Roni's stomach plenty of opportunity to gurgle and groan. A pain stitched up her side only to ease after she burped. She checked her phone — still that stupid 10:07 pm.

"Come on," she said. As if in snarky reply, the time moved to 10:08 pm.

Checking the side and rearview mirrors, Roni observed the street for signs of anybody coming. No need, though. The street was empty. The sidewalks were empty. From one house a few mailboxes back, a blue light flashed out from the downstairs window with no other lights on. Probably someone fell asleep while watching television. She wondered what that life must be like — so free of worry, so oblivious to the idea that there was more than one universe, more than one reality, so free from concerns over this world that a person could fall asleep while watching inane and innocuous television shows.

She glanced at her phone — 10:13 pm.

Crap! She was late.

Half-falling and half-jumping out of her car, Roni scurried across the street and onto the sidewalk. Every inch of her skin tingled, shooting off nervous energy like a fireworks display. All the sounds around her amplified in her ears — her clicking footsteps, the rustle of her coat, the chirping crickets, and the hooting of an owl. Loudest of all — her breathing.

As she neared the house, her pace slowed. The outside porch light was on, bathing the front yard in yellow light. The laughter of two old ladies dribbled out from the living room. Amazing. Gram had only met Jane a few minutes ago and already the two were carrying on like old friends.

Bright lights crossed the yard as a car turned onto the street. Roni dashed forward and crouched behind an old Toyota in the driveway. The car cruised right by without indication that the driver noticed anything wrong.

Roni counted to ten, forcing a sense of calm, before scampering along the side of the house to the back. With careful, slow motions, she placed one foot on the back steps. As she increased her weight on that foot, the wooden step groaned. She waited. When nobody called out and no lights clicked on, she brought her other foot down on the next step. Another groan. Another wait. Twice more and she reached the back door.

If Gram did her job right, not only did she have Jane chatting it up in the front, but she also had managed to unlock the back door without getting caught. Roni swallowed against her tightening throat as she reached out for the doorknob. Unbelievable — it turned. Gram had done it.

Roni opened the door enough to slip inside and brought it to a close as softly as possible. Crouching in the kitchen, she listened. Jane and Gram continued to chat. Nothing to indicate Jane had heard the door open or close.

Staying low, she crept across the floor until she reached the open archway leading to a short hall and then the living room. Her thighs burned from the prolonged crouch and duck-walking — she would have to get back to doing yoga before trying this again.

She paused at that thought. Again? She had no intention of ever doing this again. Did she?

Gram's voice cut into her thoughts. "Really, Jane, it's fine. I don't need any tea."

"Nonsense," Jane said. "A delightful new friend deserves some hospitality."

Crap. Roni looked around the kitchen for a hiding place. Under the kitchen table might have been an option if it had a tablecloth large enough to cover the sides. She might have been able to contort her way into one of the lower cabinets if she had the time and flexibility. In the pantry might have been worthwhile if she didn't have to cross the entire kitchen to get there. Which left an unpleasant option.

She stood straight up, made a fist, and waited at the side of the archway. Once Jane walked into the kitchen, Roni planned to clock the lady on the head and make a run for it. Ugly and distasteful, but probably effective.

Jane's footsteps came closer. Roni had never punched anybody before. Summoning the courage she hoped resided deep within her, she pulled back her fist, ready to strike.

With an embarrassed laugh, Gram said, "Please, don't make the tea. I appreciate the offer, but well, if I drink tea this late at night, I'll be in the bathroom for hours."

Jane halted. "Oh, I'm so sorry. I didn't even think about that."

"It's okay."

"Look at you, turning all red. There's nothing to be bashful about. If we old ladies can't be honest with each other in the privacy of our homes, then what the hell is the rest of the world going to do? Me, I've been fortunate. Got a bladder as tight and strong as if I were in my twenties. I can't boast about the rest of me — more aches and pains than I'd ever thought possible. So, forget about the tea."

"Thank you," Gram said, and Roni released a shaking breath. "You mentioned a blanket you made?"

"Oh, yes. Made it for my son a few years ago. It's up in our guest room."

"I'd love to go see it."

"Come with me."

And like that, Gram had Jane going upstairs. Hands shaking, Roni took a moment to count to ten. Once she had regained her self-control, she strode down the hall and into the living room.

She moved quickly and with purpose. Gram wouldn't be able to keep Jane up there staring at a blanket for long. Roni went straight to where Jane had kept her photo album. She pulled out a volume and flipped through the pages until she found it — the second ticket stub.

Pulling back the plastic that covered the page, Roni did not even flinch at the ripping sound. She picked the ticket stub loose, put it in her pocket, closed the photo album, and set it back from where she had snatched it. Having that tiny scrap of paper in her pocket sent warm bubbles of excitement through her blood. She had done it.

As she walked back to the kitchen, she heard Gram and Jane clumping down the stairs. Gram hit each step with a strong thud to warn Roni, if necessary. Roni grinned as she headed out of the house.

A few minutes later, after she had crossed a few backyards and popped out on a side street, she slid into the driver's seat of her car. Almost ten minutes went by before Gram came walking toward the car. She acted casual. Just out for a night stroll.

When she got into the car, Roni wanted to tell her that everything went well. She wanted to describe how it felt to sneak around and what a good job Gram had done diverting Jane. But before Roni could utter a word, Gram pointed at the steering wheel. "You going to drive us away from your crime or are we going to sit here and wait for the cops to show up?"

Roni drove them back to the bookstore in Olburg and never said a word.

CHAPTER 19

After dropping Gram off for the night, Roni lucked into a parking space one block from her apartment and walked in the opposite direction. Two blocks later, she sidled up to a stool at Connor's Corner Bar. Near midnight and only a few customers — the heavy drinkers not willing to call it quits on a weeknight. A few of them eyed up Roni, perhaps hoping to get lucky, but thankfully, they read the situation right and returned to their drinks.

Roni ordered a shot, downed it, and ordered another. She wanted liquid fortitude to get her through the night — and only liquids from this universe. With any luck, the alcohol would provide a better sleep aid than any pills.

"You okay?" a grizzled man said from the end of the bar. He must have been near-seventy and had a beer gut to prove that he had spent most of his years in one bar or another.

"Fine," she said, though her shot spilled on her hand as she attempted to bring it to her mouth. Throwing it back, she ordered two more.

"Care to talk about it?"

She glared at him. "Do I look like I want to talk?"

Sipping a beer, he said, "No, ma'am, you do not."

"Then why are you bothering me?"

"People don't usually come to a bar like this to be alone. They come to spill their guts, sometimes their drinks, and not be judged. Or to drown their sorrows, as the saying goes. Is that why you're here? You broke up with a boyfriend or something?"

Roni swung her foot out and slipped off the stool. Her legs wobbled and the room took a short detour before lining up with her vision. Four shots in quick succession on an empty stomach — not a smart idea.

The man shook his head, and a few other men stared at her. "You all think you know what's what," she said, her words not quite crisp and clear. "You sit here in this pit and drink away, and you think you got it all under control, figured out, that you know the way the world works. Right? There are rich folk and poor folk and hard-working folk. But you're wrong. There's worlds and worlds and worlds out there. You can't ever figure it out because the rules are not set in stone. It's all in flux. One day, you're struggling to find a job and have a good, normal life, and then BAM! Next day, nothing makes sense. Pretty soon you find yourself breaking into an old lady's home to steal her memories." Roni laughed at that. "Memories. Got to steal some since I ain't got enough of my own."

The men watched her as they would the television. She certainly wasn't the first to get drunk too fast and monologue about things that made no sense. She wouldn't be the last. For them, she was the entertainment for the evening.

She thought about ordering another shot but held off. Four was already three too many. Stumbling out of the bar, she let the night air refresh her senses. With her head clearing, she weaved her way back to her apartment.

By the time she reached her door, her stomach had decided that rushing alcohol through the body might not have been such a good idea. She clamped her mouth shut, fumbled with the keys, shoved open the door, and darted to her kitchen sink. The booze burned coming up as much as it had going down. Afterwards, however, she felt better, clearer. Which only served to bring back her jumbled thoughts over what had happened that night.

It had been thrilling — if she wanted to be honest — but the way Gram spoke bothered her. So nonchalant. As if robbing people had become second nature and only a slight inconvenience to the day.

Roni guessed that dealing with rips between universes year after year jaded a person towards other matters. After all, what better justification for any crime than trying to save the universe?

She meandered into her living room. Shoving aside a pile of rumpled clothes, she made room on the couch to plop down.

"It's over," she said, her voice hollow in the late night.

At some point in the next day or two, Elliot would track down Darin. Gram and Sully would join him and together, the three of them would stop the current madness. None of that, however, involved Roni. She had done her part, and she had nothing left to offer the group.

Gram knew that all along. She knew Roni did not have magic powers like the rest of them. She knew Roni would not be casual about thievery. The whole talk of legacy and decisions meant nothing. Gram had put on that act because she knew Roni would never join.

Roni rubbed her throbbing head. Where were these thoughts coming from? She and Gram had not gotten along much lately, but Roni knew better than to think so ill of her. Yet it felt like the truth. Not in some mystical, clairvoyant way, but rather, it seemed to Roni that she could assess Gram better lately.

"Or maybe I'm still a bit drunk," she muttered.

She let her body fall to the side, her head resting on the clothes pile, and she closed her eyes. Something poked at her side. Trying to ignore it, to let sleep take over, she wiggled deeper into the clothes. But that only made the object poking her dig in more.

Sighing, she sat back up and tossed a cushion aside to find out what lay underneath. Her photo album — blue with thin lines of gold swirls. Though she knew she would grow maudlin if she looked through the book, especially half-drunk, she opened it anyway.

The simple album contained the only photographs Roni owned depicting her with her parents. Ten pictures. That was all she had.

She knew every part of the photographs. She knew the way her mother's hair curled up at the ends in the one at the beach and how her father's hand squeezed her mother's side in the one from a New Year's Eve party. But of all ten, the best one showed her mother holding baby Roni in her arms while her father gazed on mesmerized by the beauty of the ladies in his life.

The rest of the album was empty.

One blank page after another.

A thought burst forth in her head — something so strong and obvious as she thought it that she could not conceive how she had failed to think of it before. Her lack of memory, her lost time, had to be connected to Gram and the Parallel Society. It wasn't normal to lose so many years of memory — not unless there was a birth defect or a physical trauma. Mental trauma could cause amnesia but not like this. Could it?

And like that, she settled into the idea quite easily. Tomorrow, whether Gram wanted it or not, Roni would accept her position in the

Society. She would learn all she could about the Society, she would do her best job as their librarian, and she would have access to all those books. If the answer waited for her in there — and she felt more and more confident that it did — then she would find it.

Thinking about that huge room full of old journals and diaries and maps, Roni whispered, “This might take years.” That did not sit well. The idea of spending so much time wrapped up in the Society that she might end up like the Old Gang churned her stomach — or was it the alcohol?

But would it be so bad to spend that time in the bookstore? She would be able to learn all about the other worlds. She would get chances to help people like Darin, and in the future, she would be able to help them the right way instead of this mess they were cleaning up. And with some more honesty in her heart, she admitted she had nowhere else to go. At least, the Society would give her a reason to get out of the apartment in the morning.

She closed her eyes and sunk her head back into the clothes pile. Tomorrow morning. She would deal with these questions tomorrow morning.

CHAPTER 20

The phone rang. Roni jolted awake, her head foggy as she scanned the room — her apartment. At least she made it home safe — she checked around the room again — and alone.

Picking up the phone, she licked the film from her teeth. "Morning."

"Elliot found your boyfriend," Gram said.

Roni held the phone away from her ear and turned the volume down. "Okay. Thanks for letting me know."

"Are you not listening? We know where Darin is. It's time to get to work."

After a pause, Roni realized that Gram waited for her to say something. "Good luck."

"Don't you want to know where Darin is? How else do you plan to find the place?"

That woke up Roni's brain. "Why would I have to be there? I did my part. I got the ticket stub. There's nothing else for me to do except leave the rest in the hands of those with powers."

"Having powers doesn't mean ... oh, never mind. Darin is holed up in an abandoned house bordering Kaneslow Cemetery. You know where Kaneslow is?"

"Near Reading."

"Right. Should take you about thirty, forty-five minutes to get there. On the left side of First Street as you come in from the south, you'll see a diner. We'll meet you there."

"But what can I do except get in the way?"

She could hear Gram's disapproving breaths. "You made me a promise that you would see this to the end. Well, it isn't over until

Darin is dealt with. Are you a woman of her word or not?"

"Oh, for crying out loud. Does everything have to be a measure of my worth to you?" She couldn't believe the words had come out of her mouth. From the long pause, Gram apparently had the same shock.

At length, in a stoic tone, Gram said, "The thing that has taken over Darin may end up being all bark and no bite. I've seen it before. They all boast that this world is ripe for the plucking and they'll be the ones to take it. Sometimes they are a serious threat. Sometimes they're nothing but talkers. But sometimes, and I fear this is the case with Darin, they are more like an invasive species of plant. They're like kudzu. They come in and their mere presence starts to effect the surrounding area. They multiply and pretty soon, your world doesn't look like it once did. They seem harmless but they can be the worst of all."

"Okay, okay. No need for a full-on lecture. You want me there, I'll be there. Okay?"

"Elliot's the one insisting you come along."

"Jeez, I'm just waking up. I'll meet you at the diner as soon as I can."

Without waiting for a response, Roni ended the call. She brushed her teeth, splashed water on her face, and dug a few semi-clean clothes from the pile she had slept on. Then she checked her phone to find the fastest route to the diner, and off she went.

The drive offered no troubles other than her splitting headache. She had downed a couple of ibuprofen but either they had not kicked in fast enough or she needed more.

The town of Kaneslow looked like many Pennsylvania towns — a steady mixture of modern homes and stores with buildings from the original colonial settlements. Sprinkled in between were modern homes done in a colonial style.

She parked outside the diner — affectionately called the First Street Diner. Inside, she found Gram and Elliot at a booth near the back. Elliot had a plate with the remnants of eggs, toast, sausage patties, and hash browns. Gram had a cup of coffee.

"Where's Sully?" Roni asked as she slid in next to Elliot.

"He'll be here," Gram said. "He never lets us down."

Roni couldn't tell if Gram meant the comment as a fact or a slight. She opened her mouth to set things straight before they got any further, but Elliot spoke up.

"Let me tell you what I know so far. Sully won't care about most of this, and since he will probably stay in the back, he has no need for these details."

Gram nodded. "He's always been good at improvising, anyway."

"And he likes it that way. Makes it more exciting."

A brief grin. "It does fill him with life, doesn't it? Okay. Tell us what you've got."

Leaning in on his elbows, he lowered his voice. The conspiratorial nature of the move woke Roni more, sending an excited tingle across her skin. "On the other side of town, they have three churches all next to each other. Each one has a cemetery, and as far as I can tell, the land bleeds one into the other, so it's really like one enormous cemetery. In the woods surrounding the cemetery, there is an abandoned house.

"Now, that place has been here long enough to have built up some bits of legend around it. As far as I could learn chatting with the locals, it once belonged to the Stoltz family — husband, wife, and a little girl. All those acres of cemetery were the Stoltz farm.

"Apparently, Mr. Stoltz was quite a respectable man. Church-goer, stern and fair, and a hard worker. All good attributes in the 1700s. But something went wrong. Nobody saw it coming. There was no build up, no slow change in behavior. Just one night, he snapped. Killed his wife and his child while they slept. Slit their throats, then shot himself."

Taking a sip of coffee, Gram said, "You thinking Darin chose that place because of its energy?"

"Possibly."

"Energy?" Roni said. "Like auras and stuff?"

"Nonsense," Gram said. "Elliot is suggesting that there might have been a universe tear in the house. If Mr. Stoltz stumbled upon it and got infected by it — much like Darin, except this would have been by accident — then that would explain the sudden shift in personality and behavior. Either he was taken over like Darin, or more likely, contact with another universe drove him mad."

Elliot said, "It might still be going on, too. The legends I heard all suggest the house is haunted. Brave and stupid kids try to spend the night there but never make it. A few were never seen again. Those kinds of stories."

"Hold on," Roni said, her brain playing catch-up with the words her ears relayed. "Are you telling me that all those haunted house tales you hear growing up, that those are really people getting caught up with rips between universes?"

"Sometimes. Most times, really. In this case, I see all the hallmarks of a universe tear. Plus, it would explain why Darin zeroed in on the place. Because that's where he is."

"I don't get it. Why would he hide like a criminal on the run? He left us all full of himself and ready to take over the world."

Gram tapped one finger on the table. "Remember what I said? Some of these beings are all bluster. Maybe that's the case with him."

"No," Elliot said. "This one is dangerous. Maybe not *take over the world* dangerous, but he's got some serious strength and anger. I think that move he did at the zoo, transforming himself with those wolves, that must have taken a lot out of him. He's not hiding in that farmhouse so much as healing. And when he is ready, he will strike again."

The waitress finally noticed Roni had joined the table. She slapped a menu down, poured coffee, and walked off. Roni pushed the menu aside. The greasy aroma of all the food around her was bad enough, the thought of eating food threatened to send her running to the bathroom.

Frowning, she asked, "Why would he be attracted to this tear? It's not his universe. Is it? Can there be more than one tear into the same universe?"

"Good questions," Elliot said. "The answer will not be so good. Basically, we do not know. We think it might be possible for there to be more than one tear, but we have never seen it. We have seen that oftentimes beings are attracted to the tears themselves, but we've never put it to a test, so we cannot say definitively."

Gram added, "The Society doesn't have the time or resources to conduct deep investigations on these kinds of questions. It's one of the big drawbacks to keeping the group so small. The answers might be in our library of journals and such, but well, you've seen that room. Perhaps such questions will be answered by those who take up the call after us. Not really your concern though, since you'll be leaving after this is done."

Sully arrived in time to prevent Roni from snapping a response. He shuffled his feet as he approached, his face unshaven and his remaining hair sticking out at odd angles. He slumped into the booth with a hiss and a wince.

"You okay?" Roni asked.

"Just my back," he said. "When you get as old as me, see how well you do." The waitress came by right away this time. "Bagel, toasted, with a shmeer on the side."

Gram rolled her beaded necklace between two fingers and inspected Sully closely. Her face turned livid. "Are you serious?"

"What?" He looked to Roni. "What's she on about?"

"Don't pretend you don't know what you did. Is this really how you want Roni to see this group function? After all our years of hard work, is this really what you think we should be doing now? Screwing things up like this?"

"You know who's screwing this up? The waitress. She never poured me any coffee."

"You didn't ask for any, and don't change the subject."

Roni pushed her coffee across the table. "Will someone tell me what's going on?"

Gram arched an eyebrow at Sully, but when it became clear he wouldn't open up, she said, "This genius was supposed to be in his workshop —"

"I was in my workshop."

"— making a new Golem for today. Instead, he fell asleep."

Stabbing the air with his finger, Sully said, "First, I didn't have the clay to make it. I used up most of what I had to make the one a few days ago. You all think I'm some magic wizard that can create supplies from thin air. No. I need more clay. Second, I've been telling you the wiring in my workshop is bad. Not enough power for what I need. So, I had troubles there. Third, I am an old man and I need rest to do good work. Should a doctor be so tired he falls asleep in surgery? Should a pilot skip a nap and crash a plane? The work we do is more important than those, so yes, I went to sleep. Look at the bags under your eyes and Roni, too. You both could use a few more hours rest."

"Never you mind Roni and me. We're here, on time, and ready to do our jobs. But I guess we won't have a Golem to back us up in case there's trouble. And when isn't there trouble?"

Elliot broke in. "Stop it. Both of you. Sully, from now on, please keep us informed when it comes to your clay orders. We could have purchased more last month easily. Lillian, we will be fine without a big Golem. I have the fullest confidence that Sully can still be an asset. Besides, with any luck, it won't matter because Roni is going to talk Darin in."

Sputtering, Roni said, "I am? No, no, no. That's not a good idea."

Putting up his hand to quell any further protests, Elliot remained calm. The waitress arrived with Sully's food, and they all sat quiet until she left. Gram shifted forward with a clear intention to speak her mind, but Elliot raised his hand again.

"Let me speak," he said, and Gram sat back. "There are many reasons this is a good idea. We have several concerns to deal with in this situation. Obviously, we wish to return this creature from whence it came, save Darin's life, and close any other tears we might find. But more important than all of those things, we must protect the people of this town from exposure to all of this." To Roni, he added, "Sometimes we are lucky and our cases take us into remote parts of the world where we can act freely, but more often, we are in situations such as this one. Plenty of people attend those churches and visit those cemeteries. If we have Roni talk with Darin, if she is successful, we can achieve all of our goals without causing any contamination of the townsfolk."

Gram shook her head. "Roni's never done anything like this."

"We all began as such."

"But she doesn't know the first thing —"

"She is the only one of us with a connection to the victim. That is why the wolf creature Darin offered to have her join him. Somewhere inside, there is a tiny spark of the original Darin left. It is why we acquired the second ticket stub, and it is why I think Roni will succeed."

Roni said, "I think Gram's right. I don't know what I could possibly say to him that would make him give up. What could anybody say?"

"If you're going to be part of this Society, you will have to take risks. You will have to dig deep into your soul to find those words you need."

"Well, you said it right there." Gram lifted her chin. "Roni has no intention of being one of us. We couldn't have put a more welcoming embrace, considering the situation, yet she hems-and-haws, unsure of herself, unwilling to commit. This is not the kind of person we want in the Society."

Elliot thumped his cane on the floor garnering a few surreptitious glances from other diners. "If your granddaughter does not even try —"

"She's made her decision."

"I have not," Roni said with enough force to quiet everyone at the table. Even Sully looked up at her in surprise. "You all seem to think I should be acclimating far quicker than I am. I'm sorry about that, but that's the way it is. I didn't get eased into this. Perhaps if, while I was growing up, Gram had prepared me for this Society and all that it entails or, at the least, given me a hint that things might not be the way I thought they were, well, then maybe I'd be able to decide faster."

Elliot took hold of Roni's hand. "I'm sure it has been quite difficult for you. I wish we had the time to do all of this right. Sully and I have wanted to tell you the truth for years, but your grandmother kept saying you weren't ready."

"That's not true," Gram said. "I never said that she wasn't ready. I said that I didn't want to burden her with our responsibilities." To Roni, she added, "You've had an unfortunate childhood and you've been aimless for a long time. I didn't think you needed to be bothered with all of this. Look at you — caught with this big decision which will impact the rest of your life, yet no time to think about it because we've got Darin Lander to deal with. This was what I wanted to avoid."

"There is no avoiding. Sully and I told you as much more than enough times."

Roni knew she would be unpacking all that she had heard for days, but at the moment, Darin needed help. "Is there another plan that doesn't involve me lying to Darin?"

Elliot said, "You do not have to lie to him. I never said such a thing. But you are the one who must talk to him."

"I just don't think —"

"You must try. If you do not, we might perish. Not just me or Sully or your grandmother, but all of us. Whether on purpose or by accident, this version of Darin has the potential to destroy the world as we know it. Not overnight, of course — at least, I hope not — but as time goes by. Maybe months, maybe a few years. Who knows? Right now, though, this is the only opportunity we will get to stamp out this trouble before it truly begins."

Roni knew she had no real choice. Part of her knew it all along. "Fine. I'll try. When do we begin?"

"Right away."

"Hold on, hold on." Sully put a hand on his plate. "I still have my bagel to finish."

CHAPTER 21

As they drove to the cemetery, all four in Elliot's Lincoln, Roni could not stop her knees from bouncing or her fingers from tapping. Her nerves firing off reminded her of sitting for a final exam in college — one that she had not prepared for. Strange. She could remember a sensation like that even when she could barely remember the faces, names, and events of her past. It had never bothered her much, this lost time, but now she found herself thinking about it more than ever.

"Just ahead," Elliot said.

He drove under an iron gate with the words Kaneslow Cemetery on the arch. A gravel driveway led to a small parking lot. A red Subaru Outback sat at the end of the lot. As they got out of the Lincoln, Roni spotted three men standing by a grave — an elderly man, a younger man and a boy.

The morning sun rose high enough to cast shadows off the gravestones, and Roni's skin chilled. They were more than shadows. They marked other lives — people and families and histories she would never know. Each one like a universe unto itself. Each one a book in the cavern.

"Come," Elliot said, and Roni shook off her dark thoughts.

He led the way along a white stone path. After a short distance, they crested a hill and soon they could no longer see the cars or the three men by the grave. Roni wanted to rush ahead even as she wanted to rush back to the car, but neither would do. The Old Gang moved at a slow and steady pace, and she would have to get comfortable with it. No way could she manage this alone.

Up ahead, she saw a thick tree line — the beginning of a forest that wound its way around several towns and eventually connected with

Norris Acres Park. Just inside the tree line, a silhouette of a farmhouse partially hid. A one-floor rancher, small, probably a single room with bed, stove, and table all smack up next to each other. Practical for a farmer centuries ago.

The closer they walked, the more the house struck Roni as a dead and rotting beast. The windows were cracked or missing. The wood had split in some places, been eaten by insects, and hollowed out in others.

When they reached the tree line, Elliot halted and pointed at the ground. "Blood."

Roni had to crouch down and squint to view the two spots Elliot had indicated. They definitely were there, but without touching them, she had no way to know if they were fresh. She didn't really want to know, either.

They entered the woods. The leaves shushed as the wind blew through — a thousand librarians angry at their trespass. Sunlight speckled the ground but not enough to warm the air. The temperature must have dropped five degrees, maybe more.

Many of the trees surrounding the house had been removed to create some space but not all of them. Shadows covered the area well enough. As they stepped towards the front of the house, Roni noticed she could barely see the cemetery.

Gram swung her big bag over her shoulder as she looked at the building. "Sully, get to work."

Roni expected his usual sass, but instead, he nodded and walked deeper into the woods. The seriousness in his steps, in the way he focused on the ground, in the fearful glance shot back at the house, spiked Roni's heart rate. She wanted to throw up.

"You are going to do fine," Elliot said, nudging her shoulder. "Just talk with him."

A wood porch large enough for two rocking chairs with an overhang had been built up to the front door. The warped wood looked like subtle waves on calm waters. But Roni knew better, now. Nothing calm awaited her. Vicious monsters swam the waters ahead, ready to strike.

She stepped forward.

"Darin?" Her voice sounded tiny in the forest. She cleared her throat. "Darin?" More forceful this time, but it still felt small. "I came here to talk. That's all. I want to make sure you're okay. I want to help you figure this out. For everyone's sake."

Sully returned with a mass of sticks cradled in his arms. He set them on the ground in a haphazard pile and walked off again.

Chiding herself to stay focused, Roni said, "Please, come out and talk with me. You know we're not going to leave. This isn't about how you're going to beat us. It's about how this will end. I should be angrier than ever with you, but I'm not. I only want to talk, to help, to make this better. That's it."

Nothing. Not a sound.

Roni glanced back at Elliot and shrugged. He offered a consolatory nod — she tried. Lifting his cane over his head with one hand, he began circling the air in front of him with the other.

But a loud squeaking broke the silence. The front door opened inward.

Elliot lowered his cane. He and Gram stepped up on either side of Roni. Through the open door, they could see nothing more than darkness. They walked ahead together until they reached the steps onto the porch.

Darin's deep voice boomed out. "Just Roni."

Roni put her foot on the first step, but Gram's hand shot out. Clenching Roni's arm, she said, "Don't go in there."

"Why am I out here then?"

"This isn't a game. There is real danger inside that house. I know we don't get along that well lately, but I don't want to see you hurt."

"I have to try." Roni's confidence began and ended with those words. As she climbed onto the porch, her heart sank into her gut, her chin quivered, and her mouth went bone dry. Like a painted line leading into the house, Roni saw dark blood — something had been dragged across the wood. Barely above a whisper, she repeated, "I have to try."

Her stomach gurgled and a burning sensation coursed through her lower abdomen. She kept her mouth a thin line and focused on not flinching from the discomfort. Part of Darin had been changed into a wolf, and Roni knew that with animals, particularly dogs, she had to show as little fear as possible.

Crossing the threshold into the house, she fought to remain still. A putrid, rotting odor threatened to knock her down. Her legs wobbled, desperate to whip her around and sprint off into the woods.

The glow of low coals from a once hearty fire burned in the hearth. A plain, wood table had been placed a few feet away. On that table, Roni saw the body of a man — split open, his innards hanging off the side. Next to the body, she saw the head of a fawn. In the back corner, Darin sat in the dark.

"I thought it would be easier," he said. "Apparently, merging with the wolf was a one-time experience. Back home, we merge and depart without thought. We take the best we can from each other and attempt to give off the worst. Some of us can even force two others to converge on a point." He gestured to the table. "It doesn't work in this world."

Roni shifted so that she faced Darin fully and could not see any of the horror on the table. Breathing through her mouth to avoid smelling the severed stomach, she said, "No matter how many times you try, it won't ever work. Our worlds are too different."

"But I'm here. I'm fine. And it worked for me."

"Like you said — a one-time thing."

"Unless I can figure out a way to change that. I have time, and I'm sure I can find your most intelligent people."

"Why would they help you?"

"They won't have a choice. I can think of countless ways to threaten them, their families, anyone they love."

"Or you could admit what you know is the truth. That this world isn't right for you. That you should go back to your home."

Darin jumped to his feet, his wolf mouth snarling. "When I was young — a boy, you would call me — I was little more than the size of a thumb. Just a glowing ball of energy. I'd bounce around, merge with other young ones, and I stupidly believed I had been born into a beautiful world. But my mother, for lack of a better word, she wanted me to be something I was not. She cared about that kind of thing. She would chase me around, watch every move, every decision, every aspect of my life. It got to the point where I found it difficult to function. So, I left. And I don't have the time or interest to explain how my world works, but suffice it to say, I did not excel."

"Most people don't — at least, not in the way we think we should."

"I mean something different. But while I had no hope of achieving the higher planes — and don't bother asking — I did learn to take better aspects of a merge and discard the worst. I could fight off multiple threats, and I knew some of the best places to rest, heal, and prepare for the next outing.

"I also started to work. My mother kept tabs on me still and I knew she would be disappointed when she saw to what lows I had achieved. It gave me the only happiness I ever had — watching her fall apart because of me."

Roni inched back toward the door. She needed fresh air. "Your mother won't see anything you do here."

He moved towards her. Blood had splattered across his clothes and speckled the fur on his neck. "What you just said is the biggest problem I have."

"Then go back. She's there. Waiting to be humiliated by you."

"You don't understand." He looked pained and frustrated. At least, Roni thought that was how he looked — she never had to read a wolf's facial cues before. Darin's yellow wolf-eyes narrowed as if he struggled to force out the words. "I have no mother."

"But you just said —"

"That wasn't my mother. That was Darin's mother. We — my species — we do not have mothers and fathers. We split and reform. Do you see now? Darin and I are blending in a way that shouldn't happen. I can't tell where my life ends and his begins. We are one being now."

"What about the wolf? He in there, too?"

"The wolf cannot think at a high enough level to merge our thoughts that way. So, now you understand. Now, you must leave."

Roni edged back further. "You know I can't do that. I'm here because you can't continue like this. I'm here because that man you are part of, Darin, he doesn't deserve this."

Darin bent closer, his canine breath hot and foul. "There's no point in trying to save him. We are entwined. There is no going back."

She tried to hold her ground, but her legs stepped toward the door anyway. "I know it's not the same, but lately, I've felt like I had two people entwined within me. One wants desperately to forget all of this ever happened. One wants to embrace it all, jump off into the excitement of it. It can drive you to do dumb things, erratic things. But it doesn't have to be bad. I'm sure there are ways we can gain control over our competing selves. Maybe we can help each other figure it out."

"That's your solution? You think we can talk our way through the problem and find some happy balance that still involves me taking control of your world?"

"That's not happening, and you know it." She pointed to the table without looking at it. "This isn't going to change. We can't be merged like that."

A creak of wood on the porch caused Roni and Darin to freeze. He cocked his head as his wolf ears perked up. He snatched a glance at the back window. A Gram-shaped figured darted by.

"I see," Darin said with a low growl. "You don't mean anything you are saying. You've only been stalling."

"No," Roni said. "I don't know what they're up to, but I had nothing to do with it. I was sent in here to talk with you, to try to find a peaceful solution."

"Liar." His lips lifted to reveal his long fangs. Saliva dribbled down through the fur on his face and onto the floor. "You are a stupid, insignificant, worthless piece of meat. That's the truth you must learn. You are nothing but food to me."

"So now you're all wolf and going to start eating people? What happened to changing us all?" Roni's hands trembled at her side. She felt the warped porch underneath her as she continued backing up. She had no clue what words tumbled out of her mouth, but she figured as long as they were speaking to each other, he wasn't killing her — that seemed like a good choice.

"You disgust me. You pretend to care about Darin or me or us, but you're nothing but a manipulator."

With a bark, he jumped forward forcing her back. Her foot reached the end and missed the stairs. Flailing her arms, Roni smacked into the earth. She scrambled to her feet and dashed for Elliot.

Darin towered at the edge of the porch. Muscles he never had a few nights before now bulged through his shirt. His fingernails had thickened and grown longer.

Roni stood behind Elliot. He leaned on his cane and watched. His old, stained shirt made him appear scrawny. What had she been thinking? How could these three people — so old they were ready to sit in wheelchairs at a retirement home — how could they be the saviors of all? Sure, Roni had seen them in action before, but not like this. Not against a beast like Darin.

It was one thing to prepare for a fight on home turf with special rings in the walls and magic forces ready at hand. Even then, they had narrowly survived. But this — this creature outclassed them. Roni was the only one of the Society who could move with any sure speed, and she had no doubt that Darin could chase her down without getting winded.

"I shall give you one chance," Elliot said — even his accented voice sounded weak. "Come with us peacefully, and all will be fine."

Darin barked twice as his answer. Then he inhaled hard, his chest widening as it filled up, and let loose a long howl. By the time the single note faded, four wolves entered from deeper in the woods. They snapped their jaws, growled, and barked.

Roni felt urine trickle down her leg. "We're going to die."

CHAPTER 22

Elliot patted Roni's arm. "I shall take care of this," he said. "You go help Sully."

"But —"

"Go." His voice suddenly firm and dangerous. He stepped closer to the porch, letting the wolves flank him. Pointing at Darin with his cane like Babe Ruth showing where he would hit the next homerun, Elliot said, "I do not wish to harm you. Heel your wolves now. There will be no more chances after this."

Darin paused, and Roni had the time to think that maybe he had changed his mind. But a swipe of his claw through the air sent the wolves into a frenzied attack. Roni backed away, her eyes stuck wide open, as she witnessed Elliot's incredible reaction.

The first wolf thrust into the air, and Elliot ducked, jabbing his cane upward to catch the wolf's gut as it passed overhead. Two more came in from the sides. A sweeping motion of the cane halted their approach. The fourth barreled in full-speed with its teeth bared. As Elliot finished his sweep, he let his momentum carry him to the ground. He rolled backwards and onto his feet. This gave him plenty of distance to swing his cane hard enough to crack the attacking wolf's skull.

"Roni!" a voice called from behind. She spun around to find Sully with another armful of sticks. "Yes, yes, he's amazing. But at his age, he won't keep that up for long. He's counting on us to finish this. Come. Help."

Behind her, she heard the grunts and smacks and growls turn to bites, but she pushed it from her mind. She had to help Sully.

"What do we do?" she asked looking at the pile of sticks.

"Find the big ones." He grabbed a thick branch and drew lines in the dirt. "Two legs here. Arms here. Body and head. Put the biggest branches first, then put on all the sticks. Then tie them together."

"Right. Big sticks, little sticks, tie it all together. Wait — tie them with what?"

Sully reached into his coat pocket and tossed out a handful of zip-ties. "Hurry."

As she picked up the ties, she snatched a glimpse of Elliot. With one wolf dead on the ground, the other three increased the pressure. One after the other, sometimes two together, even all three. Attack after attack. And Elliot fended them off with a swirling cane and a well-trained fist.

Roni grabbed the biggest branches she saw and placed them on the ground. Frantically, she spread the smaller sticks all over the skeletal form.

"No, no," Sully said. "That's a mess. That won't do. Do it right or we'll lose whatever time Elliot buys us."

Moving fast, Roni picked up the sticks and laid them into the proper positions. Blood dribbled on her hand from the numerous cuts she received but she kept going. Elliot cried out and she saw him deflect one wolf with his cane while clutching another by the neck. The third, however, bit into Elliot's calf.

Roni doubled her efforts. As she worked, Sully sat on the ground with a pad and pen. She knew he would be writing in Hebrew, that she wouldn't be able to read it, but she wanted to watch him. No — she had to finish the stick-Golem.

With the zip-ties, she gathered up each limb and tied them into bundles. When she finished, sweat and blood mixed in her palms. "Is this good?"

Sully scowled. "No."

"What's wrong? The legs and arms and body are all tied up."

"But not together. The legs aren't attached."

"I didn't know."

"What are you thinking? How's it going to walk without attached legs?"

"I'll fix it."

Sully peeked up at Elliot and shook his head. "Not enough time."

Elliot had maimed a second wolf, but the two remaining sensed his flagging energy. They stalked closer, and though he swiped with his cane, they barely flinched. Sweat dampened his head. His footprints left behind splotches of blood.

Darin laughed — a full-throated barking laugh. "You're pathetic. Far past your prime. If you're what I have to worry about, then once I fix the merging process, this world will crumble."

Two metal chains with spiked ends whipped around the corner of the building and lodged into Darin's back. Gram leaned away from the porch, putting all her weight into holding Darin still. He bellowed and the two wolves on Elliot pivoted away. But Elliot lunged forward, tackling both — one with his body, the other with his cane.

"Roni!" Gram's voice strained to be heard over Darin's howling cries. "Roni, help us!"

Having no idea how to help, Roni rushed forward anyway. She kept a wide berth around the wolves. Elliot used his weight and the last of the strength to keep the animals locked to the ground.

Darin swiped a claw in Roni's direction, but another chain shot out and wrapped around his wrist. Gram yanked that wrist back.

And Roni saw it — Darin's stomach. A flicker of amber light.

That had to be it. She knew it like an instinct. But no, if the answer were that simple, surely Gram would have said something, would have known. She shoved the idea away.

But it refused to leave. And in that second, the idea took her by the chest and shook her inside. It yelled at her that she had ignored her instincts too often and where did that ever get her? If she had listened in the beginning, she would have gotten rid of Darin from the start.

Well, nothing else is working, she thought.

Storming up the steps of the porch, she made a fist and punched. She yelled, her face inches away from Darin's snout, her eyes manic and wide. Her fist hit him in the gut, and as she had guessed, it kept going — straight through and into his abdomen.

Darin roared. He tried to grab her or push her, but Gram kept him restrained. Roni plunged her hand further in, holding back the urge to vomit, until she hit something pulsing hot. At first, she thought it might be his heart — maybe his innards had reshaped along with his outward appearance. But no, she knew what she grasped onto. It could only be one thing.

She yanked her arm free, causing another howling shriek, and staggered off the porch. Blood and bile dripped from her forearm, the smell ripe and vulgar. In her palm, she held the glowing ball.

All eyes lifted to her. The wolves ceased their struggle and watched her every move. Elliot stared in shock. Even as Gram held Darin back, her attention fell on Roni.

But Roni turned her focus on the glob in her hand. Something rested inside it. A small, rectangular object. Roni's face dropped open. "Oh, man."

She threw the glowing energy onto the ground. It splattered like a ball of paint. Darin screamed and tried to intervene, but moving forward meant tearing his back to pieces.

Roni crouched down. On the ground, she saw the ticket stub — Darin's ticket stub.

"No!" Darin lunged forward.

His skin tore and blood shot out his back as he freed himself. Gram fell over, her chains dropping to the ground. The wolves jumped hard, taking Elliot by surprise. He couldn't hold them back as they raced to join Darin.

Roni bent down and snatched the ticket stub before bolting off around the house. She wouldn't get far. She knew it. But she had to try. If she survived this, that would have to become her mantra — try, try, try.

Cutting around the corner of the house, she didn't dare look back. She could hear how close they were. If she darted into the woods, Darin and the wolves would get her easily. Another corner and she came up the side of the house. Whatever backup plans Gram and the others had waiting, Roni hoped they were ready.

She turned the last corner and saw Gram standing near the porch stairs. In front of her like a shield, she held a book. No, Roni realized — *the book*. The book that Darin had fallen into originally.

"Throw it!" Gram said.

Roni tossed the ticket stub into the air and kept running. As she zipped by Gram, she saw the book being opened. She dove to the ground, scrambling for the nearest tree, and wrapped her arms around its trunk.

When she looked back, she saw the two wolves spinning in the air as the book vacuumed them in. The ticket stub had already fallen into the book as did numerous leaves and rocks. Though Roni felt the strong winds, she did not have to fight to keep her position. They were in a large, open forest and Gram had pointed the book away from them. Roni was safe behind the book.

Darin, however, had to fight to stay in this universe. He dug his claws into the ground and moaned as he climbed his way back towards the house. Once close enough, he bit down on the porch railing.

After a few moments, Roni could see that Darin had secured himself well. The book would not be taking him back. Gram must have come to the same conclusion. She closed the book.

All went quiet.

CHAPTER 23

For several minutes, nobody moved. Roni's pulse beat against her neck and her heavy breathing matched that of the Old Gang. Elliot had managed to get to his feet but he leaned hard on his cane. Gram held the book to her chest and closed her eyes. Roni couldn't be sure if she prayed or simply needed rest or both.

Crumpled on the ground by the porch, Darin whimpered. His wolf hair fell out in clumps. His snout receded back into his head.

"Is that it?" Roni said, her voice cutting into the silence like a car backfiring during a church service. "Did we save him?"

Gram opened her eyes and looked over Darin. "Perhaps. Elliot?"

Dabbing at a cut on his forehead, he said, "I suspect the creature attached itself to the ticket stub. It was the man's emotional core, and thus, it became the core of the creature — its heart. By ripping the ticket stub out, Roni essentially ripped out the heart of the beast."

"So, it's over?" Roni asked.

Gram watched every motion Darin made as she approached him. "Darin? Are you okay? How do you feel?"

His shoulders shook, but when she reached out to touch him, he whirled around with a maniacal grin on his face. "I feel damn good."

His arm circled over Gram's elbow, locking her against him. With his free hand, he slapped Gram upside the head. Dazed from the blow, she could not stop him when he plucked the book from her weakened hands.

Elliot lifted his cane and started a circle with his hand, but Roni knew there wasn't enough time for that. Though feeling spent of all her strength, she charged. Darin shoved her aside as he stepped forward. She flopped onto the ground next to Gram.

To Elliot, Darin said, "You're not so bright. The ticket stub was not the heart of me. It was the heart of old Darin." Turning back to face Roni, he laughed. "You threw away the man you wanted to save. And now I have this book, this door into my old homeworld. I have to thank you all. With this, I don't have to bother experimenting on ways to merge beings. I can simply open this and bring in my own kind."

Gram threw out a chain but Darin sidestepped the attack. His fingers slid along the book's cover, tracing the corners with affection. Roni saw it in the man's eyes — he was going to open the book and point it at them.

She had nothing to grab onto. If she ran for a tree, he would open the book long before she got there. The porch was too far away. Her only option would be to grab Gram's leg, but after all the energy they had spent to get this far, she didn't think Gram would be able to hold onto anything long enough to save them.

Roni tried not to think of that horrible Hell tunnel of flesh and faces she had seen before. Trying not think of it only made the image stronger in her mind.

"Goodbye," Darin said.

But he never got the cover open. Two arms made of sticks and branches rose behind him. The stick-Golem stood a foot taller than Darin as it locked him in a thorny bear hug.

Thrashing his legs, Darin tried to break the Golem apart. He wriggled his shoulder and thrust his head back into the mass of branches. Bits of wood spit off into the air, but the Golem did not release him.

Roni helped Gram to her feet. She trembled out a smile, but Gram shook her head. Darin had not given up yet.

As Sully walked around the scene to reach Gram, Darin pushed off the ground, stomped on the Golem's feet, and bit at the twigs near his mouth. His exertions only fueled his rage. Holding the book tight in his arms, Darin took a different tactic — he dropped. He lifted his legs off the ground and let all of his weight carry him down.

The Golem's arms and back could not move fast enough to accommodate the sudden shift in weight distribution. Two loud snaps of wood and Darin hit the dirt — free. He popped to his feet, spun around to face the Golem, and opened the book.

With splintering cracks, the broken arms of the Golem tore free of its body and soared into the suction of the book. The Golem's feet rooted into the ground, keeping the rest of it safe. Darin closed the book.

"I'm leaving here," Darin said with his back to the group. "If any of you try to stop me, I'll open the book, and you will find out how hard it is to live in another world."

He walked by the Golem, sneered at it, and kept going. Roni looked to the Old Gang for some sign of what to do, but they watched him go. They were motionless and exhausted.

"Well, I'm not giving up," she said. Digging in her pocket, she pulled out the second ticket stub. "Darin! If there's any part of you still in there, you'll want this."

He stopped.

"Can you feel it? Your father's ticket stub."

He whirled back. "How did you get that?"

"You *are* in there, aren't you? The creature in you said I threw you away, but I didn't believe it. Not entirely. If it were so easy, he would have done it long ago."

"Shut up," Darin said, but Roni thought he said it to himself. He smacked the side of his head. "Shut up. I'm in control."

"Come here, Darin. Come get your father's ticket stub. You remember that day, right? One of the best of your life."

Darin took three quick steps and halted. He stood to the side of the stick-Golem and leaned in. To Roni, he looked like a man lured by a Siren call while another, invisible man attempted to hold him back.

He stuttered another two steps and reached out. "My dad's ticket." Then he struck himself on the cheek. "Your father is dead and I am all that matters to you now."

She waved the ticket back and forth. "Courtside seats at a 76ers game. Remember? Your mother and father were proud of you and wanted to celebrate. They couldn't afford tickets for all three of you, so you had dinner together. Then just you and your father went to the game."

Darin staggered closer. She had no idea what to do once he arrived. She need not have worried.

Sully crossed his arms with one hand on each shoulder. He closed his eyes and recited Hebrew while bowing three times. What remained of the stick-Golem sprang into action. Keeping one foot with its roots held in the earth, the Golem locked its other leg around Darin's waist. It moved faster than before, and Darin had no time to react.

Elliot hobbled to Roni as fast as his injured feet would take him. "Come," he said, taking her by the hand. They scurried off to the tree line and waited.

Gram stepped before Darin. She opened her big bag and pulled out another book. "It didn't have to be this way," she said.

He spit at her. "Of course, it did."

She opened the book.

No wind. No whoosh of air. No vacuum pulled at everything in sight. And from the tree line, Roni saw only cold darkness inside.

Darin opened his eyes. He looked at Gram and then the book. As it dawned on him that he would not be sucked into oblivion, a smile crept up his mouth.

"A dud?" he said. "Your book is a dud. It didn't work! Ha!"

Gram's eyes narrowed and her voice chilled. "Not all universes are the same."

A gray and black marbled, seven fingered hand burst forth from the book. It stretched across the area on an elongated arm with multiple joints. Boils and open wounds covered the bizarre appendage.

The hand opened wide enough to encompass Darin's entire head. He screamed — a muffled sound under the palm of the hand. It pulled him back, breaking through the stick-Golem without effort.

Darin managed to get his feet under him and attempted to run off, but the hand shoved his head to the ground. He bawled in pain and fear. He kicked and yelled. As the mottle-skinned hand dragged him across the dirt and stone, he let loose a long howl that lacked all the strength of the wolf. Clutching his book, he continued to squirm on the ground.

If he thought to open the book, he failed to act on it. Not that it would have mattered. The seven-fingered hand never ceased retracting.

In seconds, it drew him down into the book Gram held.

She closed it and shook her head.

CHAPTER 24

Hours later, as midnight approached, Gram led Roni, Elliot, and Sully through the twisting maze of the caverns. They stepped off the main path and went up a short incline until she finally halted by a wall with two chains hanging loose.

"Everyone doing okay?" she asked.

Elliot had spent the car ride home healing himself and then Sully. Roni said she did not require his aid. Though she did have a few bruises, she thought it would be better to avoid getting reliant on the old man.

From her bag, Gram pulled out the book that had captured Darin. It had green vertical lines down the front and wide black spaces between. She reached for the chains, paused, and lowered her arms.

Turning to Roni, she said, "This is your victory. You do the honors."

Victory. Roni didn't know if she agreed with that word. They had won, yet they failed to save Darin. Gram told her that Darin had died the moment he entered the book the first time, but that did not relieve her uneasiness.

Still, they had saved their world and their universe, so she recognized that much of a victory. Taking the book, she moved in close to the wall. She reached up for the first chain. At her touch, it snaked down and locked itself around the book. When she brushed the other chain with her finger, it too wrapped around the book and then punctured the spine with its sharp end.

Gram motioned in the air, and both chains tightened up, securing the book against the cavern wall. The Old Gang clapped their hands and Roni blushed.

"Speech! Speech!" Sully said.

Roni knew she could not avoid this part, so she decided to make the most of it. "I know this has been a difficult few days for you all. I've not been clear-headed or easy to get along with. All of you probably have had some idea in your heads of how I would be when I learned about the Parallel Society. Gram, most of all. Yet none of it turned out as any of you could have planned. I certainly didn't expect any of it."

Elliot chuckled. "You did perfectly fine."

"I don't know if this is a typical week for you guys, and I'm not sure I want to know. But I also realized that I've been fooling myself into thinking I can go back. I can't. When Darin broke in here and went into that book, it was over for him. Same for me. You can't unlearn what you've learned. And here's the thing I really have to admit — when we drove home, beaten and tired, I had a smile on my face. We had won, and that felt really good. Special." She stepped in front of the group. "I don't want to lose that feeling."

Sully put out his hand. "Does this mean you'll join us?"

"Yes." She took his hand. "If you'll have me."

Elliot and Gram stepped forward with arms out and hugs ready. "Happy to have you!" Elliot said.

Gram held her tight. "I've been so worried you'd leave us."

"What?" Roni's throat tightened. She wanted to scream. "Why didn't you say so? Why did you keep pushing me away?"

"Because this is a commitment for the rest of your life. You had to make the choice to join us despite the bad. I'm glad you enjoyed the feeling of victory, but there are tough times in this business. A lot of them. We had to make sure you had the thickest skin possible for it."

Roni accepted the answer but did not believe it entirely. She had too much firsthand knowledge of Gram's tough side to buy that it was all an act for Roni's benefit.

"Well," Sully said, "now that's all settled, it's late and I'm tired. Good night." He walked off.

"I think I shall join him. Sleep sounds like a good idea." Elliot followed him away.

Gram held Roni at arm's length. "You're going to make me proud, right?"

"Of course," Roni said.

"Because we still don't know who hired Darin, and that troubles me. Things may not settle down anytime soon."

"Don't worry about me. I'll do my part."

"You've got a lot to learn, but I think you can handle it."

"I can't wait to get started."

Gram's face brightened. "Good. You saw the Special Library. Your first task is to organize and catalog that mess. Should only take a year or two. Maybe three. But that's the beauty of having a job for life. You've got time. So, you do like the boys and get some sleep. I've still got to hang the books we used for those small rips from the farmhouse. Then I'll sleep, too. Work starts at six tomorrow morning."

Roni forced a smile as they walked back to the elevator. She did not want to look too eager. After saying goodnight, she left the bookstore and headed to her apartment. The smile on her face became one of anticipation and determination.

What she said about the thrill in victory had been true, but it was not the reason for her decision to stay. It was the library. That special library held all the knowledge of the Society. That was the reason she joined the group. If answers were to be found anywhere, she would found them in those books — answers to all her lost time.

Her smile faded. She had to be ready for what that meant. She had to prepare.

Because she had a dark feeling that Gram knew the answers already.

BOOK ON
THE ISLE
THE PARALLEL SOCIETY BOOK 2
STUART JAFFE

CHAPTER 1

Veronica "Roni" Rider sat in the breakfast nook of Elliot and Sully's apartment. Living on the fifth floor of the *In The Bind* bookstore, the two old men had been part of her family for decades. Along with Gram, they made up all that Roni had left. Which made her problem all the more difficult.

"You should talk to her," Sully said, pushing his glasses up his nose. He scratched at the white tufts that ringed his head. "She's your grandmother, after all, and that's important."

Elliot laughed — a powerful sound that denied his age. With exacting motions, he scrambled eggs in a small pan. "We are talking about Lillian, correct? Roni's Gram?"

"Phooey, to you. Yes, of course, Gram can be prickly about things at times, but this is her granddaughter and the future of the Parallel Society."

Roni had been joining the boys for breakfast most every day for the last year — ever since she had discovered the truth about the Old Gang. Lillian "Gram" Donaugh, Elliot Kenwana, and Sully Greenbaum were no ordinary trio of elderly folk. Not at all. They had been saving the universe for decades.

"That's my problem," Roni said. "What kind of future will the Society have when all Gram will let me do is library work?"

Sully wagged a finger. "You're our researcher, our librarian. Where else should you work? I make Golems, so I work in the studio with the clay. Gram's gifts are the chains and books that bind the tears between universes — that's why her office is the entrance to the caverns that house all those books. And Elliot — well, his abilities don't really get an office here."

Elliot laughed louder than before. "If I was not healing you every few months, you would have died ages ago. Besides, I do not think Roni is complaining about her work environment." Though Elliot had been an American citizen for over twenty years, his Kenyan birth and London upbringing made his speech exact and his insights worldly. "It is more the work itself, yes?"

Accepting a plate of eggs, Roni tucked into her food — easier to focus on eating than on the truth of Elliot's words. "I don't want to seem ungrateful."

As Elliot settled at the small table, Sully rose and went about pouring mugs of coffee for the three of them. "Nobody'll think you're ungrateful. You want more responsibility. That's admirable. Shows real chutzpah. And you should get it, too. You need to learn more about what we do so that you'll be ready when the time comes."

"That is absolutely right," Elliot said. "Because Gram and Sully and I have our powers, you might be mistakenly thinking that we have magic over life and death. But this is not true. We are mortal, and we are old."

"Listen to him. Elliot's done a marvelous job of healing Gram and me for years, but we all die eventually. You have to be ready to take over."

Roni set down her fork. "Then help me talk with her. If the only other members of the Parallel Society support me, then she'll have to listen."

Elliot twitched his eye towards Sully. "That would not be advisable."

"He's right," Sully said and slurped some coffee, hiding his eyes behind the mug. "In fact, Gram will only dig her heels in deeper if we get involved."

Roni shook her head and chuckled. "Cowards."

"No," Sully said. "We're simply smart. Trust me. When she's ready, she'll ask us our opinions and then we'll support you. But to do more will only get you less."

Roni pushed away from the table with a firm motion. "You're right. How can I go about learning to save the universe, if I can't even approach my grandmother with a simple request to have more responsibility in this outfit?"

"What? Now?"

"Why not? She'll be up. Heck, she'll be downstairs already, probably going through the bookstore inventory to see what to order."

Sully gazed at the refrigerator. "I haven't even toasted my bagel yet."

Leaning over, Roni kissed the top of Sully's head. "Enjoy your breakfast, boys. I've got to go chat with Gram."

Elliot patted her arm. "You will do fine. And when we come downstairs, if we must, we will clean your blood from the floor as if it never had been spilled."

Roni and Sully stared at him in shock. But then Elliot's face broke into a wide grin, and all three laughed. For Roni, though, the nervous energy beneath their mirth cut straight into her chest.

She took the elevator to the first floor, its close confines like a coffin pressing in. When it came to rest with a hard bump, she considered opening the panel that housed the button for the secret floors beneath the building. She could simply go down to the Grand Library and get to work.

No. She had to deal with Gram. A year was more than enough time. Too much, in fact.

Walking toward the front of the bookstore reminded her that she had grown up here. The smell of the old books, the feel of the narrow aisles, the sound of the hushed voices — from the baseboard molding that she had carved her initials into when she turned fourteen to the dent in the metal shelves of the Fantasy section where she had smacked her head after running (and falling) at age seven — every inch of the place belonged to her childhood. She knew it all.

Or she thought she did. Until she learned of the endless caverns beneath, the secret rooms on secret floors, and that her Gram and the Old Gang were powerful heroes battling amazing worlds, she had really known nothing about the place.

Gram manned the front counter with a large ledger open before her. Though not an all-out technophobe, Gram insisted on doing the books by hand. A stout woman, she kept one hand following the ledger numbers and the other clenching her beaded, crucifix necklace that sat on the shelf of her prominent chest.

Lifting her head, she nodded. "Good morning, Roni."

"Morning."

Roni's legs weakened. She could still turn toward the basement stairs and catch the elevator one floor below. But Gram would wonder why she had taken such an odd route. If Gram didn't stop her to ask then, the question would arise later in the day.

The OPEN sign hung in the doorway, but nobody would bother coming inside for a few more hours. It was a rare day that anybody arrived before ten o'clock. So, Roni couldn't use customers as an excuse.

"Something on your mind?" Gram asked.

Roni trembled a smile. She had been standing still long enough to be noticeable. In fact, she realized, she stood next to the big table — a large, square oak table that ruled over the center reading area of the store. Many of the big conversations in her life had happened at this table — starting with the first big one, the day Gram told Roni that her mother had died in a car accident and that her father had been institutionalized.

"I haven't all day," Gram said. "What's this about?"

"Well," Roni said, and to her surprise, her voice sounded firm.

"Well what?"

"It's been a year since I've learned the truth about you and the world and everything. I've spent this year in the sub-basement, cleaning up the library, organizing the books and maps and all of it, and that's been fine."

Gram straightened. "But?"

"It's time I get more involved. I need more responsibilities. I need to learn how to do everything so that I'm ready."

"And what exactly do you mean by *everything?* You want to go out fighting creatures with us?"

"Yes. But also, I should be introduced to the various contacts you have. I know there are religious leaders and other people all over the world who report to you when they spot trouble. How are they going to know to call me when ... that is ..."

"When I die?"

"I've done my year of penance. Shouldn't I be allowed to join the Society in full?"

With a firm snap — a well-honed maneuver — Gram closed the ledger. Roni lowered to the nearest chair at the big table. Her mouth dried.

"Let me understand this," Gram said, and Roni's throat closed up. "You've decided that after a measly year, that you deserve to become a full member of the Parallel Society — the most important group in this entire universe, the one group of people protecting everybody. The fact that I'm the leader means nothing to you."

"I only meant —"

Gram put up a hand to silence Roni. "You think because you've decided that you're bored with the task I gave you, that your penance, as you put it, should be over. Let's look at what caused your penance. You brought a date into this building and let him discover the hidden caverns."

"I didn't let him do anything. I didn't even know about any of that stuff at the time."

"Nonetheless, you knew that nobody was allowed in my office, but you allowed him —"

"He broke in."

"Under you guard."

"I wasn't a damn sentry."

"Watch your language." Gram stepped out from behind the counter and loomed larger. "After we rescued the man, Darin, from the book he fell into, you were supposed to get rid of him. Instead, you ended up — unwittingly again — aiding him into become stronger and more of a problem. Finally, with Elliot and Sully's help, we stopped Darin from potentially enslaving our world. And we all almost died doing so. During that time, you couldn't make up your mind if you wanted to join us. When you finally decided to be part of the team, I made it clear that you had no special powers other than your mind. You're smart and you love books. This makes you ideal to be our team researcher. I figured with all the journals and reports from centuries of the Society's existence at your fingertips, you'd be enjoying all there was to learn for several years to come. Penance? That was a gift."

"Meanwhile, you three are doing the real job of the Society and you never once call upon me for help. The idea that I'm your team researcher is a joke."

Gram marched to the edge of the table. Her stern glower lightened. "Is that what you think?"

"Just last week, you and Sully went off to Argentina, and two months ago, you sent Elliot to Poland."

"Dear, the reason we haven't called for your help on jobs is because there haven't been any. Those trips were more about keeping strong network ties with those that help us. It's a big world, so every bit of help is appreciated. But going a year without trouble is not unheard of. Longest we've gone was five years, and I'm sure some of the Society members from centuries past went even longer. Other universes crashing into ours is not a weekly event. Thank the Lord for that."

Roni frowned. The idea that she had not been excluded left her in doubt. She wanted to believe Gram, but that proved harder all the time. After all, Gram had lied to Roni from as far back as she could remember. No matter how much justification she wanted to grant Gram, the lies remained. Clearly, nothing as threatening as Darin had occurred in the last year, but nothing at all?

Clinging to her anger, Roni said, "That might be, but I still need to meet the people that you network with. I still need to know more about how to do any of this job. If a meteor strikes tomorrow and kills you three off, then I barely know anything. The Parallel Society would be ruined."

"It's a good thing there are no apocalyptic meteors on the way."

"Joking isn't going to change my mind."

Gram's gentle smile turned into a thin line. "Nor mine. You have an important job to do, but allow me to be clear — you work for us. Not the other way around. The Parallel Society has been operating far longer than we have written records for, and there is a method to keeping the whole thing going. So, stop worrying about yourself and how all this affects you, and start working for all of us."

"That's not at all what —"

"Enough of this. I'm all upset now. Please mind the store until the boys come down. I'm going to my apartment for a rest. When I return, I hope to find you in the Grand Library where you belong."

Without waiting for Roni's response, Gram shuffled toward the elevator. Her apartment took up the other half of the fifth floor opposite Elliot and Sully. Roni waited until the elevator closed before she punched down on the table. The smack's dull echo died around her leaving a lonely silence.

"Well, shit," she said.

Chapter 2

Roni spent the remainder of the day working as usual — sifting through old journals, organizing ancient books and diaries, taking scraps of hand-drawn maps and attempting to make sense of the twisting, winding caverns beneath her. But unlike her usual workdays, her thoughts did not fill up with the wonder of the library. Instead, she replayed her conversation with Gram.

More like a lecture.

No matter what angle she looked at it, Roni returned to the same result — Gram did not trust her. Gram had kept the truth of the universe hidden despite knowing that at some point Roni would have to take over. She had kept the gang's current cases secret, claiming that nothing had happened in the last year. She had kept Roni isolated in the library, away from all the other secrets she must be holding.

By the time the day ended, Roni had worked herself into a quiet rage. She tramped out of the bookstore without a word to anybody and headed to the 1st Street Bar. After two shots of whiskey and a beer, she relaxed enough to take a cab to Cody's Saloon. Several more drinks and she found her way to Nicki's Corner. By that point, midnight had come around. That's when she met Frank.

Young, fit, and handsome — though she had enough sense to question if he really looked that way or if the alcohol had made him that way. He bought her a beer. "It's late for a girl to be drinking on a Wednesday night."

"Late for anybody," she said.

He smiled and her body tingled. "Very true."

With that auspicious introduction, she spent the next hour chatting away about movies and television shows. She wondered if he read books — one of the few passions in her life — but reminded herself not to care about him in that way. There would be no more romantic relationships in her life. How could there be? She had a monumental secret. If she got close enough to a man that she might reveal the truth about the world, she would put that man's life at risk. Darin died because of that secret, and they had only dated twice.

"Frank," she said, interrupting his observations on the comedy of *Seinfeld*, "there are only two reasons people are drinking hard in a bar on a Wednesday night. Either they're a drunk or they're looking to get laid. I'm not a drunk."

Roni followed the cracks along the bedroom ceiling as she listened to the gentle snoring of the stranger beside her. Dim light peeked through the window blinds. Morning would arrive soon. Much of the previous night blurred together, but she knew enough. She drank too much, met up with Frank, and topped the night off in his bed. Twice.

With a gentle motion, she rocked her head from shoulder to shoulder. No pounding pain. No blistering fire from the sounds of the rustling pillowcase. Other than some dehydration, she fared well. No major hangover. If she were religious like any of the Old Gang, she would thank the Lord for small favors. As it was, she merely marveled at her body's resilience.

After a few minutes, she jiggled the mattress but Frank continued to snore. Good. Peeling back the white-and-gray striped comforter, she eased her legs free. The floor chilled her feet and she involuntarily hissed. Autumn in Pennsylvania could create some brisk mornings. Holding still a moment, she waited until she heard the snoring resume. A few breaths later, she rolled off the mattress and onto her feet.

Rising on her tiptoes, she leaned over enough to see the side of his face — not bad looking, certainly nothing to be horrified by. She had done worse.

Throwing on last night's clothes, she padded in bare feet across the apartment. Like a thief in reverse, she slipped out to the hall and eased the apartment door shut so that the lock made a meek click. Sitting in the stairwell, she put on her socks and shoes, stuffed her bra into her handbag, and checked her cellphone — 7:02 am. She hurried downstairs, out the building's front door, and fast-walked her way along the broken sidewalk on Arbor Street.

She had not been in the northwestern part of Olburg in years, but she recalled a corner diner a few blocks over — the Olburg Chestnut. Inhaling slow and deep, letting the cool morning air fill her lungs and clear her head, she eased her pace. As she neared the corner, she knew the old eatery remained — she could smell the frying bacon and fresh coffee. A hard-looking lot shuffled their way into the diner — truck drivers, road crews, and other blue collar men and women seeking a hearty start to their day. None of the business suits came here. They all grabbed a donut and coffee on their commute to Philadelphia. The people here were those that kept the local world running.

Except one man.

He wore a pressed suit, leaned on a black cane with a silver handle, and played with his mustache styled from the 1920s. Though he merely waited on the sidewalk, Roni's instincts kicked in — she had no doubt that the man waited for her. As she neared, his head jerked in her direction, and he fashioned a dark grin.

"Ms. Veronica Rider? Yes?"

He had a smooth voice with an odd accent — not one she could place to any particular country. She brushed by him and entered the diner.

The hustle of waitresses blended with the chimes of silverware and the sizzling of the griddle. Laughter, mumbled conversation, and the call of food orders drifted along heavy aromas of pancakes and eggs. A sign up front stated: *Please seat yourself.* Only problem: no seats available.

Standing at the door with the cold air from outside fighting the warmth of the diner, Roni scanned around for signs of anybody about the leave. The odd man from outside entered behind her and stood quietly. Like a passenger on a sinking ship, she searched again for a table to save her. Nothing.

Refusing to look back, she said, "You a lawyer?"

As if insulted, he said, "Never."

"Good. Thought you might be serving a summons."

Two men wearing jackets with *Stoltzfus Plumbing* on the backs tossed some cash on their table and walked off. Roni nabbed their booth near the back and waited as a young man hustled to bus the table. Once he left, another young man set the table with paper placemats (complete with ads for local businesses), silverware wrapped in paper napkins, and two thick coffee mugs. The man in the nice suit settled in opposite Roni. She thought about making a scene, but that required too much energy. Instead, she nudged her mug toward the aisle, and as if by magic, a waitress walked by and filled it with hot caffeinated goodness.

"You want something to eat?" the waitress asked.

Roni didn't bother looking up. "Two eggs, over easy, and some toast."

"And you, sir?"

"Nothing, thank you."

Once the waitress left, the man unrolled his napkin and set about placing his knife, fork, and spoon in the proper positions. Roni sipped her coffee. Under other circumstances, she would have told the guy to go away. If he refused, she could easily get one of the many strong men to escort the guy out of the diner — probably throw a few punches, too. But that morning, she wanted to simply sip her coffee, find her way home, and curl into her own bed. Her body needed to recalibrate.

But then the man spoke again. This time, his voice deepened, and the words he said spun the world around her head. "We need to talk about the multiverse, your grandmother, and the rest of the Parallel Society."

CHAPTER 3

The incessant rumble of the busy diner ceased. The clatter of dishes, the chimes of the main door opening, the conversations muddling together, the cellphones beeping and singing and chirping — all of it simply disappeared as if somebody had forgotten to add sound to the picture. Roni stared at the well-dressed man opposite her as the coffee in her stomach threatened to return.

"What did you say?" she finally managed, and with those words life around her returned to normal volumes.

"Oh, yes, I'm well aware of the truth. Surely, your grandmother explained that there were many of us out there in the world who had learned — or, at least, had believed. Not many as in thousands or such, but certainly more than a few. Perhaps a hundred or so. Maybe less."

"Must have slipped her mind."

"Well, then, allow me to be direct so as to avoid further confusions."

Roni lowered her hand beneath the table and clenched a fist. She didn't know if she wanted to punch this guy or turn her anger upon Gram. Instead, she listened.

"My name is Kenneth Bay. I am the current emissary of the being Yal-hara."

"*The being?*"

Kenneth raised his pointer finger. "Please. Permit me to finish before you ask questions. It will save time." He waited until Roni sat back and gestured for him to continue. Stroking his mustache as he exhaled, he went on, "Thank you. Yal-hara is from another universe. One night, a tear in her world opened beneath her while she slept, and it deposited her in our world. Until that moment she knew nothing of the multiverse. She was a teacher, actually. She instructed the young in basic skills — what we call reading, writing, and arithmetic.

"This all occurred in the year 1907 in the Sahara Desert. She nearly died, but a nomadic tribe came upon her and took her into their care. When the Parallel Society of that time arrived and captured the rift into one of their books, Yal-hara was twenty miles away and being treated like a god. It would take her many years to find her way out of the desert, learn enough languages to survive, and create a source of wealth — all the while keeping hidden from mankind."

"Why hidden?"

"No interruptions, please. However, to answer your question — not all beings that come here can pass as human. Eventually, Yal-hara learned of the Society — this was in 1932. At that time, they were using Paris as their homebase. She sent her emissary to contact the Society, and it did not go well. They attempted to assassinate her. I suppose they thought that the most prudent course of action — dispose of the problem. But their rash decision drove her into deeper hiding."

Roni opened her mouth but held back her next question. She opted for a sip of coffee, though she doubted Kenneth Bay had been fooled.

"By 1944, Yal-hara had settled in America. Turned out that the turmoil Hitler had caused also created enough chaos to benefit her travels. Nobody bothered her. The war took the lives of all but one member of the Society. That woman, Grace Covington, relocated to Philadelphia — no easy feat when you consider the dangers of moving all those books. Eventually, she met your grandmother and passed the torch. Yal-hara spent her days educating herself on the world and learning all she could about the multiverse. But, of course, that subject is not widely known, and she could not easily approach your Gram, as I believe you call her. After the Parallel Society had reformed to its full complement, Yal-hara decided to risk exposing her existence. She sent her newest emissary, my father, but unfortunately, the meeting did not go well. The Society made it clear that they had little interest in Yal-hara's story and only wanted to send her back into the multiverse — any book would do. Though better than before — after all, your Gram did not attempt to kill Yal-hara — they still did not want to help solve the actual problem. This was unacceptable. Yal-hara had learned enough about the mulitverse to know that some of the worlds were dark and terrible places."

Roni shuddered as she recalled gazing into the open book Darin had fallen inside. It stretched downward like an esophagus while anguished creatures wrenched their bodies against the membrane wall. At the bottom, she saw hurricanes blasting across while thunder cracked the air. It had been enough to destroy Darin's sanity.

"Once again, Yal-hara went into hiding. However, she always maintained an eye upon the Society. It was then, and remains now, her only real hope. But she is growing old, and with that, her desperation grows, too. I took over from my father as her emissary, and against my advice, she attempted to infiltrate the caverns through Darin Lander. You are quite aware of the results."

"So that was all you?"

"Not me. Yal-hara. And while the entire endeavor was regrettable, the one positive was your inclusion into the Society. After careful observations, Yal-hara and I both agreed that you represent a new and much needed perspective on the Society — one worth reaching out to for help. That's precisely why I am here. She has waited a long time for someone like you — someone caring and open-minded. Can you imagine how hard it must have been to live for over a century as the only fully-sentient, non-human being on this planet? And please, don't bring up chimpanzees. I know they're sentient, but they are mindless twits compared to Yal-hara. All she asks is a small favor that will help her immensely."

"Sure. Because everything you've told me leads to a *small* favor."

Kenneth laced his fingers as he rested his arms on the table. "You're wary. It's only natural. You should be. The only thing that lends credence to my words is the fact that I say them at all, that I am aware of the Society and the books and the caverns and Darin and the rest of it, but why should that be enough?"

Roni couldn't tell if he mocked her. Before she snapped out a response, he sighed and pulled a torn piece of paper from his coat. Her eyes widened. On the table, sitting between her half-eaten eggs and a mug of coffee, Kenneth had placed a map fragment depicting part of the caverns.

"How did you get this?" she asked.

"Yal-hara gave it to me to give to you. I never questioned how she acquired it. I assume that if one lives as long as she does, enough things happen that one ends up with all sorts of oddities in one's possession. Regardless, that is part of a map detailing some of the route to the Book on the Isle."

Roni looked closer, her fingers tapping the edge of the table. Much of the map looked like many of the others she had seen in the Grand

Library — one tunnel after another snaking through and looping around and looking no more organized than cooked spaghetti on a plate. But on this map, there was an open section with a small circular island in the middle. The words *Book on the Isle* had been printed neatly next to the circle.

"If you are willing," Kenneth said, leaning closer, "Yal-hara would like you to find the Book on the Isle and retrieve a kyolo stone. They are plentiful in the world that book leads to — you may be able to simply reach in and pluck one off the ground — and they are quite distinctive. With that stone, Yal-hara can create a simple compass that will lead her to a rift back into her universe."

Holding her breath, Roni reached out to touch the map. With so many gaps in what she had to work with, this fragment could be infinitely important. Certainly, Yal-hara believed it offered enough to guide her to this book — which suggested it would fill in a significant part of the overall mapping of the caverns. Unless, Roni held the same wishful thinking as Yal-hara. But before Roni could defeat her own hopes, she would have to take this paper to the map room in the Grand Library and see how well it fit in.

Holding the map in her hands, however, she paused. "Why is Yal-hara handling things this way? Why not come directly to the bookstore and talk with all of us? No matter what had happened in the past, Gram would help if —"

"Really? Have they helped you?"

"Me? I'm not stuck in somebody else's universe."

"You have Lost Time, don't you?"

Roni's muscles contracted. "How do you know —"

"It's not an unheard of phenomenon. From what I've been able to discern, nobody from any universe knows the exact cause — or causes, it may be more than one thing — but this kyolo stone might be able to help you, too. Perhaps it can lead you to some answers — ones you grandmother withholds from you. Just as she would withhold her aid to Yal-hara."

Folding the paper, Roni gave a short nod. A lump formed beneath her ribs and wormed its way into the pit of her stomach, but she placed the paper into her pocket. "I'll look into this," she said.

Kenneth's shoulder dropped an inch as he grinned. "Thank you." He rose from the table and slid his business card towards her. "Call me when you're ready." Straightening his coat, he walked away.

Roni sat motionless as she watched the strange man exit the diner.

The torn piece of paper weighed down her coat. She took a deep breath — best not to raise her expectations.

Hard, though, when the man had mentioned her Lost Time. She had always thought that was a name Gram gave to her missing memories, but now it appeared to be something more — chalk it up to another lie from her grandmother. But since those lost memories revolved around the accident that stole her mother's life, Roni couldn't stop the excited questions racing through her mind — all centering around the promise of that piece of paper.

Her phone rang and she jumped. Glancing at the screen, she read — *Gram.*

As she swiped to accept the call, she placed her other hand under her thigh to stop its shaking. Nothing could be shaking — especially her voice. She had to make sure the Gram did not suspect anything out of the ordinary.

"H-Hello?" *Damn.*

But luck came her way. Gram was so wrapped up in her own purpose for calling that she made no reaction to Roni's nerves — or perhaps, she assumed Roni was nervous because of the call. It all reduced to Gram's two word reply. "You're late."

CHAPTER 4

Although Olburg was not a huge town, it still took Roni twenty minutes to reach the bookstore. She burst in with a dismissive wave at Gram. "I know, I know. I'm here now."

Behind the counter, Gram crossed her arms underneath her large bosom. The scowl on her face deepened. "Are you wearing the same clothes as yesterday?"

Without slowing her pace, Roni said, "That depends — do you want me to go home and change or do you want me to get to work?"

In the aisle leading to the elevator, Roni weaved around a young woman. "Excuse me," the woman said, "I'm looking for —"

"Check with the woman up front, please."

"But —"

Smiling, Roni hopped into the elevator and closed the door. On her way down to the Grand Library, she patted her coat pocket, checking that the paper had not disappeared. Out of the elevator, she stepped into the main room and flicked on the lights.

She paused as the Library came to life. Despite all that she thought about being isolated from the Old Gang, she had to admit that she loved this place. Designed like the smoking room of an old estate, the main part of the Grand Library encompassed a far larger amount of space than such a room would require. When she took on the job of researcher for the Society, books had been stacked in dusty piles while papers were strewn about without much care. After a year of steady work, however, Roni had transformed most of the ill-used shelves into categorized, logical order. The wood gleamed, the light glittered, and the books had begun to discover their homes.

In addition to all the journals and diaries of the previous Parallel

Society members, she had found numerous volumes of non-fiction written by Society members. Some of them were descriptions of how physics worked in different universes, some detailed the various powers different Society members had possessed throughout history, and some narrowed their focus to analyzing a specific location of the caverns or a single book chained to its walls. While all of these tomes excited the bookworm in Roni's head, she had come to love the room off to the right even more — the map room.

She had only started focusing on that room in the last four months. Her initial hope had been to take all the maps drawn by various expeditions and create a single, giant map of the caverns. But this proved far more challenging than she had expected. The maps were all different scales and styles. Many were fragments like the one in her pocket while others could not even be called a fragment. Some were nothing more than a rough sketch in a journal with barely a description of the surrounding area to orient the reader. In the end, Roni decided to create two versions of her Master Map — one on her computer and one on paper.

Taking all the completed, half-completed, and hardly-completed maps she had available, she used her computer to rescale everything to a uniform size. That took a long time until she got the hang of it. She then printed out the scaled-maps and went through the tedious job of figuring out how they connected. Like the early stages of tackling a complex jigsaw puzzle, she searched for the smallest connections between map pieces — especially anything that might resemble the ends. But after several tries, she realized she lacked key parts.

Roni stared at the map. Clenching the fragment, she searched for anything that it could connect with. Why give her the fragment if it couldn't be found? But with approximately half the wall covered in the paper maps and knowing that she had far more map than wall space, Roni had the sinking thought that this island holding a single book might be located far into the as-yet-unmapped portions of her project.

Except the fact that Kenneth Bay brought her the map fragment suggested the island would have to be near enough to reach; otherwise, it made a poor bribe for her help. Kenneth and Yal-hara had to know that Roni would use the fragment to locate the island — that's what they wanted her to do — so, it had to be in an accessible location.

Roni took the fragment over to her scanning table — an expense that bothered Gram but that she acquiesced to after Elliot and Sully defended the purchase. Upon scanning the fragment into the computer and having it rescale the image to match the rest, Roni started by letting the computer attempt to find where the fragment connected with the whole map. As expected, it came up empty. Well, it actually returned over four thousand results which pretty much meant the same thing. There were simply too many gaps in the overall map.

She then spent over an hour going through the four thousand plus possibilities. Most were easily discarded, but some required several minutes of failed attempts to make the fragment fit. Even as she rotated and flipped the image on another attempt, part of her questioned if it would fit any of the map. The possibility existed that the fragment sat in the middle of a missing section with no connection to any of the current edges — like a puzzle piece for the center when all she had was the outer-frame.

Taking a break from the computer screen, Roni walked over to the map wall. Her eyes roved over the endless corridors and tunnels, the steps and drops, the widening spaces and narrowing fields. Somewhere in all of that mess, a single book sitting on a tiny island awaited her. She read off the names of the various spots that previous Society explorers had discovered and marked. Things like Stalactite Plains, Connor's Corner, the Cathedral, and Soft Slope — each name written by the hand of the cartographer, probably at the location itself.

Roni's mouth dropped open. She whirled back to the scanner and picked up the map fragment. There. In tiny script, neatly scrawled on the bottom edge — the name Gerald Waterfield.

She hurried back to the main room and brought up the library catalog on her computer. Typing in *Gerald Waterfield*, her fingers tingled and her lips lifted at the corners. But no results came from her search. That didn't mean anything yet — Roni had only digitized the Library holdings she had placed on the shelves. She had years of work ahead of her before the whole library could be searched via computer.

In the back corner of the main room, the old card catalog gathered dust. Much of it no longer corresponded with the actual locations of books, but for the moment, Roni only wanted to confirm the book's existence. After a short rifling through a drawer of typed and hand-written index cards, she found it:

> *Waterfield, Gerald. The Journal of Gerald Waterfield. incl 4 maps and 7 plates. Society member 1807-1842. Loc: Row 21, WAT*

Roni snagged the card out of the drawer and worked her way through the Library. Many of the shelves had been moved throughout the years. She had moved several herself. But she doubted many would have shifted the books far from where they had been shelved.

As she walked up and down several aisles, she wondered at the immense effort required to move the entire operation from Paris to England to America. All those books in the caverns chained to the walls — where were they held in England? How did Grace Covington, the leader of the Society at the time, even know about the caverns in Pennsylvania? And with Gram, Elliot, and Sully nearing the ends of their lives, did that mean that Roni would someday be responsible for moving everything again? She thought over the map and all its missing parts. Moving all the books in those caverns without an accident destroying universes would be impossible.

At the end of one aisle, Roni found ten stacks of dust-covered books piled as high as her chest. On the wall, small gold plates marked the old row numbers — 19, 20, and 21. She walked back to her work desk and dragged her chair to the ten piles of books.

Though she wanted to rifle through it all to find Waterfield's journal, part of her could not resist organizing the books into ready-to-go piles that she could come back to later. Despite the extra time, she managed to get through three-quarters of the books in under an hour — getting distracted only when she came upon a book with Grace Covington's name on it. Turned out to be a biography rather than a personal journal. She set that book to one side and continued on.

And then she found it. A leather bound journal that smelled of long years outdoors by a campfire. The pages crackled, instantly bringing images of a hard-faced man of good upbringing, exploring the underside of the world, aware that he did his part to save so many lives and that so few would ever read his words or know his contribution. Roni clutched the journal against her chest like a schoolgirl in an old film.

Returning to her desk with the book and her chair, she settled in, intent on approaching her find carefully. While the pages were stiff, they did not break under her touch. Good. She had no desire to bring the journal upstairs to the floor where Elliot and Sully repaired old volumes of all kinds.

Before she read a single word, she sifted through page after page. Waterfield's sharp-angled script and messy use of ink would be difficult to decipher, but she had read enough journals from further back than the 19th century — she could handle this one. Searching deeper into the book, she finally found the key page she sought — the torn page displaying the rest of Waterfield's map. To be sure, she retrieved the fragment and matched it up with the journal. A perfect fit.

Picking up the journal to get the rest of the map scanned into the computer, a yellowed card fell from the back of the book, flipping to the ground like a fallen leaf. The library checkout card. As she picked it up, she made a mental note that the checkout system would have to be digitized as well. Setting the card into the sleeve on the journal's back page, her heart jumped.

The last person to check out the book — *Elliot Kenwana.*

CHAPTER 5

For several minutes, Roni stood immobile in the middle of the library, the old checkout card held tight between her fingers. Her mind blanked. She kept seeing the clean, steady penmanship that men rarely possessed. She only knew one man who wrote like that — Elliot, of course.

Closing her eyes, she tried to think straight. First, she needed to confirm that this wasn't a coincidence. Perhaps there had been another Elliot Kenwana with excellent penmanship. She didn't believe it, but going through the thought process provided her body and brain with an action. She walked over to several book piles throughout the room and randomly opened books. None had been checked out by Elliot. While that did not prove anything concrete, it did suggest that he was connected to all of this — whatever *this* was. After all, if he had simply been a curious reader, she would have found other titles he had explored. That would have made her feel better. She inspected more of the books, but after twenty minutes without finding Elliot's name, she decided that would be confirmation enough.

Resisting the urge to race upstairs and confront the old man, Roni walked the journal over to the map room. As the new map fragment scanned into the computer, she reorganized her thoughts. It would do her no good to approach Elliot without more information. She had to attack this problem like a police detective. Whenever possible, a detective interrogated a suspect with enough knowledge of the truth that they had a good shot of catching a lie. Roni knew so little at the moment that, no matter what Elliot said, she would never be able to separate fact from fiction.

Why am I assuming that he'd lie to me? That thought troubled her. Gram would lie. Gram had lied. But Elliot? She always thought of him as the most honest man in her life.

After the scan completed, Roni once more sent the image through the computer program to find matches to the existing map. Only 2900 results this time. Better than before. But over the next few hours, she ended up in the same place. The fragment did not connect with any part of the map.

The grandfather clock standing against a support pillar chimed six o'clock, and Roni's stomach rumbled on cue. Arching her head back, she smacked the arm of her chair. The entire day had gone, and she had made so little progress. The island in the lake could be practically anywhere in the caverns, and she had come across nothing that pointed to why Elliot would have an interest in any of this.

Except for Yal-hara. If Roni could believe even part of what Kenneth Bay had said, then at one time, Yal-hara asked the Old Gang for help and they refused her. Except that didn't make much sense. Roni couldn't see Elliot turning away any living creature.

Which left Roni with a baffled mind, an empty stomach, and a need for answers. No point in stalling further — her claims at a detective's approach sounded good, but she knew better. No secret evidence would be revealed unless she started kicking over stones. She had to deal with Elliot.

Stepping out of the elevator onto the main floor, Roni planned on inviting Elliot to dinner. A nice, public place would keep their conversation calm — not that she thought Elliot would raise his voice, but as a precaution against whatever secret lay beneath. Plus, she needed to eat. But when she walked toward the big table in the center of the room, she found Elliot, Sully, and Gram all dressed nicely and ready to leave.

"What's the occasion?" she asked.

Gram flipped open her compact to check on her hair. "Nothing at all. For many years now, we've made sure to get together for a nice dinner at least once every month. It's a good way to keep our team strong and our morale up."

Placing a tweed hat on his head, Sully said, "Oh, we've made a mistake. You should've been asked to join us. How could we do such a thing? You're part of the team now."

Elliot gave Sully a squeeze on the shoulder. "You are absolutely right. Please, Roni, accept our apology. We did not intend to exclude you. Rather, we have been doing this dinner for so long that we all simply got ready to go without thinking about it. It is our old habit."

Snapping the compact shut, Gram said, "Boys, don't pressure her. I'm sure she has a million things more fun to do than spend an evening stuck with three old folks like us." She looked at Roni. "Of course, dear, if you'd like to join us, you're more than welcome."

Roni could not read her face. Did she want Roni to join or not? A piece of Roni broke inside — how had things devolved so far between them that she would even question if Gram wanted her around? Worse than that, Roni knew exactly when this change began — a year ago, on the night she first learned of Gram's powers, the caverns, and the Society. Once the Old Gang's secret had been revealed, much of the warmth and stern caring that made up Gram's foundation disappeared.

"Maybe next time," Roni said. "It's been a long day."

Gram raised an eyebrow but said nothing more. As the Old Gang left the bookstore, Roni thought she had made the right choice. She didn't want to be sitting through a long meal while itching to speak with Elliot privately, and she didn't want to talk about Waterfield's journal with Gram and Sully until she had more information at hand. Besides, Roni was the New Gang — a gang of one for the moment, but the New Gang nonetheless. She would be better off getting comfortable with that fact.

Having the bookstore to herself, she ordered a cheesesteak, retrieved the Waterfield journal from the Grand Library, and settled at the big table in the main room. Reading while eating, surrounded by the quiet of the closed store and the blanketing aroma of old books, she allowed herself to relax — not entirely, but enough.

The journal had many entries covering a wide variety of topics, but she found three key details within Waterfield's words. The first had nothing to do with Yal-hara nor Elliot's possible involvement. Rather it focused on the nature of the caves themselves —

> *I must admit that I have pondered these caverns at great length. The rest of the team seems accepting of the structure and shows no more curiosity, but I find that infuriating to say the least. I requested the opportunity to perform certain experiments upon the cavern walls to determine how it can be that I find references to these very caverns within the diaries of Society members from over a hundred years past. This is simply impossible when one considers the verifiable fact that the Society has changed locations throughout the world on numerous occasions. How can it be that*

we all utilize the same caverns?

Roni jotted down a note, marking where she could find this entry again at a later time. But as she read on, she could not stop her own curiosity —

I've been denied my request. Short-sightedness appears to be the common ground for my peers. They fear that interfering with the cavern walls might cause damage to our purpose. Since we do not understand the cavern itself, they reason that we cannot comprehend how our actions upon it might behave. But is not that the very point of experimentation? How are we to learn if not by trial?

Well, it has become apparent that I have another resource for information. The Grand Library has several volumes by Mr. Augustus Kincaid who grappled with the same concerns. According to the good gentleman, the caverns must exist within a universe of their own. It is that simple. When we step through the entrance into the caverns, we leave our universe and walk through to another. The caverns universe, therefore, is the storage container for all the breaches we investigate and attempt to close. Fascinating as a hypothesis, but one that requires deeper attention to prove valid or false. Of course, I shall never divulge to my teammates that there is this information. They would argue that such information makes experimentation unrequired.

Roni wrote down the name Augustus Kincaid to deal with another day. The next entry she found useful had been written one page before the map Waterfield had drawn. He described a seven day journey through the caverns which ended with the discovery of a narrow river. He named it for himself — Waterfield River. None of his teammates joined him on the expedition, so he chose to return before traveling the river. A month later, despite his teammates refusal to help, he found his way back to the river. This time he brought supplies to build a simple raft and took to the water.

Roni then read:

The waters of my namesake carried me through tunnels upon which no other path could be taken, and following a rather

> *unsettling patch of rough currents, I was deposited into a massive lake with a lone island in the center.*

With her hands shaking from adrenaline, Roni could barely write her notes. No wonder the map never matched up with anything she had already scanned through — it never would. The access to the lake involved a river, not a path. Clearly, Waterfield found a route back because he lived to complete his journal and shelve it in the Grand Library — *and why couldn't that route be used to get there?* — but for the moment, Roni reveled in the idea that all she needed to do was find the river.

The last entry she read that made a strong impression came only pages later. Waterfield navigated his raft to the island — *"a circular clump of empty sand no bigger than the parlor room of a home."* Almost empty. In the center, a stone pedestal had been built. Sitting on the pedestal, Waterfield found the Book of the Isle — a single volume chained to the stone.

He wrote:

> *I cannot account for the sensations that overcame me, the thoughts that grew within my mind, but I had the undeniable urge to open that book. What kind of universe would be so special that it received an island all to itself? Quite naturally, I considered the possibility that the book accessed a most dangerous universe, one that should never be opened. And yet, my heart denied this. I could feel a loving embrace, a warmth of welcome that no evil could ever produce. Since it was my instincts that brought me to this place, despite the disagreements with my fellow Society members, I chose to adhere to my instincts once more. I opened the book.*
>
> *I discovered Heaven.*

The front door rattled as Gram unlocked it, and the Old Gang bumbled inside. Roni closed the journal and grabbed her notes, but Sully had already stumbled further in.

"You had quite a bit to drink," she said with a lighthearted chuckle. She slid the book into her bag, but Sully's brow knitted downward.

"Whatcha reading there?" He burped and pointed at the bag.

"Nothing important."

"Don't be like that. It's good to be a reader. I've always loved that about you. And you've got strong taste. Good taste."

Elliot stepped over and steadied Sully. "You have had too much to drink. Leave Roni alone."

"Since you won't drink, I gotta do it for both of us."

Gram laughed. "You didn't have to do it for me, but you did anyway."

Roni shouldered her bag. "Well, you all need to get some sleep. I'll see you in the morning."

As she walked by Sully, however, he dipped his hand into her bag and pulled out the journal. "Well, well, let's see here. *The Journal of Gerald Waterfield*. Who the heck is that?"

Roni spun back and snatched the journal — but not in time. Elliot had frozen. He stared at Roni, his eyes glistening as his jaw shivered.

CHAPTER 6

Holding onto the table for balance, Sully waved his hand in the air. "What's with you two? Somebody tell me who Gerald Whatever-his-name-is is?"

From behind, Roni heard the hardline tones of Gram upset. "He's the man who discovered the Book on the Isle."

The words sobered Sully fast. "Oh. Isn't that where Elliot ... oh, I see." He looked to Roni and shook his head. "You shouldn't have done that."

"Done what?" Roni said, her focus still on Elliot. "What is this island to you?"

Elliot brushed a tear before it could fall. He glanced upward, perhaps gaining strength from above, and opened his mouth to respond. But Gram stepped between them.

"We will not be discussing that island," she said. "Elliot, help Sully get upstairs before the poor man can't stand anymore." With a meek nod, Elliot did as instructed. Gram then turned to Roni. "You need to forget about the Book on the Isle. You need to forget about Waterfield and anything you read in his journal. The man was a crackpot, and his writings have done more harm to members of the Parallel Society than any other journal in our library."

Roni's blood heated fast. "Another secret. I suppose I should get a list of books that I'm banned from reading. It'll make it easier for you to hide things from me."

"You should know better than to question me about things you aren't informed on."

"How can I be informed when you won't tell me anything? You want to keep me trapped downstairs, but you are being pigheaded to think that you're protecting me. Not after a year of knowing the truth about our world. If anything, you put my life in greater danger. How am I supposed to make informed decisions, to lead the next group of the Society, when I know so little? I guess I'll have to do like Waterfield and explore the caverns myself."

Gram slammed her purse on the table. "You will not. To do so is to risk death, and I won't have it. Whatever your problems with me, they do not give you the right to break ranks, to go off on your own, make your own choices with any of this."

"You don't get to tell me —"

"I damn well do. Being the leader of this group says so. If you defy me, there will be serious repercussions."

Roni's face dropped. "Are you really threatening me? What was the point of taking me in after Mom's death, of raising me to be strong and independent, if you're going to treat me like this?"

"The fact that you ask such a question, once again shows me that you are not ready for the greater responsibilities of the Society. We cannot be selfish. We cannot go off on our own like Gerald Waterfield and ignore the others of the team. To do so invites disaster. And any disaster involving the Society can mean disaster for all of mankind."

"Then why not work with me instead of against me?"

"You sound just like Waterfield. You're happy to cooperate as long as we all go along with you. Well, that's not the way this works."

"But —"

"That's it. This is done. No more talk about Waterfield or the Book on the Isle. I don't want you mentioning journeys into the caverns because there won't be any. And above all else, you do not speak a word of any of this to Elliot. The poor man has suffered enough. Now, go home before I really get mad."

Roni saw the cold fury in Gram's face. There would be no reasoning with her that night. But Roni did not want to be reasonable. With a huff, she stormed across the room, flung open the front door, and stomped out.

The frosty night air slammed into her with a strong wind. Hugging her arms against the chill, she trudged along the sidewalk. Her thoughts raged.

Gram had no right to impose her will upon them. Being the leader did not make her a dictator. Worse, she acted like she knew everything, had all the answers, but if that were true, then she abandoned Yal-hara purposefully. And what purpose could warrant trapping a being in our universe when it doesn't belong here?

Oh, that old woman had so many secrets held close to the vest — and she dared to criticize Roni for being selfish!

Roni walked onward and tried to calm her anger. She thought about the cavern with all those books leading to all those universes. Each streetlight she passed under, each flicker of television or computer screen in a window, each car driving by with its headlights flashing over her — all the lights like universes spread out before her. And all she needed to do was find one small light sitting on an island.

But then she thought of Elliot and the horror on his face when he saw the journal. As much as Roni wanted to ignore all Gram had said, her final words about Elliot echoed — *the poor man has suffered enough.* Roni wanted to ask him, but she had dredged up something dark, and she couldn't do that to him. At least, not unless she had no other choice.

And I do have a choice.

She had Waterfield's journal, after all. He had made the trip to the Isle by himself. So could she.

Except she didn't want to. She did not have the gene for becoming an explorer, mounting expeditions into uncharted territories. The only reason she looked into any of this was Yal-hara. It was a moral choice, not one of discovery, not one of defiance.

No, she thought as she glanced back toward the bookstore. The moral aspect of it — helping Yal-hara find her way home — was only one part. Mostly, she wanted to get the kyolo stones to help her with her lost memories.

Perhaps, then, she was selfish. But before she attempted to traverse the caverns alone, before she took steps against Gram's wishes that could never be taken back, before she gambled everything, she figured she should at least try her only other source of information one last time. It had been years since she really tried to talk to him, to do anything more than sit by his side, to attempt to get through. Yet it seemed like the right thing to do.

Nodding in the chilly air, seeing her breath plume out in vanishing vapor, she thought, *Okay then. Tomorrow morning, I'm going to visit my father.*

The Belmont Behavioral Hospital had been constructed in West Philadelphia, and if not for a small sign out front, there would be no way to know the building's purpose. But Roni knew. Whenever she drove this way to visit her father, whenever she passed beneath the gates and parked in the visitor section, whenever she heard the echoing click of her shoes or smelled the hospital aroma of disinfectant blended with disease, she could not avoid remembering why this building existed.

"Ms. Rider, good to see you again," the front desk nurse said.

"Uh-huh." Roni didn't mean to be rude, but visiting her father never settled well within her. She had no room for small talk.

The nurse handed over a clipboard and plastered on a smile. Roni knew the routine. Sign in, wait to be called, then get escorted to the visiting room where she would sit and wait for somebody to bring her father out. Meanwhile, other visitors spoke in low voices with their loved ones. Some of the patients responded. Others gazed off half-dead. For Roni, it was always a coin-toss which version of her father would appear.

An orderly opened the doors, wheeled Mr. Rider into the visitor's room, and stopped at Roni's table. "Your father's been doing real well lately. I'm sure he's excited to see you today." The orderly patted Mr. Rider's shoulder and walked off.

Growing up, Roni's image of her father centered on his shoulders — big, broad shoulders that she could sit on at a parade or when she was tired of walking. Muscular shoulders that never weakened no matter how many times she asked to be swung through the air. The shoulders of a powerful bear.

But seeing him now, she shuddered. All the strength had left him. His arms, once thick enough for Roni to do chin-ups on, had become thin reeds. His eyes sank into his skeletal head. Worse, she saw no light behind them, no spark of cognizance.

Yet she had to try. "Hi, Dad. It's Roni. You been doing okay?"

No response.

"Things for me have been unusual. I mean, a year ago my biggest problem was that I had no direction in life. Remember that? Gram always bickering that I needed to pick a career already." Roni snickered. "I was so stressed out about all that, but I'm telling you, that was easy street. Now, the fate of the universe depends on me."

His mouth dropped open an inch. Odd. But Roni figured it was nothing more than his drugs kicking in.

"Anyway, I'm sorry I haven't been here more often. I suppose you get it. Not like you signed yourself in here because you thought you were spending too much time with me. I mean, let's be honest. After mom died, you fell apart and you couldn't be bothered with me. Oh, don't worry. I don't hold it against you. Really. I did at one time, but I'm all grown up now. And ever since my life has changed, this last year, well, my perspective on a lot of things has changed, too. After all, nobody is what they seem on the outside. I grew up thinking Gram and Elliot and Sully were the cutest, little old trio. Never would I have guessed they were heroes. They really are. Call themselves The Parallel Society."

His head turned towards her. His eyes focused on her.

Roni tried to speak more, but her throat constricted. Nodding and smiling like an eager child, she finally found her words. "It's true. You know about it? The three of them go around closing up rifts with other universes. Strange, though, that they always talk about it in those terms — universes — when really they only fix things on Earth. I wonder if there are rifts billions of miles away from here. There must be. Maybe there's another Society on another planet out there."

He shifted in his wheelchair an inch, leaning closer as she spoke.

"You understand what I'm talking about, don't you? You do. I can see it. Now that I'm thinking about it, I shouldn't be surprised. They offered a job to Mom. She turned it down, of course, but no matter how wild a life she led, she always came back to you. So, she probably told you about Gram. Did you ever learn about the caverns? You'd be amazed to see them."

His hand reached out and found her wrist. Though his grip shook, she could tell that if he had more strength, he would have held her tight. In a whisper, he said, "Stay away from the caverns."

"Dad? You hear me?"

With more force, he said, "Stay away from the dark thing in the caverns."

"I'm not in the caverns. Not regularly. I'm just a researcher. You don't have to worry. I'll never see the dark thing."

Tears brimmed on the edges of his eyes. "The dark thing — the hellspider — it will destroy you."

Roni's muscles froze. "What?"

His head drooped as his eyes rolled.

"No," Roni said. "Come on. Tell me."

"The hellspider," he said in a slow drone. "Leave it alone." Then his eyes closed and he snored.

Roni stayed for twenty minutes more, trying to bring her father back. Twice he lifted his head and looked about the room, but he never regained lucidity that day. Eventually, the orderlies wheeled him off to his bed.

Driving to Olburg, Roni tried to make sense of everything he had said. Except none of the parts appeared to connect with the bits of information she had acquired. Even if there had been a connection, it might have been nothing more than lunatic ravings. *A hellspider?* She couldn't fully trust anything he said. Yet she couldn't dismiss it either.

Not that it mattered. Gram now knew about some of it — enough that she had shut down the whole thing. Roni had built up an idea that she would present all her research to the team, that she would then explain about Kenneth Bay and Yal-hara, and that Gram would be so impressed, she would insist on Roni leading the charge into the caverns. That would never happen now.

"Damn it," she yelled in her car. Turning on the radio, she blasted classic rock for a few miles but flicked it off before the first song had ended. That was her career in the Society. Over before it began. Not even a one-hit wonder.

She found a parking space on the street several blocks from her apartment. As she strolled home, she tried to let go of the failure and stress. If she could accept her position as the librarian and not the adventurer, she would do far better. And why not? She never wanted to go into the caverns in the first place. Never wanted any of it. Why not simply hole up in the Grand Library? She could be of great assistance to those equipped to deal with the other universes, yet she should never have to bloody her hands.

Chuckling, she picked up her pace. That sounded good except for the part where she would have to be under the thumb of Gram. Plus, one day, Gram would find somebody to take over — not Roni, of course, because the researcher can't be the leader — which would leave Roni being under the thumb of yet another formidable Society member. No, that wouldn't work either.

"Finally, you are home," a voice called out.

Roni looked up and all she saw ahead of her was trouble. Elliot waited for her in the doorway.

CHAPTER 7

As Roni opened the door to her apartment, Elliot brushed through straight for the center of the room. With his cane, he pushed aside the robe and dirty blouse discarded on the floor. Standing between her old television and her worn couch, he lifted the cane shoulder-height with his right hand. His left traced a figure eight repeatedly.

Roni knew not to speak while Elliot cast a spell. She gently closed the door before going down the hall to the bathroom. When she returned a few minutes later, the air around Elliot's hand shimmered. She leaned against the wall and waited.

The shimmering increased its frequency right before Roni heard a pop. Then her ears clogged up as if from the pressure of sitting in an airplane changing altitude. Rubbing her ears, she tried to get them to clear, but nothing helped.

Lowering his hands, Elliot turned towards her. Despite all the sounds around her being muted, when he spoke, his voice cut through the thick gauze in the air. "This spell will not last long, so I advise you to be honest with me. For the moment, nobody can hear what we say. Anyone attempting to snoop on us will know nothing."

"Who would be snooping?" Roni asked, her own voice louder than she expected.

"Not everybody in the world that knows the truth agrees with the Society. We have our enemies."

Roni wondered where Yal-hara and Kenneth Bay fell in that dichotomy — friend or foe. She had accepted them at face value — mostly because of the map fragment — but seeing the deep concern in Elliot's eyes worried her.

Placing both his hands on the top of his cane, Elliot tilted forward.

"Now is the time when you must tell me all that you know about the Book on the Isle and how you came to know it."

"I just stumbled upon it. I was working in the Grand Library like always, and I came across Waterfield's journal. You were the last to check it out, so I got curious."

Elliot shook his head. "Even without powers I can see that you are lying. I have known you since you were little, after all. Do not try to deceive me. I shall offer you one more opportunity. Tell me the truth." His stern expression cracked for an instant, and beneath it, Roni saw mournful sadness.

"I'm sorry," she said. "Here's the truth." And she told him everything that had occurred since Kenneth Bay sat down across from her in the Olburg Chestnut.

When she finished, Elliot gave a thoughtful grunt. "Yal-hara. We never did the right thing with her. We wanted to, but there was no way to pinpoint her specific universe. Not that we know."

"Why couldn't you just open the book that captured the original rift? Let her go through."

"Because we never did capture it. It disappeared on its own as if that universe merely grazed ours instead of intersecting it."

"Yal-hara says she needs this kyolo stone to find another rift to her universe. That with the stone, she can find her way home. Is that right? Is she telling me the truth?"

"Maybe."

"But these stones are everywhere in the Book on the Isle. She said that. Is that much true?"

"It once was true, but I have not been to that place in many years."

Roni pushed off the wall, her head cocked in disbelief. "You've been there? You've seen the Book on the Isle?"

Closing his eyes as if the words might cause him to scream, he opted instead to nod.

A dark thought struck her. "What's the hellspider?"

Elliot's eyes snapped open. "Hellspider? I have never heard of that."

"I thought we were going to be honest here."

"I am. I have never heard of nor have I ever seen something called a hellspider."

She believed him. "What about my Lost Time? Yal-hara said that the stones she wants could also help me with my memory."

"I don't know."

"How can you know so little about this when it's obvious that you're connected to it all?"

"Because I have never met Yal-hara, so I cannot confirm the truth of her words. I am assuming that you also have not met her."

Crossing her arms, Roni said, "Just her guy, Kenneth Bay. He called himself her emissary."

"I know him. His father, Roger Bay, was the man I dealt with on the few occasions Yal-hara reached out to us."

"If you worked with them before, then you should know whether I can trust them."

He chuckled. "You most certainly cannot trust them. But that does not mean they have lied to you. Yal-hara has been stuck here for a long time, and she wants to find her way back to her world. That much is true. Whether the kyolo stones can save her, whether they can help you, I do not know. I doubt Yal-hara knows for sure, either."

"So this is all a gamble?"

"Perhaps a better way to say this would be that Yal-hara is making a highly educated guess."

Roni walked to the couch and slumped into its lumpy cushions. "Then I have to try, right? I have to go to this Book on the Isle and get some of those kyolo stones. And I have to prepare myself for the fact that it might not work — at least, not for me."

"The Book on the Isle leads to a wondrous place."

"Waterfield wrote that it's a paradise."

"Indeed, it is. Possibly the most extraordinary world I've ever seen. Yet such worlds of beauty and peace can do more harm than the dark, evil worlds." Elliot's gaze lowered. "A world of paradise gives hope. And hope — real, pure hope — is destined to be destroyed."

"Maybe," she said, a dread excitement building as a bonfire grows from a single flame. "But knowing the place is real, confirming it because you've been there, that sort of means I have to go now. I can't turn away. I have to try — for Yal-hara and for myself."

Roni heard a high-pitched whine followed by a pop similar to the one earlier. Elliot shuffled toward the front door. "The spell is done," he said.

"Thank you for telling me this. It's going to help me make this decision."

"Do not lie to yourself. You have already made that decision."

"I suppose I did. That's it then. I'm going to the Isle."

"Good. I assumed as much when you first mentioned the Isle. That is why I have taken the liberty of packing supplies for the trip. We should get started right away."

"We?"

"I expect you to come along. It would be too lonely to do it by myself. Now, get some clothes together and we will be off."

Roni grinned. "Shouldn't we sleep on it? I mean, I could use some rest before hiking into a cavern for days."

"The longer we wait, the more likely that Gram and Sully will attempt to stop us. Who do you think I was casting that spell against?"

"The spell is over. Shouldn't you be quiet about it now?"

Elliot blushed. "I am old. I forget things. Maybe I am also too paranoid. But Gram has strong feelings about this subject, and she will not want me going to the Isle. So, we must be on our way. If you are too tired, we will find a place to rest once we are out of Gram's reach. Okay? Good. Now, let us begin."

CHAPTER 8

An hour later, Roni walked down the stairs from the main floor of the bookstore into the basement. The Grand Library was further below ground, but this low-ceiling, musty area filled with boxes of old periodicals and dusty dictionaries led to the door with the medieval padlock — Gram's private office. Normally, the door remained closed and locked, but Elliot had already used a spell to "pick" the lock.

The last time Roni entered this room without permission, she discovered the caverns and her whole worldview shifted beneath her feet. She had been terrified to go in there. This time, however, she went in willingly — with a purpose.

Fluorescent lights hung from a tiled ceiling which only added to the utilitarian style of the room. Like an old 1970s cop show, the room appeared to be a metal box with metal shelves for the numerous books Gram collected. But unlike any room elsewhere in the world, a large hole in the back wall opened into a cavern.

Elliot stood by this hole. He wore a long winter coat and a tweed, newsboy cap. Roni shouldered a backpack as she approached.

"All set," she said. She had clothes for three days and a folder with hardcopy printouts of the maps. "There are missing chunks," she said. "The maps will only help us so far."

With a grandfatherly smile, Elliot tapped the side of his head. "This still works. I shall get us to the river, and the river will get us to the Isle."

"Just in case, I also brought this," she said, pulling out Waterfield's journal. "I haven't had the chance to read it thoroughly, but I'm guessing there's more in here to help us."

Bringing such an old and irreplaceable text should have caused her deep worry — it was risky, to say the least — but nothing could be more essential than the words of a man who had already made the journey. Such vital information far outweighed her concerns over possible damage done to the journal.

"Yes," Elliot said. "That is a good backup, in case something happens to me."

Roni didn't like his tone, but she let it pass. Elliot stepped forward, and Roni glimpsed the cart behind him — a wagon with a metal rod to pull it, wooden crate sides, and four rugged wheels. Inside, she saw jugs of water, boxes of food, camping gear, and clothes. An uncomfortable sensation crawled across her skin.

"Wow," she muttered. "I never thought to bring any of that stuff."

He snickered. "Don't feel bad. My first trip into the caverns, I didn't even have the sense to bring a change of clothes. We were only going to fetch an empty book from a specific spot, and we only planned to be gone a few hours. But I fell, slid down a muddy incline and splashed into a puddle the size of this room. The water was cold and the air cool, and there was no easy way back up. Gram and Sully had to carefully climb down, which took a half-hour, and then we had to walk far out of our way to get back to where we were originally — which required most of the day. I could not do so sopping wet. So, I striped down and proceeded for several hours in the nude."

Roni laughed. "I'm sure Sully never let you live that down."

"Nor your grandmother. She kept threatening to take my picture."

"I can't imagine that, but I'll take your word for it." With a shrug, she added, "I guess that's all we need. Let's go."

"One more thing." Elliot reached into his wagon and pulled out a leather-bound journal. "A proper researcher will document her experiences."

Roni kept her eyes on the journal in case she cried. She accepted the gift as a priceless heirloom. Passing her hand across the top, she noticed the silk ribbon used to mark her place and smelled the rich aroma of the pages. Holding the journal at her side, she stepped in close and hugged Elliot with her free arm.

"Thank you," she said.

"I can think of no greater honor than to take this first big step with you. Now, let us begin."

Before Roni heard Gram's voice, she heard Gram's footsteps. Turning towards the doorway, she saw the familiar scowl. She could feel everything falling apart.

Gram gripped the cross around her neck. "I don't know which of you two to be more angry with. At least Roni's been consistently defiant from the start. But you. How could you go behind my back like this?"

"I am not behind your back," Elliot said, his tone more forceful than Roni had expected.

"Really? So, it was merely coincidence that you cast a dampening spell when you went to my granddaughter's apartment."

"Not at all. I wanted our conversation to be private. Leading this group does not give you the right to know all that we think, feel, and do. It most certainly does not give you the right to spy on us."

Caught between two angry old people, Roni scooted out of the way.

Though Gram had to lift her chin in order to meet Elliot's eyes, she seemed the larger of the two. "I was looking out for the safety of my granddaughter and you, for that matter. But everybody is hellbent on doing whatever they want. That won't work. We have to be united or we will lose any battle we encounter."

"I agree. Yet you seem to consider the word *united* to mean that we follow your rules at all times."

Roni cringed, bracing for the tirade Gram would unleash. But instead, Gram stepped back with a disappointed grin. She glanced at Roni. "I didn't want to believe him, but Sully told me that you saw things this way. And now I hear it from my own teammate, too." To Elliot, she added, "Do you really think of me as a dictator? Come now, you know me better than that. I admit I am strong-willed, but I have a duty to maintain the strength of this group, the safety of us, as well as that of the entire universe."

Elliot placed his hand on her shoulder. "That duty belongs to us all. Whether she knows it or not, I am sure that Roni would be taking this journey alone, if necessary. I would not let that happen."

To Roni's further surprise, Gram's chin trembled. "But she wants to go to the Isle."

"I know."

"Are you sure you're ready to face them?"

"I have hid for too long." Elliot glanced back at the opening to the caverns. "And for Roni, this is not about my past."

"Oh?"

Roni stepped in front of Elliot. "This about Yal-hara."

Gram laced her fingers as her face darkened. "I see. You're after the kyolo stones."

"You know about them?"

"It's a myth. Yal-hara is old and desperate for anything that'll get her home."

Roni looked toward the caverns. "I'm still going. I'll find out for myself if it's a myth."

Gram opened her arm toward Roni. "Then we all go — together." Roni stared at her grandmother, trying to piece together what had happened. "Come on," Gram said. "I expect a hug."

Rushing over, Roni wrapped her arms around Gram. "You're really okay with this?"

"Not at all. But this is clearly something the two of you need to do, and I will not sit upstairs while you both risk your lives."

"But there's nothing —"

"Oh Lord, my dear, you must learn this right away — any trip into the caverns is a risk to your life. Any single step in there must be treated with cautiousness and respect for danger. Understand?"

She nodded. "I will."

"Good. Then I have only one question." Gram pointed at Elliot's cart. "What the heck is that?"

Elliot knocked his cane against the cart's tires. "What? It is strong and easy to pull. You do not expect me to carry all of these items."

"That thing won't last one day in the caverns. Once you get beyond the well-worn paths, there's rugged terrain and muddy areas — you know all about those. I would be shocked if those tires didn't pop flat within a few hours. And also —"

"Okay, okay. What do you suggest?"

"Sully, of course."

Roni laughed. "Sully's going to carry all of this?"

"No, not directly. But the moment I realized what Elliot was up to, I got Sully working." She cocked her head toward the door. "Sully? You coming?"

From further in the basement, Sully's voice rang out. "You people are so impatient. I'll be there in a second."

A moment later, he walked into the room. Behind him, on a rope, he brought in a full-sized donkey-golem made of clay. It had a broad, flat back and thick legs. Its head lacked a mouth but it did have eyes. Somewhere in its clay body, Sully had written Hebrew words on a slip of paper — a spell to create life from a non-living thing. He would have slipped the paper into the donkey form, whispered an incantation into its ear, and the donkey-golem would spring to life.

"One of these days," Sully said, huffing as he walked, "you will give me more than a few hours' notice and I'll be able to create a beautiful creature instead of a mere semblance like this."

"As long as it can haul our gear, I don't care if it only has half of a head."

Patting the donkey-golem's flank, Sully said to it, "Don't listen to that old crab. You're more than labor to us. We appreciate all the hard work you're about to do."

Gram stepped in front of Roni and Elliot. "Come on, now. Quit gawking and help load her up."

Although nothing that had happened went along with Roni's expectations, part of her warmed at the idea of Elliot and Sully joining her. Even Gram's presence gave Roni a small sense of comfort. The Old Gang knew the way to the Isle, and they knew the dangers to be found in the caverns. At least, she hoped they knew.

When they finished packing one section of the donkey-golem, Gram made a motion with her wrist. A thin, metal chain flew out of her sleeve. The chain wrapped itself around the gear, securing it to the donkey-golem.

After they had finished transferring all of the supplies, Gram gestured towards Elliot. "Last chance. You really want to do this?"

"It is long overdue."

Gram gazed back over the team. She seemed to be weighing this final decision in her head. At length, and without further word, she led the way into the caverns. Elliot followed and Sully came up with his donkey-golem nudging along.

Roni stopped at the edge. She had done this before, yet it felt new. This was her first foray into the caverns as a member of the Parallel Society. This was her first time setting foot in the caverns having read that it existed in another universe. Whatever they encountered in there would become part of Society history. The idea filled her with a sense of importance — and dread.

Swallowing down her rising dark thoughts, she entered the caverns.

CHAPTER 9

For the first half hour, Roni could not have been more awed. Once they traveled beyond the small portion she had experienced a year ago, the caverns treated her with one astonishing view after another. Enormous ceilings with thousands of stalactites — sharp like teeth. Books leading to other universes hung on chains, dangling in the air like muted wind chimes. Winding paths spiraled off into the dark, and narrow crevices had been worn smooth like glass.

In every direction, no matter how high up or how far away, Roni saw books. Endless books. Each one chained to the walls, chained to themselves, or lined up behind tightly wound chains. Some books occupied huge sections of wall by themselves while others had been crowded together, shoved into tiny spaces, locked away like prisoners. Each book opened to a rift into another universe. Hundreds of years of the Parallel Society capturing these rifts, putting them in these magic books, and housing them in these caverns. It looked full, yet Roni had seen the maps — there was room for hundreds of thousands more. Maybe millions.

The cavern air maintained a steady coolness — warmer than the autumn air outside in Olburg but chilly nonetheless. It smelled fresh, too. As if all the moss of a forest had found its way into the stone surrounding them.

Lighting from various decades had been strung along the pathway revealing the history of those who came before like striation patterns. Modern, small rectangles that cast enormous bright, pale light in one section. Bulky, brass lanterns that needed to be lit with matches in another. One section required Gram to spin a crank for a few seconds until dim amber lights came to life.

Further in, the lighting stopped, but the strong glow from massive numbers of phosphorescent rocks created an unreal beauty to guide their way. Shortly after, they reached a section of pure dark. Sully handed out flashlights. With slow, cautious steps they made their way through until they reached an area that resembled a playground — filled with nooks and tunnels and overpasses.

Sunlight bounced around. Elliot glanced back at Roni. "There are a lot of sections with natural light like this. As far as we know, nobody in the Society has ever located the source. Perhaps you'll discover it someday."

But no matter how beautiful the sights, no matter how amazing the history, eventually, the excitement lessened. They trudged along through more and more dark sections with little to see. They stayed quiet, focusing on the next step, and the next, and the next. The click of their walking, the jangle of their equipment, the clump of the donkey-golem echoed into the distance making a unique, cavern music. But even that sprinkling sound could not relieve the drudgery of doing nothing but walking.

By the time Gram called the day to an end, Roni's mind had become a dull blankness nearly as dark as the lightless cavern sections. Scanning the area, she saw that Gram had picked a concave section of a large rock wall for their rest. A knee-high edge of stones had been formed by previous explorers. It took a crescent shape, and Sully went to work building a fire in the center — he had brought wood for this purpose but also warned that as they went further, they would be wise to pick up anything usable for the future.

Once he had a steady fire going, he removed a cooking pot, several bags of vegetables and meat, a box of spices, and a jug of water. "I hope you all are up for some stew. If not, you can eat it anyway because I'm not taking requests."

Elliot and Gram examined the map printouts Roni had brought. They murmured to each other as they pointed out various sections.

And Roni — she rubbed her sore shoulders as she rested on a large, flat rock. Flexing her toes, she knew to keep her boots on and laced. If she took them off, chances were her feet would swell to the point that it would be difficult, if not impossible, to put her boots back on.

After about twenty minutes, she rose and dug out her new journal from her backpack. She hovered a pen over the first fresh, blank page. She wrote:

I don't know what to write.

Bemused, she took a breath and gazed at the Old Gang. They all acted so calm and in control. She wondered how many times they had ventured into these caverns. Maybe one day, she too would act the same.

Resetting her pen to paper, she wrote:

My head is too full to know the best way to begin. Having spent a year reading the journals of other Society members before me, I feel that I should offer something profound in these pages. Maybe someday I will. Others have written journals that are poetic, vivid, and just far better than anything I could write. Still, this is my duty, I suppose, and I want to do it. I want to let the future Society members know what our lives were like, and as my experience grows, to know what I learn so that readers can learn, too. But as far as my first day hiking goes, I can only say that I am happy to finally be on my way. My feet ache and my muscles are cramped. I stink. Yet I can't wait to get back at it tomorrow. To whoever will read this, I hope my first entry is enough.

She read over her words, grabbed the page, and nearly ripped it out. But before she could do so, she heard a strange sound. Something nearby hissed. Roni bolted upright and caught Gram staring at a spot off to the left. Snapping her fingers, Gram pulled Elliot and Sully's attention.

A bone-white creature skittered onto a rock. It had the wrinkled, scrawny look of a furless cat and an overall alabaster coloring. On some parts — especially around the mouth — the skin bordered on translucent. Though no bigger than a terrier, the creature's movements reminded Roni of a gorilla. Black, raisin eyes darted from Roni to Gram to the boys. Once again, it hissed, revealing a mouthful of teeth like jagged rocks.

"It's okay," Roni said as if talking to a frightened dog. She smiled at the creature and moved closer. "We won't hurt you."

"Roni, freeze," Gram said. The creature backed away at the harsh voice.

Sully said, "Perhaps I can —"

"No. You stay by Roni. Keep her safe."

Roni looked over at Gram. "Safe? It's just a little —"

The creature jumped onto a rock closer to Roni. She stumbled back, unable to stop the surprised screech from escaping her lips. Just a short sound, but enough to scare the creature. Sully put his hands on Roni's shoulders, steadying her with his firm stance.

The creature thrust out its chest and hissed. Gram moved towards it, her arms out as if she intended to tackle the thing should it leap forward. Locking her eyes on the creature's every movement, Gram said, "Elliot, get me the green book from the donkey-golem."

Elliot nodded and cautiously backed away. Gram stepped forward. The creature rocked its shoulders before moving in a tight circle. It clearly did not like the situation, but it also did not appear willing to back down.

"Elliot?" Gram said. Her right arm lowered and her hand pulled into her sleeve.

"Got it," he said, coming up to her side. He held a large green book similar to all the books chained to the walls.

Roni saw Gram's wrist twitch and she put it all together. "Don't do that," she said.

But Gram's arm had already begun its motion. She snapped out her hand and a chain flew from her sleeve. It caught the creature's ankle and tightened around the bone. As the creature shrieked, Gram transferred her end of the chain to her free hand. Then she shot out another chain. This one caught the creature around the chest.

Crying like a lost child, the creature leaned back, pulling uselessly on the chains. Though Gram could not hold her ground like Sully, she had no trouble keeping this small creature under control.

Gram cocked her head back. "Open the book!"

Elliot held the book facing the creature and pulled back the cover. Roni reached up for Sully's hand and braced herself. She had seen books opened before — they could vacuum in everything around them.

But nothing happened. No whoosh of air. No howling winds. No vortex pulling one universe into another.

Elliot planted one foot against a rock behind him. "Now!"

Yelling like a warrior, Gram swung the creature straight into the open book. She released the chains, allowing the entire package to pass into the pages. The sound of the creature screaming weakened as if it fell down a long shaft. Elliot shut the cover and Gram hurried over to tie a fresh chain around the outside.

Roni wrenched free from Sully. "What the hell did you do?"

"Watch your language," Gram said.

"That thing was just scared and you tossed it away like it meant nothing."

"That thing is a relic — a living relic. You remember what that is?"

With an impatient sigh, Roni said, "Yes. A relic is an object from another universe that gets stuck in ours."

Gram took the book over to the donkey-golem and roughly made room to store it. "Well, relics can be living things, too. Yal-hara is a relic, and so was that thing. It doesn't belong here."

Stomping over, Roni said, "And does it belong in that book? Is that where it came from?"

"Of course not. This book opens to an empty universe. I use it for all the things that I cannot place anywhere else."

"Shouldn't we at least have tried to find where this thing came from? You just tossed it away. Threw it into — what? What's *an empty universe?* Unless that's a euphemism for a thriving ecosystem, I'm guessing that creature is going to die floating in emptiness." She looked to Elliot and Sully. "Are you guys really okay with this? Is that how you've all been handling things? Just sweeping the relics under the rug?"

Sully stabbed a finger in her direction. "Young lady, you should learn to close your mouth and open your ears. You don't know what you're talking about right now."

"I know that murdering a creature because it's in our universe isn't right."

Gram's stern brow eased as she approached. She hooked her arm through Roni's. "Let's take a little walk. The boys will clean up."

Though anger urged Roni to rip her arm away and yell more, the sensible side of her prevailed. She had not seen Gram like this since before she joined the Society. A dim light deep inside her warmed at her grandmother's kind touch. It had been too long. Patting Gram's hand, she nodded, and together they went for a walk.

At first, they stayed silent. Their footsteps echoed around them. Just as when Roni was little, Gram had the ability to time things right. Before the silence grew uncomfortable, Gram spoke in a calm, soothing voice.

"I know this part is going to be hard for you. It was for me, too."

"You can't possibly convince me that —"

"Shhh. Let me speak. The first thing you must understand is that in order to protect our universe, we must get rid of all relics as fast as possible. Remember that each relic brings with it the threat of germs, bacteria, even seeds of invasive species — all of which could wipe us out, if we are not careful."

"What about Yal-hara?"

"Some relics, like her, predate my involvement with the Society. Any damage those relics would do has already been done."

Remembering that Gram had a private stash of relic alcohol, Roni snickered. "Is that why you don't mind having vodka from another universe in the bookstore?"

"You can laugh at me, but yes, that's true. Now, pay attention. These caverns are not part of our universe."

"I know. I read about it in Waterfield's journal."

"What you may not know is that there are no living things in this universe. I do not know how the caverns came into existence. I believe our Lord provided them, but that doesn't mean He made them. However it happened, the caverns are here to house the books. Nothing more. When we come across a relic, especially a living relic, we must dispose of it as fast as possible — because if a relic can devastate our universe, mankind dies; but if it devastates these caverns —"

"Then everything dies." Roni paused as she looked at all the books hanging from the walls. "All of it. Holy shit."

Gram smacked Roni's hand. "Please. I'm not stupid enough to think you don't cuss all the time, but I don't need to hear it."

"Sorry." A thought hit her, and Roni faced Gram. "If the caverns are a different universe, doesn't that make us relics in here, too?"

"You understand now. We are just as dangerous to everything in here. It is why we must be extremely careful — not only to protect the caverns, but to protect ourselves. We don't know how large the caverns are, but it has been suggested that they connect all universes. If that is true, it stands to reason that there are other Parallel Society-type organizations out there, and if we come across one, then they may try to dispose of us, fearing the damage we may cause in here."

"So you got rid of that creature both to save the caverns but also because it might try to throw us in a book?"

"Exactly."

All the sounds bouncing off the walls, the glorious symphony of clicks and drips and unidentified tinkling tones, no longer brought joy. Roni shifted on her feet. Could there be another Society out there? Watching her? Waiting to chain her up and toss her away?

"Let's go back," she said. They turned around and walked toward the campfire. "If we're potentially damaging the caverns by being here, then why are we doing it? I don't mean this time, I get that we're helping Yal-hara, and I guess Elliot, too — and you've got to explain that one to me soon — but what about all those expeditions of the past?"

"For hundreds of years, I doubt anybody understood what damage they might cause. It's only been in the twentieth century that the concept of the multiverse has come to be. I've tried to limit our exposure in here as much as possible. I can only pray that you will have the sense and ability to put rules into place that will further protect these caverns."

"Me?"

"As you've pointed out numerous times, we're getting old. You know you're taking over for us eventually. This is one thing you need to start thinking about."

When they returned, Elliot and Sully had cleaned up all evidence of their meal. Sleeping bags had been unrolled, and both men had curled up for the night. Gram indicated one of the bags for Roni.

After everyone wished pleasant dreams, the Old Gang fell asleep fast. But Roni could not. Her mind swirled with all that had happened and all that Gram had said.

On the one hand, she felt thrilled to have come so far, to have seen deeper into the caverns, to have witnessed a living relic, and experienced her first day of adventure. On the other hand, Gram had finally given in a little and offered Roni a touch of responsibility. And what was it? Find rules that more or less shut down her access to the very thing that makes everything exciting and worthwhile. On the other, other hand, she accepted the seriousness of her task and would do her best. On the other, other, other hand, the whole thing ticked her off. Because once again, Gram had taken charge, and in doing so, changed the way the entire trip had gone.

Roni punched her pillow a few times and thrust her head down. Sleep would not be coming soon, and every sound threatened to attack her as if she were the dangerous relic. A small voice in the back of her head wondered if they shouldn't simply turn around and go home.

CHAPTER 10

When Roni woke, Elliot and Sully had already begun to pack up for the day. Waking in a cavern disoriented her — no sunlight, no change in temperature, nothing but another hour. Gram nibbled on a pumpernickel roll nearby.

Roni stood and felt an unwelcome pressure below. She crawled over to Gram. Whispering, she said, "Um, I have to go to the bathroom."

"So? Go. You didn't have a problem yesterday."

"That was all number one. I have to really go, this time."

Gram winked. "It doesn't make a difference. Go behind a rock and let loose."

"But what about everything you said? Isn't it dangerous to leave our business here? Germs and bacteria and everything?"

"Dear, if poo is going to destroy this universe, it would already have happened. You think the Society members of a hundred years ago thought about such things?"

"I guess not. It doesn't seem right, though. Shouldn't we be better?"

"We try to be. When it comes to this, unless you brought a doggie poop bag, you've got two choices. Either go behind the rocks and do your business, or take one of my empty books and squat into that."

Roni opted to go behind the rocks. She thought she'd be a hypocrite if she crapped into another universe — even an empty universe — to be clean in this one. As she headed off, Sully called her name. She looked up and he tossed over a roll of toilet paper.

Shortly afterward, the group finished packing and they started on the day's hike. This time, the allure of the caverns had faded. Roni still found interesting rock formations and unusual ways light bounced around, but the excitement and majesty of her first steps drifted further behind.

Each minute brought pain — her feet had blistered and her muscles ached. She grew thirsty but avoided taking more than the minimum of water. Partly because she wanted to ration what they had, and partly because she decided that morning to avoid going to the bathroom as much as possible.

Elliot put up a hand to stop the hike. Using his cane, he drew a line across the dirt at his feet. "Our maps end here. We may have to go slower from time to time because it has been many years since I have traveled this way. It will all come back to me, so please have patience."

"Of course," Sully said. "We understand."

Roni wanted to yell that she didn't understand, that nobody would tell her what was Elliot's problem with this Isle, but she stayed quiet. As they powered onward, she pulled out her journal and attempted to keep a rough detail of the path. She figured that even if her entries never became worthwhile reading material, at least she could provide useful maps.

"Good idea," Sully said, walking side-by-side with his donkey-golem. "If the world this Book on the Isle leads to is half as wonderful to view as I have heard, we will certainly want to know how to get back."

Roni thought about what she had read in Waterfield's journal. When he discovered the book, he wrote down what he saw when he looked inside.

> *A marvel to behold. Bright with gold and silver. People much like ourselves, only filled with light and joy. They dressed in flowing gowns that declared their freedom as much as the happiness upon their faces. From my vantage point, I witnessed a gorgeous fountain in the center of a town that seemed to be in an agrarian utopia. A true fantasy lifted from one of our children's books, only nary a witch or evil giant in sight.*

For the next hour, their path led them along the base of a cliff. Roni kept expecting rocks to fall from above, but nothing so dangerous occurred. Even the books above her were chained tight against the walls.

Later, the ground sloped downward — a smooth descent that slowed their progress. The path spiraled downward as if they navigated their way through the inside of a long tube. Books swung from chains above them. Some hung so low, Roni and the others had to duck in order to pass.

Until they reached the halfway point.

Gram gasped and they halted. "What happened?"

The pathway forward had all the chains jingling against each other, but no books. Some chains had been torn free from the ceiling. Some of the links dotted the ground. But every last book had been removed — only the chains remained.

Elliot slid his cane across several of the hanging chains, creating an eerie music. "I have never seen such a thing. Sully?"

Pushing his way forward, Sully inspected the chains. "I haven't. But this doesn't look natural."

"Of course it's not natural," Gram said.

"I only meant that the books didn't fall, the chains didn't rust or weaken. And if I had to say, I would wager that these books were violently ripped loose."

Gram nodded. "So it wasn't somebody like us — somebody with the kinds of powers we have."

Sully's focus drifted toward Roni. "We must be extra careful."

Roni wished she could muster a light comment, some way to dismiss the fear circulating amongst them, but she only managed to swallow hard against her dry throat.

They proceeded further down. All the chains without books swayed like nooses without bodies — a threat hanging with each one. At the bottom, the ground leveled into an open plain of rocks. Thankfully, the books there remained. A few were missing from the lower sections of the walls, but the majority of the spaces had books properly chained — as far as they could tell. The ceiling of this cavern section rose so high, it became lost to the dark.

Unfortunately, the ground could be seen with total clarity. Relics like the living one that had stumbled upon their campsite the night before littered the ground. Only these no longer lived. Hundreds of pale corpses had been spread across the dirt, each one twisted in an agonized position. Their foul odor rose in the air.

Gram covered her mouth. Elliot looked away. Sully glanced downward and shook his head.

"What did this?" Roni asked.

Patting her cross against her chest, Gram said, "We will find out. Elliot, please locate the source of this evil."

Stepping forward, Elliot lifted his cane horizontal over one of the corpses. He wrinkled his nose at the sharp stench. Closing his eyes, he raised his hand and also held it horizontal to the corpse. After a few quiet moments, he lowered his hands and stepped forward, placing each foot with care. When he stopped walking, he lifted his cane and hand as before. This continued for several minutes. Each time, he moved deeper and deeper into the slaughter.

While they waited, Roni tried to jot down notes in her journal, but finding the words to describe this horror failed her. She kept seeing the living relic Gram had tossed into a book and wondered if that creature had been escaping whatever had caused this. Everywhere she looked, she saw accusing glares as if the dead might rise and point at her and blame her for the death of their friend.

Don't be stupid, she thought. She had done nothing wrong. If anybody, Gram deserved such glares, yet that wasn't even true — Gram did not mass murder these creatures.

By the time Elliot returned, Roni needed any distraction from the surrounding death. "So?" she said, the eagerness in her voice mimicked by the hopeful looks from Gram and Sully.

Elliot's grim countenance answered before he spoke. "I cannot get a clear reading. All the books around us, all the books in these massive caverns, they lead to near-infinite universes. It is too much to narrow my focus. When I know which book we are searching for, I can handle it. One universe is difficult, but possible. Here there is simply too much pulling me in all directions. Especially because there is a good, logical possibility that these once-living relics came from one of the books now missing."

"Thank you for trying," Gram said. "Let's move on. We've still got plenty of hiking to do, and Lord knows I don't want to smell these things any longer. Everybody be vigilant."

With that, they left. Roni wanted to ask why they didn't dispose of the bodies. Shouldn't they be worried about contaminating the caverns? But evidence pointed out that despite Gram's warnings, the caverns had been exposed to much over the centuries, and while it behooved them all to be better custodians, Roni would not have to worry over every germ.

They trudged onward for several hours until Gram finally pointed to a trickle of water running off of a large boulder. "We'll camp here."

Once they had eaten and settled in, the Old Gang again fell asleep with ease. Roni, however, could not shake the heaviness in her thoughts. The dead relics troubled her, but more, her mind rattled through scenarios of her future — none of which ended with good results.

She was expected to learn how to do things yet Gram withheld too much information. Then, when she finally did learn a few things, Gram contradicted her rules with blatant disregard in her actions. Roni had always been a believer in the idea that one had to know the rules before breaking them. It helped to avoid stupid mistakes. Yet it seemed that one day she would be inheriting all the responsibilities of the Parallel Society with no firm grasp on the basics. And no matter how many times she played that idea, she couldn't help but wonder if part of Gram wanted her to fail. Maybe it helped Gram still feel useful.

Roni rolled onto her side, but she could not clear her mind. Yet at some point in the night, her thoughts became her dreams, and the hours slipped by. The next thing Roni knew, Elliot nudged her awake.

He smiled at her scrunched face. "Hurry up. We are close. Today, if I can still find the entrance, we will arrive at the Book on the Isle."

Twenty minutes later, they had the campsite clean and the donkey-golem packed. Elliot moved with an exuberant step as he led the way further into the caverns. Despite his excitement, Roni kept her own expectations low. Good thing, too. It would be three hours before they reached a dark passageway with a hole in the side.

"Here, here," Elliot said, waving a flashlight. "Be careful. This is rugged."

The ground angled downward on a series of large rocks poking out at odd angles. Roni did her best to help Gram and Elliot work their way to the bottom. Sully's ability to hold to the ground like a redwood rooted for five hundred years kept him stable. He guided the donkey-golem.

Before they reached the bottom, Roni heard the gentle sound of water streaming over stones. She smelled the freshness in the air and felt the moisture surrounding her. "This is really it," she said.

"Yes," Elliot said, beaming his flashlight across the water. "It has been a very long time, yet this looks the same as when I last saw it. How wondrous."

Roni walked to the edge and knelt. "Is it safe to drink?"

"Absolutely."

She smiled and dunked her head in the cool current of Waterfield River. It felt like all the ugliness they had seen washed away. She drank a little — tastelessly fresh. When she resurfaced, her whirling thoughts settled. Not far away, they would find the book. She would reach in and pluck out a kyolo stone. Her first big mission, and she would not only succeed in helping Yal-hara, but she might be able to help herself recover some memories. She wanted to cheer, but Gram would not appreciate that, so Roni dunked her head once more.

"Enough already," Gram said when Roni came back up for air. "This is not the time to start bathing. We've got a lot of work to do before we get on the water."

"We do?"

"Sure. We can't possibly take the donkey-golem with us, and that means we can't take all our supplies. Time to make some hard choices."

CHAPTER 11

As Gram pulled items from the donkey-golem's saddle bags, Sully brought out two inflatable rafts and two air pumps. Elliot joined Gram separating needed items from those that would stay behind. So, Roni inferred where they expected her to work. Grabbing a raft, she got busy unrolling it, attaching the air pump nozzle, and then pumping over and over to inflate the raft.

"Everybody gets to keep one change of clothes," Gram announced.

Roni kept pumping. "Just pick something from my bag. It doesn't matter."

At length, she and Sully finished the rafts and set them in the water. All four helped load their limited supplies on the two rafts. Then Gram pointed at Sully. "You and I will take the back. Elliot and Roni, take the lead."

As Roni climbed into the front boat and Gram took the back, Sully and Elliot picked up the supplies staying behind and put them on the donkey-golem. Sully leaned over and whispered to the creature. Snorting, the donkey-golem turned around and clambered up into the dark.

When Sully climbed in his raft, he said, "Our things will be waiting for us back at the bookstore."

"Is everyone ready?" Elliot said, taking the front position. "Then let us begin."

Pushing off the shore, Roni had the urge to point out that they had begun days ago, but instead, she used an orange, plastic paddle to help guide them along the river. Unlike hiking through the caverns, traveling upon the water filled the air with constant sounds. The simplest babble of water over stone echoed and amplified. Paddle strokes and subtle splashes became long-lasting noise. Even the groups' breathing played back upon them.

"Be careful ahead. Duck," Elliot said.

Roni scooted lower in the back of the raft, and a moment later, they passed under a rock bridge that reached close to the water at parts. If she hadn't listened, she would have cracked her head against the stone. The current picked up as they curved off to the right. The next section opened wider, and to Roni's surprise, there were numerous chained books to be found.

"How did these get here? I mean, do you guys regularly use rafts to find places to chain these books?"

From behind, Gram said, "Not our doing. Possibly not even our Society. Don't forget that the odds favor there being other Societies from other universes." She gestured with her oar. "You can see some pathways going off, so this river isn't the only way to get in here."

Something in the air above squeaked. Roni popped on her flashlight and caught a glimpse of a bat-like creature flapping its way from one stalactite to another. Once it came to rest, it stretched out its wings — all four of them.

"I guess you can't really catch those relics," Roni said.

Sully chuckled. "You'd be surprised what we can accomplish."

"Should we stop, then, and take care of those things?"

"Oh, so now you want to throw relics into books?"

"I only want to do our job. And I doubt those creatures want to end up like the dead ones we saw yesterday."

"No," Elliot said. "We must keep going. Relics like those have their own fates to follow."

Gram said, "C'mon, Roni. You're the one keeping the journal. Make a note, and we'll come back someday to take care of it. There's only so many problems we can handle at once."

Roni agreed — partially because she understood how difficult it would be to catch flying creatures so far above them, partially because she knew Elliot needed to keep on track, and partially because by the time they had finished chatting about it, the river had already pushed them towards a new section of the caverns. Roni noticed the current had strengthened, and Elliot concentrated on steering. They bumped hard against something — a rock, most likely — and Elliot shoved them off to the right. The noise level increased, too. The constant echo doubled, then tripled, then quadrupled the river's growing rage.

"Left! Left!" Elliot bellowed over his shoulder.

Roni tried to paddle the way he wanted, but the raft heaved upward and splashed down like hitting cold steel. The jolt sent electric sparks up her spine. Her fingers clenched involuntarily, and for two seconds, she could not get her body to follow her commands.

"Your other left!" Elliot said, not having time to look back.

They smacked into an outcrop of stones. The hit spun them until they were facing Gram and Sully while zipping backwards down the river. Sully's flashlight jittered across their faces, and Roni saw how ghost pale they both looked. Water flooded over the edges of the raft, soaking her as she fought the current to turn them around — she needed to get them going in the right direction, and she didn't want to see Gram's fear any longer than necessary.

The bottom dropped out from under her. One moment, she dug her paddle into the water, and the next, the water disappeared and they fell. Only a few feet, but her stomach rose straight up her throat. This time, she had the luck to raise her body before slamming into the water. Though this saved her from another spine-wrenching jolt, the action also left her unbalanced. Her body fell sideways, folding over the edge of the raft. As she raised her head to get back, she saw the cavern wall — right before it smacked her in the forehead.

Bright lights flashed before her eyes as the pain radiated across her face, down her back, and through her legs. The metallic taste of blood wet her mouth, and the side of her tongue throbbed. Something grabbed hold of her and yanked her back into the raft. She gazed upward. The dark image of Elliot with the darkness of the cavern behind him tilted as he looked upon her.

"Are you okay?" he asked.

She had no idea how many times he asked the question, but her head finally cleared enough for her to nod. "I will be," she said, reaching for her plastic oar. "Get back up front. We need to watch where —"

The front of the raft flew upward as if it skied along a ramp. Elliot tumbled onto Roni as a loud pop burst out followed by the hissing of air leaking from their raft.

"Quickly," Elliot said as he scrambled toward the front. He wrapped the head of the raft in his arms, hugging it tightly as he attempted to slow the loss of air. "Grab what you can. Toss it to Sully."

Roni threw her backpack onto her shoulders and picked up a box of food. She looked back, but didn't see Gram and Sully. The floor of the raft dipped deeper into the river and the fast-moving waters pooled in.

"It is of no use," Elliot said, letting the front go. He gathered two boxes, one on each shoulder, stuck his cane under one arm, and hopped into the water. It went up to his chest, but he managed to hold his ground.

Roni had no choice but to follow. Her head only came up to his chest under normal conditions, so she held her breath as she jumped in. The box broke free from her grasp as if a giant tore it away. Water rushed up her nose. Sputtering, she thrust her hands outward and attempt to spin around so that she floated on her back with her feet leading the way.

Too dark to see anybody, too noisy to hear anything clearly, she rode the river until the current eased off. When the waters no longer threatened to pulverize her against the rocks, she rolled over and swam to the shore. Coughing, she crawled out. Then the cool air sent shivers across her skin.

"Elliot?" she gasped. "Gram?" From her water-logged backpack, she pulled out a penlight and flashed it upriver. "Sully?"

"Over here," a voice called out — Gram!

The Old Gang paddled to the shore with Elliot hanging on the side. They all climbed out and flopped onto the gravel edge.

"Well," Sully said, "that definitely didn't go well. Remind me, no whitewater rafting with you lot."

Gram chuckled. "We still have the one raft. That's good."

"And we lost half of our supplies — including my change of clothes, I might add."

"Complain all you want once we get back on the water. Come on. Help me with Roni. She's been through a lot."

Roni waved them off. "I'm fine. Soaked, but fine. Just give me a few minutes."

"We can't stay here."

Gram's odd tone sent a different shiver across Roni's skin. Sully reached toward Elliot to help him reorganize the raft. As they made room for all four, Roni used her penlight to scan the cavern. She didn't smell or hear anything irregular, but her skin continued prickling long after it should have eased back.

"Is something out there?" she whispered.

A pale red light formed on the cavern walls. Roni snapped off her penlight as the red grew brighter. The walls themselves appeared to thin — as if they were flesh with lights behind the skin. Chained books swung from these skin walls and a deep rumbling rose on the air. Roni and Gram hustled to help with the raft, and in less than a minute they were ready.

As they pushed off, Roni caught sight of several chains without books. Gram noticed it, too. She then pointed near where they had stopped. Holes big enough to fit a kid's plastic pool dotted the ground. In the distance, Roni saw a shadowy form stretching up towards the ceiling. She swore it moved, and she wondered if those holes in the ground had been made by the shadow's feet. What kind of creature could make such a mark?

Shaking off the winding path her mind had taken her, she looked again. Yes, there was a shadow, but it did not move. Perhaps no more than a flicker of light, but it was no creature. It couldn't have been.

Sully paddled in the back while Elliot steered up front. Moments later, the river curved off and the horrid sight disappeared behind them.

Roni stared at the dying red embers in the distance. "Will one of you explain that to me?"

Digging a blanket out of their meager supplies and handing it to Roni, Gram said, "That was another universe. From the looks of it, not a place I'd like to visit."

"Are you serious?"

Keeping his focus forward, Elliot said, "Do you really think this is a time we would choose to joke with you?"

"I meant that ... well, I don't know. How could that have been a separate universe?"

"We do not know how any of this cavern works exactly, but from what I have read and seen, I believe this river acts as a conduit between caverns. In other words, the caverns that hold the books are not all one endless structure but rather, it is a connection of structures spread over many universes. The river is one method of traveling between them."

"You're saying we're not in our own universe anymore?"

Sully said, "Our cavern isn't even in our universe. I thought you knew that already."

"I did. I do. I just — this is a bit much to take in." Her body wobbled, and Gram held her to make sure she didn't flop backward into the river. "So, we saw part of a universe in that section of cave, and we're now in another universe? And this whole cavern system is several universes?"

Sully grinned. "See that? You're smart, after all."

Gram said, "It's another reason we don't worry about

contaminating the caverns too much. They are a mixture of universes by their very nature. Though it's still good practice to keep our end of things as clean as possible."

Holding the blanket on her shoulders a bit closer, Roni said, "How do you know all this? From what I saw in the Grand Library, none of you have spent much time down there."

"We did when we were younger, back when we had a librarian. And as far as we know, well, it's what's written in the books. I've often thought that much of it all is educated guesswork."

Elliot added, "There have been some attempts at using the scientific method to test out our ideas. While nothing conclusive has been determined, this is the best explanation we have so far."

"Best thing is to remember that the caverns are dangerous on more levels than we even know. Don't explore it lightly."

Roni looked up at Elliot. He knew how difficult this journey could become, yet he not only offered to help Roni, but he encouraged her. She opened her mouth to ask him directly or to point out this fact, but then her mouth closed. Elliot had turned back with a broad smile.

"We have arrived," he said.

CHAPTER 12

Rock walls spread out in all directions to form an enormous cave too far across to see the end. The river let into a lake that filled most of the cavern space. Large enough to create real waves, the lake must have been several miles wide. Oddly, the air felt warmer and smelled salty.

Elliot whooped — a strange sound to hear coming from him. "We made it. I do not think I ever truly believed I would see this place again. But we made it."

As the water pushed them closer to one wall, Roni noticed ledges with stairs running alongside. A few of these stony paths led to openings, but she could only see darkness inside the passageways — if that was what they were. The echoes of the cave had changed from the rest of the caverns. Perhaps because of its size, their voices echoed less, the sounds dying off quicker. Perhaps not — Roni did not know auditory physics. She only knew for certain that the quality of sound had altered.

Something else bothered her. She could not pinpoint her discomfort until Sully said, "Where are all the books?"

Not a single book had been placed on the walls. These books, however, had not been ripped down by unseen hands. They simply never existed in the first place. No chains hung from above, no marks in the walls, no shelves — nothing to indicate that a book to another universe had ever been there.

Roni thought about something she had read in Waterfield's journal. Some books, some universes, were more powerful than others. Some required more chains. Some had to be buried in stone. But the Book on the Isle had to be alone.

"This whole cave," Roni said, "and the lake and all of it — this is to contain only the one book. It's a prison."

"No, dear," Gram said. "It is an oasis."

"Over there," Elliot said, pointing toward the center of the lake. "Everybody, please help."

Sully dug out two extra paddles and handed them over. Roni leaned across the right side of the inflated raft while Gram took the left. With all four digging into the water, they moved exactly where Elliot indicated. Despite the extra muscle and the increase in speed, they still traveled for a half-hour before Roni saw it — the Isle.

More like a glorified sand dune — at least, it appeared so in the dim light produced from their flashlights and two shafts of daylight ricocheting in from parts unknown. The closer they came, the less she saw on the isle. From afar, she thought she saw brush, maybe a tree, but with every paddle stroke, Roni realized the isle truly lacked all but sand.

And a pedestal.

When they hit the shore, Elliot swung his legs over the front of the raft. Roni got out to help him bring the raft up into the sand. As Sully and Gram worked their way over the sides, Roni followed Elliot inland for several feet.

There, toppled like a fallen tree, the remnants of a stone pedestal lay. The sand surrounding the stones had been disturbed, too. But they weren't footprints — not human ones anyway. In fact, the more Roni inspected the area, the more her stomach churned. The prints were holes in the ground. Not as large as a kid's plastic pool, but similar in shape and depth.

"It is here," Elliot said as Gram approached. He stood a foot from the top end of the pedestal. Pointing to a chained book, he said, "This is it."

Roni gestured to the marks in the sand. "Something found your oasis."

Gram patted her cross as she stared at the prints. She then gave a short nod. Roni fought hard to keep her face still. She tamped down any excitement rising from the mere idea that Gram would acknowledge something she said as valuable — especially because that excitement bothered her. She didn't want to care what Gram thought. She couldn't. Not when she had to be on her own.

Sully arrived and set right the pedestal's stone base. In order to keep her cool, Roni launched into helping. Gram picked up the book and looked it over. As Roni handed stones to Sully, she heard Gram and

Elliot talking.

"I don't think you should do this," Gram said.

"You know I must. Why come all the way out here if we are not going to open the book?"

"That was before we saw the conditions of this place."

"So what if the book was knocked over? Anything could have flown in here and done it by accident."

"You don't believe that. And even if you somehow convince yourself of it, Lord knows I don't believe it. I'm not sure I can condone the risks you're going to take."

Elliot pecked at the sand with his cane. "I find it amusing that you speak as if you have a say in the matter."

"I'm still the leader of this team." Gram stepped in front of Elliot and spoke in a harsh whisper that Roni and Sully could hear even easier than the previous conversation. "We are here because of Roni, not you. All of your issues with this place are a side matter that I am happy to see you address, but that is not the mission."

"Not for you."

"Elliot, please don't do this. Don't start making poor decisions because you feel guilty."

"It was my poor decision that cost me —"

"I know that. But you are not alone here. This isn't all on your shoulders, and it isn't about you. Sully is here. I'm here. You care about us, right? And most importantly, Roni is here. I know you care about her. Are you willing to put her at risk just so you can feel better about something so far in the past that you're not even that man anymore?"

Elliot puffed his chest and gazed over Gram's head. "I do not expect you to understand, but I must do this. Roni has her own mission, one that I can help her with, but even if she decides against, I will still go."

Brushing sand from her hands as she stood, Roni presumed a dark cloud would form over her head when she said, "Go where?"

Gram turned around with such shock on her face that Roni stepped back. Elliot also looked at her like she had mushrooms growing out of her nose. With the top of his cane, he bumped the book in Gram's arms and said, "In there, of course. We go into the book."

Chapter 13

If Roni had eaten anything substantial in the last day, she would have thrown it up twice over. She paced the sandy isle while Elliot sat near the pedestal. With his eyes closed, he meditated. During the entire trip, she had assumed she would reach into the book with one hand, grab the kyolo stones, and that would be it. Never did she think they would physically enter the books. Why didn't anybody tell her? She wanted to shake Elliot, yell at him, get him to smile or get some words of confidence from him, hit him, hug him, anything to shock the energy out of her system. She paced faster.

During these minutes, Gram and Sully conferred near the raft. Roni's attention volleyed between them and Elliot and the book. It had a tattered cover of red and black circles. Two holes remained from where the original chains had kept it bound to the pedestal.

Roni could picture the thing opening. The horrors she had seen when gazing through a book flashed in her mind. Yes, she knew that Waterfield's journal described it as a paradise. And yes, Elliot would not be jumping into a book that led to a nightmare. But those points of reason did little to assuage her growing unease.

"We're ready," Sully said as he walked towards the pedestal.

Elliot snapped awake and jumped to his feet. He gave a slight bow toward Sully, then Gram, then Roni. "I thank you all for helping me in this endeavor." Before Gram could speak, he raised his hand. "I know you believe that you are doing this not for me but for the Society. Perhaps that is true. Perhaps you are, and I am being naive. But I thank you anyway."

Gram flicked her wrist and a chain fell from her sleeve. And it continued to fall. The non-stop ringing of metal on metal as it piled at her feet sounded like coins dropping from a slot machine. When it finally finished, she handed the end to Sully. He wrapped it around himself and used the teeth-like clamp on the end to secure it. Elliot pulled out the other end of the chain and offered it to Roni.

The cold metal weighed more than she anticipated. Gram must be worried about the strain. Roni refrained from making any comment — she didn't need the Old Gang knowing her fearful thoughts, and any word from her might betray the shaking in her legs. As she locked the chain around her waist, she could hear it jangling in her hands. To hide the sound, she asked Elliot, "What about you?"

Gram released another chain. This one, though equally thick, was much shorter. She handed one end to Elliot, and as he secured it, she clamped the other end to Roni's chain. "You two will have to take care of each other."

Sully shoved one foot into the sand, then the other. He closed his eyes, mouthed a few words, then leaned back slightly. Roni knew he could summon the strength of a golem to root himself to the ground, but she had no clue how long it would last.

As Gram settled the book upon the pedestal, Elliot nudged Roni's arm with his cane. "Time for us to go."

They walked towards the pedestal, and Roni's throat tightened. She wiped her palms against her sides. Brushing the chain, she felt its weight tugging behind.

"Listen close," Gram said. Her voice took on the same tone she used years ago when laying down the rules for a sleepover. Only with this, if Roni broke a rule, serious consequences would follow — not a grounding or a loss of television privileges, but injury or death. "You are to tug on the chain three times every five minutes to let us know you're okay. If you fail to do so, we will yank you right back here and that'll be it. No going back in."

"Hold on," Roni said. "Do you mean tug on it three times in a row at the end of five minutes or three times throughout a five minute period?"

"I mean three times in five minutes. What's so hard to understand?"

"I don't want you pulling us back if we're not ready."

Sully forced out a laugh. "Okay, you two, keep this simple. Three times in a row roughly every five minutes. Clear enough?"

"Thank you," Roni said.

Gram shot a harsh glare at Sully before continuing. "If you run into trouble, just keeping tugging over and over as fast as possible. Is that clear enough? It will be to us. Roni, you get in there, grab your kyolo stones, and wait for Elliot. The less you interact, the safer for you and for that universe. Elliot, do what you must but don't you dare put Roni at risk."

"I would never put her at risk."

"You already have by bringing her here."

"I am only going to talk with them. Nothing more. There is no risk to be had."

"Nonetheless, you know what to do if you have to."

Elliot nodded. "Of course."

"Good luck," Gram said and rested her hands on the book. She gripped it tight. Roni got the distinct impression that Gram considered throwing the book into the lake. But her shoulders dropped with a sigh. "Good luck," she whispered and opened the book.

Roni flinched, but all remained still. Nothing but quiet. A thick mist rolled over the edges of the book, and with it a strong smell of thyme.

Reading the confusion on her face, Elliot said, "Not all universes depressurize when a book is opened. Some are close enough to our world — or in this case, to the world of this cave. It is no more than opening a door."

"So, we can walk in and out without any trouble?"

"Exactly."

Putting words in action, Elliot stepped toward the book. Roni did not wait for the chain to pull her along. She hurried up to Elliot's side and clasped his hand. His excitement vibrated in his fingers, and the corners of her mouth lifted. Several stones had been piled into a small step. Together, they climbed up.

Though the book looked about the width of a library dictionary, Roni could not see how they would fit in. But when Elliot placed his left leg inside, the rest of him smeared as if his image flickered on ruined film. He didn't scream or show any sign of pain. The colors of him ran together and poured into the book.

Roni followed — had no choice with the chain connecting them — and to her shock, she felt nothing. Despite the bizarre picture she had seen, experiencing the effect caused no sensation at all. She simply walked into the book.

She did her best to hold back any expectations, yet her mind kept thinking, *this isn't what I expected.* They had entered the center of the town Waterfield described so vividly. The fountain, the trees, the buildings — all of it stood before her.

Except all of it had died.

The town lay in ruin. The colors of paradise had vanished. An overcast sky lent a gray filter over the place, muting the air with its somber pall. Bare trees and crumbling buildings abound, each one forming its shape through a thin veneer of gray fog like shadow puppets. A chill wind picked up dead leaves and spread them across the chapped ground like a careless vagrant. Even the once beautiful fountain had been toppled over, and the stagnant water in its basin smelled foul.

Elliot let go of Roni's hand as he walked further. She looked in the windows and down a few alleys, but she did not see signs of people. Not even a sound. Only the clinking of their chain.

She glanced back to see the chain stretching right into a ragged opening in the air as if a child had cut out part of the world with dull scissors. Inside the opening, Roni could see the forms of Gram and Sully but as if viewing them through gauze.

Turning back, she walked further into the town. One house, its front door hanging askew, caught Roni's attention — it looked official with two pillars out front and papers attached to a board standing to the side. Symbols on the papers did not match any language she knew. As Elliot came up behind, he pointed to one paper with the writing in large, bold script.

"It is a command to evacuate the town," he said.

"You can read it?"

"I spent a long time here once." He rubbed his eyes and sniffled. "I learned the language."

"Does it say why they had to evacuate? Where they went? Do they give anything to say what happened here?"

"No. And it would not. The people of this world would simply gather their things and start walking until they reached another town."

"And the other town would take them in?"

Elliot's voice cracked. "They were good like that." His legs wobbled and he lowered to the base of the nearest pillar. With his head in his hands, he tears flooded and his shoulders shook.

Roni stood next to him. While she waited, she gazed at the ghost town. In particular, she looked at the dusty ground. Stones of various shapes and sizes littered the area. Which ones were kyolo stones?

After several minutes, Elliot showed no sign of calming down. Roni rubbed her hand along the back of his shoulders. "It'll be okay," she said. "I'm sure they followed the evacuation order."

"I doubt it." He dabbed at his eyes, his voice shaking, and he forced a long inhalation. "I said that the people of this world would pack up and go, but not the people of this town. They were different. They put their souls into making this place as perfect as they could. I don't see how any of them would leave."

"Something bad must've been coming. A plague, maybe, or a terrible storm."

"They would have stayed. They would have faced whatever calamity came their way." Using his cane, he stood. "Do you understand? They stayed, and they stood their ground."

Roni's eyes widened. "And they lost."

"Yes."

"The whole town?"

"It appears so."

"I'm so sorry," she said. She lifted the end of the chain and yanked three times on it — that would appease Gram for five minutes. "What do these kyolo stones look like? I was told they're everywhere."

Elliot paused with a disapproving glare.

"What?" she said. "I came here to fulfill a mission."

"And you found something else. We cannot ignore the tragedy that happened here."

"I'm not suggesting we do. But we should grab the stones we need first. That's our main reason for being in this place."

"Only for you. And you know that to be the case. You know that I came for other reasons, yet you never once bothered to ask me why I want to be here."

Roni's face flushed. "I was being respectful of your privacy."

"You did not want to burden yourself with the concerns of others. You think I do not see what you have become this last year? Sully and I have ears. We have eyes. You think that we did not notice how all of our breakfasts helped you avoid your grandmother? After all, when you and Gram fight in the bookstore, we know it."

Trying to hold back her desire to scream at him, to tell him that she had spoken the truth, that she respected him and that it hurt to think he doubted her sincerity, she gritted her teeth. Because no matter how much truth she spoke, he also spoke the truth. Attempting a calmer tone, she said, "We're here now, and we're alone. Please, tell me what happened."

Elliot leaned on his cane and squinted into the fog. "Do you remember my wife at all?"

"Of course. I loved Auntie Janwan." An image flashed in Roni's mind — Auntie Janwan standing in a kitchen, her body firm and strong, her dark skin glistening with the summer heat. She was baking cookies and she coated the whole house in a sweet, lovely aroma. "She made the best lemon snaps."

Rubbing his belly, he said, "I must have lost twenty pounds after she died."

"It was cancer, right?"

Elliot kicked at the ground. He eyed her as if she had said something profound. "Pancreatic cancer — that was the story we told everybody, but not the entire truth. The real reason she died was because she was a living relic in our world."

Roni glanced at the town buildings. "Auntie Janwan came from here?"

"Oh, yes. This land and our world are closely compatible, but it turns out, that after decades of exposure, her system finally overloaded and shut down."

"Another lie." Her face scrunched as she held back her tears. "She was one of the few memories I could trust, and now you're telling me it was all a lie."

Elliot's hand snapped out fast, smacking Roni upside the head. "Do not ever call my wife *a lie*. She was one of the most beautiful creatures in any world — inside and out. And she loved you. Are you still so childish that you cannot understand the need to perpetuate an untruth when we must protect the secrets of the Parallel Society?"

"Of course not. I'm sorry. It was just a gut reaction. I didn't mean it like it came out."

"Pay attention and maybe you will learn." Rolling his shoulders, he pressed more onto his cane as if he needed it to help him hold the weight of his memory. "When I was thirty-four — which seems like lifetimes ago — back then, I was impulsive and a bit reckless. I had yet to learn more than a few simple tricks I could perform and a few general healing principles, but I thought I had harnessed the greatest forces of the universe. I had not been with the Society long, yet each day brought such wonder and excitement that I grew impatient to learn more. And of course, like you, I was kept away from all the action that I was sure went on without me. Gram had me taking care of the bookstore's ledgers while I also helped keep guard over her office and Sully's workshop. You can imagine how I felt about bookkeeping and guard duty.

"I complained to your grandmother once. After she lectured me for an hour, she showed me the Grand Library. We had a librarian back then — Lydia Schuck — and I was permitted to check out one book at a time. A few months in and I discovered Gerald Waterfield's journal. His descriptions of this paradise world would not leave my mind. Our world was no Utopia, especially for a black man, yet in this journal I read of a world that sounded unreal to me. Unreal and wonderful."

"Yet you went, so part of you must've believed it was real."

"Certainly. According to Gram, no book that makes it into the Grand Library can contain lies. So, I began stocking supplies and a year later, I was ready. My night finally arrived, and I waited for Sully and Gram to go to sleep. Then I snuck into the caverns and used Waterfield's maps to find my way here. When I entered the book, I saw a paradise that made Waterfield's descriptions no more than a braggart's poor rendition of another man's achievements. I could describe this place for months, and still, I would not adequately convey to you the incredible, unimpeachable beauty this world possessed."

Elliot shuffled several steps over. "That fountain was the heart of the town, pumping life into every moment. Its waters could heal people, and it radiated an energy that people craved. An energy of love and kindness. Every town in this world has such a fountain, and as a result, they did not have wars or power grabs or oppressive regimes."

Roni could see that Elliot had become lost in a memory, but she also had an uneasy sensation crawling along her arms — as if someone spied on them. She wanted to get her kyolo stones and leave. "Is that when you met Janwan?"

"Right over there. Next to the fountain. She was with some of her friends, laughing and smiling, and I was taken. I ended up spending the next year here — falling in love and earning her love."

The air around them shifted, and Roni's nerves spiked. She heard something. An animal, perhaps, only it sounded unlike any animal she knew — a throaty breath like a stallion forcing air through its nose followed by a series of clicks.

As she scanned the gray surfaces surrounding them, she said, "Please tell me you know what that was."

Elliot gripped his cane in both hands like a warrior's staff. "I have never heard that sound before."

"We should go."

"Not until we learn what happened here."

Again that horrible combination of breath and clicks.

Roni edged towards the opening that led back to Gram. But if she jumped back in there, Elliot would be left alone. She edge closer to Elliot. But if she stayed, she had no special powers to help him. She would be in the way.

"Please," she said. "We have to go. If you must come back, we can regroup and come in with some sort of plan."

Strong legs thumped against the ground in the distance — a lot of strong legs. Elliot stepped forward, towards the fountain, towards the sound.

Roni grabbed the chain connected to him and yanked him back a step. "You can't go that way. It's my life you're risking, too. Now, help me pick up a few kyolo stones, and then we're leaving."

"We have to know what happened."

"Whatever's out there making that sound, that's what happened."

Elliot's eyes closed as he offered a single, gentle nod. "You are right. You need the kyolo stones. They are smooth and crimson." He smiled at a memory. "They always make me think of gumdrops."

"Where do we find them?"

"Probably at your feet."

Roni gazed down. Numerous stones covered the ground. But all were gray. She bent down and touched one smooth looking stone — gray dust bunched into a small pile as her finger pushed it aside. Underneath, she saw the dark red coloring. Snatching it up, she held it between her thumb and forefinger. "Is this one?"

"Yes," Elliot said. "That is exactly what you seek."

Sweeping her hand in a wide arc across the ground, she discovered over a dozen kyolo stones mixed in with pebbles, rocks, and a few stones of varying colors. She picked out seven kyolo stones and placed them in a small pouch that tied to her belt loop. Her body relaxed slightly — she had succeeded. When they got back to the bookstore, she would contact Kenneth Bay, deliver the stones, and find out how to use them to recover her Lost Time. It had been a difficult trek, but feeling the stones bumping against her thigh made it worthwhile.

Standing, she said, "Okay, let's go back and ..."

Elliot walked away from her — his end of the chain unclipped and dragging behind him like a metallic tail.

"Sonuvabitch," she muttered. Grabbing the chain around her waist, she yanked on it three times. Then she unclipped it, letting it clatter on the ground. Five minutes. She could get him back before then. Even if she had to knock him in the head to do it.

With fists clenched, she followed him down a street lined with cracked lamps. He halted in front of a fallen tree blocking his way. The top of it had smashed through the window of a two-story home. When he turned around and spied her, he scowled.

"You have your stones. Go back to Gram and Sully."

"I'm not leaving you here."

"You can all come back for me in a few days. I will be fine."

Answering his statement, the deep breath and the rapid clicks. Roni marched down the street with her hand extended. "Don't mess around. Come on. Time to go."

"You are not my mother."

"I'll be a police officer in a second if you don't get moving. I'll bend your arm behind your back and break it, if you make me."

Elliot raised his cane. "Do you really think you have the ability to stop me? Go back to Gram. She knows the rest of my story. She will know what to do for me."

Roni stopped in the middle of the street. Elliot was right, of course — she could not follow through on her threat. She had no special powers. Elliot would never hurt her, but if he was determined to stay in this universe — and clearly, he was — then she could not stop him.

"Please," she said, throwing on a puppy dog look that had always melted his heart when she was a child. "I need you."

"Nothing bad is going to happen to me. I promise I will return. In fact, when I get back, I will explain to you why ..."

His voice trailed off as his gaze lifted from her face to something behind her. Her muscles locked and her pulse quickened. She could feel its presence looming over her. The fear registered on Elliot's face which caused Roni's stomach to knot. And then she heard it — the throaty breath and the hard clicks.

CHAPTER 14

Roni turned around like a windup toy running low on power. Her arms hung out but they barely moved. Her fingers had locked spread apart. Her eyes refused to blink.

The creature clung sideways to a lamppost. About the size of Roni's torso, it looked like a late day shadow — grayish-black with a soft, uneven outline. It had numerous legs, at least six, but such details were difficult to discern. The creature looked out-of-focus. She could see the way its body segmented like an insect, the way the lower-body had more hair, the way the upper-body looked hard like a carapace, the way its head combined both hair and shell. And its eyes — beads of red shimmering behind the filter that surrounded the creature.

Roni knew exactly what she looked at. The legs, the black hair, the shape of its lower- and upper-body, the demon-like eyes — it all added up to one horrendous name.

Hellspider.

"Walk to me," Elliot said, barely above a whisper. "Slowly."

Roni moved her left foot back, and the hellspider opened its mouth, bared its needle-teeth, and growl-hissed at her. She did not move the right.

"It is okay," Elliot said.

She could hear him moving his arms and pictured him holding his cane up as he prescribed a spell through the air. But a new sound broke her growing hope. Off to the left, a second hellspider clattered over a pile of brick rubble. Another set of clicks announced the arrival of a third hellspider. This one maneuvered along a wall until it looked down from the second floor.

"Elliot? Are you ready yet?" she said.

"I am trying, but I need more time."

"We don't have it." With hellspiders on three sides and a fallen tree behind them, they were pinned. Roni guessed that the creatures had not attacked yet only because they were not sure what to make of Elliot's hand motions. But that caution would not last long. "Forget the spell right now. We've got to get somewhere safe."

The first hellspider once more growl-hissed. The other two launched towards Roni. Without thought, she dropped to the ground. Not a good move. The two hellspiders fell upon her. Every part of her body ignited as the creatures pummeled her with their legs.

But it only lasted seconds.

She heard Elliot grunting, and looking upward, she saw that one hellspider had been thrown back into the rubble pile. Elliot smashed the end of his cane into the second creature.

"Stand," he said.

Roni clambered to her feet as the lead hellspider lowered from the lamppost. Elliot grabbed Roni's hand and guided her toward the nearest doorway — a house on their right. The hellspiders rushed behind their leader, and all three approached. But they did not attack. Cocking their heads, their eyes followed Elliot's cane as he waved it left and right.

Edging toward the door, he said, "When we get inside, run for the back exit. And pray there is one."

Roni opened the door and inched into the entrance. She moved aside and watched as Elliot cleared the jamb. Not waiting for his command, she slammed the door shut. Through small windows at the side, Roni saw the hellspiders jump at the loud bang of the door. She raced down the hallway, following Elliot through a kitchen and toward the back door. They hurtled over a few wooden stairs, crossed a backyard, down an alley, and emerged on another town street.

Waving with one hand, Elliot said, "This way."

Roni hurried to catch up. They jogged across the street and up several blocks. At each corner, Elliot peeked around the edge before leading them further along. When they reached a building that poked outward into the street like an overstuffed belly, Elliot stopped. He touched the building at a spot near his knee, and a round door slid aside.

"Go in," he said.

Roni ducked as she entered. Once inside, Elliot sealed the door with the touch of another unseen button. They were in a store — Roni could tell that much — but the grime-covered windows let only dim light through. A stench of rot permeated the air.

"Into the back," he said.

She kept close as he led the way through an aisle of boxed goods — smiling faces on brightly colored cardboard, each mouth ready to devour bowls of food. Crossing to another aisle, she saw open tables with mounds of rotted and molding fruits. At least, she thought they were fruits. The label did not matter. She had seen enough to confirm they were in a grocery.

When they reached the back of the building, Elliot pressed himself into a corner. "I will get us out of here safely, but you must make sure I have time to do so. Can you do that?"

"I don't really have a choice."

"Not if you want to live."

In his right hand, Elliot held his cane at a slight angle. With his left, he traced a complicated pattern in the air. Roni could not follow all the movements, but the sharp downward motion that began it repeated several times. She wanted to ask him how long he needed, but she also knew better than to interrupt — doing so would only require him to start over.

Guess I'll defend him until this works. Or I die. One or the other.

She needed a weapon. Rushing along the back of the store, she glanced up each aisle. At the end, she discovered the source of the horrible stench — the corpse of a rotund person, half their belly excavated by bugs and animals. A shelf had collapsed, much of it leaning on the body, pushing more of its foulness into the air. But on the far side of the mottle-skinned form, she saw something that made her want to scream in frustration — a metal pole. A weapon. Sticking out from the darkness beneath the shelves.

She looked back at Elliot. Maybe she could find a knife or something equally sharp. No. She wouldn't last ten seconds fighting hellspiders with a knife. But that pole would give her distance.

Gripping the shelf, she tried to lift it. No luck. It had been bent and wedged in where it fell. She tried to think of another way to move it, but she had to assume the hellspiders would be upon them any moment. No time to be squeamish.

She rolled her lips into her clamped mouth and held her breath. Squatting next to the body, she cringed as she reached over the decomposing flesh. Her finger graced the edge of the pole, but she could not snag it.

"Shit." She got on her knees, swallowed down the urge to vomit, and pressed against the corpse until she could grab the pole. With the metal in her hands, she shot back away and stumbled into a display of crunchy food in burlap-type sacks.

The reek wafted over with her, but at least she had the pole. About three feet long, it must have been used to keep the shelf up. Long enough to give her some room to fight. It didn't weigh much, but banging it on the floor showed her it could take a few hits and not bend.

She rushed back to Elliot. Though his eyes had closed, he continued motioning through the air around his cane — never once accidentally bumping it. When she was a teenager, she once walked into his apartment while he meditated. He took no notice of her, so she stood in the doorway and watched him for a while. The serene look on his face at that time left her feeling the same — calm and at peace.

Sitting in the back of a grocery, Elliot displayed none of that ease. His brow wrinkled as he concentrated, and his motions lacked all the peaceful grace that teenage girl once saw. Elliot was worried and trying hard to finish before the hellspiders arrived.

But he could not rush those hands or the results. Planting the end of the pole down, Roni stood a few feet in front of him, and she waited. *I am the last line of defense.*

More accurately, she was the only line of defense.

A loud whine of metal from the front reverberated throughout the store. She gripped the pole in both hands and crouched in a stance she hoped would be good for fighting. Three bangs followed, and the door careened into the store, smashing through several shelves of glass items. They shattered, riddling the floor with tiny shards that tinkled like a chandelier.

Then Roni heard it. Deep, throaty breath. Rapid clicks.

In the dim light, she found it difficult to make out the details of the far aisles. She had to assume that at least one hellspider would come from there — thought she could hear it, too. She caught sight of another as it vaulted atop the shelves and gazed down at her. And the third?

She heard it charge from her left side. She had thought she could see that side fine, but what she mistook for a shadow now moved like a stampeding bull. Jumping back, she swung the pole and clocked the hellspider in the side of the head — all luck, but it worked. The hellspider slid across the floor and smacked against the wall. Though still conscious, it wobbled as it struggled to stand again.

The other two growl-hissed as they took the offensive. Roni whirled back, letting the pole take the lead. The hellspider from above dodged her attack and regrouped at her left flank. Watching it carefully, she heard the other one too late. From out of the dark, it launched towards her. Two shadowy legs bashed against her — one connecting with her hip, the other knocking her in the head.

She dropped to the floor. The metal pole clanged and rolled away. Rubbing her temple, she tried to sit up, but another shadowy limb slammed into her side. She fell to the floor.

From her back, she lifted her head. All three hellspiders closed in. They opened their greedy mouths. Saliva dribbled off their teeth. They were hungry.

Roni thought of the corpse on the other side of the store. These things had eaten everyone — or at least, the parts they wanted. Roni and Elliot were warm, fresh meat.

The lead hellspider reared back on four legs and jumped into the air. Roni thrust her arm up as if she could stop the attack. To her shock, the hellspider froze in the air. It hovered above her, wiggling its legs without effect. Then it slid in an arc downward to the ground as if stuck on the outside of a glass dome.

A dome?

She looked behind her. Elliot stood with his cane held high above his head and his left hand glowing pale red. His arms shook with effort and his face betrayed the deep concentration he exerted. Roni had a million questions flooding her mind, but survival instincts kicked in.

She jumped to her feet. "Can we leave now?"

Elliot walked forward, and Roni stayed close by his side. As they moved, the invisible dome moved with them, pushing the hellspiders back. Growl-hissing erupted from the three creatures, but they retreated each time Elliot stepped ahead. Though slow-going, Roni moved at Elliot's pace.

Proceeding up one aisle, the field around them shoved boxes aside. Even the shelving bowed away from them. When they reached the exit — now a ragged hole where the entranceway had been — Elliot turned back to face the hellspiders. Two of the creatures shot forward and rammed the dome. They only succeeded in bruising their heads.

"Outside," Elliot said, his voice strained.

Roni obeyed. When she stepped onto the sidewalk, she felt a warm tingling as she walked through the dome. Looking back, Elliot had one foot on the wall and the other in the store. Easing backwards, he ducked. His hands stretched forward, and the tip of his cane still worked inside the store.

"Be ready," he said.

Ready for what?

Motioning a different pattern in the air, Elliot scurried backwards in her direction. His hand still glowed, but the light dimmed. As he came near her, the hellspiders made more noise before crawling through to the sidewalk.

Roni finally saw it all — like an open umbrella the dome would not fit through the opening in the wall. Elliot had to get Roni out and then himself before he could contract its area of effectiveness. Now, with the closed dome in his hand, the hellspiders moved freely. They bolted toward Roni, but Elliot had already reached her. He opened his palm, spun his hand in the air, and she heard a sizzle as the dome reformed around them.

But Elliot stumbled into her arms. Sweat soaked his brow. The hellspiders scratched at the dome, growl-hissed at it, and paced around its perimeter. Though they could not find a way in, they seemed to understand that Elliot would not be able to hold the dome forever.

"Come on," Roni said, ducking under the arm that held his cane. "Lean your weight on me, and we'll get back to Gram and Sully."

Limping up the street, Roni guided Elliot toward the opening to the book and the caverns. They had to go around the block. Having seen the difficulty Elliot faced getting them safely out of the store, Roni thought it best to avoid passing through the house again.

The hellspiders never let up their attacks. Either the creatures weren't too bright and thought they could muscle their way through the dome, or they were smarter than expected and they were testing for weakness. Or they were starving.

One other possibility came to mind, and it bothered Roni the most — the hellspiders might be attacking simply to keep the pressure on. To intimidate.

As they turned the corner, all thoughts of hellspiders vanished. Roni stumbled, nearly fell to her knees, as she stared at the empty street. How long had they been? Certainly more than five minutes. But the idea that Gram would truly reel in her chain, that she would close the book, that any part of her could sacrifice her own granddaughter — Roni's mind went numb.

Elliot shoved her as he moved ahead. "Get to the pathway."

"What pathway?"

"The gash floating in the air — our way back through the book."

Of course. The book was still open. Roni could see the opening in the air — the pathway. Hobbling onward, they reached the halfway point in the street, when the pathway shimmered as if behind a clear waterfall.

Her heart jolted. Was that what it looked like when a book closed?

But a figure stepped through. A boxy, stout figure with a large chest and a stern, determined expression — Gram. She had a chain crossing over her front to form an X. It stretched back through the pathway, presumably to Sully. As Gram took in her surroundings, the hellspiders stopped attacking the dome.

Before Roni could think what to do, her instincts kicked into action. She burst through the warm tingle of the dome and sprinted towards Gram. "Go back!"

Gram smiled at her, but the smile faded fast. Roni didn't need to hear the growl-hisses and the thundering of twenty-some feet chasing behind her. Waving for Gram to turn back, she pressed onward.

But Gram did not listen. She released a new chain from her sleeve and spun it over her head like a cowboy preparing to lasso a calf. Her eyes locked just behind Roni.

It might work. If Roni could run straight by Gram, the hellspiders would follow. Gram could strike with her chain, whip it across all three, and hopefully injure them enough for Elliot to make it to the pathway. Yes, Roni could see it all happen as if they had planned it that way all along.

Then Roni tripped.

She hit the ground hard, rocks and dirt finding their way beneath her damp clothes as she tumbled forward. The hellspiders raced by her, but two of them made tight arcs and curved back. The lead hellspider continued after Gram.

Tasting blood on her lips, Roni rolled onto her feet. With one hellspider on either side and no metal pole in hand, she did not see how to get free. From the corner of her eye, she caught sight of Elliot, but he was too far away to rescue her. Gram had a hellspider of her own to contend with.

Roni's right leg shivered. Her left fingers tapped. Her heart raced.

She never saw the signal, yet both hellspiders lunged after her simultaneously. Her fingers curled into fists. She had no expectation of defeating them, not dealing with both at once, but she hoped to get a couple of solid punches in first.

Right before she pulled back her arm to strike, she heard Elliot scream as if far away. Thinking of him falling under those tooth-riddled mouths angered her more. She roared and swung her fist.

But she never had time to connect.

A single pulse of sound erupted like a flash of lightning. A sound thick as clay, sharp as razor. It shook Roni's limbs, shuddered her muscles, jarred her teeth. Though it lasted less than a second, she covered her ears and dropped to her knees. The ground lifted beneath her as she lost all sense of balance. With her cheek pressed into the dirt, she saw that the hellspiders had suffered even worse — one stumbled like a drunk, another lay on its back wriggling, and the third dragged itself using only three legs.

She heard nothing.

All sounds had fallen away. Not even a ringing in her ears. Simply silence.

She rolled onto her back. Gram crawled on all fours. It seemed she tried to get near Roni, but her disorientation had her weaving away as much as towards her granddaughter.

Roni attempted sitting up but only succeeded in flopping onto her side once again. Her new angle gave her a view of Elliot. She had to be hallucinating — Elliot stood firm and unaffected.

He surveyed the scene, dropped to his knees, and dug into the ground. Roni reached out to him — tried to, but her hand fell to the ground. He pulled something from his shirt and buried it. Rubbing his face — *tears?* — he stood. She tried to call him but could not make a sound.

Working hard with his cane, he managed to move closer towards her. Agonizing step after agonizing step. The pain wrinkling his brow, the sweat dripping off his chin, and the blood dribbling from his nose all told Roni that she did not hallucinate. Elliot must have created a hellish force.

She tried to smile — *a hellish force for a hellish spider.*

When he finally reached her, he bent down and clipped the end of his chain to one that Gram had tossed across the ground. Roni could not recall when Gram had done so, but there the chain waited. He then tied an end around her waist and secured it.

"Now, Lillian," he said, though Roni only saw his lips move.

Though Gram still weaved and wobbled, she had enough control to grab onto the chain and tug it repeatedly. Seconds later, the chain reeled into the pathway. In another universe, Sully had to be digging his feet in hard as he pulled all three of his friends back to safety.

Roni had the barest awareness of dragging along the ground. When she slipped out of the book and onto the sand of the Isle, her imbalance helped her a bit — just another disorientation. The change in the way the air smelled, however, woke her senses faster.

Her hearing returned to the level of a muted undersea sound, but it was enough. She heard Gram yelling, "We're through. We're through. Close it."

Sully dropped the chains and hustled over to the book. He snapped the cover shut before a single hellspider could escape.

CHAPTER 15

Roni kept her eyes closed, feeling the cool grains of sand along the back of her neck, beneath her fingers, and under her legs. She wanted to move and not to move. If she kept her eyes closed, she could be at the beach hearing the soft waves under the cool night stars. But she heard Gram to her left sitting up, and to her right, Sully helped Elliot do the same.

"Is everyone okay?" Elliot asked.

Roni heard Gram brushing sand off her clothes as she stood. There would be no reprieve. Roni opened her eyes. "I'm okay. What did you do to us?"

Elliot sat with his bare feet in the sand. While Sully knelt behind him and massaged his temples, Elliot said, "I used the power that I had hoped I never would have to use. I learned of it in one of the old journals in the Grand Library. You see, you are not the only one who ever steps foot in there."

"We've all made use of the Library, too," Gram said as she walked over to the book. With a practiced hand, she created chains and wrapped them around the cover like ribbons around a Christmas present. "I'd still like an answer to Roni's question, though. I've never seen you do that before. I'd like to know if there's going to be some residual effects. Like this ringing in my ear — how long is that going to last?"

"There has been no permanent damage, I promise you. As to the reason why you have never seen me do this before, it is because creating that particular shockwave, the kind that disoriented those creatures, puts great strain upon me."

Sully said, "He's underselling it. The words *great strain* mean it damn near killed him. Maybe when he was a younger man, but at our age, he shouldn't be creating that kind of thing."

"It was, as you have probably begun to surmise, a loud blast of sound. It self–calibrated to cause maximum damage to those creatures while harming us the least possible."

"That was the least possible?" Gram said. "I'll pray we never have to experience it again."

Elliot leaned over towards his side. Sully held him as his stomach convulsed. But after three fruitless heaves, Elliot continued down until his cheek rested firmly in the sand.

Roni had made it to her feet. "Any idea how long it'll take him to recover?"

"What's the rush?" Sully said. "You have somewhere special to be?"

"Sorry, no. I'm just happy to be done with this. We have a long walk home, and I'm looking forward to a hot bath. That's all."

Gram crouched near the pedestal, poking at a hole in the sand. "We're not leaving yet."

"I got the kyolo stones, so the mission is over. It's what we came for. Of course, we'll wait for Elliot to feel better, but —"

"I'm not talking about Elliot." She looked to Sully. "I'm sure he'll be fine. In fact, we need him to be fine. Look at these marks."

Roni did not need to inspect the holes that had caught Gram's interest. She already knew. "It's another hellspider, isn't it?"

"I'm afraid so. From these marks, I'm guessing it's a much larger version. You said you saw something when we were on the river, and we all saw the dead relics and the missing books. And now these footprints. When I went in that book to get you out, I saw what those creatures had done to the place. We can't let that thing remain free in these caverns."

Sully said, "Of course not."

Roni spit sand off her lips. "Are you losing your mind in your old age? Elliot and I barely survived fighting off those hellspiders. You didn't fare much better. And now look at him. He can't even sit up. There is no way we can go fighting a mama hellspider without Elliot, and he's in no shape to do anything."

Brushing off her hands, Gram walked toward the raft. "Elliot can rest in here while we paddle. If we move the supplies around, he'll fit. It might be a little scrunched for us, but we'll manage."

"Listen to me. We are too weak to take this thing on." Roni wanted to mention her father's warnings, but she held back. Gram had already made up her mind and mentioning the ravings of a man in a mental hospital would only stir her anger. Roni had enough anger for the both of them. She figured if she got Gram equally upset, they might cause a seismic event.

"Dear, I'm not a fool. I know what we are facing."

"Then why —"

"We are talking about entire universes. Each book out there represents billions, maybe trillions or quadrillions, of lives. Probably even more. Infinite lives. You were in that world, you saw what the hellspiders did. How many universes is enough before we act?"

"I'm not saying we should allow the hellspider to go destroying universes. But running into a fight down a man — particularly, the only one of us who has managed to stop these things — it seems a bit idiotic."

"We don't have a choice. This is the job."

"I thought the job was to protect our own universe, and we can't do that if we all end up dead."

Gram tilted her head with an understanding grin. "I know this is scary. I'm at the end of my life as it is, and Lord knows, I'm terrified. But what do you think happens if we allow this cavern, this incredible and impossible cavern, what do you think happens to our world if this place is destroyed? Come now, I know you. You are not a heartless person. Rather than fighting me on this decision, you should be helping me figure out how to make it work."

With his head still against the sand, Elliot said, "May I weigh in on this?" Using Sully to assist, he managed to get into a sitting position. "Roni seems to have forgotten that I am a healer. It will not take me long to be ready."

"You see? He's going to be fine."

"I did not say that. I will be ready, but there are limits to how much healing I can do to myself, even under the best of circumstances. And even if I were to be as strong as I was twenty years ago, do not expect me to use that sound blast again."

Sully approached the raft and wagged his finger. "He's got you there. Both of you are right and both of you are wrong. With an answer like that, Elliot would make a good Rabbi."

Though she smirked, Gram said, "Right or wrong, I'm still the leader of this group. So, let's get this raft ready. Elliot, you rest. When the time comes, we'll need you to do everything you can."

Straightening her back as if she tried to grow a few inches, she stared at Roni. For a moment, Roni's chest withered as it had so many times when she was younger and had to endure her grandmother drawing a line in the sand. But this situation was different. She was no longer a little girl who had made a mistake. In fact, she knew she was right. She understood Gram's position, but a leader had to make tough choices — and in this case, the decision was between losing several universes while they regained their strength versus fighting now, losing, and watching *all* the universes be destroyed. She wondered if Gram sought to go out in a blaze. Unfortunately, Roni also recognized that the Old Gang would stick together. She could not let them face the hellspider alone. So, doing her best to avoid meeting Gram's eyes, Roni helped Sully prepare the raft.

By the time they were ready, Elliot had managed to stand with the aid of his cane. Gram walked him to the edge of the water, and Sully assisted him into the raft. After a little finagling, they all managed to find a space, gather their oars, and push off onto the lake.

Roni watched the sands of the Isle recede and wondered if all her experiences with the books in the cavern would be like this. Every book she had encountered led to horror. Even the one that had promised to be a paradise — it came the closest to killing her. The whole world had become like that. On the surface, the world offered opportunity and a chance for happiness. But beneath the façade resided an ugly truth. The world was like all the others out there. It promised one thing and delivered another. It was a fairytale — on the surface a pleasant children's story, but beneath, a dark and sinister gaze into the abyss of mankind's heart.

And yet she still wanted to save it.

Perhaps it was Waterfield's journal. Perhaps it was seeing the way Elliot and Sully and even Gram fought for it. Perhaps it was nothing more than the survival instinct. Whatever the case, deep in her core, she would continue to fight for their world. Having learned the truth and joined the Parallel Society, she felt a duty, if not an honor, to fulfill this task.

But Gram was wrong. Her decision would most likely cost the lives of many universes and that might include their own. Roni wanted to take over, but she doubted Sully and Elliot would follow her. They trusted her well enough, but after decades of being part of the Old Gang, their allegiance went to Gram. Understandable, but frustrating.

"To the left," Gram said, pointing toward a rocky ledge poking out over the water.

Working together, they maneuvered the raft to the ledge, so that Gram could safely step out and tie them off. Getting Elliot onto the ledge proved more difficult. But they managed.

They could only walk single file down the narrow tunnel. Gram led the way with her flashlight while Sully brought up the rear. Elliot managed a slow pace using his cane in the right hand and the wall on his left side. Behind him, Roni stayed ready in case she needed to catch him should he fall.

"If you want to take a rest," Roni said, "just say the word."

Breathing heavily with a wheeze when he inhaled, Elliot gave a slight nod.

Sully said, "Quit worrying about him. He's been in great shape his whole life. I'm the one that needs your concern."

Roni looked back to wink when she noticed that the tunnel receded into darkness. She had not realized they had come so far. Only a few minutes later, the rocky walls smoothed out. Several steps after that, they became tiled walls like an old New York City subway.

"Are we in another universe?" Roni asked.

"Very possible," Gram said, flashing her light over the group. "Often a change like this indicates a new universe. But nothing is a guarantee."

The tunnel continued straight onward, never once curving left or right. Though not prone to claustrophobia, Roni found the cramped quarters disturbing. She kept thinking that should the hellspider attack now, they would be helpless. Yet Gram pushed forward. She seemed to quicken their pace, pushing them as fast as Elliot could handle. Roni wanted to say something, wanted to scold the woman for having no compassion, but anything that slowed them down meant they would spend that much longer as easy targets in this awful tunnel.

As if treating her thoughts like prayers, they came to a crossroads. The corners between each tunnel had been flattened, and a bench had been carved into the stone. Above each bench, a carved face gazed down. Not human faces. Nor animal. Rather, they were in amalgamation of both that left Roni with a disquieted sensation roiling in her gut.

Gram pointed to one bench. "Have a seat. Let's rest and figure out which way to go."

Elliot plopped down. The collar of his shirt had warped loose with sweat. As Sully peered into each tunnel, Roni sat next to Elliot and held his hand. His fingers would not be still — they danced against her while his other hand gripped his cane as if it were a life preserver. To see this man who had always been a paragon of health tremble before her churned her thoughts into a dark future — the reality that Death waited for the Old Gang. While everybody faced dying eventually, the strain on Elliot made his passing more concrete, more certain.

"He can't go on like this," Roni said.

Leaning forward while attempting to smile, Elliot said, "I am fine. Just a little winded. It is not easy hiking day after day, not at my age."

Gram crossed her arms and gazed down to appraise him. "You know what we've got to do. I'm trusting you to tell me if you're not up to the task."

"I have always been up to the task."

Roni looked between the two as if watching insane people self-diagnose. "Look at him. What part of him looks ready to take on a hellspider? Is it the way he can hardly breathe? Or perhaps you find his sweat-stained clothes more convincing?"

Elliot raised his shaking hand to quell any further arguments. Leveling a firm stare at Roni, he said, "Our job is not to live forever. We are here to fight, to protect our universe. We are sentinels, guardians, soldiers. You have to accept a lot of hard truths in order to be an effective member of the Parallel Society. Please, do not make them harder for me, Gram, or Sully."

Despite his conviction and sincerity, Roni could not believe all that Elliot had said. She suspected that at least part of him acted out of loyalty to Gram and nothing more. Yet despite her misgivings, she backed off. Outnumbered in this debate and outmaneuvered by Elliot, she had no choice but acceptance — after all, she still needed them to guide her back home.

Even as she nodded her acquiescence, she crossed to the opposite bench. With a silent vow, she decided that upon their return, she would rely only upon herself. Maybe someday she could have a team like the Old Gang, but until that day, the universe would still need protection. And these old folks seemed determined to kill themselves.

Gram stroked Elliot's cheek. "You are sure you can handle this?"

Roni huffed. "Now you suddenly care?"

Gram did not bother to look back. "Before, you said you could not find this creature. Won't it still be that hard?"

Elliot raised his cane and hand. "At that time, I did not know what I sought. But I have faced these creatures now. It will still be difficult here in the caverns, but I believe I can manage. And besides, after all this arguing, it would be a waste not to try."

For ten excruciating minutes, Roni sat on her bench, arms folded, and watched Elliot strain through his motions in order to locate the hellspider. She could not decide what she hated more — her inability to prevent this, Gram's willingness to push Elliot, or the way Sully had remained silent throughout the entire debate. The stone faces above mocked her like a group of adults gazing down at a foolish child.

As if bursting into the air from beneath the ocean, Elliot gasped. He dropped his cane and slumped back against the stone wall. Sully raced to his side. In that instant, Roni saw how the last ten minutes had strained Sully as well.

"Are you okay?" he asked.

Though woozy, Elliot managed to say, "The hellspider can be found at the end of that passageway." He pointed to the West. "Good luck." With nothing more, he passed out.

Sully gazed up at Gram, a mixture of anger and understanding combating upon his features. "I will stay here and watch over him."

There was no room for debate in his tone. Perhaps Gram agreed with him, too. She bent down and picked up the cane with a gentle touch. As she handed it to Sully, she said, "Of course. We can't leave him here alone, and I can think of no better than you to protect him. Roni and I will handle things just fine." She looked at Roni, and with a doubtful expression, she said, "Isn't that right, dear?"

Roni could barely open her tense mouth. "Absolutely."

"Then let's go." As she stepped toward the West passageway, she turned to Sully. "Give us at least a half hour. If we don't come back —"

"No need to finish that," Sully said. "We've been down this road too many times. I know what to do."

Flashing a warm smile, Gram said, "You always make me proud."

As she headed down the tunnel, Roni followed. That final comment buzzed in the air between them like a World War II bomber waiting to drop its payload. Roni had too many emotions juggling within her. In the end, she shoved it all down to be dealt with later. Those bombs had to drop sometime. But for now, they had a hellspider to find.

CHAPTER 16

For such an old woman, Gram sure could set a strong pace. Though they only had their flashlights to see by, it was enough for Roni to catch the anger in her grandmother. Fine with her. She had just as much anger and more to spare.

Before they had time to boil over, the tunnel ended with a wooden door. Gram inspected the door from top to bottom with her flashlight. She then placed her hand on the wood, followed by an ear. Looking back at Roni, she shook her head. "I'm not picking up anything."

"You have another power?"

"Lord, no. I only mean I don't see anything, I don't feel anything, and I don't hear anything. If it's not safe to open the door, I'm not getting any indication."

"I guess we'll just have to try our luck."

Brushing her sides with her hands, Gram said, "Unless you, perhaps, read something in Waterfield's journal that might help."

Despite all her anger and frustration, part of Roni recognized how difficult it must have been for Gram to admit she needed the expertise of the researcher. It didn't change the overall problems, and it didn't solve their troubles, but Gram's passive admission eased the pressure. Even if only for a little while.

"Waterfield never got this far. Remember, for him, the Book on the Isle led to a paradise. He had no reason to go exploring further. And he lacked the support of his teammates." She hadn't meant to throw that jibe, but once it was out, she could do nothing more about it.

Gram flinched but covered it up by turning to the door. "Then it's like you said. We'll have to take our chances." She reached for the handle.

They walked into a ballroom-sized space with piles of books making mountains along the sides. In the center of the room upon a stone platform awaited a chair carved in stone. Either a throne room or a courtroom — Roni couldn't tell which. The carvings on the walls and the architecture of the platform had a distinct flavor to it — like something dwarves made in a Tolkien novel.

Their footsteps echoed in the open space, and Roni breathed easier now that she had escaped the tunnels. The air smelled stale. Sharp too. Roni thought that odd. Running her flashlight beam across the ground, she discovered the source of the odor — old droppings from above. Arching her ear upward, she listened for the telltale squeaks of bats or batlike creatures. She heard nothing.

"Whatever caused this mess," Gram said, "it happened quite a while ago. You can see how dry it all is. And fresher business doesn't dry out the air."

Roni fought back the urge to throw up. "We're breathing crap?"

"Dear, we've been breathing it for days now. Not a lot of air circulation in these caverns."

Roni clamped her mouth shut. But breathing through her nose only intensified the foul odors. Not breathing seem like a poor choice. She opted to switch back and forth, a few breaths at a time — she would've preferred a gasmask but never saw one in the supplies Sully and Elliot had packed.

Gram played her light over the book piles. "Looks like we found the missing books."

Looking closer, Roni spotted torn chains still hanging from the spines of several books. "Great. We've confirmed that this is where the creature's taking those books, and that means we've done a good job of reconning the situation. Let's go back, get Elliot and Sully, strengthen up, and return here when we're ready to fight."

"Not yet. We only know that this is where the books have been stored. We don't know for sure that your hellspider is what brought them here."

"It is not *my* hellspider."

"I don't see any of those large round marks on the ground. Do you? Anything to indicate the hellspider."

"Are you saying there's some other kind of creature out there that's stealing these books?"

Gram shrugged. "We have to stay open to all the possibilities."

They walked deeper into the room, and Roni sensed greater

pressure from the large open space as she neared the chair. *More likely a courtroom,* she thought. Facing judgment while sitting in that chair surrounded by this huge space would be maddening.

Once on the platform, she had no doubt the room had been set up to intimidate. "We shouldn't be here," Roni said.

"Nonsense. We are the Parallel Society. It is our duty to be here."

Roni's skin prickled. She thought she heard something — a rustling of clothes or bristling of hair.

Gram turned in a slow circle. "I don't see any other doors or passageways out besides the one we used. Unless these hellspiders can squish their limbs like an octopus, I don't see how the big one would be able to get through the tunnel."

As the answer hit Roni, so did the sound — a deep breath like a foghorn, rapid clicks like an amplified centipede. All from above. *Oh, shit.* Shrinking under her suspicions, Roni raised her light to the ceiling. Gram's light joined in, and they moved along the uneven surface searching for the source of the noise.

"We should go," Roni said even as she continued searching.

"Not until we're sure."

"We know exactly what's up there."

"Really? Tell me then — is there just one or a hundred up there? We have to know what we're facing. Then we go."

Several feet from the end of the room, they found it.

The hellspider clung to where the wall and ceiling met, blending in with the rocks and crevices formed by the cavern. Too far away for Roni to get a clear idea of its size, she could see enough to be sure of one thing — this one was definitely bigger.

Roni put her mouth to Gram's ear, and softer than before, she said, "We need to leave right now."

Keeping her light on the hellspider, Gram eased back, quiet step by quiet step. Her breathing quickened. Roni followed, her chest tightening until she remembered to breathe. She inhaled with an audible gasp and snapped her hand over her mouth.

With a shaky beam, she brought her light upon the hellspider. Two large, long legs unfolded out of the crevice and clamped onto the ceiling. The creature pushed and emerged from its hole. Hanging upside down, it gazed upon them with horrid red eyes. Roni stood still like a mouse caught between the paws of a cat — knowing it needed to break for freedom but terrified that the cat would pounce.

It held its stare, and she had the passing thought that the hellspider might have been as surprised to see her as she was to see it. However, she did not think any form of amicable understanding crossed between them — indeed, she had the distinct impression that the hellspider was sizing up the form of threat she posed. Still, there was an instant, the briefest of flashes, in which Roni thought perhaps the hellspider decided there was no threat. In that sliver of time, she saw the creature inch back towards its crevice in the ceiling.

But then Gram released one of her chains.

Roni snapped her attention toward the gentle rattle as its echo amplified throughout the room. Gram grabbed the loose end to quiet the noise, but it was too late. The hellspider's limbs stiffened as it cocked its head toward the new sound. It raced across the ceiling, chunks of stone dropping to the ground where it released its footing. In seconds, it had reached the front of the room, crawled down the side, and blocked the only exit.

Gram faced the hellspider, feet in a wide stance like a gunfighter at high noon. The hellspider shifted on its numerous legs and glowered down upon them from its ten foot height. Roni's feet became as solid as the stone around them — she couldn't move.

She had seen monsters before — the creature Darin had become, a giant hand reaching out of a book, and most recently, the three small hellspiders. But she had never set eyes upon such a truly monstrous creature. Its sheer size pulled it out of her memories of scary stories told late at night.

Having so few memories to cling to, she marveled at the idea that this ten foot colossus could bring forward one of the darker images within her. Even as her heart pulsed with uncertainty, another part of her, a part rarely touched upon, sparked. That same part of her hopeful enough to send her into these caverns searching for kyolo stones. That part of her determined to get back to her world so that she could use the stones to unlock her memories — hopefully.

Gram twirled the chain at her side. The hellspider swayed as if locked in strong air currents from its height.

"I don't want to hurt you," Gram said even as she set one foot behind to brace herself. "But you don't belong here. If you let me, I'll help you. If you can show me what book you came from, I'll send you back there. If you don't want that, that's fine, too. There are other worlds I can send you to where you'll do no harm. The choice is yours, but that is the limit of your choice. You do not get to stay here."

If the hellspider understood a single word she spoke, it never showed it. Roni, however, caught Gram's response — a slight drop of her shoulders. Disappointment. Perhaps even a touch of regret. But not enough to stop her from attacking.

Like a stagecoach driver whipping her team of horses into action, Gram snapped out her chain at the hellspider. For one glorious second, Roni saw the future unfold before her. She saw the chain grab into the heart of the creature. She saw how Gram's magic subdued the creature. She saw the strength of her grandmother and the way the old woman never faltered as she sent the hellspider into a book she held.

But that was all in her mind's eye. None of it happened.

As the chain sailed forward, the hellspider moved with astonishing speed. It snagged the chain out of the air with one leg and took control with two more. Moving with grace and agility, it rolled its body toward the left with a ferocious motion that rippled down the chain. Gram never had time to react.

Power released from the chain, up Gram's arm, and sent her flying across the room. She slammed through a pile of books and crashed to the floor. As the books opened, the mayhem began.

Storms clashed within the room. One book sucked air into it with tremendous force while another blew air out shoving over a pile of books. In front of Roni, an open book spewed out rain and hail into the air with such force that she could hear it rattling upon the ceiling. Another book culled all of that water and ice back into it. Lightning flashed out of one book while the howls of strange creatures echoed from another.

The hellspider worked its way around the raging winds in its effort to reach Gram. Wiping the rainwater from her face, Roni found her legs. She rushed across the room toward her grandmother.

"Close the books!" Gram whipped out chain after chain trying to lock down the open universes.

Roni pivoted to the right and started shutting the covers as she passed them. But for every book she closed, the strong winds knocked open two more.

The hellspider crept along the wall working its way up and over piles of books. It paused to observe Gram's movements. Like an astronaut in zero-gs, the hellspider pushed off the wall and sailed across the air. Roni could see the trajectory. The hellspider would land right beside the stone chair, and it would be in a perfect position to attack Gram.

Flashes of light and heat burst toward her right. An open book spit out plumes of fire and smoke. Roni leapt over, plucked up the book, and pointed it at the space where she expected the hellspider to drop.

Fire shot out of the book. The cover vibrated in her hands, and the heat built up against her palms. She had a brief moment of satisfaction when she saw understanding cross the red eyes of the hellspider. It knew the trouble it was in.

As it landed in a sea of fire, Roni heard the creature shriek. The sound of its pain brought her own pain to the forefront of her mind. Her hands felt as if they were on fire. She dropped to her knees, determined to keep that book open as long as it took to protect Gram. Tears streamed down her face. She opened her mouth and roared her anguish. Through blurry vision, she finally saw the hellspider escape back up the wall and toward the ceiling.

She dropped the book using her elbows to close the cover.

"That one," Gram said, pointing toward a book that threw large puffy white snowflakes into the air.

Roni scurried toward the book and plunged her hands in between its covers. Cool air and icy flakes soothed her immediately.

Leaning back, Gram's face turned red as she struggled to tighten a chain around one book while a winged-beast flapped and thumped an escape attempt. "When you can hold that book of fire again, let me know. It's all we've got so far that'll work."

Though Roni said nothing, she gaped at her grandmother's cruelty. Knowing the pain Roni had just endured, Gram made no effort to locate a different book to utilize. Or simply let the hellspider go. They did not have their full team, and they had sustained injury. They were in no shape to continue the fight. Besides, the hellspider had been hurt, too. It sat on the wall licking its burns. It showed little interest in them anymore. Yes, they needed to capture it and place it in a book, but Roni thought it would be better to regroup, reorganize, and then return.

Huffing and sweating, Gram tossed aside the latest chained book. She paused to kiss the cross around her neck. "Now, Roni, while we still have a chance."

A ridiculous statements — they had no chance.

The hellspider lumbered across the wall toward the back, hanging above a tall stack of books that had managed to stay standing. Stretching toward the pile with one of its back, singed legs, it snatched a book off the top. With a deft maneuver, it tossed the book into the air and caught it with its front legs. Holding the book out the full length of its legs, the hellspider opened the cover.

A mild breeze puffed out against the dark hairs on its face. It squinted, and for a moment, Roni thought the hellspider would do its work for them. She could see it simply walk into the book and all would be well. But she knew that was nothing more than wishful thinking.

Emitting a deep, grinding noise, the hellspider's neck elongated towards the book. Roni flinched backwards, her hands breaking free from the soothing cold. The creature opened its mouth. And continued opening its mouth, unhinging its jaw like a serpent, until its orifice measured twice the size of its normal head.

While Gram continued to chain down books, Roni watched the creature inhale the air of the book. The wind whipping around the edges of the cover howled like a ghost. The hellspider widened its mouth, and the wind it inhaled strengthened. Roni wanted to ask Gram if she knew what was happening, but she didn't dare turn away.

Another hellspider, this one small like those Roni had fought alongside Elliot, now burst forth through the book and hovered in the air between book and mouth. It lasted only seconds, but Roni swore she saw an odd look on the new hellspider's face — perhaps confusion, perhaps fear. Flailing its many limbs around like a rag doll in a hurricane, it tumbled into the mouth of the larger hellspider.

A snap of the jaw. A snap of the cover. All went quiet.

Lifting one of its burned legs, the hellspider watched as its blistered skin healed. Roni glanced at her own reddened hands — they would take weeks to heal, at least. Though she could not be sure, she swore the hellspider appeared to have grown as well. Not much — perhaps less than an inch — but enough to be noticeable. With its newly healed leg, the hellspider reached down to swipe another book.

"Fuck that," Roni said.

With an enraged war cry, she swept up the fire book and sprinted toward the hellspider. The creature took no notice of her, occupied by its own healing process. She reached the bottom of the pile of books that towered above and began climbing.

Progress slowed as half the books she stepped upon slipped beneath her feet to tumble toward the bottom. Turned out that a pile of books did not create the sturdiest of structures. Too many wobbled like her heart. What began as a bold reaction settled firmer into self-doubt with each step higher. When she passed the halfway point, Roni wondered how much range the fire book needed. The sooner she could open it onto the hellspider, the happier she would be. But her calculations were unnecessary. The hellspider had noticed her.

It scrabbled down the wall and onto the top of the book pile. Roni heard Gram's chains shooting out and wrapping up books as they fell to the ground.

"Come on a little closer," Roni said. "Come on now. I've got a little something for you."

She climbed up another book, and the hellspider reared back, hissing and clicking. Moving sideways like a crab, it dropped down several feet and narrowed its red eyes on the perch beneath Roni's foot.

"Oh. Is one of your friends in there?" Risking a fall that would end her, Roni scrunched down and picked up the book that held the hellspider's interest. It had a green leather cover and weighed more than the fire book.

The hellspider sidestepped again, dropping lower, almost parallel with Roni. Clearly this creature wanted to leap forward and grab the book, but it had learned a healthy appreciation for its foe.

Holding both books, Roni could not decide what to do. Part of her wanted to burn the creature as before. Part of her wanted to burn the green leather book. But as the hellspider inched closer, the answer clarified before her.

Holding up the green book, she said, "You want this? Come and get it."

Like a puppy offered a treat from a stranger, the hellspider approached with its fear and desire fighting out upon its face. Roni watched each footfall. The closer it advanced, the more its massive size loomed over her. Her throat tightened, and she hoped the creature could not sense her deception or worse, her fear.

One more step. That was all she needed. One more step, and she thought the hellspider would be close enough.

"You're acting a little unsure. How about this? How about I set this book down so you can pick it up?" Putting words to action, she placed the green book upon a sturdy section of the pile. Then she backed away a few steps.

The hellspider lurched forward. Its sudden movements sent a mini-avalanche of books tumbling downward to the floor. As it took hold of the green book like a greedy child on Christmas morning, Roni opened her own book.

Flames belched into the air. The hellspider shrieked as fire engulfed it. Cradling the green book, the hellspider skittered up the wall onto the ceiling, smoke trailing off its burnt limbs.

Roni shut the fire book. If her hands had been burned as before, she did not feel it. While Gram took care of locking down the damage created, Roni kept her focus upon the hellspider.

At first, she thought the creature would open the green book and inhale the smaller hellspiders within as it had done previously — heal before it went on further. But the hellspider had had enough of Gram and Roni. With a slight limp, it gingerly worked its way across the ceiling until it reached the crevice from which it had come. Without hesitation, it crawled in and disappeared deeper into the caverns.

For several minutes, Roni did not move. She stared at the hole in the ceiling, and she breathed. She might have spent hours in that position, but rain fell upon her. The arrival of cold water upon her face snapped her attention away from the ceiling. Gram had opened a book of rainstorms and used it to extinguish the few books that had caught fire after Roni's attack.

Carefully, Roni descended, making sure not to send any more books spinning to the floor, causing more problems. By the time she reached the bottom, however, she had a new focus for her concerns.

Before Gram could say a word, before she could touch her cross or offer a conciliatory smile, before she could raise an eyebrow or cross her arms over her large chest and glare down, Roni lifted an index finger and pointed it at her.

With a sharp scowl, Roni said, "This is all your fault."

CHAPTER 17

Neither woman spoke a single word as they handled the remaining books. Roni sifted through the piles, separating out the unchained books and stacking them for Gram to deal with. Thankfully, the majority had managed to stay closed — many had retained most of their chains, and many more were difficult to open at best. They resisted. Feeling the covers pull back against her grip, Roni pictured a muscular arm on the inside looped around a ring bolted to the cover.

As she watched Gram working, she wondered if some of those chains could create that resistance. Or perhaps, whoever created the books themselves could imbue them with different properties of strength.

After an hour, Gram chained the last book. Without any acknowledgment or word of any kind, she turned on her heels and walked back through the tunnel toward Sully and Elliot. Part of Roni did not want to follow. She knew what was expected of her, and that alone made her not want to comply. But thinking about the books and their creation only served to increase her frustration over Gram's leadership.

As they trudged through the tunnel, as stone gave way to subway tile, Roni struggled to put her thoughts in order before she spoke. It would have been difficult under any circumstance, facing down Gram had never been easy while growing up, but part of Roni's mind remained back in the courtroom filled with books. They were now chained down. They were secured. But none of those books — at least, none that she was aware of — came from that room. Many of them had been stolen from other parts of the cavern. Didn't they have to be returned?

She supposed not. At least, not by them. Few of those books, if any, had originally been placed by Gram and the Parallel Society. Many would have been secured by other groups from other universes. They had done their part to protect the cavern and those universes held within the books. Perhaps it was somebody else's problem to get the books back where they had originally been stored — if that was what was required.

Perhaps that was simply more evidence of Gram's poor leadership.

By the time they entered the small junction with benches, Roni had worked herself up enough. "You are not facing up to reality," she began.

Elliot and Sully lifted their heads, their expressions revealing joy at seeing their teammates again yet shock at the scowls they witnessed. Sully got to his feet and opened his mouth. A swift gesture from Gram silenced him. She whirled around, taking the center of the room.

"Until just over a year ago," Gram said, "you didn't even know what reality actually was."

"And now I bring fresh eyes to this reality. Or maybe other, more seasoned Society members may have simply grown complacent."

Clearing his throat, Elliot said, "Your hands are injured. Come. I will heal them. I promise I am not too weak for that small task."

Roni hesitated, but mentioning her burned hands, only ignited their pain once more. Trying to maintain a position of strength on her face, she settled next to Elliot and put out her hands. He lifted his cane to the side of her hands and began motioning a curious circle over her injuries. In seconds, she could feel the pain subsiding.

Though she already felt the fire of their speech dwindling, she knew it was important to continue the argument. Even if in a calmer voice. "I have no doubt you have been a fine leader to this group for a long time. But by your own admission, you brought me into all of this because I am the future of the Society for our world. There's an implication to that — the idea that you've passed your prime in that position."

"Ladies," Sully said, with a grandfatherly smile and a gentle waving of the hands. "The two of you are family. There is no need to fight. We can talk about this and —"

Gram arched an eyebrow toward him. "I need you to do what you're best at. Build us a golem."

"With what?"

"Stones, of course. Lord knows, there are enough around."

Gesturing to the meager pickings on the floor, he said, "I suppose. If I had a pickax, I could make a real golem, but with just the loose rocks, it won't be much."

"Make do."

Roni said, "Unless fire is an option."

"It's not," Gram said, whirling upon her granddaughter. "You would know that if you spent your time focusing on your job and not trying to do mine."

Roni tried to stand, but Elliot tapped her shoulder with his cane to keep her in position. She twisted her head to give Gram a sharp look. "You're not doing your job well. After Elliot's injuries, we should have stopped. It's that simple. When we got to this room you split the group — another bad decision. And when you and I spied the location of the hellspider, we didn't go back to regroup, strengthen up, and come up with a plan. No. We bumbled in there and nearly got killed. Your Ahab-like obsession nearly cost all of us our lives unless Sully could find his way back on his own. And no offense, but I don't think he's up to the task."

Sully chuckled from the floor where he piled stones into the shape of a man lying on the ground. "I think none of us would be up to the task of getting back on our own. Except perhaps Elliot."

Holding her commanding position, Gram glared down at Roni. "By the foolish look on your face, I can see you are still wondering about why Sully can't make a fire golem. Think about it, dear. How is he going to write his spell on a piece of paper and stick it in a golem if that golem is just going to burn it all up? It would kill itself."

Roni slouched back against the wall. As Elliot's hand motions changed direction and pattern, she was reminded yet again that she had no powers. Apparently, she didn't even understand the basics. But that didn't mean she was wrong.

Jutting her chin toward Gram, she said, "Just because I don't know every detail of being in the Society doesn't mean I can't assess your leadership."

"They say everybody's a critic."

"So now I'm a cliché?"

"No, dear." Gram said. "You are just young and inexperienced. Your heart is in the right place. That's worth a hundred people who know all the rules and details. But that does not make you the leader you will need to be. The role of the leader is so much more than simply barking out orders and gaining a benefit here or there." She raised a hand though Roni had not intended to speak. "It is my job to make sure the team is at its most effective level. It is my job to make sure the team is at its best readiness. With the fact that there are sometimes years between events requiring our attention, I have to stay on these boys to make sure they keep practicing their abilities. I have to learn and stay up on the best tactics and military strategies. I'm also responsible for monitoring the entire world, looking for anomalies that might require our attention. That's not all. I also act as a liaison between the Parallel Society and the few religious leaders and government leaders out there who know of our existence. When we have to travel abroad, who do you think is responsible for all the legal hassles involved? It's not like it's an easy matter to take a book containing an entire universe inside it across borders. And that doesn't even touch the surface of what I must do. Because sometimes we end up in a situation like this — out in the field, dealing with an adversary we know nothing about. It is my job to stay a few steps ahead, to improvise, and always, under all circumstances, to make the hard call." Gram's stern look faded, and briefly she warmed into the grandmother Roni had grown up with. "You know I love you. That never changes. And it's with that love that I tell you, you are not ready yet."

Roni did not respond at first — a good leader did not speak rashly. She weighed Gram's words, deciding which ones were worth responding to, and most importantly, what response would sway Sully and Elliot to side with her point of view. With the Old Gang staring at her, waiting, she felt like a defendant on a witness stand. Perhaps even an unfortunate soul forced to sit in that hard, stone chair in the courtroom.

At length, she said, "The Parallel Society is an old institution. It is vital to our survival. All institutions develop traditions, behaviors, cultures of their own. And the longer an institution exists, the more complicated and ingrained those traditions become. They become rules. While they may have begun for a noble or practical purpose, nobody knows why it is still done — other than habit. In other words, just because you've always done something a certain way, doesn't make it right. You taught me that last bit."

Gram's mouth tightened into a small dot. She never liked having her own words thrown back at her.

Roni went on, "I understand and respect that you have a lot to teach me. I know that. But it is clear from the risks you have taken with our lives on this mission that some leadership skills are no longer at your fingertips. Or perhaps it would be better if I said that the leadership skills you utilize have not changed with the times. Decisions you have made on this mission, that you all seem to act as acceptable, should not be."

As Sully wrote Hebrew words on a piece of paper, he said, "You have to pay attention to experience. Experience can be the wisest teacher."

"I agree. But too much experience can lead one into thinking they know all the answers. Which is just as dangerous as not knowing enough."

Sully chuckled. "You got me there. However, I'm still with your grandmother on this one."

"Of course you are." Roni pulled her hands away from Elliot and stood. To Gram, she said, "It's abundantly clear to me now that this is and always will be your team."

Dropping her hands, Gram said, "This team belongs to us all."

"Let's not pretend. This is your team. And that's fine. In fact, it makes everything clear and easier to deal with. This is your team, and one day you want me to take over and be leader of a new team. In order to do that, I need to become a leader, and that won't happen under your tutelage. After seeing the way you've handled our lives in this mission, I'm not sure I can survive long enough to become a leader. I think I'd be better off as a team of one for now, and in the coming years, I'll find others out there, people who can replace you guys when the time is right. I will train them to work under me just like you did with Sully and Elliot."

"Stop it." Gram's stern face had returned. "You're acting like a child, not a leader. How do you expect anybody to follow you if the moment things become difficult, you bail out?"

"You bailed on us. You let us down. I suggest you help the rest of your team to safety, while I figure out how to deal with the hellspider on my own."

Roni didn't wait for a response. She blustered off, fuming more than she felt. In fact, she felt very little anger now. She had let most of it go. It had flooded out in words that she knew she could not take back. She believed most of them — that much was good. But not all. The idea of taking on the hellspider alone did not seem wise. On the other hand, she had no team, and the creature had to be dealt with. And after all, leaders had to make the tough calls. This was her first. She would find a way to take this thing on.

After two minutes of walking she realized she had not gone back down the long tunnel toward the raft. Nor had she gone toward the courtroom filled with books. This was a new path. And as she reached a T-junction, she decided to pause and regroup her thoughts.

Looking the way she had come, the urge to rush back into her grandmother's arms and blubber for her forgiveness had to be beaten back with the hard knowledge that any step in that direction would forever destroy her chances of moving forward toward her leadership position.

"Well, that sucks."

She heard a repetitive thumping coming through the tunnel. Perhaps Gram hurried after her to welcome her back, to suggest that Roni had made an important point, and that she was ready to help her granddaughter learn. Perhaps the Lord would strike down the hellspider and save all of humanity with a magic arrow of love. Roni figured both scenarios held the same likelihood of happening.

The thumping grew louder but did not sound threatening. Moments before it appeared, Roni smiled as she realized what came her way. Sully's golem jogged out of the dark until it reached her. Shaped like a person with two legs, two arms, torso and head, the golem Sully made from nearby stones had only enough material for it to reach Roni's stomach.

Patting its head, she said, "Looks like I've got a team of two."

CHAPTER 18

Bending down, Roni spotted two divots in the head of the stone golem that reminded her of eyes. She wondered if Sully could give his golems the ability to see through such markings. Possibly.

"You may be a little fella, but you're with me now. I'll do my best to take care of you."

With stone stumps for hands, the golem pounded its chest twice.

"Oh, I guess you like that idea. I do, too. I suppose I should give you a name. How about Rocky? It's a bit on the nose, but I'm in charge here. I might as well go with my gut. Rocky it is."

As before, Rocky pounded its chest twice. Roni chuckled and straightened her back. She gazed up one route and down another. Neither direction called to her as a sensible way to go.

Gazing down at Rocky, she said, "How about you decide which direction?"

Rocky backed up a few steps and considered both paths. The longer it took to make a choice, the more Roni wondered if it could weigh the decision. After all, how much brain function could a stone golem have? It didn't have a brain. Yet Roni had seen Sully's golems in action before. Many of them appeared to exhibit thought and free will.

Punching the air to the left, Rocky jogged off in that direction.

"Wait!" Roni walked in the same direction, pleased to see that Rocky had stopped until she caught up.

They entered a low-ceilinged section of cavern. Stalactites connected with stalagmites giving the sense of pillars sporadically placed in this open hall. Roni traced her fingers along the ceiling as they walked. Chained books fit snug into carved ceiling alcoves. Each one hummed with energy, creating a low frequency of tones that bordered on the musical. It was like standing in a Tibetan monastery while every monk used a different, single tone as his mantra.

At the far side of the hall several tunnels broke off in different directions — some even curved downward. As before, Roni allowed Rocky to pick one. They walked into the new tunnel, and the humming subsided. But it left behind a strange sensation like a residue of sound upon Roni's skin.

She had experienced an overwhelming number of new things on this journey — new creatures, new universes, new concepts of existence. Now humming books. Were they harmless? Or had she just been exposed to something dangerous? Perhaps even a form of radiation. Better leaders would have ensured the upkeep of the Grand Library so that such knowledge was always at members' fingertips. That would be a future project under her leadership. But she couldn't really blame Gram for that problem — it had been one she inherited from previous leaders. Which made Roni wonder what other problems she stood to inherit when the Parallel Society truly came under her control.

Calling Rocky back, Roni settled on a protruding boulder. It had a natural, banana curve that begged for her to rest against. "You know, the real problem isn't the Old Gang or even Gram. I was lashing out at them. I was angry. And, to be honest, I'm more than a little scared." She nodded at Rocky as if the stone golem had spoken. "I know. Hard to believe. But they just won't put themselves in my shoes. If I had learned about all of this, if I learned about things like you, if I had known any of it while growing up so I could be prepared, then perhaps I wouldn't feel so smothered and unqualified. But I received no training, no teaching, nothing to set me up to succeed. I was just thrown into it all."

Rocky walked to the opposite wall and crouched down on its haunches.

"You think I'm going to be rambling on for a while? Maybe you're right."

Rocky put out one arm and made a rolling motion.

"Okay, okay. I'll get on with it. The point is I was unprepared, and yet I was expected to behave like I had been one of the Society for my whole life. Gram wants to be the leader and to set down the rules, and I am to be obedient and blindly follow. But I can't. I have to be responsible for the entire planet, the entire universe — which don't get me started on that. I have so many questions on how we're supposed to handle things beyond our own planet and nobody has given me an answer to that. I've even started looking in the books of the Grand Library and nobody has answers to give me written down or otherwise. That's why I'm so mad. It's not that I want to be off here on my own, but I already am. I already was. They float around me like ghosts — like they're there, visible, but they won't give me anything of substance."

Rocky plunked its head down between its arms.

"Too poetic or am I boring you?" Roni's tone snapped Rocky's head back up. "That's better. What's the point of having a little golem of my own, if you're not going to pay attention? Look, the real problem for me, for all of us, is that the truth is coming after us. I don't mean that like some metaphysical answer, or some spiritual answer, or even the number forty-two. I mean that before I learned about all of this, the truth was a certain reality I understood. And then I discovered the caverns and the Parallel Society and all of it, and now the truth is something different. It's more truth. And seeing the way things have been run here, the way things have been set up to avoid getting too deep into these caverns, the way Gram has dealt with the hellspiders and other relics from other universes — well, I think there's a further level of truth that even the Parallel Society has not witnessed yet. That's what I feel coming our way."

Roni grew quiet, and after a few minutes of silence, Rocky popped to its feet. Nudging her leg, it gestured for her to follow. It then led the way further down the tunnel. Roni did not think her golem friend had a specific destination in mind, though it seemed to move with purpose.

"You smell something?" Of course not. It didn't have a nose. "I mean, do you see something?"

Rocky kept a steady pace ahead.

As Roni followed, her mind wandered back to her earlier words. This was more than some kind of performance anxiety, something an athlete might experience before a big event. It wasn't a simple matter of self-doubt. Of questions like *will she be ready?* Or *will she be capable?* Too much riding on her ability to make the right decisions. And what of the Yal-hara? Wasn't that the ultimate truth? They had a duty to that living relic.

Roni did not truly care if she had to wait to lead the group. She didn't really want it in the first place. Deep down, she felt she was better off alone. But Yal-hara was counting on them.

No. Once again, Roni tried to evade the truth.

The truth — the real truth — was that she did not care who led the group, or what happened to Yal-hara, or if the hellspiders were freed or imprisoned. She had not come down here to impress Gram or convince her grandmother that she was capable of greater things. Perhaps on some level those things existed in her mind, but none of that scratched the real truth.

She stopped walking. Without looking back, Rocky stopped as well.

"I did this," she said, needing to hear her voice, "because I want to get whatever help the kyolo stones will provide for my lost memories. And now that I have the stones, I want to get back to Yal-hara and have her deliver on the promise."

And there it was.

Not only had Roni spoken the truth, but she knew that it rested at the core of all strife between her and Gram. More than any fight over leadership, she suspected Gram would hate the idea of Roni remembering.

Why?

She never had a suspicion of Gram. Her grandmother never once said or did anything to suggest that there were secrets to be hidden. Gram was not a bitter woman, and though tough, she did not seek out confrontation or drama. So why would Roni instinctually feel that Gram did not want her to remember?

If Roni wanted to look at it from the point of view of love, then she considered that Gram worried the discovery might be upsetting — perhaps, devastating — and so she wanted to spare her granddaughter. Yet after discovering her entire reality was false and learning of the incredible, bizarre nature of true reality, there really couldn't be anything in her mundane memories that would shock her. If, on the other hand, Roni took a cynical viewpoint, a darker one, then perhaps Gram knew more about her mother's death than she had let on. Perhaps, Gram had been involved — even if only tangentially.

Roni shook off these thoughts. She had the kyolo stones, and they would hopefully reveal something of her memories. When that time came, Gram's place in all of it would be revealed. No point in working herself up now when she had no knowledge of the actual answer.

"And I better remember that Yal-hara made no promises. She only suggested the kyolo stones might help." Roni knew from a lifetime of disappointment not to grow too excited about the possibility of getting her memories back.

Stretching her arms, she looked back the way she had come. She heard the *thump thump thump* of Rocky running up to her side. Tugging on her arm like a little child, the golem gestured deeper in the tunnel.

"I'm coming. I'm coming."

Rocky's urgency did not cease. Then Roni heard the deep, foghorn moan. Her skin prickled.

CHAPTER 19

The blood pumping through her system froze in place. She could not move. How had the hellspider found her when she didn't even know where she was? And why? Did this creature seek vengeance? Was that possible?

As her thoughts roiled her stomach, a feather fluttered within her — a glimpse of a memory from her Lost Time. Her father.

They sat in a park. The one that backed up against the Olburg Elementary School. He looked young, fit, ready to be the best version of a dad one could ask for. Several children played on the jungle gym, and though Roni wanted to join them, she could not move.

Her father stroked the back of her head. "Fear is a funny thing. See, in one way it's one of our most important instincts. It is something so basic, so part of us, that without it, we never would've survived long enough to evolve into human beings. But the modern world isn't filled with lions and panthers and things that are hungry to eat you up. So when we're threatened, those two ideas come into conflict — the new world reality versus the old world instincts. And for a lot of us, our body does not know how to react. We shut down. We freeze. Here's the thing — it doesn't matter what you do when you're afraid. It's only important to do something. Don't allow yourself to stand still. Even if the choice you make is the wrong one, it'll be better than standing there waiting to be destroyed."

From what she could remember — and that was, of course, not much — her father often spoke to her like this. He took something as simple as being shy around new kids, and turned it into some big lesson far beyond her capability of understanding at that age. Standing there in the cavern, she got the sense that he might have been trying to prepare her for moments like her current one.

Even as she pushed aside that notion, she realized the memory was right — she had to do something.

With Rocky close behind, Roni hustled along the tunnels until they returned to the low-ceiling cavern. She scanned the area with its numerous paths — which one had they come through?

"Any idea how to get back to Sully and the rest?"

Rocky lifted its head to check all the possibilities. Then it checked them again.

"Guess I shouldn't expect too much from somebody with rubble for a brain." The ceiling hummed with its many books, and when the low moan of the hellspider echoed into the chamber, Roni could feel vibrations in the air rippling off each book.

"We definitely can't stay here. When that hellspider gets closer, I don't want to see what kind of damage those vibrations can do."

Bouncing her finger from one direction to the next, she ran a quick game of eeny–meany in her head. When she finished, she pointed at a tunnel on the left.

"Looks like that's the one."

She wanted to run, but she knew that would be dangerous in a dark cavern. Too many opportunities to twist an ankle or break a bone. But she couldn't casually stroll, either. Moving as fast as she dared, she headed along the tunnel with Rocky staying near.

The passageway curved sharp in one direction and then the other like a switchback on a mountainside. Though the walls opened and narrowed, and the ceiling raised and lowered, Roni never encountered a junction or even a branching off pathway. With her pulse beating hard and her heavy breaths bouncing off the walls, the steady *thump thump thump* of her golem created a rhythm to their pace. Beneath it all the throaty moan of the hellspider followed by its distinct clicking continued its threat that soon, very soon, it would arrive.

At length, the passage ended in a space no bigger than Roni's apartment bedroom. Shelves had been dug into the stone walls, and chained books filled them with no apparent order.

No doors.

No tunnels, passageways, or alcoves.

No way out.

The hellspider's numerous legs crunching stone as it progressed through the tunnel grew louder. Roni spun back to face the only direction she could go. *Don't stand still. Don't stand still.* If she returned up the passageway, she would smack right into the hellspider. So, that option was out. A quick glance at the walls and the floor convinced her she could not dig a solution.

Books. If she could find another book that opened up into a world of fire or lightning or anything that would inflict harm, then she could fight back. Rifling through the shelves, Roni did not find a cover bearing the symbol that she had seen on her previous fire book. Nor did she find a symbol that indicated lightning.

But she had no way to know if the symbols on these books used the same language as those on the books from her part of the cavern. Considering that the various groups doing the same work as the Parallel Society came from other universes, it would be a lot to expect them to share a common language. Besides, even if she found the book, she soon discovered that these volumes had been chained numerous times. They barely budged when she tried to pull them.

She did not have the time to start cracking them open in an effort to locate a useful one.

Responding to the latest, and loudest, series of noises from the hellspider, Rocky stepped into the entranceway and raised its fists. Like a deer knowing full well that a hunter stalked nearby, Roni gazed up the passageway even as she inched towards the back of the room. Her mind raced through possible ways to escape — their number were few and none seemed good. Worse, the more she strained for an answer, the more her mind conjured images of her horrid demise. She repeatedly pictured the hellspider disemboweling her, decapitating her, or worst of all, it would open its unhinged jaw and inhale her.

Four obsidian legs reached around the edges of the entranceway to grip the wall. More legs followed, and Rocky took several steps backward to put itself between Roni and the hellspider. Accompanied by that incessant clicking, the hellspider entered the room.

The stone golem launched toward the intruder. Yet even as the hellspider got its bearings, it had no trouble swatting Rocky aside. The golem slammed into a wall of books. Turning its red eyes upon Roni, the hellspider approached.

As her gaze lifted to keep focus on the creature's eyes, her heart sank. She had no escape. She had no weapon.

Her palms grew sore, and when she snatched a look, she saw that her fingers had clenched into fists. As the hellspider gazed down upon her, she mustered all her inner–strength to maintain her composure. Yes, she was scared. But she didn't have to show it.

The hellspider leaned down bringing its face closer and closer. Roni noted an unpleasant, musty odor — like a horse that had rolled around in its own manure.

She could not say whether the next moment came from bravery, inspiration, or stupidity, but before Roni had formed a clear idea of what to do, her body reacted. She punched the hellspider in the jaw.

Its head wracked to the side and the hairs on its face bristled. The rest of it, however, remained still. As it turned back toward Roni, its red eyes narrowed and an angry huffing flared its cheeks.

With so many legs on her opponent, Roni never saw the attack coming. She had fixated on its face, and the two legs that shot forward came low and out of sight. As one struck the air from her lungs, the other shoved her back against the wall. Then the beating really began.

Roni had taken a punch or two in her life, but nothing could have prepared her for the assault she endured. One leg after another pummeled her body. The hellspider struck her in the chest, the arms, the thighs, the pelvis, and of course, the head. It was a jackhammer attempting to break through her bones. The ferocious beating made it difficult to catch her breath, and she worried she would die of suffocation long before any internal injuries took their toll.

Like a boxer, the hellspider exhaled with each jab thrown. Blood dribbled down Roni's face. Her mouth filled with its coppery taste.

She slumped to the ground, and mercifully, the hellspider let her. In moments she found herself lying flat on the stone floor. Everything burned and throbbed and ached, and she had grown numb to the worst pains — at least, she thought so. She cringed at the idea that sometime soon, the full torrential pain would ignite. Unless she died before that unpleasant moment arrived.

Through swollen eyes and a filter of blood, she watched as the hellspider climbed up the wall and onto the ceiling. It positioned above her, making slight adjustments until it centered directly overhead. Roni thought of old wrestling shows that featured costumed stars like Hulk Hogan standing on the ropes of the ring ready to jump through the air and slam onto their opponent for one final big move.

Roni listened to the crowd. The cheers, the boos — sounds that signaled the end.

Obliging her thoughts, the hellspider hissed long and loud before dropping through the air. She saw its multi-limbed body flip over like a cat ready to land on its feet. But it was Roni's head that the hellspider aimed for. The dark figure grew fast in her view, and she had one flashing thought — *I wish I had gotten to find out what I can't remember.*

That was when Rocky saved her.

The stone golem shot out from the side, hurling its body through the air and T–boning the hellspider. The creature flailed out its legs. Knocked off target, it skidded against the floor to the right of Roni.

Too injured to move, Roni simply watched as her stone golem scrabbled atop the hellspider, throwing a flurry of punches. While Rocky did not have the strength to damage the hellspider significantly, the little golem moved fast. Like a dog overrun with fleas, the hellspider twisted and turned and rolled back upon itself in an effort to rid its skin of this irritating bug. But Rocky would not be deterred.

The stone golem ducked, jumped, and maneuvered every way possible to evade the hellspider's lumbering attacks. As the two creatures wrestled on the ground, Roni felt her consciousness fading.

The hellspider thrust back against the wall in an attempt to slam the stone golem, but at the last second, Rocky dismounted and let the hellspider injure itself. Not wasting a second, Rocky lunged back into the fight. Irritated, angered, and possibly hurt a little, the hellspider pivoted toward the entranceway.

Roni saw the creature slinking down the tunnel with Rocky throwing punches on its back. When she could no longer see them, she could hear them — sounds of stone against stone, hissing and moaning, angry cries and multiple grunts, even as the sounds disappeared.

Roni coughed, and blood spurted from her mouth. With each breath, her chest felt as if somebody stood on her sternum. She wondered if she had broken most every bone in her body. She wondered if she would feel Death coming or if she might simply fall asleep and never awaken.

A tear welled in the corner of her left eye and dribbled back the side of her face. She had never given much thought to dying, but she never thought she would die alone.

CHAPTER 20

The trickling stream made for a peaceful sound, and the warmth covering Roni eased her pains. In fact, she felt little pain. Concentrating on her feet and working her way up her torso all the way to the top of her head, she discovered only the barest throb. Turned out, death wasn't so bad.

She heard the shifting of cloth and smelled the rich aroma of burnt wood. She knew that smell. Only one man she had ever met brought that comforting aroma her way — Elliot.

Opening her eyes, she saw Elliot's gnarled cane above her. His free hand brushed the air back and forth over her head and down to her belly.

"Do not struggle," he said, with a gentle smile. "You sustained quite a large number of injuries. Let my healing do its work."

She tried to speak, but moving her mouth to form words sent crushing pangs through her jaw.

"Close your eyes. Rest. You are safe."

She had questions, but her exhausted body forced her to obey Elliot's commands. Her eyes closed and her mind shut down. Only for a few seconds — at least, that was how it felt. However, when she opened her eyes again, Elliot sat nearby on a large stone eating an apple.

With minimal effort, she managed to sit up. Gently prodding her jaw with two fingers, she discovered no pain. "You're amazing," she said.

Elliot chuckled. "I have had a lot of practice. I must say, though, you were pushing my abilities. I am not a young man anymore. Please, do not get so torn up again."

"It wasn't something I planned."

They sat in a small crater like a fire pit unevenly dug. A pathway passed above them. The stream — not much more than a brook — entered from a hole in the pit wall, meandered along the ground, and disappeared on the opposite side. Leaning back on her elbows, Roni noticed her stone golem standing on the path, keeping guard at the entrance way.

Elliot nodded. "That little fellow saved your life more than I did. It brought you here. Probably dragged you, even carried you, and set you down by the stream. He tucked you in close to the wall so that the hellspider would not easily find you. Then that little golem ran back to us."

"Amazing it found you. We were a bit lost."

"I suspect it hiked every tunnel until it found the right one. By the time it brought me here, you had been gone for six, maybe seven hours."

"Then why are you the only one who came? Something happen to Gram and Sully?"

"They got into an argument. When the golem reported to Sully, we knew that we were partly responsible for your situation. Sully blamed Gram, and she did not take it well."

"I can imagine."

"The two of them can bicker for a long time. I figured it would be better if I came here alone and took care of you right away." Setting the apple core aside, all mirth left Elliot's face. "That is not accurate. They are not bickering like they often do. They are fighting about you and your welfare. Whether you realize it or not, we all love you very much. I fear the Society is falling apart."

"I'm sorry."

"It is not your fault. The cracks are in our foundation." His throat convulsed as if he fought back the urge to throw up. "The fault is mine."

"I doubt that."

"You are wrong." Resting his cane across his knees, Elliot turned his head away and focused on the stream. "When I first came out to the Book on the Isle, I thought I had made a discovery akin to the Fountain of Youth — something so profound that it would upend all our understanding of the universes. Of course, I could not share this with the world, but for us few in the Parallel Society, I could impart what I learned. Think of the wonder of it all. A world of shimmering beauty. A culture built on love and hope and strength through community. These are things we give lip service to, but the people of that universe truly lived. Arguments are not a bloodsport. Business is not war. If one thing benefits the individual, then it can benefit all. But when I returned with this incredible paradigm shifting news, my words were dismissed."

"Gram can be that way."

"It was more Sully's doing. I think he feared I had succumbed to a Siren call. As it turned out, he was partially correct."

"You went back?"

"First chance I had, I left our world and entered that wondrous place. The people living there welcomed me in without hesitation. They threw a feast in my honor, and the evening stretched on as if it had no end. So much of it blurred together. Songs and dancing and laughter. By far, one of the most joyous nights of my life. And then, right by that fountain, I met Janwan. I fell in love with her immediately. It was not simply an infatuation. It was like meeting part of myself and knowing instantly that we belonged. She was the daughter of one of the town elders — Dorarnosk. I had more than a little fear when I met him. Big man. Full of muscles. But I soon found out that he was a kind and warm-hearted sort. The moment Janwan confirmed that she loved me, I became part of the family. All had fallen into place. All was well."

"Until?"

Squinting upward, Elliot cleared his throat. "A golem appeared."

"From Sully?"

"Who else? It came with a letter — Sully and Gram wanted to remind me that I had a job to do. I wrote back with two sentences: *I can be replaced. Go on without me.* But a few days later, another golem arrived. A few days after that, another. And another. And another."

"Hold on," Roni said as she pictured the scene. "How did they find you in the first place?"

"A map, of course."

"But —"

"I am not some adventurous explorer like Waterfield. I would never have gone walking through the dark caverns nor braved the river currents without knowing where I was going. No, I had a detailed map that he had drawn. But, and please do not be angry with me about this — you see, I destroyed it. I have always had an excellent memory. Still do, even at my age. So, I knew I would remember the route. Sully and Gram, though — I figured they would not be able to find me or send golems after me, if they did not retain the map. I returned for a weekend, gathered the last of my things, destroyed the map, and returned to my wife.

"I thought that would end it all. Gram would find a replacement for me, Sully would get over his disappointment and eventually come to understand, and I would remain in paradise with the woman I loved. Except that woman knew me better than I knew myself. After a year, she convinced me that I needed to return to the bookstore, that I needed to set things right with Gram and Sully, and that only then would I be able to truly live in peace.

"She was right. And if it had gone as she had laid out, I would never have the burden of guilt that weighs on me daily."

Elliot paused, and though he attempted to hide it, Roni spotted him pushing the tears from his eyes. She got to her feet and approached him. The bruises on her body caused the barest of aches. Gesturing to her ease of movement, she said, "You're more than the team's medic. You're a freaking miracle worker."

Shaking his head, Elliot said, "I couldn't save Janwan from cancer."

Roni lowered to Elliot's side and leaned her head on his shoulder. "I loved Aunt Jan so much. I hated seeing her decline. But, if you don't mind me asking, why didn't your skills work? It couldn't have been her age — she was only in her forties or so when she died."

"I tried, but as I have since learned, I need to know the anatomy of a creature in order to heal it."

"Wait — Aunt Jan wasn't human?"

"Patience. We are getting there."

"I'm patient, I'm patient. Get on with it."

"Shortly before we left for Pennsylvania, her father visited with me. Now, Dorarnosk could intimidate a lion, and even though I came to know him as a good man with a gentle soul, I knew he could rip me in two, if he wanted to do so. When dealing with such a powerful man about his daughter, it is always wise to be cautious."

"Is that your way of saying you were crapping your pants?"

Elliot snorted a laugh. "Not literally, but yes. Anyway, Dorarnosk met with me in private and begged me to leave Janwan behind. She would be here, waiting and in love, should I return. Of course, I'll return, I told him, but he insisted that I could make no such promise. In fact, he told me that he knew if I left with her, that she would never come home again. I was confused and a bit worried. How could he know? I had seen and experienced enough strangeness to be open to the possibility that some people might see into the future. But still — I found it difficult to accept.

"I said as much and he laughed at me. No, he could not see what tomorrow would bring, but he did know about the caverns and the great many universes. You see, Dorarnosk and the town elders were that universe's version of the Parallel Society. However, where we have chosen to use our abilities to close the fissures into other universes, capture them in the books, and fight back all the relics that slip into our world, Dorarnosk's group had a different approach."

Roni straightened as she understood. "They built the island."

"They did. They worked the caverns until they built up the land enough for an island. Then they flooded the place, captured their own universe in a book, and stowed it safely alone on the Isle. This would keep them out of contact from the other universes — except for the occasional visit from the likes of me."

Thinking of the hellspiders, Roni said, "Doesn't look like their plan worked."

"Isolation rarely does. Not in the long run. But back then, Dorarnosk had no reason to believe the end of his world was only a few decades away. He was simply a father who did not want to lose his daughter. And he had done his job to protect their world. I told him that he should understand then — I had a duty to the Society. I had to return and make sure that somebody qualified could replace me. I had to set things right — not only for the sanctity of my friendship with your grandmother and Sully, but also to complete my job, to make sure that our world was in good hands from the encroaching worlds.

"Dorarnosk said he understood that fine, but he also knew that when Janwan experienced the vastness out there — all the universes, all the people and creatures — there would be too much to keep her interest. Why would she want to return home? I tried to explain to him that his home was a true paradise, that while Janwan may be intrigued by our world or some other world, she would soon find out that her home was the best place to be. Not so, he told me. People always want to move beyond where they are. Once they taste the rich possibilities, they forget about their homes. Maybe not long ago, not when people were few and the worlds spread far apart, but now — he knew in his heart that she would not return. So, he asked me to make a promise. A simple one really — just that I watch over her, protect her, do all I could to provide her with a good life. Of course, I made the promise."

Roni wanted to ask a few more questions — namely, she wondered if Janwan ever learned of the promise or if she ever regretted leaving — but she could see how difficult this story was for Elliot to tell. Best to keep as quiet as possible and let him speak.

"We left shortly after." His voice tightened as he went on. "I did all I could to fulfill my promise. I tried to give her a happy, good life. In some way, I believe I succeeded. But in the end, pancreatic cancer had its way. In another life, I would feel no guilt over that fact. People get cancer. It is the way things are. But not in all worlds. Cancer does not exist in the world she came from. I thought she would be immune to our diseases the way a cat and a human do not share the flu. Different species generally do not get sick from the same things. And while we were both humans, we came from different universes. She should have been fine. And it is not as if cancer were a contagious disease. She should not have become sick. I will never know exactly what happened, but my guess is that her DNA altered after living here for so long. Perhaps if I had stayed in her world, my DNA would have altered. Perhaps I would have been the one to get sick.

"But I learned then that the only way I could heal cancer or any such illness would be to know the person's DNA — the full code."

"And that's kind of impossible."

"It seems unlikely. Certainly impossible for me." He sighed. "Well, it happened the way it happened. She got sick, and she died. I returned to face her father. The moment he saw me, he knew. I dropped to the ground and begged his forgiveness, begged him to give me some way to make up for thinking I knew better. He cried and walked away. And then, before I left, I made the situation worse. I did something which shames me — I stole a hairpin. A piece of Janwan's life from before she met me, before I lured her away and destroyed her. I took this object to our world, creating a relic. Gram was not pleased."

Roni couldn't help but let out a sharp laugh. "I'll bet."

"She made me promise to return it. And so, for the second time, I promised. But time drifted onward, we had missions to accomplish, and Gram had her stash of relic alcohol. I never felt too bad about holding onto a memory for so long. When you brought up the idea of going to the Book on the Isle, I took it as a sign that I should fulfill my word."

"Except you were too late."

"I should have listened to Gram and rid myself of the relic immediately. I should have listened to Dorarnosk and encouraged Janwan to stay in her universe. They knew more than I did, had experienced more, but my youthful arrogance led me astray."

Roni stiffened. "Are you saying I'm arrogant?"

"Nothing wrong with arrogance. At times. We need that kind of surety to be bold. But it can go too far. It can make us believe we know all the answers. But do we?"

"I never said I knew everything."

"Good. Then you will understand that while I agree with you regarding your need to be better educated in the world of the Parallel Society, I do not agree with your running off. Sully, Gram, and I have a lifetime of experiences to offer. We are the greatest textbook you could have to learn your trade. Most of all, you must accept that the tasks we are assigned are far greater than anything we can do alone. The Parallel Society has always operated as a team because a team is the only way to protect our universe. You need to respect that."

"I do. I always have. Heck, my little team with that golem proves it. I would have died without its help. Which, I suppose, means that I need to thank Sully, too. But see, that's the thing. I'm not really a part of your team."

"That is not true. You have made yourself to feel that way."

"A year. A full year and none of you went out of your way to share anything with me. I won't argue this again. Whether you all agree with me or not doesn't change things."

"Then what are we to do? You see now that you need to be with the team — I hope — so, rather than run away again, tell me what we can do to make this work better."

Roni jolted as Elliot's words sunk in hard. On her feet, she spun to face him. Ideas layered atop one another with increasing speed. "You're right. I do need to be with a team." She beamed at him. "But the Old Gang ain't it."

"That is not what I —"

"We can win this. We can defeat the hellspider. Come on. Get up. We've got to go see the others. I know what we need to do." The thoughts racing through her mind threatened to overwhelm her.

"At least tell me what you plan before I go walking all the way back. If we know Gram is going to refuse you, then maybe we can —"

"Stop doubting me. I know what I'm doing, and Gram will agree."

"She will not let you go find a new team."

"That's why we're going to make one."

CHAPTER 21

Stepping back and forth over the stream, Roni paced the sunken area. She had wanted to rush back to the junction, but Elliot insisted she stay — she still had healing to do.

"Besides," he said, "when the stone golem informed us of your injuries, Gram and Sully headed back for the raft. They went for food and supplies and were to meet me here."

The fact that they had yet to show bothered Roni. But Elliot promised they were fine. He pointed out how long the tunnel to the raft had been, and as extra insurance, he sent the stone golem back to retrieve them. There were a lot of twisting turns in these caverns, and the little guide might be what they needed at the moment.

Twice, Elliot attempted to get Roni talking about her plans. But she dissuaded him — she only wanted to go through the arguments once. She then pointed out that they could take this time to make a more hospitable place for their meeting. Elliot agreed.

Together, they cleared away many of the rocks and stones and found other busywork to kill the time. As they lugged across four of the larger, flat stones to be used as seating positions, Roni prepared for every argument she could think of — every objection, every debatable point. Gram would not like this, yet Roni saw it as their last chance to save whatever relationship they still retained.

With the meeting area set up, Roni and Elliot fell into thoughtful silence. It did not last long. Within minutes, the *thump thump thump* of Rocky announced their guests' arrival.

Ready for the fight to begin immediately, Roni was shocked when Gram entered with tears wetting her face. The old woman scurried down, her arms open and her face betraying grandmotherly love. She wrapped Roni in a strong hug and patted her down at the same time as if to ensure that all the body parts were where they belonged.

"Are you okay?" Gram said holding Roni's head between her hands. "Is anything still broken? Did Elliot do a good job for you?"

Stomping his cane once on a stone, Elliot said, "Of course I did."

Pulling away from Gram's hands, Roni smiled. "I'm fine. Elliot did a wonderful job." Looking over her shoulder, she added, "And thank you, Sully. Your little golem is the real hero."

"Happy to hear it," Sully said, lowering his face to hide a bashful grin.

Before this reunion could derail Roni's plans further, she gestured to the meeting area. "Please, everybody have a seat. We've got some important things to discuss."

She saw the change on her grandmother's face — a hardening, a closing off of the warmth and love to be replaced by her wrinkled stoicism. No matter. That was the face Roni had expected to deal with originally.

As the Old Gang settled on the stones, Roni gathered her final thoughts. Her mouth tasted stale, and she wondered how long it would be before she could once again brush her teeth. Nobody ever mentioned such things about their long exploring journeys. She made a mental note to add such suggestions to her journal.

Looking from Elliot to Sully to Gram, Roni made sure she had their complete attention. "Facing the hellspider on my own, with nothing more than a short stone golem, has made it clear that being part of the team is vital."

Gram snorted. "Any of us could have told you that."

"Please. Let me speak. Because, well, my experience also made it clear that we were never a team."

"Don't be ridiculous. The three of us have been a team for decades and you've been with us for over a year."

"Gram!" Roni's fingers rolled into tight fists. "Not another word."

Her tone sent a shockwave across the room. The boys sat straighter, and Gram's eyes widened as her mouth tightened into a dot.

"This mission started without a team," Roni continued. "I was the one asked to go find the kyolo stones. Not the team. I was the one who did the research, and I pretty much intended to go do the whole thing on my own. Of course, I now know I never would have succeeded, but the point is that I never felt part enough of this team to bring it to you. Elliot joined me, but not the Society, just the two of us.

And even we had different missions in mind. I sought the stones, technically for Yal-hara but really I want them because her assistant indicated that I might be able to access my memories with their help. Elliot, on the other hand, cared nothing about that mission. He wanted to return to the Book on the Isle, the world the love of his life came from and where the people he had hurt resided. He sought their forgiveness, and more importantly, he wanted to return the relic he stole."

Roni paused, and she smiled inwardly when Gram did not take the opportunity to speak up.

"As we tried to leave, the two of you showed up," she said, gesturing toward Gram and Sully. "You bullied your way into our mission, joining without being asked, and Gram took over as if we were all one united group."

"I did not," Gram said, crossing her arms tight. "I am the team leader, and I saw half of my team leaving on a mission that had not been sanctioned. I knew enough about how pigheaded you could be, so I didn't dare try to stop you. But as a responsible leader, I could not let the two of you go off without support. That's why we were there."

"It doesn't matter why you think you came. That's not the point."

Placing his hand on Gram's back, Sully said, "She's right. We were not asked to join, and though I agree that you and I had the best intentions at heart, we have to admit that there really were three teams along on this journey — Roni, Elliot, and the third team, you and I."

Before Gram could get started again, Roni spoke louder. "After we reached the Isle, after we had entered the book and discovered the horrible truth of what the hellspiders had done, our missions were over. I have acquired the kyolo stones I sought, and Elliot found that there was nobody left to apologize to. He buried the relic and bid his farewell. But now we had the hellspider to contend with — a new mission that none of us wanted. And it's in a part of the cavern that probably isn't even our jurisdiction. Yet here we are."

In a strong voice that suggested not only agreement but also encouragement, Elliot said, "You have done an excellent job of detailing out how dysfunctional we have been. And as you point out, the hellspider is out there. Whether or not we have jurisdiction, as you put it, does not matter. We are here, and it is our duty as members of the Parallel Society to protect the caverns — thus, protecting our world."

"I absolutely agree. That creature is out there and it must be stopped. We all now know that it will take a functioning team to succeed. So, I propose we do just that — form a new team. One that works. The four of us can come together as new. I tried to be part of the Old Gang, but I'm not. I wasn't there for all those decades, going on adventures with you, facing terrible creatures with you, and celebrating victories or mourning our defeats. I can't be part of that. It's too far set in stone. But, if we agree now to form a new team, then the four of us can reorganize and begin our mission against the hellspider as one."

Lowering her hands, Gram said, "How do you propose we do this?"

"We start over as equals. No history, no assumptions based on past missions, we forget what we know of each other, and give each other the benefit of the doubt. Now, I'm not talking about some fairytale amnesia or anything like that. What I am suggesting is that we rely on each other's talents and ignore what we assumed to be true about each other. The three of you think you know me. But you don't. You can't. I barely know myself — how can I, when part of me is missing? You think you know each other, but you don't. You only know each other in terms of the Parallel Society. If we can give each other a clean slate, I think we'll be on our way to forming a strong team together. And our first step towards that must be electing a new leader." She didn't want to, but she couldn't help it — she looked right at Gram. "Not you, not me, not unless the team decides it."

With robotic motion, Gram turned her body to look at each of the men. They shriveled under that stark gaze. Roni did not blame them. Change was always difficult. And in the case of the Old Gang, the three of them had well–defined roles to play. Gram had led for so long that the idea of willfully giving it up was a purple cat riding a dinosaur — it made no sense.

But Roni believed that certain instincts could override the comfort of habit. In this case, the instinct of survival. "We can argue about this all day. You can try to intimidate the boys, but none of it will change the situation."

"I was not —"

"You might not know you did it, but you did. It doesn't matter. The fact is that none of us will get out of here alive without the others helping. We have no choice but to form a new team. It's up to the three of you. You decide. Either give up your old way of seeing things, of doing things, of the way you think, or we die. What's it going to be?"

With her accusations plainly laid out, Sully and Elliot looked at the ground. Gram stared at them, perhaps expecting one or both of them to turn to her, to ask for forgiveness, and to pledge their support towards her. Then Gram's face changed. It softened. Not as before — not filling up with grandmotherly warmth — but rather with understanding. Roni could not believe her words had changed these three titans of her universe.

She could almost see Gram's thoughts as if they were written in a bubble over her head — *the Society comes first.* She saw Gram watch the shame on the boys' faces, and Gram seemed to recognize her role in the current situation. Probably didn't want to admit that Roni had been right, but part of her clearly accepted the truth of Roni's final statements.

Patting her chest, Gram said, "Okay. I agree. Let us form this new team."

Sully and Elliot nodded as well. They tried not to exude relief, but there was no mistaking the change.

Elliot walked over and put his arm around Roni. "You are a smart and brave woman."

Sully clapped his hands. "Here, here."

"Boys," Gram said. "Let's not inflate this girl's ego." Sully and Elliot chuckled, but they also ceased with their praise. Gram continued, "Since we're going to start a new team, then as has been pointed out, we need a new leader. So who's it going to be?"

Not wanting to lose momentum, Roni jumped in. "It seems to me there is only one good choice." She pointed to Sully. "You're the only one who's been impartial in this whole mess. I came for the kyolo stones, Elliot has a whole personal history with the Book on the Isle, and Gram had her own mission in all of this as our previous leader. You, however, have done nothing but support us all. For that matter, I would not be alive at the moment if not for your little golem."

Sully pushed his glasses up his nose. "I don't know about this."

Elliot laughed. "I agree with Roni. You are the best choice. And you would hem and haw for hours if given the opportunity to weigh this decision out. It is a good thing you are not the one who gets to decide who leads."

Gram added, "You have my vote, too."

"Then it's settled," Roni said. "Sully is the leader of this new incarnation of the Parallel Society."

All eyes turned toward Sully. Smacking his palms against his knees, the old man stood with a grunt. "Very well." He walked over to Roni and gestured for her to take his seat. "I will accept."

Gram chuckled. "Oh Lord, I think I feel a little relief. It's kind of nice not being the one in the hot seat anymore."

Sully smirked as he thrust his hands into his pockets. Standing with his slight stoop, he reminded Roni of a politician — not the sleazy kind, but rather somebody like Churchill who could rally the troops and get an entire country behind him. She hoped.

"The first mission of this new group is obvious," Sully said without a hint of shaking in his voice. "We must either imprison or destroy the hellspider. I would like to hear from Gram and from Roni details about the previous two attacks that you were involved with."

As Roni opened her mouth to speak, Gram puffed. "I don't want to tell you how to do your job, dear, but as the only one here with true experience leading, I must point out that going over what we already know is only wasting time. That hellspider is out there, and it doesn't need to go over everything to figure out how to come after us."

Elliot sat up to the edge of his rock. "You are not the leader anymore. Sully is. If he thinks it is worth our time, then we will go over the details of the previous attacks. Besides, you were the one who taught me that it never hurts to take the time to organize thoughts and actions."

Gram stared at Elliot, her eyes wide, her head pulled back, and one hand unconsciously reaching toward her cross. "I was only trying to offer a suggestion from my experience. But if our new leader sees things a different way, then that is the way we will do things."

With as much detail as she could recall, Roni went through the events as she had witnessed them. She told of the way they had first encountered the hellspider in the courtroom. She outlined the way the creature moved, how it disrupted all the books, how it suffered from fire, and how it inhaled the smaller versions of itself. She went on to share her recollection of the second assault. As she detailed the abuse she had endured, she caught Gram cringing. It always felt good to see the grandmother side of her come out — even if only for a moment.

When she finished, she looked toward Gram. "Did I miss anything?"

"Not that I can think of."

Rocking back and forth on his feet, Sully kept his head down and his brow furrowed. His tongue poked out from time to time wetting his lips. He said nothing.

After a few minutes of this, Gram said, "What are we doing? Is he simply going to stand there or do we have a plan?"

"Patience," Elliot said. "You have never really spent enough time watching him create a golem in his workshop. This is how he thinks. Give him a moment."

As proud as Roni felt for both Elliot and Sully, her impatience matched Gram's. Perhaps it was a family trait. Thankfully, she did not have to wait much longer.

"This room you call the courtroom — it has only one exit, yes?"

"Only one we can use," Roni said. "The hellspider came in and left through a hole in the ceiling."

Sully's head snapped up, and he had a spark in his eye. "I know what we'll do. We'll need more stones, and of course, that courtroom. And unfortunately, one of us will have to lure the hellspider out."

Though nobody said a word, Roni knew that task would fall to her. She would be the bait.

CHAPTER 22

Roni stood in the middle of the humming cave. It's low ceiling and numerous books lodged in stone pressed down harder than before. She envied Atlas who only had to carry one world. The Parallel Society dealt with so many worlds, so many universes.

Maybe this wasn't such a good idea. When Sully had presented his plan, it sounded strong. Perhaps Roni would have supported anything the old man said — after everything she had gone through to reform the team, part of her didn't want to undermine Sully's newfound authority. Yet if they failed, it not only meant the end of her life, but probably the end of numerous other worlds. That seemed a great deal to heap on the four of them.

But if not them, who? They had not seen another person in the caverns. And while the Old Gang had told her that Parallel Societies existed in one form or another throughout the various universes, she had seen little evidence of it. Not that she doubted them, but those groups were not here. They might be doing great work within their own universes, but that did not solve the problem of the hellspider.

That trouble belonged to the New Gang.

For the tenth time, Roni checked that her laces were tied tight. She did not want to trip while running for her life. Although Elliot had given her a clean bill of health, she wondered how quickly her body could jump back into action. The others had gone through Elliot's healing in the past, and they seemed comfortable and secure with his approval. However, they were not the ones standing in the middle of a cave waiting to be attacked by the hellspider.

All four of them had examined the path Roni would have to run. They cleared away anything that might trip her up — every stone, every root, every twig. With a clean route and a solid plan, everything would be fine. Provided she could run fast enough. And if she couldn't — well, she had memories of her previous encounters with the hellspider.

Naturally, because life loves to be cruel, those horrible memories were the ones she could not get rid of. She could feel each strike to her body, and she could bring to mind the way the hellspider threw her. She could feel the heat radiating off its body. And those red eyes — those she would never forget.

Her father had been right. He had warned her — had tried. But it was difficult to believe words coming from a man institutionalized. And that made her wonder why he was there in the first place. A dark thought entered her mind — could Gram have had her father committed as a power-play? No. Roni didn't want to think so poorly of Gram. Besides, Gram had supported this new gang — with a few harsh comments and some grumbling thrown in, but she did come around. She was not a power monger. It must be difficult, having always been the one in charge, having always had the responsibility — letting go could not have been easy. Gram liked to control things, but she wasn't cruel. Certainly not enough to put her son-in-law into an asylum for all these years. Certainly not cruel enough to deny her granddaughter the chance to be raised by her father.

Her thoughts could not change reality, though. Her father was institutionalized. Yet, he had spoken the truth about the hellspiders.

Strange. She had been a child swaddled in a series of ever-thickening blankets — warmed and comforted by the lies that surrounded her. Now that the truth had been revealed — albeit only partially — those blankets had become a tangled mess which she struggled to clear out of. Only it seemed that each time she threw one blanket away, she found another waiting in its place. Unlike a tunnel of thought that shined light at the end to guide one along, Roni had the distinct impression that when she finally pulled away the last blanket, there would only be darkness.

She smacked her leg — these kinds of thoughts would get her nowhere. She needed to either concentrate on the moment at hand or, if that chilled her heart too much, she should dwell on whatever happy memories she could surface. As she pondered which option to take, the decision disappeared.

She heard the moan.

Once again, its deep-throated rumble caused vibrations in the humming air. Stepping out from behind a wall of stalagmites, the hellspider approached with its head brushing the ceiling. It took cautious steps. Its head turned from side to side as its eyes roved around the cavern.

Good. Roni liked that the creature remembered she could be dangerous. At least, she hoped that's what made it so careful.

"That's far enough," Roni said putting out her hand like a police officer stopping traffic.

The hellspider halted and cocked its head.

Roni spotted the way its feet dug into the ground, ready to launch forward. She heard the way it controlled its breath like an athlete preparing for a difficult maneuver. Inhaling through her mouth to avoid the creatures distasteful odor, Roni said, "You are one ugly mother —"

She had only intended the insult to relieve her stress. But the hellspider reacted as if it had understood her. It reared back and bellowed its foghorn tones. The ceiling shook. The humming grew louder, and Roni's head began to ache. She had no idea what the humming books could do, and she did not want to find out.

She didn't want to hang around to be disemboweled, either. Speaking far braver than she felt, she said, "You haven't killed me yet. Want to try? Come on you ugly piece of crap."

The hellspider roared again, and this time Roni did not wait. She whirled around and sprinted away. From behind, she heard another angry bellowing followed by the rapid-fire pounding of the hellspider's legs.

As she raced through the tunnels, adrenaline poured through her veins. She could see the clear path with ease. Each footfall landed exactly where she wanted it. Sweat drained out of her, and she could taste the blood in her system as if it had to go through her mouth first. Though she knew it was all in her head, it seemed real enough. And anything that encouraged her to keep running, she would take.

When she zipped through the junction, she felt the corners of her mouth creep up. *This might work.*

The hellspider grunted behind. With any luck, it would be more exhausted than she was — so Roni kept running.

Bursting into the courtroom, she saw the far wall moving up quickly. As planned, she put out her arms and kept running. Dear Rocky grabbed hold of her right arm and spun her ninety-degrees, lifted her off the ground, and eased her back down, slowing her momentum until she rested against the right side wall. Less than a second later, the hellspider crashed into the room, skidding to a halt in the center. Three legs pressed up against the stone chair on the platform. As it spun its head toward the back, a large golem made of stone stepped into the entranceway and disassembled into a mound of rocks that blocked the hellspider's exit.

From behind a book pile, Gram stepped forward, planting herself between the blocked exit and the hellspider. In her hands, she held a book with the emblem for fire on its cover. "Remember me?"

CHAPTER 23

As Gram opened her book, Roni saw the new expression on the woman's face — a mama bear protecting her cubs. Fire streamed out of the book as if from a flamethrower. The hellspider vaulted into the air but did not seek purchase on the walls — instead, it shot backwards, towards Elliot. Though several books burned on the floor, Gram had made it clear earlier that nobody should worry about putting them out. The books only held the rifts to the universes, they were not the universes themselves. Losing a book only meant that the fissures leading one universe into another would reopen. Not a good thing, of course. But an acceptable loss under the circumstances.

As the hellspider soared through the air, Elliot fumbled with the book in his hand. Roni wanted to scream that he should drop his book and use his cane — a weapon he felt far more comfortable wielding. But, after the exertions of sprinting through the tunnels, she had yet to catch her breath.

The hellspider body-checked Elliot, sending them both somersaulting across the floor.

Holding the ribs on his left side, Elliot used his cane to get back to his feet. Roni wished she could dart across the room, punch the hellspider, and assist Elliot in an escape. But that wasn't Sully's plan. Everybody had a job to do, and everybody faced dangers. This was not the time to defy the leadership.

Thankfully, Rocky did not have a specific task. Roni's heart jumped as she watched the little stone golem leap across the room. Launching off a stack of chained books, Rocky twisted in the air and planted its feet hard on the hellspider's back. Roni didn't know if a stone golem could feel cocky, but Rocky sure seemed overconfident. It knew it had gotten the better of the hellspider once and clearly aimed to do it again.

The hellspider, however, had the ability to learn. Rocky scampered along its spine, dodging limbs and throwing punches whenever it could. But Roni could see the difference — the hellspider did not panic. It did not wrench around searching for the source of its discomfort. It knew exactly what it was dealing with.

Though Rocky's tactics were less effective, they did provide a distraction. Elliot swung his cane hard as if trying to knock the hellspider's head across a baseball field for a home run. The loud crack of cane against bone was followed up with a satisfying groan. But Elliot made the mistake of trying to repeat the maneuver.

As the cane cut through the air for a second strike, the hellspider ducked its head while simultaneously punching out with its front limbs. Elliot shucked backwards into a pile of chained books. The hellspider used its momentum to tuck its head down and roll onto its back. It continued until it had returned to its feet — but Rocky had been slammed hard against the floor. Prodding the golem's legs, the hellspider tested to see if it had killed its little enemy.

Having stones for brains, Rocky did not know to play dead. The little golem bounced up to its feet, grabbed onto the hellspider's leg, and attempted to crawl up the creature's back.

The hellspider did not flinch. Using two of its legs, it grabbed hold of Rocky and swung the golem hard against the wall. Stones and pebbles smashed out in different directions.

Roni gasped — unsure if the rubble came from the wall or Rocky.

With all the confidence of a well-trained soldier, Gram stepped to the corner across from Roni. "Get into position, dear."

Roni moved before her ears had deciphered the words.

With a voice strong enough to carry across the room and back, Gram said, "Hey! Are you so afraid of me you have to go mess around with all my friends? I'm waiting for you." As the hellspider glowered at Gram, she whispered to Sully, "Get moving."

The hellspider stepped towards the chair in the middle of the room. It kept its focus on Gram, moving forward with tentative steps. Sully scooted across until he reached Roni.

"You holding up okay?" he asked.

"I'll be fine."

To Roni's right, a small pile of rocks had been pre-set in place. Sully grabbed these rocks, and surrounded Roni's feet with them. One by one he placed them until they formed a mound up to her ankles. From his pocket, he removed a piece of paper with Hebrew writing. He then closed his eyes and whispered some guttural words into the paper before folding it into a small square.

Handing the paper to Roni, he said, "You won't become a golem. Just put it in your pocket or on your belt, someplace where it won't get lost."

"Doesn't it need to be in the stones?"

"Only if I want it to be alive. But not for such a short and mindless task. Don't worry. You'll be fine."

Roni wasn't worried — not about that. Placing the paper in her back pocket, she felt the rocks on her feet compress as if an invisible hand had tightened her shoelaces beyond what was comfortable. Sully scrunched his brow. "Something wrong?"

"Hurry. Go help Elliot."

Nodding vigorously, Sully hastened along the room, staying close to the wall. Roni had never seen such doubt in Sully's face before — but then, he had never been the leader before. Looking at Gram holding a showdown of will with the hellspider, Roni wondered how long it would take until their new leader had such confidence.

Perhaps she had been wrong to oust Gram. The fearlessness in the cold-blooded strength of Gram could not be mastered in only a year or two. She had spent a lifetime learning how to be the anchor for her team.

No. It was too late for second-guessing. Besides, if they had not put Sully into the leadership position, he would never have come up with this plan.

The hellspider's eyes twitched as it glanced at Sully scooting along. Roni didn't have to say a word. Gram opened her book and the flames singed one of the hellspider's front legs. As the creature sidestepped the flames, favoring its other legs, Sully hustled the rest of the way to Elliot.

Roni bared her teeth. The hellspider had finally noticed its situation. It wanted to turn around and see what Sully and Elliot were up to, but it didn't dare take its eyes off of Gram. Though stuck in the middle of the room, it appeared to have figured out that Gram posed the only immediate threat.

But Roni was no idiot — soon enough, the creature would decide that it could no longer stay still. If it did not act, it would be captured. As Sully piled rocks on Elliot's feet and handed him a piece of paper, Roni picked up the first of the books stacked at her side. This one bore the symbol for a hailstorm.

Sully stepped away from Elliot, turned around, and nodded at Roni. The time had come. With the hellspider's attention on Gram, Roni had plenty of opportunity to lift her book up and aim it at the creature's flank.

She opened the book.

Rocks of ice machine-gunned out of the pages. The hellspider bolted away and Roni tried to follow, strafing the ground with hail. The hellspider scurried up a tall hill of books, out of Roni's range.

Not until she closed the book and glanced over at Gram did she know if their diversion had been successful. To her relief, she saw Sully finishing the stone shoes at her grandmother's feet. Catching Gram's eye, Roni offered a nod and a wink. Then Gram's face fell.

Roni understood immediately. She had taken her eye off the enemy. The hellspider raged down the book hill, stampeding toward Roni. With her stone shoes locking her to the ground, she could not escape.

She opened her book again but the tumultuous storm inside had dissipated. Never can trust the weather. She glanced at Gram, her eyes begging for help. Gram held back. She had no choice. If she opened her book, the flames would have burned Roni as much as the hellspider.

A tear slipped from Roni's eye right before the hellspider bowled her over. It knocked her back with such force that her ankles, lodged in their stone shoes, audibly cracked. She wailed as quakes of pain rippled up her body. A part of her brain heard the scrabbling feet of the hellspider as it climbed the wall behind and dashed toward the blocked entrance. It jumped back to the floor, appearing to understand Gram's hesitation, and turned toward Roni — it knew it was safe from the fire book.

Through blurred eyes and excruciating torment, Roni knew no such security. The hellspider moved in on her.

CHAPTER 24

When suffering pain — extreme pain — Roni knew the body could numb itself. Whether through shock or adrenaline or some other process she had never heard of, the body could will itself pain free — at least, temporarily. As the hellspider towered over her and pulled back a leg with every intent of mashing her skull, she awaited that relief from her body.

A rock flew in from the side and clunked against the hellspider's head. As it rolled its shoulders to look where the attack came from, another rock flew in smacking directly on its forehead. Several feet away Sully pitched another rock at the creature.

"Varsity pitcher, Hemsdale High, 1964." Like a pro, Sully wound up and pitched another speeding rock.

Gram switched books and opened a new one. As if unlocking a door into outer space, the open book vacuumed in everything it could grab. The hellspider slipped several feet before it could dig its claws into the floor. Books lifted in the air and pulled off the walls but all now had chains locking them to solid stone. They stretched and waved in the winds but none were lost into the vacuum.

Roni's body tried to slide but her stone shoes ended up swinging her like the hand of a clock. She howled in pain. One hand snapped out to grab the nearest part of the stone floor, desperate to stop her body from moving. If only she could be rid of these shoes.

Idiot! With her free hand she patted around her pockets until she found the paper that Sully had given her. With her teeth and one hand, she unfolded it twice and then ripped it in two.

The stone shoes crumbled apart. The individual rocks that had formed it rolled off towards Gram's book.

The relief of being freed met with new sensations of electric fire as her broken ankles shifted to new positions. Ignoring her own screams, Roni rolled onto her stomach and used both hands to claw her way toward the wall.

She dared to glance over her shoulder. Rocks and debris flew through the air each one falling into the vortex of Gram's book. The shrieking winds were matched by the clatter of debris. Only inches from her feet, the hellspider clung to the ground, desperate to find its way to safety.

For an instant, the horrifying idea that the creature might leap forward and clasp onto her ankles filled Roni's thoughts. She could see it with disgusting clarity. The large beast had the strength and mass to fly through the air for a moment. Its weight would slam upon her ankles causing high voltage to spike up her legs. The strong vacuum of Gram's book would eventually overtake the creature. But it would not let go, and in the end, it would rip Roni's feet off her legs. Then, if Elliot could not move fast enough, she would bleed to death.

But the hellspider had a different idea in mind.

With the same forceful leap Roni had envisioned, it jumped forward and *over* her — not with the intent of clasping onto her legs, but with the desire to latch onto the wall. It succeeded with two legs.

As it attempted to pull the rest of its body against the wall, the shift in position changed the pull of the book. Roni felt her body lifting off the ground, and she dug her fingers in tighter.

"I can't hold on!"

Gram shut the cover and the winds died immediately. The hellspider scaled up to the ceiling. Rolling on her back, Roni gasped for air. Sweat salted her mouth.

She watched as the creature headed for its old escape — but as it reached the crevice, another stone golem, one as big as the golem blocking the entranceway — crawled out. The hellspider backed up and hissed. The golem did not move. Instead, it disassembled itself, locking its pieces in place to seal the crevice exit.

Propping up against the wall, Roni cringed as she saw her limp feet hanging at wrong angles. As the hellspider crawled across the ceiling toward the center of the room, Roni looked towards Elliot. She wanted to hide her desperation, wanted to exude bravery, but the chemicals in her body that numbed her pain would soon be wearing off. She knew in the long run she should not become reliant on a healer, but she promised herself that she would start her self-reliance on the next mission. Just please save her feet.

Elliot caught her eye. With the motion of his hand and a single, soft nod, he assured her that when the opportunity came, he would do his best to fix her. But there was still the hellspider to deal with. Turning her attention toward Sully, she heard the change in his voice before she witnessed the cold calculations on his face.

"Everyone get ready," Sully said in a near monotone. "This is it."

Gram said, "You sure you want to do this?" Her tone did not convey doubt in Sully's plans nor did she challenge his role as leader. Instead, Roni heard authentic concern — a sense of foreboding as if Gram knew that making this decision would forever change her good friend.

Sully paused to gaze up at the hellspider. "We tried to capture it, and Roni is hurt. There's no more time. We have a plan for what to do if we couldn't capture it, and that's where we are."

Kissing her cross, Gram said, "Okay." She set down her book and lifted a different one — one bound in red and black leather.

In the far corner, Elliot picked up another book with a similar binding. Sully walked back toward the open corner and picked up a book of his own. He planted his feet hard on the ground, rooting them as if he were made of stone. With each team member stationed in the four corners of the room, all eyes turned up towards the ceiling.

"Roni?" Gram said from across the room. "You sure you're up for this?"

"Don't have a choice. Let's get this over with before I pass out."

Pride flashed across Gram's face before she turned her attention back to the hellspider. She opened her book.

The force with which this book began to pull in the room's air made the previous vacuum nothing more than an afternoon breeze. Taken off guard, the hellspider plummeted to the ground. Before the book could take it away, the hellspider positioned itself behind the chair in the middle. It griped its many legs onto the stone backboard.

The strong winds knocked Roni to the ground. She rolled forward and only stopped when she remembered to slap out one arm to brace herself. She silently vowed that should she survive this, she would invest in some training on fighting, falling, and other important skills.

The book — she had the wrong one. The red and black volume she needed sat atop the small pile only a few feet away. With the wind howling around them and pages fluttering through the air, Roni attempted to inchworm toward her book pile.

The hellspider held onto the chair with amazing strength, but it did not know Sully's plan. Part of Roni actually felt sorry for the creature. She muscled her way further toward the book pile, but she did not know if she would make it before passing out.

Over the roaring winds, Gram yelled, "I can't hold this all day. Sully, get started."

Though Roni could not see Sully from behind the pile of books, she could hear the change in noise and feel the change in air pressure as he opened his book. In an instant, there were two vortexes of energy pulling into two different books. The howling winds shifted to a shriek or perhaps it was the noise of the hellspider. Grasped by these new winds, the hellspider tumbled toward Sully. Panicking, it flailed its legs and managed to scramble back to the chair. Clinging all of its legs around the stone, it lifted its head and cried out.

Roni reached for the book pile and rolled onto her back, panting. She slipped the red and black book off the top and let it rest on her belly. No way could she crawl back to the wall, push herself up, and open the book. She would have to roll onto her stomach and hold the book open from the floor. But without the stone shoes to secure her, she did not think she would last long.

Grunting, she lolled to her side. Elliot raised his book, and as he opened the cover, he met Roni's eyes — he knew the trouble she was in. But the job had to be done. Their duty to the Parallel Society, to the caverns, to the universe, meant more than any individual. That was what the team was all about.

Opening his book, he created a third harsh vacuum. The hellspider's torso lifted free from the chair and fluttered in the air like a flag in a hurricane. Roni thought she heard Gram yelling something but the competing cacophony of storming winds made it impossible to catch individual words.

And then it happened. Roni slid a few inches.

Clutching the book to her chest, she tried to sit up. No good. Even without the pain shooting along her spine into the back of her head, her body was spent — she lacked the strength to raise herself. As she slipped further toward the center of the room, she could see the deep fear on Gram's face, the resigned sadness on Elliot's, and as she cleared the book pile, she also caught Sully's mournful gaze.

With the force of will, she managed to return to her back. Perhaps she could lift the book and open it, even though her aim would not be exact. She could do her part until one of the other books pulled her to her end. But nobody ever mentioned how heavy these particular books were — she would've had an easier time bench pressing Elliot. However, as her heart sank, she heard a sound cutting through the tumultuous noise — one that caused her blood to pump faster, one that filled her with a scrap of hope.

Thump thump thump.

Rocky appeared at her side. The little golem only had one arm remaining and lacked several of the stones that made up its head, but it was here. Wrapping its one arm around her chest it yanked her up and then spooned behind her, using its weight to lock her in place.

Cheering for the little guy as much as for her own relief, Roni set the book in her lap and aimed it toward the hellspider. She paused to think of something cool to say. But the team didn't need a cool quip. It needed her to act.

She opened her book. The front legs of the hellspider stripped free from the back of the chair and stretched toward Roni. The creature spun its limbs like pinwheels, grasping desperately for the chair, but with all four whirlwinds pulling on this creature in four directions, it could not manage to secure itself. It lifted higher in the air, hovering a few feet above the chair.

With a jerk, its legs splayed out. Roni could see the anguish on the creature's face, as well as its realization of what would come. But as Sully had said, they tried to capture it, tried to send it to a different universe, but it had refused. This was the end of the road.

Roni was thankful for all the noise thundering around her. It saved her from ever knowing the horrible sound of the hellspider's limbs tearing from its body. Though she could watch the creature crying, see its terrified face, she never had to hear its torso pull apart. She never had to hear the awful shrieking rising from her own throat. The image of limbs spinning through the air as the four books sucked up different parts of its body would haunt her long enough.

When the last piece of flesh slipped into Gram's book she slammed it shut. Elliot and Sully followed suit, and Rocky helped close Roni's book. The sudden silence rang in her ears. Only three drops of blood dappled the old chair.

CHAPTER 25

A week later, Roni sat in her car parked in the lot outside of Belmont Behavioral Hospital. She could still see the hellspider's final moments. After it had been killed and the last book closed, Elliot sprang across the room to fix Roni's ankles. He succeeded. Though sharp stings still shot up her legs now and then, it felt wonderful to be able to drive once more. Heck, walking felt like a privilege.

Elliot promised to give her another healing treatment in a few days which, he guaranteed, would clean up the last of the fixable damage. But he also warned — there were limits. Some damage could not be undone. Some would remain always.

Roni agreed with that — the mental damage alone might take forever to be rid of. And not just for her. The whole gang had barely spoken during the trip back.

Using Rocky as a movable walker, Roni had followed the gang back through the long tunnels to their raft. They launched onto the lake and paddled their way to the Isle. Elliot explained that inside the Book on the Isle they had their way home. He led them through the desolate town, towards Dorarnosk's house. They were all on edge, eyes searching for any sign or movement of the smaller hellspiders. But none were found.

Roni limped as well as she could manage. Her newly healed ankles sparked fierce flames if she walked too fast. Plus, they had to leave Rocky back on the Isle. She had already stepped through the book when she realized her golem savior would not be coming. Sully must have pulled the paper from Rocky because, after all, the golem was formed with stones from the cavern. It could not come back with them. It would be a relic. So, Rocky was no more.

"Over here," Elliot said, leading them to the ruins of a large home. Inside what might have been a private office, Elliot found the book he sought. "It will take us to a different part of the cavern. One close to home. And I know the rest of the way from there."

He opened the book and they each stepped through. That was why Waterfield never provided a map with a non-river path leading to the Isle. The way back started in the middle of an empty tunnel. From there they had a long hike, but within a day they were back at the bookstore.

Roni spent the last several days cooped up in her apartment. Resting. Though each member of the gang created excuses to stop by and check on her, she had mostly spent the time alone. Fine by her. She had too many thoughts to deal with — she didn't need more.

That was behind her now. She had finally managed to sleep through the night without seeing the frightening hairy face with those red eyes bearing down on her, ready to devour her. Driving to the mental hospital gave her something different to focus on, and for that, if nothing else, she was grateful.

Waiting outside would not make any of the day easier or better, though. She knew it. Didn't want to admit it, but she knew it.

Making sure not to take her ankles for granted, she eased out of the car and hobbled slowly to the building's lobby. She went through the process of checking in, chatting with the attendants, and eventually ending up in the visitor's room.

Less than five minutes later, a nurse entered with Roni's father on her arm. She walked the man over to Roni, helped him sit in a plastic folding chair, and smiled. Her father gazed off into the distance, his body thinner than before.

"He said he could do without the wheelchair today, but don't hesitate to call if he needs it." The nurse walked away.

For a few minutes, Roni said nothing. At first, she thought she dwelled in the peacefulness and comfort of simply sitting with her father. But her mind could be tricky, and she soon recognized that she had lulled herself into stalling.

"Dad," she said, the unmistakable tremors in her voice echoing in her head. "I faced the hellspider."

His eyes took a sharp turn towards her.

"It's okay. I'm okay. I wasn't alone. Gram and Elliot and Sully all were with me. The Parallel Society — you know it? Of course you do. Well, we had to go into the caverns on a mission, and we came across that creature. But it's gone. You don't have to worry anymore. We killed it."

He dropped his head to the side and his eyes welled. Pulling in his lips, he exhaled a long breath. With a scratchy, distant voice, he said, "You shouldn't have done that."

"I told you. We're fine." The sound of his voice fluttered her heart. She wanted to reach across the table and wrap her arms around his head, but she held off — he was speaking now, and she didn't want to frighten him back into wherever he hid within himself.

"You shed blood. It's the first step."

"Do you know what you're talking about? Do you understand what I'm saying? You don't have to be afraid for me. I'm part of the Society, and we were able to defeat a terrible monster."

"No. You have begun the destruction of the caverns."

"You've got it all backwards. We saved the caverns."

Her father's arm flashed out and gripped Roni's forearm. His eyes opened wide, and in both tone and word, Roni could see that he was momentarily lucid.

"Get me out of here," he said. "It's not too late. I can help you."

Roni twisted as she tried to free her arm. "You're hurting me."

Rising to his feet, her father inhaled sharply and thrust her aside. As loud as a warrior on a noisy battlefield, he said, "You have done a terrible thing. There will be more. There's always more. They will come and they will destroy." He paced around the room, gesticulating toward the other patients, grabbing papers and throwing them in the air. "It's all meaningless. How can we be expected to know the right thing to do? We are lied to, we are manipulated, and in the end, we nearly die trying to do the right thing which is the wrong thing. Unless it isn't which we never really know."

Two burly orderlies rushed in and wrestled her father into submission. He kept yelling about being betrayed, lied to, and yet knowing the truth. They carted him off toward his room.

Roni did not move. Her heart hammered in her chest as she tried to absorb and decipher his meaning. At what point did his words fall away from truth and into his own dementia? The only thing she could be sure of, the first words — *There will be more.* That rang true because she had thought it herself. The hellspiders would not be the last.

CHAPTER 26

Two hours later, Roni slid into the booth at the Olburg Chestnut. She tried to eavesdrop on conversations going on around her — anything to keep her mind away from the strange words her father had spoken. She checked her watch. A few minutes early. With a wave of her hand, she called over a waitress and ordered a hamburger.

That had yet to get old. After only a short time spent in the caverns, each bite of real food overwhelmed her senses with ecstasy. The simple pleasures. If nothing else, she had gained great appreciation for the nuances of life — like the succulent flavors of an old-fashioned hamburger.

"It is amazing," Kenneth Bay said. He wore another fine suit but had no cane — apparently it was for show. "One always yearns for the basic flavors of their home."

Roni glanced up at the annoying man. "Do I really want to know what Yal-hara eats?"

"Probably not." He settled in opposite her, smoothing his tie with one hand while drumming his fingers on the table with the other. "On behalf of Yal-hara, I thank you for your service. Now, if you would please complete our agreement and hand over the kyolo stones." His drumming fingers stopped as he turned his hand over.

Roni hesitated.

Before she could speak, Kenneth Bay leaned in. "I understand that you went through a difficult time in acquiring the stones. The caverns have never been the most friendly place. But we cannot help you, if you don't help us. Without Yal-hara, those stones are nothing but rocks to you. And if you are thinking about renegotiating our deal, I strongly advise you not to do so. I have been in this game a long time.

You have barely begun. You are nothing but a baby, and I can crush a baby."

"Sheesh. No need to get all dark." She set the bag of stones on the table. As he scooped them up and stood, she said, "Hey!"

Running a finger across his mustache, he gazed down at her. "This isn't hardly enough for Yal-hara or you to get what you desire. Traveling to other universes isn't easy — not when you're alone, not part of a group like the Parallel Society. Don't worry, though. Once Yal-hara has all the ingredients she needs, she'll have everything she also needs for you."

Roni clenched her jaw. She felt her emotions competing — on one side, she was like a teenage girl stood up for the prom, but on the other side, she enjoyed the relief of knowing she did not have to show up at the prom at all. "I suppose I already knew you wouldn't deliver."

"Oh, we will. But there are more items in more worlds that we'll need your help acquiring. This is a good start. Soon, we will call upon you again, and when we do, you can be assured that your efforts will be fully rewarded." He turned to leave, stopped, and looked back. He rested his hands on the table, and brought his mouth close to her ear. "No matter what, do not share any of this with anyone. It must remain secret. Especially from your friends in the Parallel Society. You failed us before in this regard — blabbing to your team about us. But they will destroy us if given a chance. And, to be clear, when I say destroy, I mean kill. If you don't want Yal-hara's blood on your hands — or mine, for that matter — then say nothing."

He left Roni to sit alone.

Chapter 27

The streets of Olburg were congested this particular day, and Roni circled the bookstore block four times before she snagged a parking space. Walking toward *In The Bind*, her jumbled thoughts and conflicted heart duked it out within her. After everything the team had been through, it seemed wrong to hide information from them. But she had already started working on how to free her father — something Gram was against. Plus, she wanted her memories back — another thing Gram resisted. Perhaps, if she kept quiet for now, it would be best.

Turning the corner, she shelved the debate for a later time when she would have privacy. She entered the bookstore and noted the lack of customers. Gram, Elliot, and Sully sat at the big table.

"Don't look so distraught," Gram said. They had a bottle of gin and a bottle of brandy sitting in the center of the table. "This isn't the first time we've had to close up the store for over a week so we could go save the universe. We always reopen and eventually the customers come back."

Sully tilted back a glass of brandy. "Yes, yes. We've been at this for a long time. You can learn a thing or two from your elders about how to run this place."

"I'm sure," Roni said.

With a wave of his hand, Elliot said, "Come. Join us."

Roni shook her head. The way the three of them sat so comfortably at the table reminded her that there newly formed team had only been temporary. "I have a lot of work to do in the Grand Library."

Sully banged his glass on the table. "Says who?"

Gram raised her hands, palms out. "Don't look at me. I'm not leader anymore — and I don't want the job back."

"Then I guess I'm still the leader." Sully pushed back his chair and stood. "This is the New Gang and you, young lady, are part of it. We're a team and it's time that you acted like part of us. Now get over here and drink some alcohol."

Trying to hide her enthusiasm, Roni sauntered over to the table. Sully gently rocked from side to side — a little drunk, apparently. He slid an empty glass toward Roni.

"We have gin, and we have brandy. Or you can make a disgusting mixture of both."

Roni chuckled. "I guess I'll opt for the gin."

Elliot jingled the ice in his glass. "Smart choice. I find it quite delicious."

"I didn't think you drank."

"There are always occasions which permit one to bend rules."

Gram lifted her glass. "I'll drink to that." After tossing it back, she reached for the gin and filled half her glass with it. Then she poured in the brandy to top it off. "Never mind what these boys say. It's delicious."

Before Roni could pick up her glass, Gram sloshed brandy into her gin. The liquids swirled around each other resembling a weak tea. Sully lifted his glass and tapped it with a pencil until everybody raised their glasses as well.

"While we have much to celebrate including the formation of this latest chapter of the Parallel Society, now that the four of us are assembled together, we should take a moment to recognize those not with us. To Rocky and all of the golems past and future — fallen heroes, each and every one. May they forgive me for the tasks I ask of them and may they always be remembered as partners and teammates of our group."

"Here, here," Elliot said.

"And," Gram said, "let us not forget to toast Sully for taking on the thankless and difficult job of herding us cats."

"Here, here," Sully said.

"Also," Roni said, surprising herself as much as the New Gang, "let's toast to a new level of honesty between us. Secrets kept from me throughout my life led to unfortunate outcomes. And to me being a bit stubborn."

"A bit?" Gram said, and the boys laughed.

"Perhaps more than a bit. But we can't be a solid team unless we build trust. That comes from sharing information, not hiding it."

"To honesty," Sully said, lifting his glass higher and dribbling a little gin onto his hand in the process.

"To honesty." Elliot knocked back his drink, as did Gram.

Roni took a short swig from her glass. She thought of her father and Yal-hara. And secrets.

The drink burned down her throat.

RIFT ANGEL

THE PARALLEL SOCIETY BOOK 3

CHAPTER 1

With her head pressed against the passenger side window, Roni rapped her knuckles against the glass and imagined her fingers around the throat of her grandmother. The green hills of Ireland rolled by as Gram drove their rental car ever deeper into the heart of the country, and though a gentle rain caused the lush grass to glisten, the beauty of this foreign country could not outweigh Roni's inner fire. When it came to driving Roni crazy, Gram had never lost her touch.

"Are you going to talk to me, yet?" she asked Gram. "You barely said a word on the flight over and we've been in this car for a half-hour now. Shouldn't I know what kind of situation I'm going into? I get that you like to be in control all the time, but you're no longer the leader of this group. A little teamwork would be appreciated."

Gram, a sturdy woman in her seventies, patted the crucifix pendant resting on the shelf of her bosom. "You have got to stop being so naïve. You think you understand everything, but then you make all sorts of misjudgments based on your ignorance."

"How am I supposed to learn anything when you won't tell me?"

The argument was too familiar, but Roni could not let it slide. Back home in Pennsylvania, things would be different. She could seek refuge at her desk in the Grand Library several secret floors below the family bookshop, *In The Bind*. She could bury her head amongst all the old journals detailing centuries of the history and events that shaped the Parallel Society. Or she could work on her favorite side-project — mapping out the endless, twisting caverns beneath the store that connected to Gram's office and housed the numerous books that were part of their sacred duty.

But this is was not Pennsylvania. This was not the Grand Library.

This was Roni's first overseas trip as a member of the Parallel Society and she didn't want to blow it.

Trying to sound more like the adult she was and not the sulking teenager of long ago, Roni said, "Sully is the leader now. He ordered me on this trip, and that means that I am part of this."

"No, dear. It means that Sully believes you are ready to learn more. Not participate. Simply observe and learn."

"That's it? Don't get me wrong. I'm thrilled to be here, but if I'm just supposed to stay in the background, then what was the point of treating this like a team? He told me I'd be a big help to you. Why send us both?"

Clenching and unclenching the steering wheel, Gram said, "You have a lot to learn. Listening should be at the top of the list. Sully and Elliot and I are not going to live forever. We're old and we're tired of running the Society ourselves. When you take over, it's essential that you understand all aspects that exist regarding the work we do."

"Which is why your silent treatment is so damn infuriating."

"Watch your language."

"Sorry, but you are acting foolish. Have you learned nothing from the way you led us before? Playing everything close to the vest does not help the team work smoothly. At least give me something so I know what to be observing and learning from."

"You never change," Gram said.

Roni could not miss the bait in her grandmother's words but locked her jaw to prevent her mouth from digging deeper. She knew she was right – they had to work together — but she had to give the old woman some slack. After all, less than a year ago, Gram had been top dog in the Society. She had controlled things for so long that she must have expected to do so until her death. But Roni's involvement in the caverns with a creature called a hellspider led to a change of leadership.

She wasn't so sure Gram had forgiven her. That Sully — short, bald, with tufts of white hair ringing his head — had taken over and showed the makings of a strong leader probably irked Gram more. He was thoughtful and considerate, even if a bit reticent about taking the role away from Gram. It helped that his best friend, Elliot, always stood by his side.

The two old men had been like uncles to Roni as she grew up, and they saw her off on this trip as if sending her away to college. Elliot, smelling of campfire smoke, had pulled her into a firm hug.

Born in Kenya, raised in England, and settled in the US, he had a deep exacting way of speaking and a broad smile that brightened his dark features. "Trust Sully and trust your Gram. I know there is much you don't understand, but we need you to be on this trip."

Elliot's words echoed in Roni's head each time she felt the fire within burning hotter. Staring at the Irish hills drifting by, she swallowed back her biting comments and exhaled long and slow. "I will stand back and observe, and I will learn. If you need my help capturing this rift, you merely have to ask."

Though Gram kept her eyes forward on the road, Roni thought she caught the woman lifting her chin in triumph.

"We will not be capturing this rift," Gram said. "It's been tried before, and so far, nobody in the Society has figured out how to do it. The rift had been stabilized, for lack of better word, and every year I travel to Ireland to make sure that the system we have in place continues to operate safely."

"Wait, so, this is a maintenance check?"

"Of a sort."

Roni put her head against the glass again. "Unbelievable. I have a lot of work to do back in the Grand Library, and you all have sent me out here to watch you look at a bunch of books and say, *Yup they're still there.*"

"What do you think the Parallel Society is all about? We are keepers of a simple and pure task — to secure these accidental rifts that open between our universe and others. It is not supposed to be about excitement and daring. We try to avoid those kinds of situations from occurring. If we do our jobs right, everything is quiet and nothing is happening. It's that simple."

"You create chains and magic books that hold these universes, Elliot and his cane can heal people and open locks and I don't even know what else. And don't get me started on Sully and his golems. What's simple about that?"

Gram's mouth tightened with a knowing smirk. "You're still upset that you don't have a special power."

"No." *Maybe.* "I'm upset because you all keep asking me to prepare to lead this group in order to go on saving our world and yet you continually try to shelter me from what we have to face."

The road twisted and curved in such a haphazard manner that Roni had long ago lost her sense of direction.

Like the sudden appearance of a lighthouse on a foggy night, Gram calmed her tone and said, "Very well. Listen carefully so that you are prepared for what we're going to face."

Roni straightened in her seat and adjusted the seatbelt so she could better pay attention in comfort.

Gram continued, "There will be at least four women at the compound. Pay attention to the layout of the buildings, and be sure to observe the power dynamics between the women. It can change more often than you think. We will be escorted into an underground room where we will find the rift. If any of the set up needs to be adjusted or replaced, I will handle it. Try to avoid talking to any of the women without being rude, unless they ask you a question directly, of course. They will seem nice, kind, possibly even warm or open-minded. Don't believe it."

Gram pulled over to the side of the road where a metal gate led to a dirt road trailing off into the hills. She turned towards Roni. "I am no longer the leader of this group, but I am the leader of this mission. Once we are there, you do what I say. Do not question me in front of these women. It could be very dangerous."

"Got it. Don't trust the women. Follow your orders. Anything else?"

"Don't show me any disrespect or attitude." Before Roni could say a word, Gram raised her hand. "I'm not saying that as the person who raised you. I'm saying that because these women will pick up on your attitude towards me. If they sense any weakness, we could be in a lot of trouble."

Reading the seriousness on Gram's face, Roni nodded. "I can do that."

"Good. Now go outside and open the gate."

Digesting all that Gram had said, Roni hurried out of the car to swing open the gate. The rusty metal whined like a bratty child. After Gram drove through, Roni closed the gate, and as she headed back to the car, she noticed a wooden sign under the protection of an alder tree.

Though weeds crept over one corner of the sign, the words could still be made out:

Croghan Abbey
County Offlay

Buckling into her seat, Roni said, "Is this a place for nuns?"

"Of a sort," Gram said as she headed up the dirt road. "They are no longer connected with the Catholic Church, though they have many of the same trappings. But don't be fooled. These women can be very dangerous. They are not to be trusted."

Driving onward, the trees thickened around them, blocking most of the daylight and cooling the air fast. It reminded Roni of the first time she stepped foot into the caverns below the bookstore — the way the temperature stayed cool no matter what the outside world was like. A chill crossed her skin.

"Got it," she said. "Don't trust the nuns."

CHAPTER 2

Roni peered into the shadowy forest as the wheels crunched the dirt and rocks below. No wonder all the old fairytales equated the forest with witchcraft and evil. Everywhere Roni looked, she saw shadows moving, lurking, watching her from the darkness. Just like discovering familiar images in the clouds, searching for horrors in the shadows proved every bit as easy.

The road broke free of the forest and led to a large, wide clearing. As they curved up a slight incline, Roni spotted a lake off to her right. To the left, a path led back into the woods. Ahead, the road opened into a large circle with a statue of the Virgin Mary in the center. With her arms held wide and open as she gazed down upon all approaching vehicles, she offered her Mona Lisa grin that both welcomed and warned all who approached.

Flower beds filled with purple butter wort and blue-eyed grass bordered the circle, and on the left, the main church rose high towards Heaven. Medieval in design, it had a bell tower up front and a long section going on out the back. To the left of the church, a colonnade walkway led to a bland, squarish building. To the right, a similar set up ended in another bland building. Off the far end of the circle, the road continued. In the distance, Roni saw a barn. Beyond that, tall corn grew in rows that stretched on as far as she could see.

The rain had ceased, and two women wearing black habits with white-trim wimples stood outside. They watched as Gram parked the car and stepped out. The older of the two women moved forward. She had a pudgy face and a stern mouth, and Roni suspected that a simple glance from her could stop a middle school classroom in its tracks.

"Lillian, it's so good to see you," the woman said.

Gram shook the woman's hand, then gestured to Roni. "This is my granddaughter, Veronica. She goes by Roni." Gram waved Roni over. "This is Sister Mary."

Roni got out of the car and shook hands with the Sister. "Pleasure to meet you."

Sister Mary gestured behind her without taking her eyes off Roni. "This is Sister Claudia. She's young enough to be my granddaughter."

Gram forced a chuckle and Sister Mary laughed harder than necessary. Sister Claudia stepped forward and shook hands with both women. She had a deceptive, gentle touch — bordering on frail.

"You'll find that everything is in order," Sister Mary said, lacing her fingers under her belly. "We take our duty very seriously."

Gram patted her crucifix. "I've never known you to do otherwise."

Both women appeared eminently pleased with each other. Gram even smiled wide enough to show her teeth — something Roni had never seen before and hoped never to see again.

Sister Claudia's eyes narrowed and with a stiff arm, she gestured toward the church. "Perhaps we should show you the rift so you may complete your inspection and be on your way."

Sister Mary's hard glower forced Sister Claudia to lower her head and step back. "I apologize," Sister Mary said to Gram. "This one is under my tutelage. She will be taking over running the Abbey when I am no longer able. As you can see, she still has much to learn."

Gram tilted her head toward Roni. "I have one of my own."

The two old women shared a more authentic chuckle before Sister Mary led the way inside.

The narthex of the church consisted of a wide, flat stone flooring, highly polished wood trim around white plaster walls, and two heavy, rounded doors made of wood with black iron straps. On either side of the doors, statues of Jesus and Mary stood. Gesturing toward the right, Sister Mary led the way to a narrow door that opened onto a narrower staircase winding clockwise downward.

Stopping at the door, Sister Mary opened her mouth and from the shape of her lips, Roni expected to hear a simple caution — *watch your step.*

But then the screams came.

Sister Mary's hand covered her mouth. "Sister Susan. Sister Rachel."

Gram leapt to the stairwell and soared downward. The two nuns flew in behind her, leaving Roni to bring up the rear. Though she had seen Gram act fast before, Roni caught a glimpse of panic on the old woman's face — a new and different kind of fear.

The screams grew louder as they descended further under the church. The narrow, spiraling staircase made each footfall dangerous. Roni felt like a bug swirling down the drain, and she let out a held breath when they finally reached the bottom.

Though not as deep as the full length of the church, the cellar stretched far enough to accommodate a small gathering. Several feet ahead, Roni witnessed the rift flickering light in all directions — a swirling cylinder of red and orange like a fiery storm. The cylinder hovered about six inches off the ground and stopped just shy of the ceiling. Eight books on eight stands encircled this rift to another universe — at least, they were supposed to.

Three of the stands had been knocked over and their books strewn across the floor. Sister Susan and Sister Rachel sat nearby nursing a bleeding head wound for one and a bloody nose for the other.

Heat radiated off the rift. Air howled around them. Weaving in and out of that noise, Roni picked up on pained screams like the cries of children being tortured. Or animals. Or even the horrid shrieks of creatures unknown. The sounds shifted as if arriving on waves.

Gram stood where the gap from fallen books had been formed. She held open a book of her own. With her left foot planted behind for support, she pushed the book forward as if fighting against a heavy storm wind.

Over her shoulder, she said, "Quit gawking. Reset the books."

Roni rushed over to the nearest bookstand and set it in place. Divots on the floor made it easy to see the correct positioning. A long chain stretched from the bookstand to the spine of one book — red leather cover with gold trim. Roni reeled it in and set the book on the stand, opening it to face the rift. A warm, yellow glow emanated from the book and the roiling cylinder of energy dimmed slightly. The howling wind lessened.

Snapping her fingers at Sister Claudia, Roni said, "Are you going to help?"

Scowling, Sister Claudia uttered a soft but quick prayer before hurrying over to set up another bookstand.

Roni docked the final stand behind Gram. Having dealt with Gram's chains before, Roni found the alligator clip that secured the chain to the stand and yanked it off. Helping Gram avoid tripping on the stand, Roni guided her back until she could set the book down. With a flick of her wrist, Gram produced a new chain from the sleeve of her blouse. She secured the chain to the stand and punctured the book's spine with the other end.

Sister Claudia finished setting her book on its stand, but when she opened it a rod of energy snapped out of the cylinder like a lance and pierced the book, knocking it and Sister Claudia to the floor. Gram and Roni raced over to reset the stand while Sister Mary attended to her fellow nuns. As Roni replaced the stand in its proper position and Gram produced a fresh book, a strange, haunted noise came from the rift.

Roni looked back. Her mouth dried from being locked open. Her eyes widened.

A young girl appeared in the center of the firestorm — her hair parted in the middle and a peace sign pendant around her neck. She stared back at Roni like some burning mirror image. Only the closer Roni looked, the less she saw of her own face. Rather, she spotted a glimpse of herself from long ago — a younger version from a time before she had been born.

But then the mirror image raised its head, looking beyond Roni. The girl's chin trembled. She lifted a hand, reaching out through the cylinder, covered in swirls of orange and red. She reached for Gram.

"Mom?" the girl said.

As Roni snapped her head around to face Gram, the final book slid into place and was opened. Roni turned back to the cylinder and the girl had disappeared. The stormy cyclones within the cylinder muted in color and intensity. The horrid sounds diminished.

With her skin paling and her eyes searching the rift, Gram stood petrified like an alabaster statue. Her eyes welled, but tears did not fall. Roni had never seen such weakness in her grandmother.

The word *stroke* popped in her mind. As she scrambled through her thoughts for the symptoms of such a thing, another part of Roni warned that this would not be so simple. She took a hesitant step closer to Gram. Her grandmother's eyes snapped upon hers. Roni froze.

"Come with me," Sister Mary said in a gentle tone.

At first, Roni thought the nun spoke to her. However, the woman put her arm around Gram and the two shuffled toward the stairs.

"Wait," Roni said, but Sister Mary kept Gram moving.

Before Roni could follow, Sister Claudia stepped in her way. "We need your help here."

"That's my grandmother. I need to make sure she's okay."

"Sister Mary can take care of her just fine. But you and your grandmother came here to help with this rift. Do you want to explain to those women why we failed to finish securing things down here?"

Roni brushed by Sister Claudia and put one foot on the bottom stair. She glanced back at the cylinder of energy and the eight books surrounding it. If three of them had fallen so easily, they needed to make sure the rest were steadied, that they would remain standing. The two injured nuns needed first-aid. That left Sister Claudia and Roni to take care of things.

Thrusting her hands into her pockets and curling them into fists, Roni walked away from the stairs. Questions bombarded her mind, and Gram's warnings echoed against her conscience.

"Thank you," Sister Claudia said, coming up beside Roni.

"Not doing it for you. I'm here to take care of this job. The moment we're done, I'm taking my grandmother and leaving this place."

"I think that's a wise decision."

Sister Claudia walked over to Sister Susan and gazed at the nun's injuries. Roni did not move. Her mind, her ears, every part of her being, tried to press through the ceiling for any hint of what might be going on with Gram. She tried to understand what had happened, why Gram so willingly left with Sister Mary, and if that thing from the rift had actually called Gram *Mom*.

CHAPTER 3

Once Roni made it clear that she would remain in the cellar, Sister Claudia sent Sisters Susan and Rachel upstairs. Sister Claudia then returned to the bookstands to start her inspection. As if she had been slapped by a loved one, the sudden change in the moment hit Roni. She gawked, frozen, her face locked in an incredulous stare. Sister Claudia adjusted an ornate wooden stand before gazing over at Roni.

With her hands on her hips, Sister Claudia said, "Is this your first time ever seeing a rift?"

With a dazed shake of her head, Roni said, "What? No. I've seen them several times. Not like this one, but I've seen them."

"Then stop acting like a child and get over here."

A headache emanated from her tight brow. She rubbed her forehead, trying to lose her frown, as she walked over to the books. In all the excitement, Roni had never taken the time to look at the books or their stands with a close eye. And though she could process the information now — each of them being different, some beautifully carved, some metallic and some utilitarian — her mind swirled like the rift.

"Did you see her?" Roni asked.

Sister Claudia kept her attention on the books. "I've seen that girl many times."

"In the rift? That girl who pushed outward and stared at me?" *And stared at Gram.*

Resetting a book with more force the necessary, Sister Claudia said, "Yes. I have seen that girl in the rift. Why is this so difficult to understand?"

"Who is she?"

"One of the Lord's chosen, of course."

"Excuse me?"

Sister Claudia strolled around the circle with her hands behind her back like a schoolmarm until she reached Roni. "I know the stories you tell each other in the Parallel Society. I've read accounts in our library about you all. But this rift is not another universe. There is no other universe. There is only the one made by the Lord. And this, the passage, this marvelous gift to us, the Sisters of Croghan Abbey, this is a conduit."

"A conduit?"

"For several generations now, the Sisters have stood vigil here, open to the glorious light of our Lord above. Through this conduit he sends his messengers."

Sister Claudia returned to the bookstands and placed a Bible on the second tier beneath the books from the Parallel Society. As if sitting a baby into a highchair, she set the Bible gently down. Her hand pressed against the cover with a soft touch. Then, with great care and kindness, she wrapped a silk ribbon around the book, tying it to the stand.

"You think this rift leads to Heaven?" Roni said.

"When these books are properly aligned, yes. But as you saw, when we fail in our duty, it opens a terrible, vengeful wrath. I don't dare utter the name of that place."

Roni's eyes snatched a glance upward. She needed to speak with Gram and hope her grandmother would be more forthcoming than usual. "That girl. The one that looks like a young version of me —"

"Did she?" Sister Claudia took a moment to observe Roni's face. "Perhaps."

Roni halted as pieces of the conversation snapped together. "If this rift is a way to connect with Heaven, and the girl is one of the Lord's messengers, then you're saying—"

"Ay, she's an angel."

The Sister's eyes sparkled as her words hung in the air. Roni struggled to keep her face from betraying her thoughts. What kind of angel would reach out to Gram and call her *Mom?* The way the Sisters treated this rift, the way Sister Claudia spoke of it, wriggled along Roni's spine. She shook her head. They were zealots.

Gesturing to the books, Sister Claudia said, "Anytime you're ready."

"Sorry." Roni got to work inspecting each one of the Parallel Society books, making sure they did their part to dampen the rift, searching for any errors or signs that a book might fail. When she finished, she would be able to talk with Gram, get some real answers, and get out of this place.

Sister Claudia followed her as she worked around the circle. "You're not much of a Christian are you?"

"Gram raised me in your faith, but it didn't take."

"That's okay. I think you'll feel different when you leave today."

"Doubt it."

"I know. I was like you — not exactly, of course, but I had my doubts." Sister Claudia's voice softened and her hard glares eased. "Even when I became a nun, I had my doubts. In fact, for the first four years, I prayed and prayed until my hands grew calloused from the rosaries and my legs were black and blue from kneeling for so long. I figured if the Lord wanted me to keep following this path, He would see how fervently I prayed and perhaps he would give me some sign or feeling or something to help me find my faith.

"I even reached the point that I was about to leave. I absolutely cannot stand hypocrisy. Makes me want to scream. So, there was no way I would be a hypocrite myself. If I did not have the faith flowing through me to my core, then I had no choice but to find some other calling in life.

"But then Sister Mary came my way.

"She brought me here with a promise — that I would only have to take one look and all my faith would be restored. Of course, she brought me down here. And as you can see, the veil is lifted here. This is the truth floating before you — there is my life before having seen the truth and now my life after.

"It's strange knowing that almost everyone in the world goes through their days with no proof that there really are angels, that there really is a Heaven. They have faith. Many have great depths of faith. But we at the Croghan Abbey — we are the chosen few. We stand before this great conduit to Heaven. We protect it. And we see the Angel. It is the greatest honor I could ever ask for and I would never dream of going back to the way my life had been."

Roni stopped next to a stone bookstand. "Why are you telling me this?"

"Because you should know that you are always welcome back. The Lord forgives, and so do we."

Roni suspected that Sister Claudia's warm openness would turn brutally cold if she were refuted. Nonetheless, it was tempting. But Roni kept her mouth closed. Especially because much of what the

Sister said rang true. Not the religious angle — Roni remained an atheist through and through — but the larger ideas sounded too familiar. The way Sister Claudia split her life into a time before learning the truth and a time after. That reminded Roni too much of her own experience. And like the Sister, Roni could not conceive of returning to a time when she did not know the truth of the Parallel Society.

Am I a zealot? she wondered.

Before she could ask Sister Claudia any further questions, footsteps on the stairs announced the arrival of Sister Susan. She entered carrying a bloody rag that she dabbed at her nose. She bowed slightly and did not move until Sister Claudia spoke.

"Well?" Sister Claudia said.

"Sister Mary is in the dorm. She asked that I inform the young lady that she may see her grandmother now."

Before Sister Susan had finished speaking, Roni bolted for the stairs.

CHAPTER 4

Roni's heart pounded when she reached the top of the stairs — from the exertion and the anticipation of seeing Gram. She banged open the door leading outside and headed for the nun's dorm. Halfway across the grass, she heard Gram's distinctive voice.

"Over here."

Roni glanced at the colonnade between the dorm and the church. Gram rested her elbows on the railing and held a shot glass in her hand. Roni hurried over. "Are you okay?" she asked.

Gram knocked back the last of her drink. "Got a little rattled, that's all. Holding back that rift takes quite a lot out of you — especially at my age."

Roni wanted to barrel into the questions bouncing around her head, but Gram looked too vulnerable, too shaken. Putting out her hand, Roni said, "Come here. Let me help you. We can go for a walk. Clear our heads."

Gram paused to look at her empty glass. She set it on the ground before clasping Roni's hand and gracelessly swinging her leg over the railing. She giggled as she stumbled onto the grass.

"How many shots of you had?" Roni asked.

"Oh, phooey. Enough to relax, that's all. I'm not drunk. I just thought that the sight of me flying over that railing and nearly falling on my rear was funny. And don't you dare start acting judgmental towards me. I'm still your grandmother. Show some respect."

"There's the Gram I know." They headed across the circle, onto the grass, and toward the wide lake. A gravel path followed the perimeter of the lake, and they decided to walk the entire way around. Glancing back at the church, Roni said, "Did that nun try to do anything with you? Say anything to you?"

"What would she try to do?"

"I don't know. You're the one who told me to be careful around them, not to trust them."

Gram rubbed Roni's shoulder. "I've known Sister Mary longer than you've been alive. She has a good heart and strong faith."

"Then why shouldn't I trust her?"

"Because these women can get kind of nutty. They don't believe the rift leads to another universe."

"I heard that story from Sister Claudia. She really thinks they have a special telephone to Heaven. But more than that is going on here. Come on. I know you. You wouldn't have told me not to trust them if it was something as benign as them being religious fruitcakes."

"Even the dumbest of religious beliefs can spawn horrible and dangerous people." Gram paused. She bent down, picked up a stone, and tossed it into the water. As the ripples expanded out, she said, "Out here, life is slow and still and calm. Except for that rift. These women have all been here too long. I've seen them come in, young and eager, full of faith and hope and a desire to do good in the world. But being near that thing changes them. That doesn't mean I can't be kind to an old woman like Sister Mary — I can even be fond of her — but it does mean that we have to be careful around them."

"The rift changes them? How?"

Linking her arm through Roni's, Gram strolled along the path again. "I've never been able to discover exactly what was going on, but I've seen the change and I can sense it. Sully and Elliot have always assumed it was negative effects from the energy pulsing out of that rift. I suppose."

"Well, the books are secure on their stands again and that rift isn't going anywhere. No matter how much wind it blows."

"That wasn't the rift. At least, I've never seen it act so violently. It's frighteningly calm, usually."

"But all that wind and the horrible sounds."

"Those are from the books we put in place. This may sound strange to you, but they are full of negative energy which sort of forces the rift to hold still. The books kind of cower the rift."

"Is that why the nuns think it leads to Heaven? Because the Society books are negative energy, they think the rift must be positive?"

"Oh, I will never claim to comprehend the minds of these nuns."

Roni discarded the further questions filling her mind. "The job is done. That's what matters. We can go back to the car and take the first flight out of here."

Gram gave Roni's arm a squeeze. "I wish it were that simple."

She pulled away and walked to the edge of the lake. With her head bowed toward the water, she clasped her crucifix, closed her eyes, and prayed. Roni waited. She had thought that once they were on the plane, she would be able to pry loose some relevant information about the girl in the rift, but between the praying and the drinking, she saw that this had hit Gram like a quake from within.

Roni came alongside her grandmother. When Gram finished praying, they watched each other through their reflections. The water distorted them.

With a defeated smile, Gram said, "You might as well ask me now."

"If I ask you, will you tell me the truth?"

"I have no choice. Not just because lying is a sin, but because you need to know. You'll be coming out here year after year for the rest of your life. You need to know what you're dealing with."

Roni walked back to where the grassy ground sloped upward. She sat and smoothed a section next to her. When Gram came over and settled in, Roni said, "Okay, then — what's the story about that girl? Why did she call you *Mom?* Did you have another daughter or what?"

Gram raised her hand to silence Roni. "You only had to ask the question one way."

"Sorry. I'm just a bit —"

She splayed out her fingers and stopped Roni again. "I suppose it's merely wishful thinking that you will ever learn patience. Lord knows I prayed to Him enough, and it hasn't happened yet." Gram glanced over her shoulder, back toward the church, and sniffled. "Doesn't look like much from afar. Sometimes, it's hard to believe so much of my life has changed in that building."

Roni stopped herself from pressing further. The woman was building up the courage to speak. Roni sat on her hands and clinched her teeth together. *Patience,* she warned herself.

"First off, you do not have an aunt," Gram said. "Maria was my only daughter as you were her only daughter. The reason that girl in the rift looks so much like you, the reason she called me Mom, is because she is also my daughter, Maria." She pressed her palms against her eyes and shuddered. Seeing Gram push back her tears kept Roni quiet a little longer. Gram went on, "I raised your mother with a full knowledge of the Parallel Society and her eventual role in it. I wanted her to be prepared, to be skilled, so that there would be a smooth transition when I retired. So, when Maria, your mother, turned twelve years old, I decided to bring her with me here — to Croghan Abbey.

"I was very proud. Partly of her — she braved the unknown with such confidence that I always felt the Parallel Society would be in great hands with her. But I also had arrogant pride in myself. Maria's successes spoke to my great parenting — or so I thought.

"It was early-Spring when we came here. I remember that because the grass smelled incredibly alive and it was so vividly green. I understood why so many fairy tales came from this part of the world. It was like walking through a painting still wet and fresh.

"Sister Mary had joined the church only a handful of years earlier, but she and I had become friends quickly. She fawned over Maria, acting as if she were more than a family friend. She was Auntie Mary, and she happily paraded Maria in front of all the other nuns. There was lots of cooing and pinching of cheeks and all sorts of silly behavior. Like I said, I was arrogantly proud. And I think Maria knew it, too. At least, she knew she was getting great heaps of attention, even if she didn't understand the full implications of why.

"Time came to get to work, so I took her by the hand and walked down the spiral staircase and brought her to the rift. I felt so full of myself. I'd impressed the nuns by showing off my daughter, and now, I intended to impress my daughter by showing off the rift. I got to work inspecting the books, and at first, everything proceeded wonderfully.

"But my pride had blinded me. I forgot that Maria did not know everything she needed to know – did not know the rules. She understood the basics of the Parallel Society, but that did not qualify her to do anything more than observe. And I failed to caution her. Out of curiosity and a desire to help, she stepped forward — and this I will never forget — she smiled at me."

With a bitter grin, Gram stroked Roni's face. "There's a specific way a child looks at her parents when she wants to show off how much she can do. It's more than pride, more than a desire for acceptance, more than simple precociousness. It's all of those things but it's also a question — a simple idea — a child wants to show that she can do Good."

Roni gripped the grass under her hands to keep from shaking her head. She understood exactly what was going through her mother's head. Maria did not want to show off or receive praise or even do Good. She wanted to feel useful. "She picked up one of the books, didn't she?"

"She wanted her mother to know that she was learning, that she would soon be ready, that she understood the importance of what the Parallel Society does, but she didn't understand. I mean, she knew that the books were dangerous, Lord knows I drilled that into her all the time, but she had no idea that this rift was so drastically different than those in the caverns under the bookstore. She lifted the book with caution and care. But that wasn't enough.

"These books — they radiate out energy at a specific frequency. It's the negative to the rift's positive. It's how they keep the rift from expanding. But the one Maria picked up had lost its ability to hold together. Spending years pushing against this rift causes the books extreme wear. She held that book in her hands and the spine tore apart."

Gram stared out at the lake as if she could see the events unfold in the air before her. "It struck out so fast. Like a snake sinking its teeth into a victim. No wind. No roars or growls or anything that we've come to expect from another universe. I have no idea how I reacted so quickly myself, but as that thing pulled Maria towards it, I whipped out a chain. I had it wrapped twice around Maria's wrist." Gram dabbed her eyes once more. "Maria cried out. Unbridled screams — the way only a child can scream in terror. She sounded so loud in the quiet of the room. I threw out another chain. Got around her waist that time. And I pulled. I could feel my muscles moving beyond their capacity. I could feel my bones digging into the ground. I screamed so hard my throat ached for three days. I was determined to save that girl — *my* girl. I suppose all mothers go through that when their child is in jeopardy, but this wasn't anything human beings evolved to be able to do. This was me protecting my daughter from being pulled into another universe.

"Seven chains. In the end, it took me seven chains to pull her out. But I did. She cried and cried in my arms, scared and shaking, she even wet herself, and I did not care because she was in my arms, and that was all that mattered."

Roni wriggled her hand free. "If you saved her, then who did we see in the rift?"

"When we got back home, I could tell she was proud of herself. Not only had she gone on her first outing to another country, but she had faced another universe and survived. Except there were little things — things that felt off.

"Pretty soon, these little things, small differences, started adding up. It was one thing for her to suddenly like strawberries when she never liked them before. Or the way she didn't mind using the bathroom on the plane, while in the past, she had been particular about only going to the bathroom at home. I could dismiss these as the natural changes of a girl growing up. But then as the year progressed, her behavior became stranger. She was more aggressive, more disobedient, and very much became the wild child that you knew as your mother."

"Isn't that called *being a teenager?*"

"I thought so, too. For the longest time. But when all the changes were put together, I saw that she was not the same. I still did not know what had really happened. I still thought I'd saved her. But a few years later, during my regular visit to the Abbey to inspect the books, Sister Mary beamed with pride. She confessed to me that the Abbey had finally been vindicated in their faith. The rift let them see into Heaven. They had been visited by an angel."

"Maria."

"The rift had split her. The girl that had returned with me, that grew up and became your mother, that Maria had been formed from the impulsive side of her. The other side of her, the risk averse side, the caring and selfless side, remains trapped in the rift — stuck at the same age and, presumably, in that same moment."

Roni launched forward and rushed down the hill to the edge of the lake. Her fingers made small circles at her temples as blood pounded through her head. Gram heaved a sob from behind, but it sounded miles away.

Roni's thoughts swirled together and spun off in all directions. She tried to hold the concept of her mother split in two, but it kept slipping away. Part of her brain felt as if she had walked out into the lake and submerged under its icy waters. The rest of her raged so fiery-hot that she would boil the lake if she touched it.

Whirling back upon Gram, Roni said, "You've known this my whole life, yet you let me think I'd lost everything. You let me think my mother died in that car accident."

"She did." Gram's brow tightened as did her mouth. "This splitting of Maria happened long before you were even so much as a thought. The Maria I returned home with, the one I raised, the one who liked to drink too much, liked men too much, liked drugs too much — that was your mother. That was the woman who held you in her womb for nine months, and that was the woman who gave birth to you. No other."

"It never ends with you. One secret leads to another and another."

"Oh, grow up. Everybody has secrets."

"Not about the nature of the entire universe. And not about their granddaughter's mother being splintered off into two beings." Roni inhaled a long, sharp breath and tried to calm down. Her mind threatened to attack Gram again — this time striking at the religious angle. But that would only provoke the woman and would close any opportunity to get more information.

Gram shuffled down the hill. "I truly am sorry. This has been a stain upon my entire life. I've prayed endlessly about this. Perhaps I should have told you. I don't know what good it would've done, but perhaps I should have. I just ... I'm ashamed."

Roni glanced away. She wanted to punch things. She wanted to rage. But seeing the distraught, broken look in Gram's eyes mollified the urge. Her fingers opened and her mind eased.

"You didn't know," she said. "Not until you saw Mom's behavior back home, and by that point, it was too late."

"I should've tried to save her when I came back here that next year. When Sister Mary started talking about angels, I knew it was my Maria in there. I wouldn't actually see here for a few more years, but I knew. I just didn't want to believe it."

Roni reached over and stroked Gram's cheek with the back of her hand. "We're here now, and we just saw her. It's not too late. We should go save her."

Gram's face turned to stone. "That's the worst possible idea." She pulled away as if stepping back from a horrid monster. "You must promise me to never do that. Do you not recall what happened only a few years ago? The thing that brought you into all of this? When your boyfriend went into one of my books and came out a different being altogether."

"He was not my boyfriend."

"We have no idea what the universe inside that rift is like. But we do know it's kept that version of Maria frozen in time. She's not aged in all the years I've come here. Lord knows what that experience would do to her brain, her psyche. You understand? Bringing her back now might destroy all that she has left. It would also unleash an unknown creature into our world. She is no longer from this universe. To bring her here would be like bringing anything from another universe here — she would be a living relic, and those are not allowed. Too unpredictable. The foreign germs alone could be devastating to our world."

"You think your daughter is a relic?"

Gram's mouth became a small dot. "That Maria is no longer my daughter. And she most certainly is not your mother."

"I only meant —"

With a wave of her hand, Gram thumped off toward the church. "I need to report in to Sully."

Roni watched as Gram walked away. Clenching her fists, Roni kicked the gravel path. She grabbed handfuls of rocks and tossed them into the lake. She threw her arms in the air and let out an exasperated cry.

How could Gram be so blind? Roni understood how horrible an experience the whole thing must have been — her only daughter, split in two, partly lost in another universe, with no way to return. Gut wrenching. But like so much that came out of Gram's mouth, that wasn't the entire truth.

Because Gram ignored the possibility of saving her daughter. She wrote off the split and focused on the living daughter she still had. But that did not change the truth — the Maria in the rift was still Gram's daughter, and in a sense, still Roni's mother. Partly, anyway. Gram's woes concerning the unpredictability of the rift did not negate the need to, at the least, attempt a rescue. Further proof that Gram no longer had the capacity to lead the group.

Perhaps Sully had assigned Roni this job because of Maria. If Sully knew about the situation — and Roni thought all three in the Old Gang knew everything about each other — then it could not have been an accident that he sent her alongside Gram. He wanted her to learn about Maria.

And that means part of my job must be to save her.

Roni stopped mid-step. She turned back and looked at the church spire peeking over the hilltops. Sister Claudia had mentioned a library. If this group of nuns behaved anything like the Parallel Society, then they would have accounts left behind by previous nuns. Somebody had to have written down something of value regarding Maria. After all, the appearance of this rift and then years later their so-called Angel had to have been the most monumental event in the Abbey.

With a more determined step, Roni headed back toward the church. She had to find Sister Claudia and gain access to that library. She had to save Maria.

Chapter 5

Roni found Sister Claudia tending to the flower beds that lined the circle drive. After everything that had happened, Roni found it peculiar that Sister Claudia would perform such a mundane task. Then again, Roni spent most of her days working in a bookstore that had the caverns leading to other universes beneath it. She supposed living with the rift bore many of the same results — the nuns had become comfortable with their situation and learned to continue living despite the miracle beneath their church.

Roni asked about the library, and Sister Claudia wasted no time leaving behind her backbreaking work. She led the way to the colonnade and building on the opposite side of where Roni had found Gram only a short while earlier. The building appeared to have been built in the 1960s — utilitarian, mostly red brick with narrow windows, and a flat roof. In style, it reminded Roni of a public high school. Inside the library, however, she discovered a far more ancient atmosphere.

Dim lighting and old wood shrouded the aisles of books with a sense of mystery and importance. Off to her right, Roni noted long wide shelves that carried scrolls covered in dust. Rolling ladders provided access to the numerous volumes on the top shelving — must have been about twenty-feet high. In the middle of this ode to lost and forgotten thoughts, a young nun sat in the center of a donut table.

"This is Sister Ashley," Sister Claudia said. "And this is Roni. She is one of our guests from the Parallel Society."

Sister Ashley bowed her head. She had a pert nose and smooth skin, and Roni wondered if such features caused jealousy amongst the nuns. Perhaps being cloistered in a nun's habit and coif actually dispensed with all that physical nonsense. Perhaps out here, these women could simply treat each other based on their intelligence, their faith, and their abilities.

"It's a pleasure to meet you," Sister Ashley said in a soft voice. "Is there something I can help you with?"

Roni asked for any writings the nuns had made about the rift. In particular, she wanted information on the angel. As Sister Ashley got to work, Sister Claudia gestured to two tables in the back where they could sit down to do their research.

"You want to help me?" Roni asked.

"It's far more enjoyable than weeding. Besides, Sister Mary told me to give you aid in any way you needed. So, here I am."

Shortly after, Sister Ashley deposited three books and one scroll on the work tables in the back. Roni had been hoping for more, but she guessed that regardless of faith, belief in conduits to Heaven or angels manifesting in physical form were still dangerous things to write down. The kinds of things that might make the Vatican no longer recognize an entire Abbey.

She grabbed one of the thick books — its dusty leather cover caused her a short coughing fit — and opened to the table of contents. The pages were thin enough to see shadows through and the print so small and tight that she considered asking Sister Ashley for a magnifying glass.

Sister Claudia chuckled. "Not what you were expecting?"

"I hadn't given it any thought. I just want to do the research."

"Of course. Discovering the truth is always a noble endeavor. I assume that's what you're after."

Roni hesitated to answer. She thought of Gram's warning and of the devotion Sister Claudia had displayed toward the Abbey. She might not have taken it kindly that Roni wanted to grab hold of their angel and remove it from the rift. Worse, Roni wanted to take this angel home with her.

"Something a bother?" Sister Claudia asked.

With a shake of her head, Roni started going through the book.

Sister Claudia tipped back her chair and with a nonchalant motion, swiped one of the other books. She leafed through it in a casual way as if passing over the endless advertisements in a fashion magazine. "I know you think we're all a little nutters here. Oh look, how quaint. The young, foolish nuns in the backwoods of Ireland are talking with the angels. But I think that's not anymore crazy then what you're believing."

Roni paused. "The rift is a hole between universes — that's not a belief, that's a fact. And I've been through one of them. I can guarantee you, it was no Heaven."

"Just because your travels took you to a horrible place, does not mean our conduit does not lead to Heaven."

"You only believe that because you saw a face in there, and you think it's an angel."

"And your grandmother thinks it's her daughter. She has no proof. If anything, she has the opposite — her daughter lived, went home with her, grew to be an adult and have a child of her own. I think your grandmother can't get her heart over the loss of her innocent daughter, the way her daughter succumbed to sin, and has projected this idea of a perfect daughter she once thought she had onto our angel. Perhaps the Lord has given the angel a similar face to ease your grandmother's sorrowed heart. After all, despite your mother's sinful behavior, despite your own rejection of the Church, your grandmother is still a devout believer. The Lord loves her."

Roni gripped the edge of the table. "I think it would be best if you left me alone for a while. I can do this research on my own."

Sister Claudia stood with a shrug. "If that's what you are thinking's best."

As she walked away, Roni rose to her feet. "Sister Claudia, you've accidentally taken one of my books with you."

Sister Claudia glanced down as if only discovering the book in her hands. "This? I looked through it already. It will not help you."

"Still, if you don't mind."

Though Sister Claudia's mouth lifted in a smile, pure venom dripped from her gaze. "Unfortunately, Sister Ashley made a mistake when she brought this book out. Not all of our texts are available for you to touch." She shot a narrow glare at Sister Ashley.

"I'm sorry, ma'am," Sister Ashley said with a motion somewhere between a bow and a curtsy.

Roni tapped the desk. "I certainly understand how precious some rare books can be. I also understand that because I'm not part of your faith, you don't want me looking through certain texts. But Sister Ashley is also a nun here. Perhaps she can help."

"I doubt that our young librarian knows —"

"Or maybe we can call upon Sister Mary for advice in this matter. I'm sure she's hanging out with Gram right now."

Sister Claudia bristled. "Sister Mary doesn't need to be bothered with this kind of nonsense. She trusts me to be in charge, and so you'll have to take my word for this decision. You don't need this book."

She started to walk off again, but Roni said, "It sucks, doesn't it? Sister Mary tells you that you're going to be head of this place one day, but she doesn't really give you the trust you deserve."

"Do not try to equate your petty little problems with those that I face," Sister Claudia said, stopping but not turning back.

"They might be petty, but if you don't allow me to look at that book, I'll have no choice. I've got a job to do. So, if I must, I'll go to Sister Mary myself. Now, maybe you're right. Maybe she'll agree that you made the correct decision, and she'll throw me out of here. Perhaps her decades-long relationship with my grandmother means nothing to her. Then again, and I'm only posing the possibilities, but perhaps she'll tell you that you're wrong. That Gram and I are here to ensure this rift doesn't destroy everything. From that standpoint, it's important that we have all the information available."

Huffing, Sister Claudia slammed the book on Sister Ashley's desk. Pointing a strong finger at Sister Ashley, she said, "Don't think I don't know what you're up to. It was no mistake that this book was in her pile. If any harm comes of this, I will hold you responsible."

Before Sister Ashley could mumble her apologies, Sister Claudia stomped out of the library. Roni stepped forward to glimpse at the book cover — an ornate illustration of two priests putting a body to rest. The cover's border had an intricate design of thorns and stems ending in roses. The title of the book — *The Abbey Tombs.*

"I'm sorry if I caused you any trouble," Roni said, trying to look closer.

Sister Ashley picked up the book and returned to the worktable. "Not at all." She peeked toward the exit, apparently looking for Sister Claudia. With no sign of the woman returning, Sister Ashley said, "In fact, Sister Claudia is right. I did put this book on your pile on purpose. I've always had an interest in the angel and the conduit, but more than that, what really fascinates me are the Abbey tombs. And I'm certain that there are answers to your questions down there."

A jolt of excitement electrified Roni's fingers. "The tombs? What exactly —"

"Let me show you." Sister Ashley opened the book and rifled through the pages with none of the care a librarian should have for such a delicate artifact. When she reached the desired page, she slapped her hand to the top of it and said, "There. Look at that."

Roni leaned over the volume — the rich aroma of old, molding paper rose around her. The text was difficult to read — the handwritten script showed little care for legibility. Plus, Roni figured it was written in Gaelic or Celtic or some other variant, none of which she knew. But there was no mistaking the illustration — a single figure, a nun, flat on her back like an Egyptian Pharaoh, with an oversized book clutched in her arms.

"What's it say?" Roni asked, the catch in her throat unmistakable.

Whispering, Sister Ashley said, "This was Sister Agnes. And the book she was buried with is called *History of Secrets*. She couldn't have been more on the nose with that." Sister Ashley's face broadened like a hungry wolf. "I've always wanted to see it, but we aren't allowed in the tombs. Sister Mary goes down there once or twice a year, but otherwise, I've never seen a single nun go there."

Roni nodded. She understood the game they were about to play. "So, if I understand this, the rule is that you are not to go down there?"

"That's correct."

"But Sister Claudia told you to help me."

"That is also correct."

"Sister Claudia is working under orders from Sister Mary — the nun who runs this place."

"Ay."

"And in order for you to help me, I need to see that book — *History of Secrets*."

Sister Ashley tapped her chin in a studious manner. "Why then, I suppose the only way to do that would be to take you down there."

"It seems like the only logical action you have available. I hate to ask you to break a rule, but you have a choice to make — you can break the one rule about the tombs, or you can break Sister Claudia's rule about helping me which also breaks Sister Mary's rule."

Sister Ashley nodded so fast and with such a wide smile, Roni wondered if her teeth might crash together. "It seems I'd best break one rule rather than two."

"If you think that's best. Then, please, lead the way. We would be better off taking care of this as fast as possible."

"Oh, indeed. If Sister Claudia were to return, then she would not let us go down there."

"Which means she would be breaking Sister Mary's order to help me and the Parallel Society. We don't want to put her in that position."

"Not at all."

Sister Ashley gathered the books together and set them on her desk. Neither woman said another word. Roni followed Sister Ashley's lead and they headed for the tombs.

CHAPTER 6

The Abbey tombs were comprised of several twisting passageways built underneath the library. Narrow and rough, they reminded Roni of certain sections of the caverns under the bookstore — the ones that had been carved out by hand. Like all of Ireland, the air felt damp and cold.

As Sister Ashley led the way by flashlight, Roni noticed long alcoves dug into the walls. Each one contained a gray, dusty skeleton draped in habit, wimple, tunic, and in some cases, armor.

"Are these all nuns?" she asked.

"Hush."

"But if they're nuns, shouldn't we be checking —"

Sister Ashley spun around, blinding Roni with the flashlight. "You best be quiet or you're going to get us caught." Her eyes darted toward one of the bodies. "Besides, it's wrong to be talking like this amongst the dead." Without another word, she resumed leading the way.

Roni considered pressing the issue, but in the end, she had to trust that Sister Ashley knew where to go. Thankfully, the majority of the bodies were difficult to discern in the dark shadows. Though the occasional skull smiling at her was more than enough to chill her bones. Worse, the air smelled stale and left Roni's mouth with a dry coating — she didn't want to think about that too much.

They came upon a heavy door with an iron ring for the handle. From beneath her habit, Sister Ashley produced a key that looked as old as the church itself. It took her five tries to get the door unlocked — the results of frayed nerves and an ancient lock.

She had to put her shoulder into the door hard in order to force it open. It obliged with a long and horrible whine as if it wanted to send waves of eerie sound across the dead. Roni glanced back into the dark and dusty shadows. If she heard a deep moan or even the squeak of a rat, she thought she would be justified in letting out a sharp scream.

"Come on," Sister Ashley whispered. "We're not down here for a show. Let's get this done."

Roni nodded and followed the nun through the door. They entered a narrow, low-ceilinged room — a private study. A plain, wooden desk and an equally plain, wooden chair had been pressed up against one wall. Next to these, a wood-frame bed with three thick blankets upon a rope lattice served as a place to sleep. On the wall opposite, two columns of shelves contained bodies on the left side and books on the right. A narrow, blackened fireplace comprised the back corner. Dark stains on the ceiling suggested a lack of adequate ventilation.

Sister Ashley centered her flashlight on the bed. "Sister Agnes lived here. The legend is that after she experienced the conduit for the first time — for the only time — she sequestered herself down here to write all her musings on what she had seen. Back then, nobody dared to say the truth — that she had glimpsed Heaven."

"Back when? How long ago did all this happen?"

"Seventeenth century, I think." She turned her flashlight toward the shelves of books and scrolls. "These are my favorite. They detail all kinds of things about life back then. It sounds wonderfully peaceful. I wouldn't mind living without electricity, but not having modern plumbing is something hard to idealize. But I can imagine life without all the noise of today. Sister Agnes did more than write about the world she lived in, though. More than just her experience with the conduit, too. She took the time to talk about her own spirituality. Very inspiring."

Roni cocked her head to the side. "I thought you hadn't been down here before."

"I said that I wasn't allowed to come down here. Not that I've never been here."

It sounded reasonable, but Roni did not recall the conversation going that way originally.

Woooooo. A horrible sound, like poorly played bagpipes, echoed around them. *Wooooo.* Roni's skin prickled.

Sister Ashley pointed to a row of evenly-spaced holes in the ceiling, each one circled by black residue that then trailed back to the fireplace. "Ventilation. Sister Agnes would have died long before she did without a trickle of fresh air coming her way. You should hear this place when a good rainstorm blows through. You can hear that sound all throughout the tombs."

Roni's gaze drifted across the bare room. She thought about Sister Agnes being down here amongst the dead and how bizarre the others must have thought her. That led to thoughts about the nuns, the Church, and —

"What is it you're thinking?" Sister Ashley asked.

With an embarrassed turn of her head, Roni said, "I'm not sure how to ask this politely."

"Then I'd recommend being honest."

"In that case, how did you end up here?"

Sister Ashley laughed. "You mean how did a nice nun like me end up in a place like this?"

Chuckling, Roni nodded.

"I imagine my story is much like all the other nuns here — at least, those that came after Sister Mary. Like most, I came to it because I had a moment — a calling. I grew up on a farm in County Kilkenny. I was not a wild one, always acted a proper child, but I wasn't particularly religious and I didn't listen to my parents well when I was involved in something. Mostly, I loved the books, and when I got to reading, I never heard a single thing my parents would say."

Sister Ashley's brightness faltered. "My father — he was a stricter sort. Spare the rod and all that. The way he went at me, my sister, and my brothers, well, I suppose I could have understood it if we were fussy or causing troubles. But we were good kids. And we were smart. Smart enough not stick around and get beaten for nothing. So, we left. Well, I did, anyway.

"I ended up on the streets of Galway which is not a place you want to end up. I saw so many other kids succumb to drugs and prostitution, and I was determined that would not happen to me. I tried getting jobs, I tried begging, I tried anything — but I always ended up sleeping in an alley.

"One day I was standing by the water watching the tide, and there were other people walking around during the day. There was a man — odd-looking fellow with a crooked nose and a long face. He caught my eye and I watched him walking along. He carried this packet of papers, and I assumed he was handing out adverts for some pub or something, but he didn't hand them out to anybody. He watched everyone and just walked right by.

"Until he came to me.

"He stopped and stared at me, and I got the strange feeling inside like he could see through all the walls I had built up from living on the streets. He handed me the paper and walked away. It was a call to church. The whole thing felt so strange that I decided to go. I walked in there and I listen to that service, and it changed me. If you've never had a calling, you can't possibly know what it feels like. And if you've had one, then I don't need to explain. It hit me then. I would give my life to the Lord. And I did."

"If you felt that strongly," Roni said, "why did you stay here when this abbey was rejected by the Church?"

"Why would I stay with a church that rejects a pathway to Heaven itself? That's like rejecting the Lord. Why would any of us do that? The real question you should be asking is why didn't more of our brethren join us here? That's what I want." Gesturing to the corpse of Sister Agnes, Sister Ashley said, "She understood. She saw that conduit and sequestered herself here and devoted her life here to the Lord. That's what I want to do. That's what all of us nuns want to do. We are here to serve the Lord. We are chosen, and I would give up everything to remain here. No Vatican, no Pope, no father or mother or friend could beat me or sway me because after all — what was my calling if not to serve the Lord? And He has provided us with this conduit to His Heaven."

Roni had never seen such firm conviction blaze in the eyes of a person. It was both impressive and unnerving. "Let's find the book we're here for — *History of Secrets*. Do you know where Sister Agnes is buried? Is she one of these?"

"Wouldn't make much sense to bring you down here if I didn't know where to go." She walked over to the foot of the bed and indicated that Roni should help her move the furniture. It was heavier than Roni had expected, but they managed to pull the bed out about two feet. They had revealed an alcove dug into the wall, and in the alcove, the remains of Sister Agnes waited.

With giddy excitement, Sister Ashley lowered to her knees and reached in. She pulled out a large book — it required both hands to hold and covered her like a shield from chin to waist. "See? The book as promised."

As Sister Ashley set *History of Secrets* on the desk, Roni approached like a hiker discovering a venomous snake in her path. The nun sneezed and waved a hand to disperse the dust climbing up from the book. But to Roni's eyes, the dust came from the desk, not the book.

In fact, she thought the book appeared rather clean.

Unlike the books upstairs in the Abbey library, this book had a black cover with a red diamond in the middle. No title, no author, no writing of any kind. No illustrations, either. Just the red diamond.

Roni's throat tightened. She had seen books like this before. The caverns beneath the bookstore back home were filled with them. "Have you ever opened this book?"

Sister Ashley's face reddened. "Oh, no. I'll admit that I've pulled it out from time to time. I've set it on the floor and looked at it, but I promise you that I have never opened it."

"Why not? If you were so eager to read the books down here, then why not open this one?"

"I want to say that I didn't open it out of respect for Sister Agnes. That's true, to some extent. But the real truth is that whenever I go to open it, I feel something — a force from the book, perhaps from within myself. I assume it is the Lord telling me to obey my vows, to stop. So, I stop."

"Until the urge to come down here strikes you again."

"Indeed." She stroked the cover three times before raising her hopeful eyes toward Roni. "But you are here now. From what I understand, you have no faith, so there should be no problem with you opening the book. The Lord won't speak to you."

"Being an atheist doesn't mean I have no faith in anything at all."

"You have no moral code."

"You know, the atheists' moral track record is far better than your own. You may not want to keep casting stones." Roni heard Gram's stern tones creeping into her own voice. She stepped back and took a cleansing breath. "Maybe I should take the book with me and look at it in private. That way your moral quandary won't be a problem."

Sister Ashley stepped in front of the book. "You cannot do that. The book belongs to Sister Agnes. It must remain here."

"No problem. I'll stay down here and read it. Why don't you go upstairs and return to your library duties — I'll come up when I'm done."

As if in answer, the Vienna Boys Choir broke into a beautiful rendition of *Silent Night*. Sister Ashley dug into her robes and fished out a small phone. She tapped at the screen for a moment and the music stopped.

"My alarm," she said. "The dinner bell is tolling. We have to go."

"I don't need dinner. I'll stay and read the book."

"We cannot be absent. And you can't stay here alone. I promise I will bring you back down. I want you to open the book. But not right now." She looked at the phone in her hand. "And please, not a word about this. I only have it because I can't hear the bells from down here. You understand?"

"Oh, I understand perfectly. It's that strong moral code at work."

Sister Ashley's pleading face darkened. With sharp movements, she set the book back on the bones of Sister Agnes. In an icy tone that sharpened her button nose, she said, "Being down here can be unnerving for some. I'll assume that has led you to speak without thinking. We will go to dinner now. Don't worry — I stand by my word. After all, honesty is part of my moral code. Tomorrow morning, you and your Gram will come by here again before heading out. I will take you down then."

Sister Ashley gestured toward the door and waited until Roni headed out. As they walked through the twisting paths, Roni attempted to memorize each turn. She listened for sound cues and even tried to leave small marks in the old dust. Anything that would help her when she returned.

Because she would return.

After dinner, she would come down by herself and find that room. No way was she going to open the book in front of Sister Ashley — not when she felt certain the book belonged in the caverns of the Parallel Society, not when she knew it led to another universe.

CHAPTER 7

Once they reached the surface, Sister Ashley rushed off to the dorms to prepare for dinner. Roni headed straight for the rental car, going over every step of the path she would have to repeat in order to get to the book. She popped the trunk and went about preparing her "tomb bag."

The trunk did not have much for her to choose from — neither she nor Gram had expected to be in this situation. She could use her phone has a flashlight, provided the battery lasted long enough, but she did not have any good shoes for the job — only a serviceable pair of sneakers. She did have her journal and a pen to record all the important details. That was good enough. She figured the tomb bag would be mostly empty going in, and probably full on her return.

The idea of stealing the book did not sit easily in her stomach, but clearly the nuns had taken the book when they should not have. It belonged to the Parallel Society, and while the Society had let the Abbey use those books necessary to contain the rift, the rest were meant to be returned to the caverns.

"Oh, there you are," Gram said, shuffling out of the front of the church.

Roni hastened to meet Gram at the stairs. She purposely left the trunk open — less suspicious than if she slammed it shut with a guilty look on her face.

Nonetheless, Gram asked, "What are you doing out here?"

"Looking for a warmer shirt." The lie came effortlessly.

"Don't bother getting it yet. I spoke with Sully. He's asked that we stay for the night to make sure the rift is secure. After what happened to Sisters Susan and Rachel, we don't want to leave with just a cursory inspection. So, you might as well pull everything out. The nuns will provide us each with a room in the dorms."

"Is that normal? To stay overnight?"

Trying to remain neutral but unable to hide true feelings from her tone, Gram said, "I've done this job many times. Either the rift is contained or it's not. There is no middle ground. I told Sully he was being overcautious, that we've taken care of the situation, but he is the leader now. We do what he wants."

"I–I'm sorry." Roni had no idea why the words left her mouth. Perhaps a little guilt nestled under her skin because of her plans for that evening.

"You've got nothing to be sorry about. It's Sully. He's too much of a novice to know the right procedure here, yet too old and set in his ways to simply ask me how I would have done it. Or perhaps he's trying to stamp his own way of doing things on this now. Who knows? Just please get our things and deliver them to the rooms."

"I only meant that —"

But Gram was already walking away. Over her shoulder, the old woman said, "Oh, by the way, Sully and Elliot are already in London. They're on their way over here."

Roni did not say another word. She knew her Gram too well — Sully and Elliot flying out to London before anything had necessitated their trip would be interpreted as a great insult. But Roni knew Sully well, too. The more she thought about it, the more she felt certain that he had assigned her to this trip not only to learn of the rift and what would be required in the future, but also because he knew the serious nature of Gram's daughter being trapped in the rift. He knew that this particular trip — especially having Roni along — would be hard on Gram. After all, every year Gram traveled here and visited Maria had to be thought of as potentially the last year she would ever see her daughter. As Gram was fond of reminding everyone — she wasn't getting any younger.

Still, Sully and Elliot should not have flown out as further back up. It only irritated Gram more, and Roni had no desire to spend more time with an irritated Gram. Certainly not for the rest of the trip.

On the positive side, Roni had all night ahead of her to get to that book. Grabbing the luggage and the tomb bag, she closed the trunk and headed to the dorms.

Trudging toward the one-story building, Roni kept catching movement out of her peripheral vision. She stopped and stared at the church, the dorm, even turned to face the lake. She saw no one. The wind rustled through the trees, the water rippled on the lake, but she saw no one. Still, she could not shake the sense that somebody watched her.

Sister Claudia most likely — glowering from some distant hiding place, ready to assert her superiority whenever she had the advantage. *Good luck with that,* Roni thought. Sister Claudia would soon find out that Roni did not cower easily.

Inside the dorm, her footsteps made dull thuds on the wooden floor. The place reminded her of a sleepaway camp cabin — only with a heavily religious theme. The main room held eight beds, each sticking straight out from the longer walls. Above each bed's headboard, a crucifix had been affixed and, beneath that, a wooden plaque with the Sister's name. Next to each bed was a low dresser. Bathrooms were off the main entrance, and at the far end, on either side, were two narrow rooms for Gram and Roni. Not much bigger than jail cells.

As she clumped down the middle of the dorm, Roni noticed that every dresser top remained bare and clean. No books, no knickknacks, nothing to distinguish one person from the other. Not even dust. In fact, only the name plaques provided any sense of individuality. She wondered if she had used the wrong word when thinking about them earlier. Instead of *zealot,* perhaps she should have used *cult.*

After resting Gram's bag on the edge of one bed, Roni went to her own jail cell and dropped her main bag on the floor. She did not want to leave her tomb bag in the open, but there was little in the way of hiding places. She glanced up, hoping to find a drop ceiling that she could stash her belongings in. Unfortunately, she saw only simple, open rafters. Really, the only viable places were under the bed or in the low dresser — and neither of those seemed particularly safe.

After a moment, she decided to roll up the small bag and stick it at the bottom of her main bag. While these nuns had clearly broken away from the Church — at least, according to Gram — it seemed a good bet that they would not go rooting through her personal things — at least, if those things were not left in the open.

"It's not much," Sister Ashley said, giving Roni a fright, "but it serves its purpose for a single night."

Roni stared at Sister Ashley, watching as the nun's eyes roved around the room. Nothing would be safe in here. "Did you want something?"

"I came to fetch you for dinner. Sister Mary, your Gram, and the rest of the nuns have already sat down to eat."

Until dinner had been mentioned this time, Roni had not taken note of the rich aroma rising through the floorboards — meaty and filling. Her stomach grumbled. She stepped toward the door. "Okay, let's go."

But Sister Ashley did not move. She glanced down — perhaps at Roni's bag — and pulled her lips in tight.

Roni motioned toward the door. "I'm ready."

"One thing first. Please, I do not wish to burden you with my troubles, but I hope you'll understand the seriousness of where we went today. I mean, Sister Mary has made the rules quite clear. Sister Claudia, too. And if you should happen to let slip —"

"I won't say anything. As far as I'm concerned, we never went down to the tomb at all. I don't even know that a tomb exists. Okay?"

Sister Ashley's tensions deflated. "Thank you. Bless you."

"You can thank me by taking me to dinner. I'm hungrier than I realized."

With a giggle, Sister Ashley backed out of the narrow room and into the main part of the dorm. As Roni closed the door, she wanted to slide a hair in the jamb or some other simple trick to ensure that the door was not opened during her absence, but she did not have the time to do it. Not with Sister Ashley standing right there.

Together they walked to the main entranceway. Sister Ashley opened a door across from the bathrooms that Roni had missed her first time through. The door led to a narrow staircase that led to a dining area underneath the dorms.

All the nuns and Gram lifted their heads when Roni and Sister Ashley entered. Sister Mary sat at the head of the long table. Sister Claudia sat at her right and Gram at her left. Sisters Susan and Rachel took the next two spots leaving the rest of the table for Sister Ashley and Roni. With choreographed care, Sister Susan stood the moment Roni sat. She hastened to a corner of the room and ladled out a bowl of stew and potatoes from a heavy, deep pot. After placing the bowl before Roni and repeating the dance for Sister Ashley, she returned to her seat.

"Let us pray," Sister Mary said.

The nuns bowed their heads and Gram did as well. Roni lowered her chin a little, but spent most of the next quiet minute watching the rigorous concentration of the nuns. They bobbed their heads as they mouthed their words, the soft swishing of their wimples like a breeze through a field of grass.

Gram's praying lacked all of that vigor and made up for it with serene contemplation. Growing up, Roni had been taught that the prayer before a meal should be used to appreciate the gifts the Lord had provided — particularly, the gift of having a hot meal on the table to eat. She wondered which form of prayer worked best.

"Amen," Sister Mary said, and the nuns responded in kind. Gram crossed herself and kissed her crucifix pendant before lifting her head.

Smartass thoughts aside, Roni found this display to feel like everything else in the Abbey — strict and slightly off. On the surface, several nuns gave thanks for their meal. Nothing particularly odd about that. But it did not sit right. Not only because of the fervent manner in which they prayed, which Roni could dismiss as simply being a different way of doing things, but because of they way it felt like a performance.

Perhaps the rift had warped the nun's minds in ways that Gram and Roni could not fathom. Perhaps always knowing that rift existed nearby felt too much like being watched continuously. Especially considering that the nuns thought of Maria as an angel. Even now, as Roni ate the surprisingly tasty meal, she could feel judgmental eyes upon her — though the nuns never looked her way. She imagined feeling those kinds of looks all the time might drive some of the strange behaviors she had witnessed.

Five minutes into the meal, Roni accepted the idea that the entire dinner would be taken in silence. But in the next moment, Sister Claudia disabused her of that idea.

"So, Roni, were you able to find everything you needed in the library?" she asked with a nasty grin.

Gram perked up. "What were you looking for?"

Startled, Roni coughed on her stew, allowing Sister Claudia to continue. "Oh, your granddaughter has taken a great interest in our angel."

This got Sister Rachel's attention. Like an eager teenager, though one with head wounds wrapped from earlier failures, she looked over at Roni. "Do you think she's real? I was too startled by what happened to see her clearly. I never have."

"Don't bombard our guest," Sister Claudia said — harsh enough that Sister Rachel instantly grew silent and lowered her head.

"Now, now," Sister Mary said. "We must always encourage inquisitive minds. Sister Rachel is excited and that's a good thing."

Gazing down at her meal, Sister Claudia said, "I only wanted to look out for our guest's comfort. I'm sorry."

"Nothing to be sorry for. We all get overeager sometimes. Sister Ashley, what books did you recommend to our guest?"

Sister Ashley squirmed in her seat. Roni could not tell whether her discomfort came from being addressed by the head nun or if she feared she might get in trouble if she said too much of the truth. Probably both.

"Sister Ashley, you've been asked a question," Sister Claudia said, clearly trying to reestablish her position.

Dabbing at her mouth with a napkin, Sister Ashley said, "Well, I chose two books and one scroll. *The Abbey Historical (1800-1900), The Abbey Historical (1900-2000),* and of course, the scroll of Sister Margaret's views on the subject."

Sister Mary appeared pleased. "I've always liked Sister Margaret's views on practically anything. I must say, I'm a bit surprised they're still sitting around as scrolls. Why have we not bound them together into a book?"

"I intend to do so. And now that I know she's a favorite of yours, I'll make it a priority."

"That's a kind thought."

"It would've been done sooner, but there's only one of me in the library."

Sister Mary gazed at the empty spots making up the second half of the table. "It is much more difficult these days to entice women into making their vows. A vow is for life. Quite a commitment." She winked at Gram. "You wouldn't happen to know any women who could use a good education and don't mind devoting their lives to the Lord, do you?"

Gram chuckled. "If I ever come across one, I'll most certainly send her your way."

As the two elder women beamed at each other, Roni wondered if Sister Mary's eyes threw the same daggers that Gram's could throw. With a snap, Sister Mary wagged her finger by her head. Roni could not tell if this was from the woman's genuine excitement over an idea or if she put on a show, but the presentation pulled everyone's attention.

"While Sister Margaret's work is wonderful," Sister Mary said, "did you consider offering anything from Sister Petra?" As a loud aside to Gram — loud enough for all to hear — Sister Mary went on, "She was a nun visiting from Brazil. Lovely woman. A bit too inquisitive about matters that had long ago been settled, but she did take an interest in our unique situation. Of course, what nun wouldn't? This was before our trouble with the Vatican. But when given the choice between following the Lord or the Church, well, that choice is easy. It's a shame they behave as they do. We have so much to offer the nuns and priests. Think of all the wonder that could fill them if they had a chance to see a real angel. Still, it's difficult for some to understand and accept. Sister Petra, for one, never did quite fit with us."

Sister Ashley said, "I'll be sure to find her book and give it to Roni."

Returning to her food, Sister Mary said, "It doesn't really matter. Just a thought. Besides, it's obvious that Roni hopes to find some secret information about our angel. Perhaps, like her grandmother, she thinks the angel is some part of their late Maria. Isn't that right, Lillian? You think the angel is actually your daughter."

Gram stiffened even as she forced a grin. "Part of my daughter. Yes."

Setting her spoon down, Sister Mary addressed the rest of the table. "I've tried. Over all the years we've known each other, I've tried hard to convince Lillian that our conduit to Heaven is not a private grave for her mourning. But the mind thinks what it wants to. Regardless, we know that the faces inside the conduit are messengers from the Lord — angels. Frankly, I have not seen one in years. They don't come as often. Perhaps the result of something the Parallel Society has done in trying to control matters. Of course, there is no real need to control it. We should let the Lord's glory spread over all of the world."

Gram cleared her throat. "Need I remind you —"

"Yes, yes. I was merely stating my opinion. I am fully aware of the deal made with the Irish government." She paused, her eyes meeting with the intense focus from many of the nuns. "I suppose you all deserve to hear this. Sister Claudia already knows, but seeing how few of us there are currently, I suppose the rest of you need to understand — we allow the imposition of the Parallel Society, giving them access to the conduit, letting them contain it and such, because in return we gain our privacy out here. Governments can be very difficult — especially when you are forging an honest path that might differ from the more traditional paths. Gaining this privacy is gaining our freedom. Without it, the Church would come in here and destroy everything we protect. They would not do it out of malice but ignorance."

Sister Claudia said, "We gain more than that. We've become the most important Abbey in the world. We're the only ones that can talk directly to Heaven."

"True, true. But we don't want to get big headed about it. We have to watch our pride."

"Of course."

Gram pushed her chair out. "I'm afraid I'm no longer feeling well. I'll see you all in the morning."

As she made a rapid exit, Roni jumped to her feet. Gram waved her back, and in the next instant, she was gone. Roni returned to the table with the nuns. She had to remain. If not for decorum's sake — something she cared little about — then for the benefit of the Parallel Society. If the nuns made any decisions or shared any thoughts with each other, somebody from the Society needed to hear it. Not that she expected anything important to happen, but if it did and she missed it while Gram was out — she would never hear the end of it.

Sister Claudia snapped her fingers and Sister Rachel went about clearing Gram's dishes. "I'm sorry if we upset your grandmother."

"She's a tough woman," Roni said. "I doubt anything you said could bother her."

Sister Claudia arched an eyebrow. "It's a pity you don't seem as strong as her. I don't mean no offense by that. I'm merely pointing out an observation. Having Sister Mary as my mentor, I've learned a lot about leadership and the world in which we live. I'm sure you've been learning much the same under your grandmother's mentorship. I'm simply trying to say that it appears you've got plenty more to learn from her."

"Don't worry about me. I'm plenty strong."

"Oh dear, I have offended you. It was just that I've seen the way you defer to your grandmother since being here, and quite frankly, it did not feel like a teacher-student relationship or even a parent-child one. It looked more like a boss and an employee. I feared you may not be getting the proper education you deserved."

Sister Mary let out a soft laugh. "That's enough now. No need to keep teasing the young gal."

Roni did not believe for a second that Sister Mary thought this was playful teasing. But instead of pushing matters, she allowed herself an awkward grin and returned to her food. *Soon,* she thought, *just a few hours and I'll have that book in my possession. Then we'll see who's strong.*

CHAPTER 8

Immediately following the dinner, Roni hastened across the colonnade to the dorm. She stormed down the aisle and knocked on Gram's door. Hearing a choked *Come in* Roni entered to find Gram sitting on the bed with her back against the wall, her legs straight out, her eyes puffy, her nose red.

"Have a seat," Gram said, patting a spot next to her.

"Are you okay? Those nuns had no right to say —"

"It's okay. I've known for a long time the kinds of people they are. Just because they wear the clothes of a nun does not make them nuns. Not in the Catholic sense, anyway."

"I still don't like it."

"I appreciate your loyalty and concern. I've actually been thinking about that a lot tonight — about you. I know you better than you think. That loyalty, that concern — it can be a good thing. You must be careful, though. It can mislead you. It can guide you down the wrong paths."

Roni worried that Gram had been snooping in her room during the dinner. If she found Roni's tomb bag, it would be years before she trusted Roni enough to take her on an outing again.

Blowing her nose into a handkerchief, Gram said, "Do you remember Princess Nanono?"

Roni thought back, the odd name itching under the dark surface of her memories. "Maybe? I'm not sure."

"You were just a little girl. Your mother would make up stories for you. She preferred it over telling you stories like *Three Little Pigs* or *The Boy Who Cried Wolf*. I made sure you learned those stories eventually, but your mother wanted to teach you lessons her own way —

everything had to be her own way. Princess Nanono was the star of her storytelling.

"You loved those stories. Each one basically had the Princess getting into some sort of trouble by making the wrong choice, and by the end she would learn her lesson. There were other characters, but I don't really remember them well — a talking cookie, I think, and a bird that was her friend. But the important part here is that you loved the stories and as you started to understand the point of the stories, you became fiercely loyal to Princess Nanono. You worried that she made so many poor decisions. And you started to write your own stories for her — ones in which she was more of a heroine than a victim. Do you recall any of this?"

"A little. I have this vague image of a calico cat — yes, its name was Petal! And sometimes it was bad and sometimes good, so I never knew which version I'd get in a story."

"Good. Then maybe you'll remember this — one morning, you came to breakfast, and you asked your mother where Princess Nanono lived. You wanted to go visit. Because your mother had made these stories up, they were not written down in any book that you would have seen. So, you believed that she was recounting tales of a person she once knew. You wanted to visit her to share your stories so that you might help Princess Nanono. It was that morning in which your mother had to tell you the truth.

"But you refused to believe it. In your mind, there had to be a Princess Nanono. No choice. Otherwise, it meant your mother had lied to you.

"For almost a year after that, you tried everything you could think of to wheedle out information about where the real Princess Nanono lived. None of us would help you because of course none of us had an answer. But you refused to believe us.

"Of course, no matter how much you wished for it, you would never find Princess Nanono. That person never existed." Gram reached over and put her hand atop Roni's. "I know you want to help me. I know you want any chance, no matter how slim, to connect with your mother. But the creature inside that rift is not your mother. It's not the woman who came up with Princess Nanono. Whatever you think is in that rift, no matter how much you wish it to be, it is not your Maria."

"Then it isn't yours either, is it?" The words slipped out of Roni's mouth before she could stop.

Gram rolled her lips in tight and looked away. With the sharp sniffle, she said, "Go to bed. Stop worrying about your mother. Get some sleep."

"Please, Gram, you don't understand —"

"No, *you* do not understand. I don't expect it, but you need to believe that you will not understand what that thing is. When we get back to Pennsylvania, maybe you'll find something in the library to help. But for now, you must accept that there will always be limits to how much of another universe you can understand. And that includes the creatures within it."

"But if it's even a small portion of your daughter —"

"Enough. Go to your room, get some sleep, and for once, just listen."

Gram's stern face offered no opening for further conversation. Not that Roni wanted it anyway. She stomped off to her room and closed the door hard. Fuming, she thought of the tomb bag. Gram simply did not understand. She had let her emotions get in the way.

Roni wished she could rush over to the library immediately, but she knew she would have to wait. A lot.

Sitting on the edge of the lumpy mattress, Roni listened as the Sisters settled in the dorm for the night. With her jaw clenched and her breathing shallow, she heard every murmured voice, every creaking floorboard, every groan of tired bodies. As the minutes dragged on, the tension in her throat grew worse. She suspected that her voice would be nearly gone by the time she managed to get started on the night's mission — an old nervous habit that hadn't surfaced in about two years.

Good thing I won't have to talk to anybody tonight.

She figured she might not have anybody to talk to for the next several days. Assuming she could complete her mission, none of the nuns would be talking to her and Gram always had enough reasons to play the silent game. Just as well. After the evening's dinner, she had little but angry words to share with any of the people surrounding her at the moment.

Roni stretched back on the bed and closed her eyes. She had earbuds in and connected to her phone. If she managed to fall asleep, her alarm would go off at 3am. By that time, nobody would be awake.

But sleep would not come.

Twice, she considered leaving early — convincing herself that surely everybody had fallen asleep. Near midnight, she even stepped out of her room and walked down to the bathroom. All were asleep except Sister Rachel. She knelt in the middle of her bed and prayed — eyes closed, hands clasped, rosary looped around. If she had noticed Roni, she did not acknowledge the fact. After using the bathroom, Roni returned to her room and attempted once more to get some sleep.

Seconds later, the alarm went off. She startled in bed, a little drool wetting her pillow. Tapping off her phone, she sat up and rubbed her eyes. She figured she had managed at least forty-five minutes of real sleep, maybe even a little over an hour. Better than nothing.

It took her fifteen minutes to fully awaken, check over her tomb bag, and step out into the main room. She kept her shoes in the bag and walked the length of the dorm in her socks. With slow, methodical steps, she inched her way toward the exit. She brought down each step gently, making sure the wood did not creak loud enough to alert any light sleepers.

The room had been split in two. The left side nuns all rattled out hefty snores. The right side slept quietly but some of them rolled or kicked or flapped out a hand.

Reaching the far end, Roni did not breathe relief. Instead, she placed her hand on the doorknob and turned it slowly. Her hands shivered, and she feared the motion might rattle the lock. The next several moments blurred together — finally turning the knob open, pushing the door out, stepping through, keeping the knob open while grabbing it on the other side, closing the door, and easing the knob back. All without making a sound. With that accomplished, she still did not breathe relief. Instead, she scurried across the cold grass until she reached the circle with the statue of the Virgin Mary and the parked rental car.

She lowered to the ground and put on her shoes. Once finished, she inhaled long and slow and allowed herself a small moment to breathe. Relief.

Roni took another moment to rub her neck, trying to ease some of the tension. But true relaxation would have to wait. She had only accomplished the first part of the evening — getting out of the dorm undetected. Now for the really tough parts.

Hustling across the grass, Roni hoped she moved with the grace of a prowling cat but suspected she clumped along more like a hungry raccoon. Her bag thumped at her side, her feet snapped a twig on the ground, and she tripped at the edge of the concrete path when she reached the library. Only the lateness of the evening saved her from discovery.

Properly humbled, she let her excitement subside so that she could focus on what actually needed to be done. She approached the door to the library like a knight stepping before an ancient ruin — respectful and cautious. In her arsenal, she had a bobby pin and a paperclip. While she lacked experience at picking locks, she understood the basic concept. Starting with a bobby pin in the bottom, she then inserted the paperclip above it, and on the first try, the lock opened. Far too much pride swelled her chest but then deflated as she understood the truth — Sister Ashley had never locked the door in the first place. Roni's picking skills remained pathetic.

An evening shower opened up as she slinked into the library. Though the rain did not hit hard, its gentle tapping against the dorm would help hide any noises she might make. She chuckled — *Perhaps the Lord wants me to get this book.*

She brought up the flashlight app on her phone and headed straight for the stairs leading downward. The late hour made the enclosed space feel tighter, darker. Under the stark, blue light of her phone, the dust and cobwebs created strange shadows and added an unnatural texture to the walls. It was like walking through an old black and white monster movie — which only served Roni an extra heaping of nerves.

She sped through the passageways, spying several of her marks in the dust to aid her in making the proper turns. At least, she thought so. Until she reached a dead end.

Tracing back her steps, she inspected the dust mark closer. Which direction did it indicate? Was it even her sign or did something else brush across the corner? Perhaps her fingermarks could have been clearer. She chose a different path which also ended up dead. Back again, and again, and again.

After several attempts, she walked upon her starting point — the staircase. Murmuring swears, she began over in hopes of finding where she had gone wrong. A full hour went by.

Roni's pace quickened as she scuttled through the passageways once more. Sweat beaded along her back even as her mouth dried with the dust of the dead.

At another intersection which looked both familiar and foreign, she stopped. Pinching the bridge of her nose, she let out a frustrated groan. This could not be happening.

Then she heard a sound that changed everything — *Woooooooo.*

Roni held her breath so she could distinguish the sound clearly.

Wooooooo. Definitely the same cry of wind going through a poorly made bagpipe.

After a few breaths, she stopped again to listen. To her right. She headed down that path until she reached the next junction. Then she held her breath and listened. *Wooooo.* Straight, this time.

Twice more she had to stop and use that horrible sound as her guide. In less than five minutes, she came upon the big door with the iron ring for a knob. The door stood ajar as if inviting her entrance — Sister Ashley must have forgotten to lock the door in her haste to reach dinner. Roni would be sure to leave it open later to avoid tipping the nuns off. Patting her bag, making sure she still held all of the things she had brought along, she entered the private study of Sister Agnes.

Everything appeared as it had during her first visit — which meant Sister Ashley had returned at some point after dinner to straighten up. Roni wondered if the young gal wanted to follow in the footsteps of Sister Agnes. Perhaps she truly intended to live down here one day — sequestered with only the books around her.

The room felt smaller than before as if it wanted to lean in and watch everything Roni planned. *Well then, watch this,* she thought, getting straight to work. She set the bag down next to the desk and positioned herself at the foot of the bed. Bending at the knees, she gripped the heavy wooden frame and lifted. It had been heavy enough with the help of Sister Ashley, but alone, Roni budged the thing only two inches. She repeated the motion — moving the bed two inches at a time.

After she had managed close to a foot, she stopped to catch her breath. She slumped onto the bed and stuck her arm toward the crevice Sister Agnes rested in. Not enough room yet.

Ignoring the dampness of her shirt against her back, Roni lugged the bed three more times. While this did not make getting the book as easy as earlier in the day, she did manage enough space that she could spider her fingers around the book's spine. The hard surface rubbing the back of her fingers had to be the bones of Sister Agnes — Roni closed her eyes and tried to wash away any image that thought dared to conjure.

Despite the awkward angle, she managed to pull the book free. With a soft yip, she dropped onto the floor and hugged the large volume to her chest — breathing hard, sweating, and hoping she had not disturbed Sister Agnes too greatly. The nuns would be mad at her for stealing the book. They would be furious if she had damaged Sister

Agnes.

Holding the book, feeling its energy pulse against her chest, Roni posed a simple question — *what next?* Her plan had been clear enough. She wanted to take the book back to Pennsylvania. After her research had proved fruitless for finding a way to save Maria, she at least could return this book to the caverns.

No. She could not start lying to herself now. Not after she had made it this far. She had done this for one reason only — to save Maria. No. Full honesty. To save Maria, her mother. The only reason this particular book could have been secreted all the way down here instead of returned to the caverns was that it held value connected with the rift.

The real question was not *what now?* But rather *what exactly is the nature of the universe contained in the book?*

"Only one way to find out," Roni muttered to the empty room.

She clambered to her feet and held the book at arm's length. Experience had taught her how dangerous a book like this could be, so she had to be careful how she went about opening it. A quick scan of the room confirmed her suspicions — the old bed frame was the heaviest object.

Roni lifted the stained mattress and looked at the rope lattice underneath. It might work.

Taking out her journal and pen, she sat at the desk and wrote a quick entry describing the events that had led up to this point. If things went badly, she wanted some record of what had happened. At length, she returned the journal and pen to her bag and set them aside.

Next, she moved the desk chair so that its back pressed up against the bed frame and that it faced the door. Roni stepped over the frame, putting one leg between the gaps in the rope. She then lowered herself to her knees. With the chair in front of her, she propped the book up against its back.

All she had to do was reach around to the front of the chair and open the book. Whatever came out of it or went into it would be facing the direction of the door — not her. If she lost control of the book and the room depressurized, she hoped the weight of the bed would anchor her to this universe. The distant voice of a long-forgotten science teacher reminded her that any system was only as strong as its weakest point.

She yanked hard on the ropes. Though they held, she thought they surely would be the first thing to snap. But everything in the room was old and brittle except the hardwoods. She would just have to make do.

She reached for the book. But stopped.

Moving fast, so as not to lose her will, she unfastened her belt and looped it around the side runner of the bed. She slipped her arm through the loop and tightened it as far as it would go. Between that and the rope and the bed frame itself, if she fell into the book's universe, she suspected her limbs would stay behind.

Blotting that image from her mind, she used her free arm to stretch out and pull the front cover open.

The book cover resisted. That suggested a different pressure level inside that book's universe — one that would suck all the air from the room until the pressure equalized. Either that or the old book had not been opened in ages and might simply be sticking. Reworking her grip, Roni took a deep breath and readied to pull harder on the cover.

The study door opened and Sister Claudia entered with Sister Ashley by her side. They took one look at the book and screamed.

Roni jolted, her heart jackhammering against her chest. As she disentangled from the bed, Sister Claudia entered and immediately sidestepped out of direct line of sight of the book. Sister Ashley followed to the opposite side.

"Are you okay? I'm sorry that I came down here without you," Roni said. "I know you think this book is part of your history, with Sister Agnes and all, calling it the *History of Secrets*. But that's not true. It's one of the Parallel Society's books and it can cause you great harm. I'm trying to help."

Sister Claudia clasped her hands behind her back. "Do not make matters worse by lying to us. We did not scream because we thought you had betrayed us. We did not scream out of fear."

"A little fear," Sister Ashley said. "I did not want to be in front of that book."

"We were taken by surprise. That's all. And now that we see what you've done, we know you have to ability to change things for us."

Roni settled on the edge of the wood frame. She frowned. "I do?"

Sister Ashley knelt next to Roni. "This is going to be a glorious day. We finally have somebody willing to touch the book and able, too. We finally have somebody who can help us."

"I'm going to help you?"

"Oh, indeed," Sister Claudia said, her eyes darkening as she lowered her head. "You're going to do exactly what I tell you."

CHAPTER 9

Sister Ashley set two flashlights face up toward the ceiling to fully light the room while Sister Claudia paced a small circle, never taking her eyes off Roni. The book remained closed on the desk chair. Wind continued to blow above filling the room with more of that awful whining.

Sister Claudia stopped and gazed down upon Roni. Her habit blended in with the murky surroundings turning her into a ghostly, floating figure. "I'm afraid Sister Mary will be quite angry, if she discovers what you've done."

Roni choked down all the sarcastic comments that crept up her throat. A sharp bite rushed back. "Perhaps you were not listening when you came in here and boasted how you weren't frightened. The fact remains that this book does not belong to you."

"Your arrogance is annoying. A little impressive but mostly annoying."

Sister Ashley stepped forward and with a respectful bow, she said, "Let us not lose sight of our purpose here."

Sister Claudia glowered at Sister Ashley for a stretched second or two. Long enough to cause Sister Ashley visible discomfort. Only then did Sister Claudia gesture to the book and Roni. "Will you please move that book aside?"

As if removing a weapon, Roni lifted the book and set it on the floor. Sister Claudia slid the chair around so that she could sit facing Roni. "I'm going to give you a choice. It is my sincere hope that once you understand the true context of the situation that you will choose to help us."

"I have a choice now? I thought I had to do what you wanted."

Sister Ashley stepped up from behind. "With the book we can

actually control the conduit."

With a sharp swat of her hand, Sister Claudia caught Sister Ashley on the chin. "Be quiet."

"What is she talking about?" Roni asked. Her stomach flipped as her mind raced to catch up with the shifting moods in the room.

Sister Claudia pressed her hands upon her knees. Her fingers dug in like claws. "As I was trying to say, you need context in order to make your decision. Be a good student, keep your mouth shut and listen." She glanced over her shoulder. "Both of you."

Sister Ashley bowed again and stepped back toward the wall. "Ay."

After a short breath to compose herself, Sister Claudia said, "This abbey has stood since the 1600s. Sisters Margaret and Agnes lived here together in the early 1800s — beginning in 1804. Margaret and Agnes were more than Sisters of the Abbey, they were actual sisters, too. Their father farmed for a time but eventually found drink to be more appealing. The mother worked hard to maintain the family. Died when the girls were young. They came to the Abbey in their early teens. More than anything, I believe that fact caused too much of the troubles between them.

"Like any siblings, they competed with each other. Even in their duties that were meant to be benevolent and giving. If Margaret sacrificed a day to help the poor, Agnes would devote a week. If Agnes spent two hours in devotional prayer, the next night Margaret would spend three. According to some of the records Sister Ashley has uncovered, this rivalry was seen by the other nuns as a healthy situation." Turning her head aside, Sister Claudia said, "Isn't that right?"

Sister Ashley took one step forward. "Ay, it is. Sister Anne, the head of the Abbey at the time, believed that the competition would bring out the best, most altruistic behavior by the sisters, and in doing so, that they would end up being models for the other nuns to follow."

"The church may move slowly when it comes to change, but at least I can say that were the two sisters in the Abbey today, they would not be pitted against each other. But the 1800s was a different time with different views.

"Now, I am not clear on how much your grandmother has shared with you about our history, but you should know that our conduit to Heaven opened several hundred years ago. For Sisters Margaret and Agnes, just like it is for me and Sister Ashley, the conduit always was. Which brings me to the last part necessary to understanding all of this

— and that part is our book on the floor."

Roni's foot slid against the book's spine.

If Sister Claudia noticed, she did not acknowledge it. "According to Sister Ashley's research, Sister Anne was the first to reach out to the Parallel Society."

"That's right," Sister Ashley said, unable to see Sister Claudia's scowl. "It's unclear how Sister Anne discovered the existence of the Society, but she wrote a letter to them and within a few months, they sent their first representatives here."

"The Society member, a woman named Caroline Grosvenor, brought that book with her. She explained that the book could be used to contain our conduit and that the Society would dispose of it later. Well, I'm sure you understand by now that we were not in favor of that approach. Sister Anne made it quite clear in her letter that we wanted to secure the conduit to protect those around it and to safely examine it. We were thrilled to have this connection to Heaven — and still are — but at the time, it had managed to injure several of the nuns and engulf two more. We are not foolish enough to think that they were brought to Heaven. It is clear from the scrolls of Sister Anne and Sister Margaret that those unfortunate souls died before they fully entered the conduit. They wanted the Society to use its specialized knowledge to help the nuns communicate with Heaven, and to do that, we needed the conduit to be stable and secure. That's all they wanted. But, of course, Ms. Grosvenor did not see it that way.

"The Lord, however, controls all and sees all. So, when Ms. Grosvenor knew we would not help her destroy the conduit, she contacted the Irish government. That did not go as she had planned. They arrived and heard what we had to say and saw what we had to show, and it was agreed that we could not risk closing this conduit. If the nuns were right and the Irish government went ahead as the Society wanted, then they would be responsible for destroying what could become a national treasure. They saw money flowing in from all those who wanted to touch Heaven. If the nuns were wrong, then surely the Society could fix matters as needed at a later date.

"Ms. Grosvenor was quite angry, but she had no power in the situation. So, with the help of Sister Anne and Sister Margaret, it was finally agreed to create the stabilizing set up we have today. In exchange, the Abbey agreed to keep the existence of the conduit private. That suited us fine. We recognized then and now that the world is not ready for such a revelation. Our sacred duty is to protect this conduit from all who would harm it, which sadly means protecting it from the majority of the world. Everything else you've heard about us or the conduit is nothing more than fabrications created by your Society."

Roni did not know how much of this to believe but found the idea that Gram had lied to her about the rift plausible. "I'm guessing this is where Sister Agnes comes in?"

"She was not about to let her sister and some woman from some Society take away the beautiful things she had experienced. At least, that is how many see it now. Other nuns in the past have suggested that it was more sibling rivalry, more pushing for power, and all other sorts of corrupt or impure approaches. But those of us who've done the research know the truth. And those of us who've seen an angel firsthand — well, we really know. It is the same *before and after* affect that you have experienced. You know it. Once you've witnessed such a thing, it forever changes you. And Sister Agnes was no different. If anything, the oddity in all of this was with Sister Margaret. How she could open the church doors to a stranger, how she could make deals with the government, instead of letting the glory of Heaven spread throughout the world — I've never understood it."

Once more, Sister Ashley stepped forward. Sister Claudia raised a hand, ready to strike. Sister Ashley backed away.

"The evening before Ms. Grosvenor left the Abbey, Sister Agnes did much like you this evening — she snuck around the dorms while everyone slept, and she swiped this incredible book from underneath Ms. Grosvenor's bed. She stole away down here — Sister Ashley tells me that this room existed long before Sister Agnes — and she made it her home."

A glance back prompted Sister Ashley to move closer. "That is correct. In that the tomb was built with this room — an unusual construction for the unusual job of tomb-keeper. I've never found another reference in an Abbey to such a position, but this Abbey has never been like others anyway."

"From here, Sister Agnes wrote her thoughts, protected the book, and led those nuns willing to follow her. Aboveground, Sister Margaret took over as Head of the Abbey, and all the sisters did her bidding. But the followers of Sister Agnes also carried out orders from below. And it remained that way until their deaths." Glancing up at Sister Ashley, Sister Claudia added, "Tell her about the vow."

Sister Ashley hesitated, her focus entirely on Sister Claudia. She nodded, opened her mouth, but flinched back.

"Well?" Sister Claudia snapped.

With an uneasy grin, Sister Ashley cleared her throat. "You have to understand that Sister Margaret and Sister Agnes knew of each other's positions. It was not like a secret spy network or something like that. Sister Margaret tolerated Sister Agnes because of the vow. It was a simple agreement — that no nun would ever touch the book. Sister Margaret, of course, wanted everyone to make the vow so that she knew her deals with the Parallel Society and the Irish government would not be broken."

"But Sister Agnes," Roni said. "Why would she agree?"

"That is quite clear. You see, Sister Agnes opened the book. Once. It did not take her life, but what she witnessed made her believe that the power inside of it should not be wielded by any nun. Possibly not by anybody in the world at all, but we can only trust ourselves to honor the vow. So that is what they did, and that is what we do.

"Since that time, Sister Margaret's side of things concluded that the book itself had created the conduit."

Sister Ashley added, "Which is why Sister Petra's scrolls point out that only the book can reclaim it. She followed Sister Margaret and thought that —"

"Enough." Sister Claudia closed her eyes, wincing as if suffering the pain of a cracked tooth. "You'll have to excuse the Sister. Her excitement is getting the better of her manners."

"You've got it wrong," Roni said. "These books are dangerous."

"Which is why we don't touch them."

"I thought you didn't touch them because of the vow."

"And that vow came partly out of respecting the danger inherent in those books. But you have the experience that we lack. Is that not what the Parallel Society is all about? Learning how to deal with these books and what they can do?"

Staying out of Sister Claudia's reach, Sister Ashley said, "I've read all that Sister Agnes ever wrote. Most of Sister Petra's work, too. That book can do what no other book can do. With the conduit held in place by the other Society books, the one you have found can pull the Angel free."

Roni rose, but Sister Claudia did not back out of the way. With their knees brushing, Roni said, "You think you can pull an angel out of that rift?"

Though Sister Claudia had to look up, she still maintained dominant strength from her position. "No. We think *you* can. You have no vow holding you back from touching the book. And isn't it what you want? To pull out the girl you saw in the conduit?"

The next few seconds might as well have been hours. Roni's head rifled through thoughts that tumbled and spun upon each other with parts of each idea being called out and spread into other ideas. In one instant, she saw the eager and open face of Sister Ashley. The young nun clearly loved her books and had an obsession with the work of Sister Agnes. Perhaps part of her truly wanted to help Roni — even if a self-interested part wanted to free what she thought to be an angel. However, in that same instant, Roni saw salivating, sharp-teethed creatures dressed as nuns. Gram had said they were dangerous, and Roni wondered if this sudden shift was more than simply self-interest but carried with it a darkness that might create a shadow over her.

After all, a year ago, her father had warned her that her actions with the Parallel Society were doing great harm. What if moments like this were the kind of things he referred to?

In the next second, Roni decided it didn't matter. She had never trusted the nuns from the start, so she would not do so now. But that did not mean she forbade herself from using the nuns. One thing was clear — this book possibly held within it the power to free whatever remained of Roni's mother. Once she had Maria out of the rift, then the nuns could think of it as a conduit to Heaven for the rest of eternity. It did not matter to Roni. She would happily visit every year to keep the rift stable. As long as she had Maria, the rest didn't matter.

But in that same second, she thought of Gram. Despite their acrimony, Roni loved her grandmother. She understood how much pain this caused Gram. Coming to the Abbey, year after year, seeing an echo of her daughter trapped in another universe — no, Roni would not be so arrogant as to think she understood. In truth, nobody understood. How could anyone? Gram endured the torture of her loss alone. No other woman in all of history could have experienced what Gram had suffered. It wasn't simply the loss of her daughter. It was seeing her lost daughter both alive and dead, a split existence, never to be made whole again.

One more second ticked by. Roni's instincts conflicted within her. She wanted to save Maria. She wanted to respect Gram. She wanted to fix a wrong from long ago. She did not trust the nuns.

Sister Claudia and Sister Ashley stared at her — expectant, hungry. Roni opened her mouth, ready to tell the nuns in a crude manner that they could screw off, but a voice stopped her. A soft, high-pitched voice. It called to her. The voice of a young girl. Trapped. It sounded like an out of tune flute.

Time sped back to its normal pace. Roni glanced up at the ceiling and heard the wind blowing through the ventilation once more. The corners of her mouth lifted. The world above, Sister Margaret's world, had always been connected with the world below, that of Sister Agnes. Connected but separate. Like two universes, each staying where it belonged.

"Maria does not belong in that rift. If you're speaking the truth, then I am obligated to take this book and pull her out. I am a member of the Parallel Society, and it is my sworn duty to keep universes from crashing into each other." Roni bent down and picked up the book.

"Wonderful," Sister Ashley said, rushing towards Roni with her arms open wide.

Roni inched to the side. "Careful. You don't want to accidentally touch the book."

Sister Ashley pulled her hands back as if threatened by a rattlesnake. "You're correct about that. Thank you for helping us. Not only are you doing the nuns a great service and helping yourself, you save us the trouble of having to bring charges against you for desecrating our tombs."

Sister Claudia snapped her fingers. "Enough chatting. Let's get this done. Come."

Before Roni could ask Sister Ashley to elaborate, the nuns exited the room, leaving Roni with the choice to follow or find her way out by herself. She followed.

As they wound their way back into the library, across the colonnade, into the church, and down the spiral staircase toward the rift, Roni fought the urge to doubt her decision. The gulf between knowing that the nuns could not be trusted and her desire to save Maria continued to widen, but she saw no easy fix. Stepping in front of the rift told her time was up. Instead, she focused her mind on how to help Maria. A lot of that would depend on what happened when she opened the book.

The rift crackled like a campfire. Its bright red and orange swirls radiated light and heat upon the room. Roni's muscles clenched and she stuttered a step. For a brief instant, she wished Gram were by her side.

But no — she could do this herself. She had to. After all, what kind of leader would she be, if she could not help her own mother?

Sister Claudia and Sister Ashley formed a rough circle with Roni. They bowed their heads. Sister Claudia genuflected and said, "Before we embark on this vital moment, let us pray."

Sister Ashley bowed her head a little more. Out of respect, Roni lowered her head. She watched Sister Ashley — her meekness, her strengths, her enthusiasm, even her subservience fit her perfectly. Her habit and coif, though — while covering her in the most utilitarian way — still managed to express some of her feminine form. Yet at the same time, Roni noticed the light circles of sweat stains on the white of her wimple.

Sister Claudia raised her head with her eyes closed. "Oh Lord, we seek your blessing and your sturdy hand as we set forth to do your work."

Having no use for prayers, Roni closed her eyes and conjured the images of Gram, Sully, and Elliot. That elderly trio had saved more lives than they could ever be thanked for. They made tough decisions, too. Sometimes, they even made decisions they knew would make the others angry. But saving people was what they did.

The things Roni had seen in the last two years, the world that had been opened up to her, even the arguments and frustrations — she saw how it all led to this moment. Ever since joining the Parallel Society, she had been waiting for some ceremony or ID card or secret handshake — something to signify that she truly belonged there, that she had earned her right to be there. But it was never something they could give her. It was something she had to take for herself by doing the very thing they were tasked to do. Not only would she soon save Maria, but she would soon prove that she had the right to call herself one of the Parallel Society.

"In the Lord's name, Amen." Sister Claudia stood and faced the rift. She gestured toward Roni as if nudging a child toward the edge of the deep end of the pool.

Time to sink or swim.

Roni walked forward until she could no longer see the nuns. Better that they were behind her. Light flashed off the rift as if it knew she meant it harm. Readjusting the book in her grip, she also set her right foot back and out, forming a sturdy stance to help her withstand the expected forces.

"Is there a problem?" Sister Claudia asked, her voice cold and threatening.

"Be quiet," Roni said, keeping her focus on the rift. "You've done your part. Leave this to an expert."

Narrowing her eyes, she opened the book.

Chapter 10

As Roni pulled open the book cover, grey smoke puffed out. But nothing followed. Dust figured to be the culprit and not some ancient mist from an unknown universe. Then the book vibrated in her hand — gently like a humming refrigerator.

She felt slight pressure upon her palms as if the book pushed against her. Or something pushed against the book in her direction. The longer it lasted, the more she equated the sensation with holding a magnet against another of equal polarity. That was it, exactly. The universe of the book and the universe in the church pushed against each other.

Her heart sank. "This won't work. This is the wrong book."

"Have faith," Sister Claudia said. "It will work."

Roni remained standing still with the book open. But its large size grew heavy in her hands. "I'm telling you, this is the wrong book. We don't want one that's pushing against the rift universe. We want one that extracts from it. Did Sister Agnes steal a different book from the Society as well?"

Despite wanting to close the cover, Roni kept it open and watched the universe in front of her. Much of the orange had slipped away, leaving behind deep crimson. Dark, smoky clouds spun by like miniature storms seen from above. It gave the rift a sense of motion as if it spun on a slow-moving pedestal.

And then Roni saw it. Crawling into view. The young girl. Maria.

As she came closer to facing them full-on, the book reacted. A blast of gold energy whipped out like a frog's tongue. Thin and long, it stretched straight to the rift. Its golden light filled the room, devouring the shadows, leaving every cracked stone and split timber visible.

"You see it now," Sister Ashley said dropping to her knees. "This is the book that created the conduit with its golden light of Heaven."

This tongue of energy had penetrated the rift and wrapped around Maria's arm. It reeled back into the book, strong and taut, pulling on Maria. In seconds, the little girl ended up hovering in the middle of the church basement, locked between two universes. The rift bulged out with her, determined to hold on. The golden tongue freed her arm and pulled harder.

Sister Claudia put out her hands. "She's beautiful. A true angel."

Crackling sparks and bulging waves rolled along the surface of the rift. The circle of books pushed all the rift's energy back in onto itself. Except for Maria. The books could not contain her. By the time Maria floated equidistant between Roni's open book and the rift, her head tore free from the rift's grasp. Even as the rest of her body remained wrapped in a menacing red blob of power, even as the golden tongue strained to pull her, even as her mouth opened wide and cried in pain — through all of it, she had the ability to lock eyes with Roni.

A fleeting second. No more. But enough to erase all doubt from Roni. This was her mother as a child. Gram's daughter. All that remained.

From behind, Roni heard Sister Ashley ask, "Now?"

For one beat of her heart, Roni heard the betrayal in that voice. She did not know what it meant, but she knew it would be bad.

"Oh, yes," Sister Claudia said. "Definitely now."

With an ecstatic squeal, Sister Ashley sprinted forward. Roni could only watch. Any effort to stop Sister Ashley meant losing control of the book — and losing Maria. Sister Claudia's gleeful laugh erupted behind.

"Sister Agnes understood what all the nuns before her failed to understand," Sister Claudia said as Sister Ashley danced around the circle of books. "This is more than simply a conduit, more than simply a way to communicate with angels in Heaven. This is a gateway to Heaven itself. Keeping this locked away, encircled by your books, is a heresy."

Over her shoulder Roni yelled, "Don't do this. Whatever you're planning, just don't." Turning her focus back to Maria, she went on, "Fight. You're running out of time. Come to me."

"She won't have to fight. None of us will."

Sister Ashley whipped off her wimple and coif, letting long locks of raven hair flow around her shoulders.

Mesmerized, Sister Claudia went on, "For centuries scholars have debated how we would know when Jesus had returned. How would we know that the time had come to create Heaven on Earth? And all that time, the nuns here at the Abbey already held the answer."

"Jesus was never going to be seen in mortal form," Sister Ashley said, her voice in a trance. "Sister Agnes knew it all along. Jesus brought us the conduit, and it is our honor and duty to bring Heaven onto the Earth."

She moved like a ballerina, and as she finished her words she bent forward and gently lifted one of the Society books out of the circle. A ripple in the air soared around the remaining books. Roni's heart sank.

And Hell broke loose.

"No," Roni said, her white-knuckled fingers trembling.

In her delirious exultation's, Sister Ashley twirled as she held the book out. The rift flashed red light like an angry storm. Its edges undulated, including those surrounding Maria.

"Help," Maria said, her voice strained, her eyes tearing.

Sister Ashley froze in an awkward stance as she stared at Maria. "Yes, my Lord. I can help. I can free you from this pain." With a jerking motion, she threw the book into the nearest group of bookstands. Two more knocked over.

Vicious winds arose as if a tornado had formed within the room. The books still operating shuttered in their stands. Sister Ashley laughed as the wind thrust her hair wildly around. Roni tried to scoot back, hoping her efforts might spool the tongue in quicker or at least bring Maria further from the rift. But the icy hand of Sister Claudia touched her shoulder.

"That won't work."

All of the bookstands lifted off the ground. The books flew about. A bolt of lightning broke free from the rift and carved a hole into the stone wall. Howls and moans and twisted cries filled the room as if the stones themselves screamed.

Roni repositioned her hands, but there was no way to hold the oversized book with one hand and attempt to grab Maria with the other. The book required both her hands to stay open, and she could not close it without giving up on her mother. She refused.

Two metal stands clattered in one corner while a wooden stand shattered against another. Sister Ashley giggled at the orchestration of noise. She looked back at Sister Claudia. "It's really happening. Isn't it wonderful?"

A large stone book stand flew through the air and clobbered Sister

Ashley in the side. She tumbled to the ground, her head banging against the hard floor. Blood splashed across the stones.

Wobbling on all fours, she attempted to stand. The strong winds and the blow to her head shoved her back down. With both hands supporting her, Sister Ashley gazed about the room. Blood dribbled from under her hair, across her forehead, and down her cheeks.

She uttered a confused gasp.

With a sharp crack in the air, the orange rift shot out a lance of energy, took hold of Sister Ashley, and yanked her inside.

Two seconds, and she was gone.

The open books shot off energy in all directions. They bounced around like bumper cars. One flew off near Roni's head and another smacked into her shins.

Amongst the chaos, Sister Claudia crossed herself. She stared at the empty spot where Sister Ashley had been. "Incredible."

"The books," Roni said. "Close the books and put them back in place."

As if speaking to a thick child, Sister Claudia said, "You don't close Heaven."

Roni gave one last glance at Sister Claudia. No help would be coming from there. She faced her mother again. "Maria, come on. Fight. You can break free."

She could not tell if Maria heard her or even understood her, but the young girl stretched her arms further towards Roni. She wriggled as if pushing through a tight space. Her face stretched back and she winced.

Another book, this one spinning like a pinwheel, cut through the air and clipped Sister Claudia on the chin. She only smiled — even as the blood slid down her throat and stained her gown. "Creation is always violent. I understand that, my Lord. I am ready. If you must take my life as you have taken Sister Ashley, I am yours." She ambled forward, a psychotic grin plastered across her lips.

In the distance, Roni heard a rumble and had the strange thought that a thunderstorm might be brewing outside. But the rumble quickly intensified. Rolling closer and closer. It became a stampede thundering down upon them.

The rift burst open.

A red wave jetted out in all directions. When it struck Roni, it lifted her off the floor and tumbled her backwards. The book flew from her hands, and as it rose, time slowed.

Not just a perceptional slowing. Time actually slowed.

She floated in the air, feeling the pull of gravity combating the push of the wave. She felt the air shoving out of her lungs. Her hair thrust back as the room tilted in front of her. But it all moved glacially.

In fact, Roni felt the slowing down more and more each passing moment — she dared not think of it as seconds. And then everything stopped. Locked in the air, unable to move, frozen in place. Yet she could still feel life around her. And with an intuitive leap, she put it together — the world inside this universe moved, but so imperceptibly slow as to be frozen in time. All the years that had passed since part of Maria had split off into the rift, yet for that part of her, perhaps only a few seconds had gone by. A minute at most. Even sound moved so slowly that Roni heard the purist silence ever in her life.

Yet her thoughts kept moving. Which suggested Maria's thoughts had continued all this time as well. How many years had gone before she realized what was happening to her? How many years did she strain and struggle with the misguided hope that she could break free? How long before she gave up?

A distant rumble struck Roni's ears — notable not only because it stood out amongst the silence but also because it sounded in real time, not slowed down. It sounded like a stampede of wild mustangs. The closer it came, the more the sound rendered into a steady thrum. She could feel it vibrating her bones, her skin, even the hairs growing on her arms.

When the thrum hit, the speed of the world returned to normal. Roni's body flipped through the air and slammed onto the hard floor. Sister Claudia shot backwards, smacking into the wall, and crashing on her hands and knees. The open books fell — several of them flapping shut, several others apparently inert. But not the big book Roni had opened.

It lay flat on the floor about ten feet away. Its strange gold light poured out, creating twisted shadows on the ceiling as it fought to engulf Maria. The young girl screamed. She braced her hands against the floor. From the waist down, she was inside the book. Tears streamed off her chin.

Roni snatched a look at the rift. Its swirling storms had settled and its deep vibrant colors had dimmed. Ignoring the throbs of pain radiating from her bones, she raced across the room and clutched both of Maria's hands. Straddling the book, Roni arched back, pulling, pulling, groaning in an effort to find a little more strength.

"Sister Claudia," she called out as she repositioned her feet. Across the room she saw the nun praying on her knees. "Get over here. Help me save this girl."

But Sister Claudia shook her head. "It wasn't supposed to be like this. I don't understand."

Sweat covered Roni's body. Her grip on Maria slipped a few inches. She looked down as the little girl stared directly into her. No mistaking those eyes — they pleaded for her life.

The gold tongue slithered around Maria, settling across her chest and on her shoulder. It constricted as it pulled her further down. Roni dropped to her knees, still clutching Maria, still pulling back, feeling her muscles strain and tear. Feeling all of her strength weaken.

"Sister Claudia. Please."

Sister Claudia stood, and through a glimmer of hope, Roni thought all would be well. But the glimmer faded as the nun bolted for the spiral staircase leading upward.

At the foot of the staircase, she halted. She stumbled backwards, her face agape. Sister Mary descended the stairs and behind her came Gram, Sully, and Elliot. All four paused to survey the situation.

Hunched over and pushing his glasses up his nose, Sully set his feet firm on the floor. "Gram, take care of those books." Gram moved around Sully and flicked her wrists. Long chains fell from the sleeves of her blouse. Like a seasoned cowboy, she whipped those chains across the room. Each one found its mark — the spine of a book. She hauled them in, tied them up, and set about placing them on the bookstands.

Sister Mary snapped her fingers at Sister Claudia and the two helped Gram reset the bookstands.

"Elliot," Sully said and his old partner needed no more.

The tall, distinguished man headed over to Sister Claudia. If she had suffered any wounds, he would heal her.

Finally, Sully approached Roni. He reached down, and with an iron grip, he grabbed Roni by the waist. She had seen his gifts in action before. Like a boulder, he could be immovable. And though she spotted the anger in his face, she felt relief at the arrival of the Parallel Society.

Until the heavy bowling sound returned. Rolling, rolling. Turning into a stampede of wild mustangs.

Roni's eyes snapped wide open. "Get out of the — "

The red wave hit harder than before. It blasted Roni off her feet, but with Sully holding her, her body twisted over his shoulder. Her ribs snapped like a chain of firecrackers. It was the last sound she heard before the wave stole all sound.

Immobilized and contorted, Roni suffered through her cracked rib cage in an unending loop of pain. An agonized shriek rose in her chest but could not escape. In this red universe, it would take decades for her mouth to open wide enough to release the sound.

From the corner of her eye, she snatched a glimpse of the book. The upside-down image promised to haunt her for the rest of her life. It remained on the floor, open, and all trace of Maria had vanished.

Roni tried to scan the area, but with her head tucked under and motionless, her limited view provided nothing more. When she finally heard the distant rumble, relief blended with terror in her heart. The wave would pass soon but the pain would only amplify.

As the rumble approached and the volume grew louder, Roni mentally braced herself. And then it was upon them. The stampede plowed across them as the wave finished its course.

The world returned to normal. Roni's legs continued to spin overhead, twisting her body, and the electrifying jolts in her chest pressed down like knives into her lungs. She screamed out, and as her body slipped from Sully's grip, she had an instant in which she saw Gram, Sister Mary, Sister Claudia, and Elliot flailing through the air. Sully arched back and watched her in confusion.

She hit the floor head first. Purple-black dots flashed across her vision.

All went dark.

CHAPTER 11

Roni's eyes fluttered open. She lay in the lumpy guest bed of the nuns' dorm. A tall, black man stood over her. He held a gnarled cane parallel to her body in his right hand while his left hand prescribed a series of motions in the air. *Elliot.*

She grinned, then chuckled. "Did you save my life again?"

"Be quiet," he said with his deep, precise voice. "You are well, but you should take it easy for the rest of the day."

Propping up on her elbows, she winced at the soreness. Better the sensation of bruising rather than the hot piercing of broken ribs cutting her apart from the inside.

Elliot snapped his fingers at her. "I told you to take it easy and the first thing you do is try to sit up. You are as stubborn as your grandmother."

"I can't let some broken bones stop me right now."

"You had a collapsed lung, too."

"I did?"

From the doorway, Sully stood with his arms crossed. "Probably a concussion, on top of that. But by all means, ignore Elliot and go get yourself hurt again."

Roni pushed herself to a fully upright position. Elliot huffed, but he stepped back and leaned on his cane. Sully's head made a slow scan as he took in the meager private room.

"Maybe we should leave you here," he said. "Perhaps a year or two stuck in the Abbey might straighten you out."

"You're not the first to suggest that one."

"I wonder why that might be?"

Roni's face wrinkled tight. "You think I wanted any of this to happen?"

"I think you lack the common decency to respect those who stick their necks out for you. Your grandmother did not want you to go on this trip. She said you weren't ready. I vouched for you. I used up some of my capital as a leader so that you would be sent on this trip. And look what you did."

As all of the events flooded back to her, Roni turned her apprehensive eyes upon Elliot. He put out a reassuring hand. "Everybody is okay," he said. "The rift is not stabilized, but we were able to create a temporary method of controlling it."

"Temporary, at best," Sully said. "Do you have any idea how difficult that was? I had to use more of my strength than I've done in years just to keep those pedestals in place. Elliot worked a shield to keep the building from collapsing upon us. And your dear Gram worked tirelessly to chain together what little we could. Many of the books were damaged. Some beyond our ability to repair from here. Some might never be useable again."

Pressing his hand harder in comfort, Elliot said, "Once we have the full complement of books repaired or created, all will be well. Until then, the rift will have to be carefully monitored."

"And Gram?" Roni asked.

"She is fine."

With a disgusted snort, Sully said, "She is far from fine. Poor woman has had to lose her daughter for a second time."

Roni's eyes welled up. "Then ... Maria's gone?"

"I'm afraid so," Elliot said, his brow wrinkling into numerous folds.

"Maria died years ago in a car accident," Sully said. He gritted his teeth tight enough to turn his jaw as white as the tufts of hair ringing his bald head. "That thing in the rift was no more than a memory of Gram's daughter. And it was never your mother. You get that straight. That little afterimage of a girl never grew up to be an adult, never fell in love, never got married, never spent an intimate night creating you, never gave birth to you, never —"

"I get it. You don't have to be a prick about it."

"Looking at the mess around here, I think I do."

Elliot sliced his hand through the air between Roni and Sully. "That is quite enough from both of you."

Plunking her elbows onto her knees, Roni lowered her head into her hands. Fighting with Sully would not solve anything. It certainly would not bring back Maria. Roni had been so close, had the girl in her arms, but now — Maria was most likely lost in another universe. Again.

Roni's head perked up at a soft high-pitched sound. The soft mewing of a cat. Faint and distant. Why would she hear that? She could not recall having seen any cats or evidence of cats around the Abbey property. And she was fairly certain it would be difficult for a cat to wander onto the property — being so far from any other homes or towns.

It came again. "Did you hear that?"

"Hear what?" Elliot asked.

"Sully?"

"I only hear you making excuses for your bad behavior."

"Do not start again," Elliot said. He stepped closer to Sully and lowered his head to speak softly — though Roni could hear them quite clearly. "It is evident that she feels bad enough about what has happened. You've done your job in reprimanding her and asserting your authority. There is no need to keep opening the wound."

Sully did not look convinced. "Until that rift is stabilized, things are not okay here. And until we can figure out what Sister Ashley's presence within the rift will do, we have no idea if that stability is even possible. Because let's face it — that universe is not like some mass expanse of space with planets and stars. At least, that's not the sense I've got from it. It acts more like a living being of its own."

Roni got to her feet. "Maria is not in the rift anymore, but she fell in that book. Shouldn't we go get her?"

"One crisis at a time," Sully said.

"But it'd be easy. We could do what we did with Darin. You build a golem, have it go in there, and bring her back."

Sully pushed off the doorjamb and straightened as much as his old back would allow. His pale skin reddened as his face tightened. "You think it's that easy to make a huge golem that can withstand the forces of an entire universe? You think it was that simple last time for Elliot to use his abilities to even locate Darin? And for that matter, the only reason we could lure Darin to join with the golem — which didn't really happen the way we expected anyway — was because we had an item personal to him. Do we have an item personal to the little girl version of Maria? The only thing I can think of is Gram herself. Do you want to stick Gram inside of a golem and throw her into another universe?"

Roni cringed as she sat back on the edge of the bed. "I'm just trying to help think through this."

"You need to stop trying to help and start to learn by listening first. Once you've got the proper knowledge of what you're supposed to be doing, then you can help."

Elliot banged his cane on the floor. "We are not going to sit here and rehash these arguments over and over. It only helps our enemies. Now Sully, you must acknowledge that Roni is a novice and that perhaps you did make a mistake in sending her here. That was your fault. And you must own the repercussions of that choice." Sully started to argue but Elliot smacked his cane against Sully's shoulder. Before Roni could snicker, Elliot faced her. "You must accept that we know more than you. You do not like authority of any kind, and we understand that. You did not like it when Gram was in charge and you're now going to be upset with Sully because he is in charge. I have no doubt that if I were in charge, you would be angry with me as well. But at least admit that your anger, your real anger, is because you know you screwed up. You went against the orders and expectations that were given to you in some hope of being the hero and acting flashy or whatever was in your head. And because of that, we are in a dangerous situation."

Roni punched the side of the bed. "Maria is partly my mother. How was I supposed to let that go? Would you have ignored her if it was your mother?"

"If doing so meant hurting my living grandmother, the one who raised and cared for me, then perhaps I would. At the very least, I would have given her more consideration than you did. And I would've talked with my grandmother, asked her to help me understand why we shouldn't go help that sliver of my mother floating in another universe. Help me understand the kind of pain she may have endured seeing her daughter's double in that rift. Just plain understand. Own your mistakes, Roni. And you too, Sully."

Elliot's gaze drifted from one to the other before he walked out of the room shaking his head. Sully let Elliot pass, then leveled a hard glare at Roni. She braced herself for another tirade, but instead, he merely muttered as he turned away. There were a lot of good things to be said about Elliot's ability to heal, but Roni decided that this time around, she would have benefited from a little sympathy for her wounds, instead.

Alone in the room, she sat with her thoughts in the silence surrounding her. But then she heard that mewing again. Only this time it sounded louder — a tiny fraction but enough that she no longer thought the sound belonged to a cat. It was more than a simple meow. Rather, it had a longer flow to it like an ambulance siren far in the distance — but not a European ambulance. An American one — with its stretched-out tone rising and falling like a leaf floating on a wave.

Coupled to the sound, came the smell — a sickly-sweet aroma like cotton candy. Roni closed her eyes, attempting to dull all her senses but that of smell. She inhaled slowly, letting the aroma drift through her nose and down her throat. It was more than sugar. She smelled some type of soap.

Sugar. And soap. Like a little girl.

Roni's knee bounced, and she gripped the edge of the bed tight. She listened intently to the silence of the room. Feeling the rush of blood pumping through her head, she opened her mouth and with a cracking voice said, "Maria?"

She waited for a response but none came. Roni had never believed in ghosts, but then again, she had believed in there being only one universe. With the latter clearly wrong, perhaps the former could be true.

"Maria?" A little stronger this time.

Roni's shoulders convulsed back, slamming the shoulder blades close to each other. Her head arched back. Like a mass of muscle spasms, it happened again. But nothing had struck her. Nobody had assaulted her. She had experienced a whack against her spine, but from the inside.

When that thought voiced in her head, her pulse shot up as if she had sprinted a hundred-meter dash. Sweat beaded across her skin. Her head throbbed and she felt nauseous.

She needed air. Stumbling to her feet, she made her way into the main part of the dorm. Elliot stood by the front door.

He glanced over at her and his face registered his concern. "You need to get back in bed."

"I need air."

Hobbling over on his cane, he said, "Then I will escort you."

"Leave me alone."

He tried to take her arm, but she wrenched it away. The sudden movement caused her to trip forward. Thankfully, she managed to stay upright. Refusing to look back — she did not want to see Elliot's pitying concern — she pushed on outside.

It was still dark. How was that possible? She glanced at her watch — 9:03 pm. She had been knocked out for a full day. More lost time.

At least, she had the cool, fresh air to fill her lungs.

And it did feel good. But her heart still raced, her head still ached, and her skin still chilled. *Is this a panic attack?*

Squatting, she let her head hang and focused on breathing. After about a minute, she thought she might be feeling better. She rose, stretched her arms, and looked over to see the church.

Gram would be in there. No doubt about it. Roni considered following Elliot's advice and returning to bed. She did not want to talk with Sully, and she certainly did not want to face Gram.

But being a future leader of the Parallel Society meant facing the hard and difficult head on. She could think of nothing more difficult at the moment than dealing with Gram. And if she indeed had suffered a panic attack, then clearly Gram was at the heart of it. Better to get that taking care of before dealing with the trouble between universes.

Roni entered the church.

While the Abbey only served a handful of cultish nuns, it had been built with a larger audience in mind. Like many of the cathedrals in Ireland — Gothic architecture intended to praise the Lord through artistry and design — it's cavernous space overwhelmed and mystified the senses. As Roni shuffled down the center aisle of the nave, she had a moment of awe at the detailed beauty found in the grand architecture. Long columns led up to pointed arches, to windowed clearstory, to ribbed vaulting which kept the high ceiling from collapsing. At the apse of the Cathedral, an enormous stained-glass window depicting the Virgin Mary surrounded by rolling hills and beautiful animals created an intoxicating view. In front of it, a life-sized wooden carving of Jesus on the cross gazed down at the parishioners. Kneeling in the front pew, Gram had her fingers laced, her elbows leaning forward on the railing, and her head lowered in prayer.

Roni knelt next to her grandmother. She heard distant cries — more lost animals or something coming from inside? — but kept her head bowed out of respect for her grandmother's beliefs. At length, Gram put out her hand and held the top of Roni's.

"It's okay," Gram said.

Of all the things Gram could have uttered, all the ways she could have vented her anger, this pierced Roni's healed chest and drove straight through to her heart. Her head dropped to the wood railing, and she let her tears fall. "I'm so sorry. I only wanted to help you. Help her."

"That's why you are going to be very good at this job. One day."

Sniffling, Roni rubbed the tears from her eyes. "Sully doesn't think so."

"Of course he does. He's just angry at himself for making a poor decision and is angry because he wants to protect me. He thinks he's failed. That's part of the job being leader."

Roni gazed up at the statue of Jesus. Her top lip curled.

"Don't be like that," Gram said.

"What did I do?"

"Don't come in here and look upon the Church with such disdain."

"I wasn't. Honest. I was thinking that it must've been hard for him. He's like Maria — stuck between worlds. Right? He was a mortal man but also a heavenly being."

"I suppose."

"I wonder — you think when people talk about feeling his presence, that they really physically feel something?"

"Of course."

"Well, we still have the book that Maria was pulled into. Maybe we can find a way to feel her presence. To bring her back."

Roni's skin tightened. *Another panic attack?*

"Dear, it's a sweet thought, but no. I have finally, truly lost my daughter."

Roni's body shuddered. Straight to the bone. The muscles on the back of her neck contracted. As if Maria had screamed the word *No!* and it threatened to rip Roni to pieces.

With a production of grunts and groans, Gram rose to her feet and settled back on the pew bench. "Sit with me."

Roni did not move at first. She feared her legs would not support her. She needed time alone to consider what had happened to her — continued to happen — but the expectant look on Gram's face meant any other plans had to be postponed. With grunts and groans of her own, she managed to get to the bench.

Gram folded her hands across her large bosom and offered Roni a genuine smile. "I know you meant well. I really do. But I want you to listen closely. I'm going to tell you a story about your mother, back when she was only nine years old, back before she ever came to this place."

The mixed odor of sugar and soap returned to fill the air. Roni had to take shallow breaths in order not to choke.

Gram said, "Your mother was a sweet, wonderful little girl. But she always had that wild side, too. The two forces battled within her all of the time. If we went to an amusement park, part of her would want to go on the roller coasters — even though she did not meet the height requirement. She didn't care. The other part of her did. The other part of her stopped her from begging to go. And yet, I would catch her eyeing those roller coasters. I could see part of her brain trying to figure out how she could get away with sneaking on for a ride yet also make sure that I would never know. And more importantly, nobody would.

"Of course, with roller coasters at amusement parks, she never stood a chance. Nobody would let her ride, and she would have to go home feeling a little left out. Yet she also seemed a bit relieved — that by following the rules, she had somehow done better.

"But there were other times when opportunities presented themselves to her. Those times her wild side won out."

Roni's head swirled, and she strained to keep focus on Gram's story. She attempted to hold her face stoic so as not to betray any discomfort, anything out of the ordinary. She probably failed, but she also figured Gram was too wrapped up in our own tale to notice.

"Once," Gram said, her voice darkening as her eyes gazed off toward the transept, "Maria and I went for a short hike and a picnic lunch at the park. It was a beautiful day — crisp air, golden leaves everywhere, perfect. Near the end of the hike, we came upon a dead squirrel. It caught Maria's attention because its belly had bloated up. She thought it looked like one of those toys that when you squeezed it, the eyes bulged out. I told her not to touch it and then moved along. Later, we sat on a blanket and had a lovely picnic. There were other families around, other children, and this was at a time when parents were not scared to let their children explore. So, while Maria and some of the other kids ran off to the woods or to play ball on the fields, I sat back with the other adults and chatted."

Gram smirked as the memory played out in her head.

"She would've gotten away with it, but she scared some of the other kids. They ratted her out. I learned that Maria went back to the squirrel. She found a stick and using a rock, she sharpened it. Nothing deadly, just enough to poke that squirrel's belly. Some of the other children who had been equally fascinated warned her not to do it. Their parents had also told them not to touch the dead animal. But she didn't listen.

"That's all. I never found out what else happened because all the screaming kids got their parents worked up, and I had to usher Maria away. I didn't want to make her feel bad for being inquisitive, so I let the matter go. But I want you to understand — she was not a perfect person. Not even from the beginning. And when that rift did what it did to her, it exacerbated the problem. That's the thing that you saw as Maria, the thing I wanted to think of as my daughter —it never was. It looked like her, but she never was whatever idealized version of her you have in your head. Never was what was in my head." Gram leaned forward, took Roni's hand, and kissed it. "She never could be. You understand?"

A harrowing shriek attacked Roni's ears. Bile flooded her throat, burning as it raced up and back down, and left behind an acrid, sick taste. Her head pounded with images from a little girl's twisted picnic afternoon.

Roni saw that squirrel — a bloated carcass, soulless and stiff. She could feel the girl's determination — using a dull rock to sharpen the stick. Fascination motivated some of her actions, but cruelty and defiance were at the core. A twisted sense of satisfaction flooded her as the gases poured out of the hole in the squirrel's belly making a wet, high tone like the mouth of a balloon held mostly closed.

"I'm sorry," Roni managed to say without throwing up. "I need to be by myself."

She hurried to her feet and rushed down the long nave until she reached the exit. She could feel Gram staring at her in confusion. Those eyes pressed upon her back hot and uncomfortable.

Once outside, she looked for privacy. She thought about returning to the lake but figured Gram might come searching for her there. The dorms and library were out — she had no desire to see either building ever again. She recalled seeing a barn further up the road from the dorms; however, she did not know if that building belonged to the Abbey or if they bordered a farm. She did not want to add trespassing to her list of transgressions this trip.

Instead, she opted to take the path leading from the library into the woods. Worst case, it was a nature trail that made a big circle. She would end up right back here, but at least, she would have time to think in the quiet. However, after a few minutes of walking, she discovered it led to the Abbey cemetery. While that held a touch of gruesome irony, it also guaranteed some solitude. She'd take it.

Walking along the path, she tried to clear her thoughts. It was a foolish attempt. No way could she stop thinking about what she had experienced since waking up.

The sounds that plagued her. The headaches and body aches. But mostly, the sense of being communicated to by word, by feeling, and by image.

Something must have happened when those energy pulses from the rift hit her. Somehow, she had connected with Maria.

Perhaps Maria's presence within the universe of the book had somehow leeched into this new connection with Roni. Or perhaps Maria never left at all. Perhaps what remained of her had been scattered into the very air Roni breathed.

Rubbing her temples, she moaned. The path opened onto the graveyard — a small but functional plot of land devoted to rows upon rows of nuns who had served the Abbey well. These people sure loved to bury themselves in a variety of ways.

Roni walked to the opposite side where she found a large oak tree. Sitting down at the base, leaning her back against its trunk, she continued her attempts to make sense out of what had happened. She needed more than simple suppositions. She needed to know the truth.

Time drifted by — she lost track. Her thoughts swam in a murky darkness that would have shrouded her even at high noon. Perhaps, she thought, she had fallen asleep for a short time, but the pain in her head had not eased — usually a rest made headaches disappear for her.

Roni got back to her feet. Might as well return. Time to find out what the Old Gang wanted to do.

But before Roni set out, she saw several lights coming her way. She heard the steady beat of an old drum. Out of the deep shadows of the woods, Sister Mary led a procession of the Abbey nuns. Three of them carried a coffin while Sister Mary hit the wide, shallow drum with a bone. As they entered the graveyard, flashlights bounced from ropes around their necks and their habits rustled the ground. The drum beat out a mournful sound.

But the procession did not stop. They went beyond the cemetery, deeper into the woods. Not following a well-trodden path but forging into an unmarked section.

Roni did not know what to make of what she saw but one thought echoed in her head as she quietly followed them — *this isn't right.*

CHAPTER 12

Leading the way, Sister Mary had no trouble creating a path through the woods despite the dark. The nuns followed her without question, though the casket made travel awkward, forcing them to weave around the denser groupings of trees. Still, they managed to stay close to Sister Mary more often than not. Behind it all, Roni darted from tree to tree. Not that the nuns would spot her in the dark, but she still thought precautions were the smart play. When the woods opened into a clearing, Roni stayed behind a tree trunk to watch from a distance.

Large stones cut like massive blocks prescribed a circle within the clearing. Some of the stones acted like oversized benches while others stood upright to form the impression of walls. On the sides of the vertical stones, Roni spotted markings — possibly Gaelic writings. Finally, after Sister Claudia started a fire in the pit dug near the middle of the circle, Roni understood — this was a pagan burial. From the soft flicker of orange firelight, her thoughts were confirmed when she noticed the graves lining the back half of the clearing.

Off to her left, two trees kissed up against each other forming a wider barrier. Roni scurried across, her heart hammering, certain every crinkling, leaf-breaking step would be her undoing. But she reached the trees. Even before peeking around the trunk, this new position allowed her to hear clearly what Sister Mary said.

"My dear sisters," Sister Mary began, "we have much to do tonight. But as we prepare to step forward into a new chapter of the Abbey, we must first turn the page on the old chapter."

The three sisters set the coffin on the ground and bowed their heads. "Sister Ashley was a dear woman to us all. It may seem that she was taken too early from us, but the Lord has a plan for all, and it is our duty to have faith rather than sadness. We few of the Abbey are the chosen. That comes with great responsibilities and greater dangers. Sister Ashley's sacrifice is of both."

Roni rolled back behind the two trunks. Glancing upward, she noticed several points where the trees left a gap. She pulled out her phone, set the camera to film, made sure to cut off the camera light, and lined up a good shot between the trees.

"Tonight, we honor Sister Ashley in the best way we can." Sister Mary stepped closer to the coffin. With a twitch of her finger, Sister Claudia and Sister Susan opened the lid. "Without a body, we must mourn her through representation." Sister Mary pulled out an old Bible — leather bound and valuable from the looks of it. She set it in the coffin with care. "She always admired this copy I kept on my desk. It is my great honor to bury it as a sign of my love and devotion to one of our fallen."

Sister Susan stepped forward. She pulled out a thin, gold necklace with a crucifix pendant. "She did not think we noticed, but she prayed more and harder than any I have ever seen. She even gave Sister Rachel a run." The nuns tittered. "I give her this so that she may continue to do so up in Heaven."

Sister Rachel went next, placing a rosary in the coffin. "I had only begun to know her, but no nun should be without this."

Finally, with a nod from Sister Mary, Sister Claudia approached the coffin. "Sister Ashley was dear to me. Just as I am a pupil under Sister Mary, I hoped one day for Sister Ashley to be my pupil. Her love of knowledge and enthusiasm for her faith left me in awe at times. I'm afraid I have nothing to place in there because the things she meant most to me cannot be represented physically. Her passion, her love, her caring."

"You are wrong," Sister Mary said. "You do have something to give."

She reached into her pocket and pulled out a tissue. After a few dabs at Sister Claudia's wet cheeks, she handed over the tear-stained tissue. Sister Claudia smiled as more tears fell. She placed the tissue in the coffin.

Another twitch of Sister Mary's finger and the lid returned. Sister Mary said, "Please Sister Susan, make sure that our groundskeepers see to the burying."

"Ay, ma'am."

"Good. Then it is time. Come forth."

Sister Claudia and Sister Susan stepped forward and kneeled. Sister Susan jerked her head to beckon Sister Rachel over. Once all three nuns knelt before Sister Mary, they bowed their heads.

"Tonight, as we mourn the loss of one, we celebrate the creation of another." Sister Mary stepped over and placed her hands atop Sister Rachel's head. "Becoming a permanent member of this Abbey is no small matter and not to be taken lightly. Heaven speaks to us. While it is true that we call the energy beneath the church a conduit, it is more of a mechanism. Because *we* are the conduit. The Angels speak through us, and in doing so, we take on the responsibility of spreading their message throughout the world. Even when that message must be kept secret. It can be a confusing conflict within, a great balancing act which will test the limits of your conscience and control, one that requires great amounts of prayer, one that will stretch your calling far greater than any other experience any other church could provide, and one I know you are fully capable of handling."

"Ay, Sister. I am ready."

Sister Mary sidestepped to the right and rested her hands upon Sister Susan's head. "To join me requires the greatest devotion for it is permanent. Like the ring you wear to symbolize your devotion to Jesus, this appointment can never be torn asunder. If you accept my blessing tonight, you will be with this Abbey until the day you die. And possibly even after that. You must be willing to walk the narrow path of your faith with the conviction of one who knows the truth. Because you have seen it. It may seem an easy choice — what nun would turn away the chance to speak with angels? But the sacrifices required will bring upon your shoulders the greatest weights you've ever felt. The loyalty required is enormous. You will never look at the world the same because you will see all those people out there who think they know better than you, and you won't be able to tell them a thing."

"I'm ready, Sister." Sister Susan said.

Roni readjusted her position against the tree, but she did not feel uncomfortable from holding the camera up. No. She heard too much in Sister Mary's speech that sounded familiar.

Sister Mary sidestepped again, placing her hands upon Sister Claudia's head. "Leadership is a difficult and lonely path. It requires devotion and loyalty, yet also a sense of duty greater than that of self-preservation. I have done all I can to prepare you. I had intended to teach you more before today, but I never expected you and Sister Ashley to hasten this moment."

As Sister Mary continued speaking words that Roni had heard coming from Gram's mouth in one version or another, something brushed the tree limbs in the woods. Roni paused her camera and brought it down to her eye. Using the zoom function, she scanned the woods.

She expected to see Sully vigorously waving her away from this scene. When she did not spot a human shape, she thought she might come across a deer or elk or some other large animal that had accidently stumbled upon the service. But again, she saw nothing.

When she finally located the source of the noise, her lips parted but no sound came from her closed throat. Three purple-black balls of smoke hovered just beyond the tree line. They were from the rift. Roni recalled seeing them dart out — one of the last things she remembered before being knocked unconscious. They did not belong in this universe, and that made them relics. They also appeared to be alive which meant they were living relics.

The way those creatures from the rift waited (the word *rifters* popped into Roni's mind), the way they appeared to be watching the nuns — it left Roni with a sense of threat. She couldn't let the nuns stay there and become targets, but she had no idea what these rifters could do. One thing she had learned from her previous encounters with creatures from other universes — knowledge of the enemy meant everything. If they even were enemies.

She moved toward the edge of the tree trunks with the intent of warning the nuns. They would not be happy to see her, they would probably yell at her for invading their privacy, they might even take their anger out on the Society. But at least they would not suffer at the whims of these living relics. Yet as she moved, sharp pain dug into her spine.

Placing a hand on her lower back, she inhaled sharply — the smell of sugar and soap filled her nostrils. She rolled back against the trunk, pressing her spine against the hard wood.

Maria? she thought. Warmth flushed over her skin like sinking into a hot bath. Tears welled in Roni's eyes, and she clutched her mouth for fear of crying out loud.

As her mind raced through the possibilities, Sister Claudia's raised voice cut into the air. "To the angels waiting on the edge of our circle, please come forth. We welcome you. We love you and are ready to receive you."

CHAPTER 13

The shock stunned Roni straight through to the ends of her limbs. She stood by the kissing trees with her head in full view should anyone look over. But even if her mind had thought to take cover, she could not. The sight before her brooked no argument towards looking away.

At Sister Claudia's call, the three purple-black creatures, the rifters, floated into the circle. The dark smoke around each one dripped off like melting wax. When the smoke hit the forest floor, it puffed and dissipated — only acting like actual smoke at that final moment. The rifters spread out, one behind each kneeling nun, and simply hovered. No sounds. No sense of sentience. Nothing to suggest thought or intention. Yet Roni's stomach turned for those ladies.

Sister Claudia stood and joined Sister Mary. "Look behind you. These are angels."

Sister Susan whipped her head around while Sister Rachel took a more hesitant approach. Both yelped.

"Do not be afraid," Sister Claudia went on. "These are angels in their true form. Not the fanciful and majestic images painted by human artists over the centuries, but their real, angelic appearance. Revel in their mysterious beauty and know that it is our divine purpose to host these immaculate beings. We will give them human form so that they may perform Heaven's duties here on Earth."

Dashing tears from her eyes, Sister Claudia returned to kneel with the others. She bowed her head. "Sister Mary, I beg your forgiveness. There were some moments — after Sister Ashley and I had reopened the conduit — moments where I lost my way. Worse still, after Sister Ashley succumbed to the conduit, I faltered. My faith abandoned me. But only for a moment. I gave voice to my fear and doubt, yet when I saw you on the stairs, I remembered why I had come all this way in my life. It will never happen again. Please, please, forgive me."

Sister Mary cocked her head to the side and smiled with such benevolence that those kneeling before her leaned back as if under the heavy rays of the sun. But Roni could see that smile, too — a hideous, macabre mask.

"We all seek the day that Heaven can spread across the Earth," Sister Mary said. "And it is only understandable and human that you would want to hasten the day. But as Sister Ashley demonstrated, the mighty purity of Heaven will destroy us all if allowed to break free. I have known this for decades. So, we must wait." Spreading her arms to include all the nuns, she went on, "This has always been our divine duty. For centuries, the nuns of the Abbey have kept the conduit stable to ensure our communication with the Angels and to make certain that the great strength of Heaven does not destroy all which we cherish but rather makes it beautiful. We all knew that someday this moment would arrive, when the Angels could leave the conduit and join us. It happened once before — centuries ago, and it led to the schism between Sisters Margaret and Agnes. It happened a second time — more recently, in fact. When it happened to me."

With gasps that came close to equaling their surprise at seeing the Angels, the nuns murmured to each other as they kept their eyes upon Sister Mary.

"I was quite young. I had only been a nun for a few years. I joined the Abbey, and after only a week, I was brought downstairs to see the conduit, to learn my duties in helping maintain it. Like many of you, I spent my early years with night duty, and it was on the fourth night that an angel came to me. Just like those floating behind you now, this angel slipped out of the conduit and floated before me. Turned out that one of the books the Parallel Society had provided did not do its job properly. And for that, I am so grateful.

"I offered myself to this angel, instinctually understanding that it needed my body as its host, but then it slipped back into the conduit — apparently the faulty book worked a little bit, after all.

"But when the Parallel Society sent Lillian Donaugh and her daughter, everything changed. The angel pulled part of little Maria into the conduit and in doing so, it created an exchange. The angel left Maria behind and it was able to join our world permanently. It came to me right away and has been with me ever since."

The kneeling nuns gazed up at Sister Mary with pale-faced awe.

"That's right. I am an angel. And in all the years since I joined with Sister Mary, I have tried to find a safe way to release more of my angelic compatriots. It is why I encouraged Sister Ashley to research our past with the Abbey. I knew she was smart, and she would be able to find the mythic book Sister Agnes stole. Oh, indeed, I knew she would sneak down into the tombs and spend time in the study. I relished the moment when she would figure out how to find and utilize the book down there. Sister Claudia, you've asked for forgiveness, but you will not get it. You have no need for it. You have done such marvelous work. You deserve praise."

"Thank you," Sister Claudia stuttered.

"The time has arrived. Pray and accept this gift from the Lord. Allow these angels entry, become one with them, so that we may take the next steps into bringing about a more heavenly world."

Sister Rachel leaned her head back and spread her lips wide. "I am ready."

"Wonderful. Give yourself to the angel, willingly allow the union. Once we are all angels, we shall return to the conduit what was taken so that it can be stabilized once again."

"I thought the books stabilized the conduit," Sister Claudia said.

"It was the child's essence, not the foolish Parallel Society books. Before Maria gave herself to the conduit, the books were all we had — unreliable at best."

Sister Susan cleared her throat. "Excuse me, but did not Sister Claudia prove the wait is over? There are three angels here — more than ever before. More than have ever even been seen. Perhaps the time to release the conduit completely has come."

"Possibly," Sister Mary said. "If so, all the more reason to stabilize the conduit. We want it to hold together as long as possible so that we can pull in the greatest number of angels. Yes. Good thinking. We must prepare."

Sister Susan lifted her head back, closed her eyes, and awaited the arrival of her angel. Sister Claudia did the same, and Roni could see the scowl on her face. That nun did not like being shown up — especially by another nun.

Without any signal or word, the three smoky masses floated over the faces of the nuns. As they lowered, appearing to be inhaled, each one of the Sisters gave out a pleasurable moan. Out of context, Roni supposed the joining of Angel and human made a rather sexual sound — even pornographic. But watching it happen filled her with dread.

A four-note sequence chimed from Roni's phone. The darn thing wanted to be helpful by notifying her that one of her friends had posted a cat picture or perhaps one of the games she played needed an update. The four nuns — now part-Angel — turned in unison to face the tree Roni stood near. They saw her face. They knew she had been watching.

Roni whirled around and darted off into the woods.

CHAPTER 14

Roni bolted through the pathless woods, snaking her way around one tree, then another, careening in the direction she hoped would lead her back to the Abbey proper. Even after she realized that the nuns could not run fast enough with their long tunics dragging in the dark of the woods, she continued to push on as quickly as possible. When she broke from the tree line, she dashed across the grass, passing the church, and headed straight for the dormitory.

Elliot stood by the doorway like a serene statue gazing at the night sky. "What's the matter?"

"Inside," she said as she rushed by him and entered the dorm.

Sully started at her sudden appearance. He snapped a book shut and hid it behind his back. Once his face registered recognition of Roni, he relaxed. "Do you want me to have a heart attack?"

Roni paused as she gazed at the poorly hidden book. She then glanced back at the doorway. "You had Elliot standing watch for you. What are you up to?"

"Just trying to get a better understanding of the women who live here." From behind his back, Sully produced Sister Ashley's diary.

Elliot walked in. "What happened? The look on your face —"

"After you both secured the rift, after you healed me, did you use your cane to scan my body?"

"My cane does not —"

"You know what I mean. However you do it, did you do it?"

"There hasn't been time and I did not observe any symptoms that would suggest the need. Why?"

Roni rushed over to the nearest window and peeked outside. "They'll be here soon. Listen carefully, and don't ask questions. Just believe me."

Her urgency had the desired effect. Sully and Elliot huddled in close, sitting on the edges of two beds, and they listened. Roni described everything she had witnessed in the woods and showed the video on her phone as well. With her heart racing, she continued to take periodic glances out the window.

"Look, I know I screwed up and that I made you angry." Roni turned toward Sully. "You can yell at me later. Right now, what are we supposed to do?"

His face paled, and his nose wrinkled as if Roni had spoken a foreign language. He walked the length of the dorm with his fingers dancing against each other under his chin. On his return trip, Roni could see the way his deep concentration mixed with his pale fear.

The urge to rush over to this old man, grab him by the shoulders, and shake him into making a decision flooded Roni's overflowing thoughts. The nuns moved slowly but they weren't sloths. Soon enough, they would arrive. Why didn't he give any orders?

"It's okay," Elliot said, moving to the side of his good friend. "I'm sure Lillian had the same troubles her first time."

His first time? She had not considered it before, but Elliot spotted the problem right away. Sully had become their leader during a moment of crisis. Decisions had already been made and he reacted to them. But after that, for close to a year, they had lived without any real trouble. All had been quiet. This was the first time they faced a situation where he had to make all the decisions.

As understanding came to her, Roni missed Elliot's quiet words to Sully. But she saw Sully nod his head and offer a weak smile.

Patting Elliot on the shoulder, Sully said, "I think it would be best if you go find Gram and bring her here. We need the team together."

"That sounds like a good idea." With orders given, Elliot rushed out of the room.

Sully readjusted his glasses and settled on the edge of the bed.

"That's it?" Roni said, gazing out the window once again.

"Your Gram is the only one of us who has had regular contact with these nuns. She's our best source of information on how to deal with them."

"When Elliot gets back with Gram, it'll be too late. We won't have time to hear what her thoughts are because those nuns will be on us. I don't see them right now, but I'm telling you they were not that far behind me."

Stamping his foot, Sully said, "I know, I know." Holding his mouth tight, he removed his glasses and rubbed his eyes. "I apologize. I didn't mean to snap at you. With all that we had to do to keep the rift from exploding, well, I'm a bit exhausted."

Roni sat next to Sully and wrapped her arms around him. "It's okay. We're all on edge. I might even be a bit scared. If we were back home, if I could be under the bookstore in that beautiful library, then I'd find out what we needed to know about these creatures and that would make me feel better prepared."

"Instead, you have to rely on me and worst of all, your grandmother."

"I can rely on you all just fine. You've all saved the universe enough times to earn that." Roni surveyed the room as she spoke. "So, the current plan is that Elliot is going to find Gram and bring her back. And we're hoping she will know something about what's going on with the nuns. That's what we're doing, right?"

Sully shrugged. "It's all we've got for the moment."

"Then we're going to need more time."

He raised his head. "You look like you have an idea."

"A stupid one, but it's better than nothing." Roni took one last peek outside — still no nuns were visible, but she could hear their voices. The words were garbled at this distance, but she could not mistake the gleeful threat of Sister Claudia.

Roni and Sully worked together to move the beds into the center of the room. They formed a circle and cleared out the middle. She stepped back to look at their work. Not terribly convincing, but they were out of time. She heard footsteps heading up to the door.

Sister Claudia and Sister Rachel stepped into the dorm with hands on hips like twin conquerors. Roni expected as much from Sister Claudia, but Sister Rachel was a different matter. From first arriving at the Abbey, Roni had seen little of Sister Rachel yet still built an impression of a meek people-pleaser who posed no threat. However, seeing the woman stand shoulder-to-shoulder with Sister Claudia, framed by the stark white wimple and shadowed by the dark black habit, Sister Rachel promised to be an imposing force.

Sister Claudia clasped her hands behind her back as she stepped forward. But where Sully had looked frightened and thoughtful, Sister Claudia looked downright terrifying. "You did a sinful thing."

"Hope you're not looking for an apology," Roni said, willing to say anything to keep the conversation going. They simply had to stall long enough for Elliot and Gram to arrive. At least, she told herself as much. The other voice inside her head promised that no amount of stalling would help.

"Words from a devil are never to be trusted — especially if they are words you no longer need to hear. Besides, you don't strike me as the kind what wants to make amends. No, with you, I only see an obstruction. Saw it when you first drove up here. Even told Sister Mary we should be done with you. You ask me, I say the days of working with the Parallel Society should have ended a long time ago."

"I might actually care if you were really Sister Claudia. Probably not, but I might."

"You see?" Sister Claudia gazed back at Sister Rachel. "Do you? They have no concept of Angels. No idea how to deal with us." Gesturing to the circle of beds, she added, "This is cute. Did you intend this to frighten us or are you offering us a nice place to rest?"

Sully tugged on Roni's arm, pulling her closer to the center of the circle. In a voice full of confidence, he said, "This is a circle of Darsha. If you are what you say you are, then crossing into the circle will cause excruciating pain to both your body and your eternal soul."

Roni's face locked in grim defiance. Anything less and she might have smirked at the ridiculousness of Sully's bluff. The best part — the bluff was also brilliant. If these women truly believed themselves to have communed with Angels, then they would not cross into the circle for fear of hurting their souls. But should they take that dangerous step into the circle, then their faith might be shaken when nothing happened — proving they were not angels.

The dilemma would hold them for a short time. Eventually, they would figure out that a circle of beds was nothing more than a circle of beds. That the circle of Darsha did not exist.

Sister Claudia meandered along the edge of the circle. She snarled at Roni. "I truly despise you."

"Feeling is mutual."

"That right there. That's one of the reasons. You come in here with this arrogant attitude as if you know anything that's been going on round these parts. I watched how you spoke with your grandmother. Set aside the respect you should show first simply because she is an elder and your own blood, but you should respect her opinion because she has been dealing with the conduit longer than you or I have been alive. You should show respect to Sister Mary because she has been dealing with it longer than any of us — even your Gram. And you should show me some respect because I've lived with this thing every day for years. And what are you? Nothing more than an apprentice who hasn't even spent forty-eight hours here. Yet you think you know everything, that you're qualified to understand anything you see. Pathetic, really."

She reached the far side of the circle and nudged the edge with her foot. Sister Rachel mirrored the actions on the other side.

"I have prayed a lot since your arrival," Sister Claudia continued. "I've been trying to understand why the Lord brought you into my life. What good could possibly come from such arrogant ignorance as yours? For a while, I thought Sister Ashley had it right — that you were here for us to use, so that we could use that powerful book without breaking our vows — that we might open the rift.

"But I was wrong.

"You see, I have respect for Sister Mary. She has shown me the error of my thinking. Our job is not to force open the rift but to help it grow and become stronger so that it can come forth when it is ready."

The more Sister Claudia spoke, the more Roni thought the magic circle bluff had been a mistake. Suddenly it no longer felt like a shield. Rather, it had become a prison. Hoping she still had some bravery in her voice, she said, "Why are you calling it a rift? I thought it was a conduit to Heaven."

With a bemused toss of her head, Sister Claudia said, "Did I? Things really are changing rapidly. Which makes me think that the idea mulling around in my head might not be so crazy after all. The Lord brought you to us, and the Lord sent us the Angels as well. I will trust these thoughts for they are guided by his angels and his will."

Though Roni really did not want to hear the answer, she still asked, "What is it the Lord's telling you?"

"Sister Mary always said that after the child had been partially taken into the rift, all became better, more stable than ever before. If you had any respect for your elders, your Gram would tell you that I'm speaking the truth. Since you are also a blood relation, then perhaps your blood will help the rift regain its strength."

"You want my blood?"

"Maybe. Maybe it's your heart. Or your bones or your brain. I don't know. We'll just have to throw you into the rift and pray for the best."

Though Sully could not stand straight, he still knew how to intimidate with his voice. "Enough. We have been polite and respectful by allowing you to have your say. Now, you will listen to us."

At least, Roni always thought Sully sounded intimidating. But she had been a little girl growing up in the family bookstore — all of the Old Gang had intimidated her. Sister Claudia, however, had no such history with Sully.

She reached down and threw aside one of the beds. "I take no commands from you."

From behind, Roni heard Sister Rachel doing the same. Sully stepped in front of Roni. He pushed backwards and to the side so that neither Sister Claudia nor Sister Rachel was behind them. "Stay where you are. I'm warning you."

Roni had no doubt the Sisters heard the shake in Sully's voice. Roni had heard it. She also had no doubt Sully shared the same thought that plagued her mind — *Where the hell were Gram and Elliot?*

Sister Rachel snorted a laugh. "The little old man is afraid of us."

"I am not afraid of a couple nuns."

"Oh, old man, we are so much more than nuns."

The Sisters stepped forward. Their eyes glowed deep emerald. As if in a choreographed dance, both raised their arms, and together, they lifted off the ground. Not far — only about a foot — but hovering nuns were still hovering nuns. Roni's heart dropped to her stomach. Any chance that Sully's bluff would continue to stop them vanished.

Sister Rachel swooped in and clawed at Sully. Thick, green veins pulsed on her face. She slammed down, clearly expecting to toss him aside, only to find that she would have had an easier time moving a steel bridge. As she swept across, her left arm lagged behind, pushing on his shoulder the extra seconds her brain needed to register the solid object she had hit.

Roni saw the woman's shoulder dislocate as she went lurching into the beds. She whimpered in confusion as she rubbed her shoulder.

Sully spread his arms back, and Roni inched closer. She pressed her chest against his back. His voice had been shaking but his body remained a mountain against all storms.

The nuns' next attack proved to Roni that the creatures inside them were somehow linked together. No way could the women have coordinated their next move without such a thing.

Sister Claudia floated higher as if she might flow overhead and land behind. This forced Sully to lift his legs in order to reposition, and the moment his firm connection to the ground ended, Sister Rachel appeared from below. She barreled into Sully, screaming as the pain ignited in her shoulder, and knocked them aside. Sister Claudia flew in and grabbed hold of Roni.

"I'm going to enjoy watching you fall into the rift," Sister Claudia said. "In fact, I'm going to ..."

She stared at Roni — stared *into* Roni. Those frosty, emerald eyes set Roni's skin tingling. Roni wanted to look away but remained locked on the nun's gaze. She felt Sister Claudia's fingers pressing into her skin, and it took a great act of will to avoid vomiting. Or crying, for that matter.

But then the nun's eyes widened. "Halt!" Sister Claudia pointed at Sister Rachel to make sure the command had been obeyed. For her part, Sister Rachel had Sully's arms pinned behind the poor man.

"What? I'm having fun."

"I see into you," Sister Claudia said to Roni. "I know what's inside you. Hiding away in there."

Roni felt Maria cringing, searching for an escape even though there was none.

With a disappointed frown, Sister Claudia said, "I guess I won't get to throw you into the rift. Not just yet, anyway."

"Why not?" Sister Rachel said. "What's happening over there?"

"You don't to get to ask me questions. Something has changed and it might help our cause. That's all you need to know. I'll discuss it with Sister Mary."

Roni couldn't help herself. "Still trying to one up Sister Susan?"

Before she even knew what had happened, Roni's face stung from the nun's sharp backhand.

"Sister Rachel, I want you to take both of these foolish heathens to the tombs. Lock them away with the dead until I have a chance to confer with Sister Mary."

Sister Rachel's green-veined grin promised to haunt Roni with nightmares for a long time to come.

CHAPTER 15

The door leading from the Abbey library to the tombs beneath closed with a thick thud. Roni slumped on the bottom stair and rested her head against the cool stone wall. Sully stood a few feet away taking in his surroundings.

As he kicked at the dusty floor, he rubbed his backside. "I do not care for these nuns at all."

"Jokes?" Roni uttered the word with more bite than she had intended. But if she held back, she thought tears would flow — for now, she'd rather be angry. "I've screwed everything up, remember? A little bit ago, you were fuming mad at me. Now, you're making jokes?"

"A little bit ago, the worst things I had to deal with were your screw ups and your attitude." Sully paused his inspection to lay a comforting hand on her head. "If you recall, a few minutes ago, I was stumbling through my first big moment as leader like a bar mitzvah boy delivering his sermon in front of his family."

"But now?"

"Ah, now is quite different. I have been trapped before. I've been held hostage, too. I've faced monsters — though never monstrous nuns but what's the big difference, really? The details might be new, but being stuck in a troubling and dangerous situation — that's fairly standard for the Parallel Society. Goes with the job."

Roni chuckled. Then sniffled. Then wiped aside a tear. She thrust to her feet and stomped back up the stairs. Banging on the door, she said, "Open up! Let us out!"

"Stop with all that racket," Sully said from below. "You really think they'll let us go after all they did to put us here?"

"I'm not going to sit around waiting for Sister Mary to decide it's a good idea to throw us into the rift."

"No, that wouldn't be good, either. Lucky for you, you've got me. Now, come sit down here again and let me think. We need to prepare."

With reluctant steps, Roni returned. "You have a plan?"

"I will soon, if you stop distracting me."

As she sat, Roni watched Sully think. He lasted less than ten seconds.

"You can't stare at me. How am I supposed to come up with a plan if you're staring at me?"

"Sorry," she said. "It's not all on you, though. I can come up with a plan, too."

"I don't think that's what we need from you."

Rather than argue, Roni lowered her head. She could feel Sully staring at her, now, and she did not like it. The longer he said nothing, the heavier his stare pressed against her. At first, she thought he merely wanted her to understand the difficulty of solving their dilemma while another teammate waits expectantly. But after a moment, she peeked up.

His brow rose even as his mouth turned down. He had let the planning slip aside. Something else rested in that look.

No, Roni thought, *I can't lie to myself. I know exactly what he's waiting for.*

Still, she refused to lift her head, refused to let the thought congeal into words. The cool darkness of the tomb wrapped around her like gentle snowfall. Cold comfort, but better than facing the myriad of problems surrounding them.

"Roni." His gentle nudge slammed into her.

"Okay, okay. What do you really need to know? You heard Sister Claudia. You're a smart man. Can't you figure it all out? Do I have to say it?"

As he often did, Sully read the moment right. He started rummaging along the walls yet continued to talk with her. "If we're going to make it through this day, then yes — you need to tell me all the specifics. It's usually the details that make the difference." He glanced up the stairs. "From the quiet, I'm guessing we'll be stuck here for a bit. You might as well get the whole thing off your chest."

Roni laughed. A deep, hearty laugh. This hunched, little man could remain so calm at the precise time she needed it. Maybe he had more special powers than she realized. She gulped and her chest tightened. She felt like a teenager about to admit that she had taken drugs or had gotten knocked up or some other possibly life-altering event.

"Maria never fell into that book. I held onto her as long as I could and when I thought I let go of her, the rift happened, and well, I don't know exactly how it went down, but she's inside me."

"Oh."

Sully's boredom tripped up Roni's thoughts. Still, she went on, "Yes, well, I can hear her in my head. Not much. Not like sentences. But sounds and feelings. I can feel her on my skin. She reacts to the things she knows about."

"I see."

He stuck his head and arms into the nearest alcove. He pulled out the bones of a long-deceased nun and placed them in a pile against the wall as he continued his macabre work.

"Why are you not taking this seriously?" Roni said, making no effort to hide her anger.

Using the flashlight on his phone, Sully squatted down to access the lower alcove. As he continued removing bones, he said, "I am taking this seriously. And I appreciate you not telling Gram about this."

"I wouldn't dare. I can see how hard it has been for her with everything that's happened. There is no reason to hurt her more. But I thought you should know. As leader. I thought you would find it important."

Poking his head out of the alcove, he dropped a thick femur onto the ground. "I understand that you think you have part of Maria in you. I also understand that you think it's important. And it might be. There's nothing I can do about it at the moment because, in case you missed it, we are trapped down here."

"There's no need to be nasty. I'm telling you this because when Sister Claudia grabbed me, she reacted to what she saw — namely, Maria. That's why she didn't throw us into the rift right away. She thinks — I don't know what she thinks, but it can't be good."

Scanning the area with his phone, Sully went on, "You've been with the Society long enough now to understand that there are all kinds of creatures out there. I fully believe that you have felt the things you say, and that you've experienced them in the way you say they happened. That does not mean that is what happened. Only a short while ago, you showed me a video of purple floating creatures —"

"That's right. And they went inside the nuns."

Sully paused and looked straight at Roni. "That is what you saw, but it may not be what happened."

"But I saw it."

"Instead of being ingested, or somehow melding into the nuns for that matter, these creatures may only look that way. In fact, they may exist on multiple planes. We've encountered similar things before. They look like they're gone, but in reality, they hover around you, wear themselves upon you like bizarre clothing. They might be mimicking your feelings towards Maria instead of being Maria. You understand?" He brushed his hands on his pants. "All I'm asking that you do is consider the possibility that what you think to be the case might be wrong. Do that. And please, don't mention this again — especially if Gram can hear. Okay?"

Roni nodded. She did not agree with Sully — in fact, she knew she was right. She could feel it deep in her bones — but she would honor Sully's request nonetheless. At least, for now.

In a simple, yet blatant attempt to change the subject, she said, "What are you looking for?"

Sully snapped his fingers, turned around, and pulled out a skull. "Not looking anymore. I think I have all the bones I need."

"For what?" But as the words came out of her mouth, she knew the answer. "You're going to make a golem out of bones?"

"I wish I didn't have to. This is a very dangerous, very bad idea. But Sister Claudia is planning on coming back. And she won't be any friendlier than she was before."

Roni moved towards the pile of bones. Cobwebs clinging to them turned her stomach. "Why exactly is this a bad idea? Besides being disgusting."

As Sully set out the bones on the ground in the shape of a person, he said, "Normally when I make a golem, I am taking inanimate objects — like clay or paper or wood — and I bring them to life. These bones once belonged to a living human being. They had been alive already. Bringing once-living things back in this way is not right. Once-living things cling to their will. Which makes them difficult to control. However, these bones are more than simply old. They're ancient. My hope is that they have been dead long enough to no longer care about what they once were."

"And if they do?"

"Then I may be creating more problems than I'm solving. But we can't sit here and wait to be tossed in the rift, can we? If you have a better idea for dealing with these creatures that have taken control of the nuns, let me hear it."

Roni gave it a moment. Then she leaned next to Sully. "How can I help?"

CHAPTER 16

Scavenging ragged bits of cloth, dried rope belts, and even a length of rosary beads, Sully gathered all he needed to tie the bones together. He asked Roni for paper and something to write with. She told him to get started putting the bones in place and she would return with his request. Though it took her several attempts, she eventually located the study of Sister Agnes — a few more times skulking around the tombs and Roni figured she would know the way to the study by heart. On the Sister's desk, Roni grabbed some paper and an old piece of charcoal for writing.

When she returned and saw what Sully had done, she surpassed her initial revulsion and landed right in horrified disgust. With the limited bones available, Sully had not created skeletons that mimicked the human form perfectly. Rather, he had slopped together bones wherever he could tie them to form a humanoid-shaped skeletal structure. He had two of the vile beings set out on the floor — both with legs and arms connected to a spine, but lacking ribs and other bones. Neither had hands and one had femurs for its forearms. Both had skulls — neither with the jawbone — and Roni would soon learn that those skulls were the most important part of the whole thing.

"Yes, yes," Sully said taking the paper and charcoal. "This will work fine."

Crouching on his hands and knees, he flattened the paper on the hard ground. With the charcoal, he wrote several phrases in Hebrew. Then he rolled each paper into a tight tube and thread one tube into each skull via the eye sockets.

Roni had seen this before — not with human bones but with other objects. All that remained was for Sully to whisper his special words and the creatures would come to life. As long as the paper remained part of the golem, it would stay intact and obey the written commands. That was the real purpose of the skulls. Without them, Sully had no secure place to leave the paper.

As he returned to his feet, the clicks and snaps of his bones made him sound like a third skeleton. "Now, we wait."

"Shouldn't you bring them to life?"

Sully pushed his glasses up his nose. "Do you want to hang out with two living skeletons? I don't. Plenty of time to animate them later."

They did not wait for long. Less than ten minutes and they heard the door at the top of the stairs being unlocked.

Sully hurried over to his skeletons and whispered into the skull of each one. When he finished, he waved Roni away. "Go, go. We must hide."

They scurried around the corner and looked back. They could spy on what happened with ease and the dark shadows would protect them from instant notice. Of course, if the nuns brought a flashlight, the hiding place would be revealed, but that did not concern them. Sully had made it clear — once the skeletons moved in on the nuns and distracted them, he and Roni would dash for the stairs and escape.

As the door opened above, the skeletons twitched. Two nuns climbed down, and the skeletons rose. The one on the left had been tied together using most of the cloth remnants Sully had found. Roni named it Rags. The other skeleton had two femurs in place of its right arm. *Femur Fred,* Roni thought, but then reduced it to simply Fred.

They were hideous creatures, lacking the elegance of many of Sully's golems and even the simple pragmatism of his more hurried creations. These abominations carried with them the sense of dust and fear Sully had during their formation.

The skeletons stood off to the side of the stairs, waiting for the nuns. Before Sister Rachel and Sister Susan reached the bottom, Roni glimpsed the cocky grins on their faces.

"Oh, sweet Roni, I hate to be the one that tell you this," Sister Rachel said, savoring every word. "It looks like Sister Mary agrees that it would be a good idea to try splitting that little girl out of you. We've never done anything like this before, though, so it might kill you."

Sister Susan giggled. "Don't worry. It won't be that bad. Probably. We are still servants of the Lord, and He would not want your deaths on our hands, if it can be avoided."

With the door above left open, dim light made it easier to see. When the nuns reached the bottom, Sister Rachel's face dropped. Sister Susan yelped as her eyes fell upon the living remnants of the Abbey's ancestry.

Roni watched as the skeletons moved on the nuns. She had expected some hissing or groaning sound, some kind of monstrous utterance, but the creatures had no vocal cords, no throats, no tongues, no mouths. Only the sound of their bones tapping against the stone flooring and against each other could be heard.

Sister Susan dropped to her knees, crossed herself, and prayed. Rags lumbered up to her and smacked her on the side of the head. Sister Rachel stumbled backwards from Fred's approach.

"The Parallel Society is a bunch of soulless witches," Sister Rachel said, her words spitting up on Fred's bones. "You hear me? Roni? Old man? I know you're watching. You are servants of the Devil, and I pray that the full wrath of the Lord falls upon your heads."

Sister Susan managed to get to her feet, and she shoved Rags backward. She then turned upon Fred, clasped his spine, and yanked him away from Sister Rachel by putting her weight into swinging him back.

Through angry tears, she said, "Are you all right?"

Sister Rachel scowled. "I'll be fine. Let's go."

"But what about Roni and Sully? We can't leave them here."

Sister Rachel's eyes narrowed, and Roni thought the young woman looked through Sister Susan straight to the corner. "They are responsible for making these abominations. They can suffer with them."

With all of this transpiring in front of the stairs, Roni and Sully never had a chance to escape. That gave Roni the time to wonder why Sister Susan acted like a frightened, meek child. Why did they not use their rifter strength? Why did they not float into the air and fight back? Sister Rachel's arm most likely still hurt, but Sister Susan would have no trouble.

"She's fighting it," Roni whispered. After all, Maria had limited control over Roni, but it felt like something she actively worked at, something Roni resisted. It stood to reason that Sister Susan might not be willing to give up complete control to the rifter inside her.

Having regrouped, Fred and Rags approached for another assault. The Sisters faced the skeletons.

Sully tapped Roni's shoulder. "Be ready. I think we might get our chance."

Rags stumbled forward and Sister Rachel had little trouble shoving him to the ground — though she winced at her sore shoulder. Fred swung his club-like arm and connected with Sister Susan's hip. She cried out, jostled to the side. Sister Rachel stepped in, took hold of Fred's clavicle and spun him off.

"Why are you taking that?" Sister Rachel said. Confirming Roni's thoughts, she watched as Sister Rachel slapped Sister Susan across the face. "You have been given the greatest gift a nun could ask for. An Angel is inside of you yet you do not allow it to reign free."

"I am not a slave," Sister Susan said. "I will help the Angels. I want to serve them. But I will not have them make me do things I have vowed not to do. You forget — there are rules to our faith."

"They're Angels. They made the rules."

"Why would an Angel encourage me to destroy and kill?"

Rags had managed to get back standing. Fred had turned around enough that it could focus on Sister Susan once again.

Sister Rachel's eyes flashed green. "I thought you were one of us." She shoved Sister Susan into the skeletons.

"No," Sully shouted as he stepped forward.

It was too late. For all their slow movement, once the skeletons had latched onto Sister Susan, they showed no mercy. They sank their top rows of teeth into her neck and shoulder. They fell upon her with more weight than she expected. And if the rifter within her attempted to fight back, Sister Susan fought harder to remain in control — even at the loss of her life.

That was the kind of faith Roni never understood.

"Shalom, shalom," Sully called out — a command word he had written to force the skeletons into disassembling. As their bones clattered to the floor, nothing more than piles of ancient debris, Sister Susan's blood pulsed through her neck. There was no saving her.

Purple-back smoke drifted from Sister Susan's mouth in gentle tendrils. They snaked around each other until they formed a smoke ball. Then the creature floated up the stairwell and disappeared from view.

Sister Rachel nudged Sister Susan's lifeless leg. "Well, Old Man, look what you've done now."

Despite the obvious state of Sister Susan's body, Sully scampered around toward her head to check if there was any chance to resuscitate her. "I thought you were merely fanatical, but now I see, you are crazy."

Sister Rachel let loose a hefty laugh. "No more than you. We both go around trying to save the world. I just happen to be on the right side of things."

Sully inched backwards. Roni wanted to step out of the shadows and warn him that he headed toward a dead end. She stopped. He had to know — he had spent the last hour sifting through every one of the alcoves for the bones he wanted.

Sister Rachel moved closer toward him. "I had thought Sister Susan's ambitions would have been enough. It certainly has been enough for Sister Claudia. But Sister Susan's faith kept getting in the way."

"Not the kind of faith you wanted?"

Moving even further down the dark aisle, Sister Rachel said, "You are awfully brave when you think your friends are coming to save you. But just like in the dorm with your fake magic circle, nobody is coming to help you this time."

In a flash, Roni understood what Sully had been doing. He had set up the perfect positioning. Sister Rachel had her back to Roni and had gone far enough down the aisle that Roni had access to a weapon. As quietly as possible, Roni crept down the aisle. She crouched and snatched up the largest bone she could find — it wasn't hard. Bones were everywhere.

Ignoring her racing pulse, Roni rushed forward and swung the large bone against the back of Sister Rachel's head. The nun never had a chance. Her body shivered upon contact and slumped to the floor.

Gasping, Roni asked Sully, "Are you okay?"

He emerged from the dark. "I don't shake that easily. Well, not often." He looked at the two nuns on the floor and the piles of bones. "What a shame."

Roni took his hand. "Let's get out of here."

"No." He pulled back. "You go ahead. Go find Gram and Elliot. I'll take care of this mess down here."

Roni wanted to argue, but Sully's tone could not be mistaken. He had issued an order.

"On my way," she said as she climbed the stairs two at a time.

CHAPTER 17

Roni tore into the open air, her mind racing as fast as her heart. She had just seen a nun die. She had just clocked another nun across the back of the head with yet another nun's bones. Being an atheist did not stop her from fearing the bad karma that might come along with these actions.

As she sprinted across the front lawn of the church, headed toward the dorms, she stuttered to a halt. Even if Elliot had managed to get Gram out of the church, they would have found the dorms empty — at least, empty of Roni and Sully. They may have encountered the nuns or they may have escaped and were hiding. If the latter, they could be anywhere in the woods. The cars were still parked outside, so Roni knew they couldn't have gotten too far.

But hiding did not sound like Gram. Especially in her current state of mind. No. Roni suspected Gram and Elliot went on the offensive — not at the nuns directly, but possibly at the rift.

Wishing she had a decent weapon, Roni approached the front of the church. At her gentle push, the door creaked open — she could not recall it having done so in the past — and she entered. The lights leading to the nave were off, but the firelight glow of the rift rose in the stairwell to the right. Softly, Roni descended the spiral staircase.

Halfway down, she heard the chanting — a steady rhythm that lacked musicality but made up for it with fervor. Her legs trembled but she continued on. At the bottom, what she saw made part of her want to race up the stairs, rev up the car, get to an airport, and leave Ireland forever. The other part of her had no choice but to stay and see this through. Gram and Elliot depended on it.

In the center of the room, the rift continued to flow, it's flashing red and orange swirls brightening at irregular intervals. The books that the Parallel Society had been able to salvage surrounded the rift. Five of them — each chained tightly to a bookstand, and each stand chained tightly to each other. The chains zigzagged and crossed one another like the moorings of a complicated tent.

Deeper into the room, near the back corner, Elliot stood with his cane planted firmly on the floor. A dome with a green-yellow hue surrounded the area. At his side, Gram sat on the floor with her right leg out straight. A long gash bled through her pants. As she nursed her leg, she glowered ahead. Two purple-black balls of smoke pressed against the dome.

Any relief Roni could have felt at seeing Elliot protecting Gram washed away under the sound of that chanting. Sister Mary and Sister Claudia prostrated before the rift. Lifting their hands and voices, they chanted foreign words that resembled no language Roni had ever heard. They lowered their heads to the ground and back up again, over and over, chanting the entire time.

With a bright pulse of red from the rift, another smoky creature emerged. It drifted across the room to join the others attempting to break through Elliot's protective bubble.

Roni's shoe scuffed the stone floor. A soft sound, really, but dissonant enough to cut through the chanting. Sister Mary paused and glanced back. Her emerald eyes flared and a mischievous grin formed. She resumed her chanting but not before whispering something to Sister Claudia.

"Run Roni!" Gram crawled toward the edge of the dome. "Get out of here!"

Sister Claudia stood, turned, and sauntered toward Roni. "I'm sorry to see you here alone. I'm guessing Sister Susan and Sister Rachel are not in good shape. I hope you haven't committed any sins. The angels will not like that."

Roni had no interest in trading quips. She had no interest in being polite, either. After all, if Sister Claudia was right, if the rifters were really angels from Heaven, then Roni's soul was doomed to Hell anyway. Might as well go in whole hog.

She stepped forward, clenched her fist, and decked Sister Claudia in the jaw. The surprise on the nun's face made the pain in Roni's hand worthwhile.

Rubbing blood from the corner of her mouth, Sister Claudia snarled. "Bitch."

"Watch the language. There are angels present."

"You'll rot in Hell." Sister Claudia charged forward with her arms up and her fingers splayed out into claws. Her eyes turned green as her feet left the ground. Roni watched her approach and punched again, but Sister Claudia had prepared for it this time. She took the blow in the side while her claws dug into Roni's shoulders. Roni yelled, and Sister Claudia tossed her against the stairs.

As Sister Claudia's feet returned to the ground, she smirked. "Maybe I'll start with breaking both of your legs. You'll cause less trouble that way."

Ignoring the bruised pains running along her back, Roni waited for the nun to be nearly upon her. Then she shot forward. She buried her shoulder into Sister Claudia's gut. The pleasure of hearing Sister Claudia's air knocking from her lungs only matched the satisfaction of tackling the nun to the floor. Roni straddled the woman, made a fist again, and pounded Sister Claudia's chest.

But as the thought hit Roni that she really needed to learn good fighting technique, the Sister bucked her off. In a flash of movement that Roni did not comprehend, Sister Claudia ended up behind her. Somehow the nun had locked one of Roni's arms against her back. She could not move without pulling the arm from the socket or breaking a bone. Pain rifled through her shoulders.

"Perhaps you'd like to feel what you did to Sister Rachel." Sister Claudia tightened her grip and Roni's shoulders burned. "Maybe I'll dislocate both arms just for the fun of it."

Bending back, Sister Claudia lifted off the floor. Roni screamed and her anguish echoed back off the stone walls. Despite the pain and the growing panic, Roni heard Sister Mary continue her chanting. She saw another purple-black ball of smoke emerge from the rift and join the attack on Gram and Elliot. Even as she kicked and thrashed, even as she recognized that she could not break free, she managed to lock eyes with Gram.

She reached towards her grandmother, stretching forward despite the pain. Gram's face dropped — scared and scarred. Roni had mimicked Maria's trapped expression. Whether she had done so of her own volition or because the being inside of her had seen her mother, Roni did not know. But it made all the difference.

Over the years, Roni had seen Gram angry plenty of times. She knew Gram's stern face, her disappointed face, her face that promised a spanking, her face that promised a grounding, and even her face of utter bewilderment. Never before had Roni seen the pure fury that contorted Gram's face at that moment. Despite the pain in her injured leg, Gram positioned herself as upright as possible. A chain lowered from her sleeve.

With a practiced motion, Gram whipped the chain out. It sliced through the dome and lassoed around Sister Claudia's ankle. A swift yank and Sister Claudia spun in the air. Her shocked yelp followed as she tumbled to the ground. Roni rolled sideways.

With her coif pulled back and her wimple askew, Sister Claudia's face twisted like a rabid dog. On all fours she galloped toward Roni. Without time to stand, Roni scooted backwards. She had no weapons. She barely had breath after being held so tight.

Gram wrenched the chain back again. Sister Claudia's eyes widened in shock as she scratched into the floor to no avail. She rolled on her back and grabbed the chain around her ankle. Pulling with great strength, Sister Claudia attempted to free the chain from Gram.

Roni scrambled to her feet. She rushed over and slammed her arms around Sister Claudia's head. She did not know how to perform a proper sleeper hold, but she had seen plenty of them in the movies. Even if it didn't work, her clumsy maneuver would help Gram — perhaps simply buying a little time. At least, Roni hoped so.

Between Gram's chain pulling hard on Sister Claudia's ankle, and Roni tightening her grip around the nun's throat, there was an instant where it seemed they had the advantage. But Roni had forgotten about Sister Mary.

The old nun stood with her arms stretched out and her head arched back. The burning glow of the rift reflected on her white wimple like a lion's mane framing her face. As Roni and Gram struggled with Sister Claudia, Sister Mary walked forward toward the rift.

Roni had seen this before with Sister Ashley. However, this time, the nun approaching did not have the cultish look in her eye of one about to sacrifice herself. Rather, Sister Mary appeared in total control.

When she reached the circle of books and chains, Sister Mary paused. "I hear you, dear angels. I hear you and I welcome you."

With green veins pulsing along the edges of her face and emerald eyes full and bright, Sister Mary took hold of the nearest chain and ripped it loose from the books.

Roni had enough time to catch Gram's terrified gaze. She wanted to say something, but only had a half-second to think a simple summation — *Oh shit.*

CHAPTER 18

An orange wave pulsed out of the rift. Roni braced herself, expecting time to slow and sound to cease. But the light dissipated like water soaked up into a sponge. Sister Mary, Sister Claudia, and Roni exchanged confused gazes.

A distant sound grew like the winding up of a helicopter blade. *Thrum thrum thrum*. As the sound grew louder, it bounced off the walls doubling the noise.

Continuing her steady rhythmic chanting, Sister Mary said, "I am here. Your vessel. Hear my voice. Let it be your lighthouse."

Another orange wave pulsed. Roni could not help but flinch. This time, however, four smokeball creatures shot out of the rift, each one making that strong *thrum* as they broke into this universe.

The creatures pivoted in the air and went straight for Elliot's protection dome. As Roni watched the maneuver, her eyes were drawn away by a dark spot forming in the middle of the rift. The spot did not move with the cloudy swirls of the rift. Instead it grew. It was a black, smoky thing — with touches of purple.

As the helicopter thrumming continued, Roni's stomach sank. Sister Mary broke into ecstatic laughter.

Roni put it all together — the smoke, the thrumming, the emergence of those creatures — and she took one step toward Gram. Sister Claudia latched onto Roni's arm and held her back. In that same moment, the creatures busted through.

Thrum thrum thrum. Each sound spat a new smoke creature from the rift. They shot out like bullets machine-gunning through the air.

Roni dropped to the floor, taking Sister Claudia with her. The rifters rattled overhead as they kept coming in a steady stream of purple-black smoke. The roar of their entrance rivaled any giant machine mankind had made. Sifting through the rhythmic crescendo, Roni could hear Sister Mary's gleeful cries.

Something metal wrapped around Roni's wrist — Gram's chain. She glanced up and snatched a peak. Her grandmother's face betrayed the desperation in her heart. Roni scrambled across the floor, but Sister Claudia latched to her foot.

Roni tried to kick loose. The nun's grip was tight. She flashed a vicious grin promising never to let go. Gram pulled harder on the chain. Roni wondered if Gram might do Sister Claudia's work for her — dislocate Roni's arm and cause serious injury.

Sister Claudia repositioned her legs to give her more leverage. "Open your mouth. Let the Angels in."

As she leaned back, the strain on Roni's leg worsened. One of these two women would soon rip Roni apart.

Not going to happen, Roni thought.

She let go of the chain. The sudden change in force sent Sister Claudia tumbling backward. Roni hit the floor hard on her tailbone and cried out. She rolled onto her stomach, popped to her knees, and raced across the floor. She could hear Sister Claudia growling as the nun recovered. The air had become thick with purple-black smoke, and Roni feared breathing in too deeply. Up ahead, she saw Gram's chain.

Just a few feet.

"I'm going to destroy you," Sister Claudia said, her voice louder, closer, more animalistic than Roni dared imagine.

Roni had the urge to glance back, to see if her ears misjudged the distance, but she kept her focus on that chain. So close.

Something touched her — a finger grazing her back. Roni vaulted forward. Her hand grabbed the end of the chain and she rolled up upon it like a scroll trying to tie itself. "Now, Gram! Now!"

The chain snapped taut and zipped against the ground as Gram pulled hard. Like a flapping fish, Roni tumbled as Gram reeled her in toward the protection of Elliot's dome. The chain spun Roni around. Skidding on her back, ignoring the burn of her tearing skin, she saw Sister Claudia stand full upright. The nun sprinted after her with a face glowing with green anger.

Roni passed through into the dome, and all the rage of Sister Claudia, all the maniacal chanting of Sister Mary, all the jackhammering *thrums* of the rifters pouring into the room — all of it muted. Roni heard her own hard breathing and little more. She felt the fire in her shoulder and the pulsing aches in her hips. Sweat covered her body, stinging her lips with saltiness.

As Gram spooled her chain up her sleeve, Roni crawled over and hugged the old woman. Gram did not hesitate to return the touch. Roni pressed her face into her grandmother's safe bosom and the strength of Gram's arms around her found the right amount of pressure to exert. The embrace lasted only seconds but it would take two libraries full of books to express it in words between them.

"Look," Gram whispered.

Roni followed her gaze. Sister Mary and Sister Claudia crouched on the floor, their arms around each other. They no longer looked joyous or ecstatic or even maniacal. They looked alarmed.

Both had bruises on their faces. Sister Mary's right cheek bled from an open gash. Sister Claudia's tunic had been torn. Tears wet her cheeks.

"How have we failed you?" Sister Mary cried out.

"Please, forgive us." Sister Claudia covered her face and lowered her head.

Roni tightened her grip on Gram's arm. "Can you save them?"

Gram shook her head. "They have those creatures inside them. The dome filters out all bio-signatures but ours. If we permit them into the dome, we will let the creature's biological signature in as well. The dome won't work for us anymore. All those things will flood in here." Gram clutched the crucifix around her neck. "I will send my prayers for them."

Roni held back shouting that she had Maria inside her. Since the dome continued to work, Maria could not be one of the rifters. But she knew the argument already — Maria, whatever she was, came partially from the real Maria. Of course, she wasn't a rifter. Of course, the dome would hold.

Without warning, a swarm of rifters paused in the air. Using that same silent communication Roni had seen before, they turned toward the nuns. Though the creatures lacked eyes or mouths or any visible sign of a face, Roni swore they looked upon the Sisters with malevolent glee.

They attacked.

Like angry wasps, the creatures dove in on the nuns. Sister Mary gyrated as one hit after another pummeled her body. Sister Claudia remained prone on the ground, shuddering under the endless attacks. The screams of both nuns vibrated through the air as their flesh tore from their bodies. Blood splashed into the air but the swarm of purple-black smoke soaked it up before it could return to the floor. Their cries worsened as their muscles tore. Soon though, they lacked throats with which to make any sound. Seconds later, bones and glistening flesh were all that remained of the two women.

Watching as the smoke creatures changed course to pile up against the dome, Roni turned towards Gram. "Now what do we do?"

Though safe for the moment, Roni understood that soon the dome would crumble. Elliot had lowered his forehead to his cane — all his strength and concentration poured into keeping that dome together. But the air glowed purple from the mass of the creatures surrounding them. The numerous rifters blocked out the sunlight. They had become a brick wall made of purple-black smoke, and soon Elliot's strength would fail.

"I am so sorry, ladies," he said, his voice weak and strained. "I can only hold on a little longer."

Roni watched the creatures pushing against each other, writhing in their attempts to break through. She imagined the pain that would come. She did not want to die, of course. But most of all, she did not want to die the way the nuns had.

A crack formed halfway up the dome. While Roni knew the dome had been made only of energy, that there was no glass or solid surface of any kind to actually crack, Elliot's weakening condition manifested in this manner. Or perhaps she was wrong — she had limited knowledge about the Parallel Society. Perhaps the dome he had created this time actually was made of a solid substance. After all, she could hear the cracking as she watched the splits spider outward in different directions.

Wisps of purplish smoke seeped through. Roni and Gram skirted backward, pressing up against one of the two stone walls making the corner. When Elliot's hand slipped down his cane, the crack widened — still not large enough for an entire rifter to slip through, but plenty of their probing, smoky tendrils found ways in.

Gram put her arm around Roni's shoulder and clasped her head with the other hand. She pulled Roni's face down to her breast and held her tight. "I'm sorry for all you've had to suffer through. Your mother and father had so many secrets, and it was never fair for you to be burdened with that mystery. I'm sorry you never got to understand about your lost time. I can only offer you my arms and my prayers. I hope the Lord can forgive us all our trespasses and I pray we shall be sent to His loving bosom."

Under any other circumstance, Roni would have been offended by Gram's words. But here, as Elliot dropped to his knees and the dome ripped into pieces, she found Gram's warmth comforting.

A storm of rifters slammed downward into the dome.

A loud bang like modern demolition.

Roni's head popped up in time to see the wall next to her break open. The stones shot outward, thrusting the smoke creatures aside. A large stone golem ducked its way in. Sully stood at the open hole in the wall.

"Care for a little help?" he asked.

CHAPTER 19

Sully's golem had dug a steep incline from the surface down toward the basement wall. With Gram using Roni as a crutch, the two managed to muddle their way to the top. Sully and his golem came out next. Elliot emerged last with his cane held chest-high and pointed at the wall — keeping the remnants of his protective dome together.

"It's okay," Sully said. "They won't come out."

Though clearly skeptical, Elliot let the head of his cane fall to the ground. Several of the rifters drifted outside, but they merely floated up the wall to enter the church again through a stained-glass window. Like dogs reacting to an invisible fence, they refused to cross further out.

As Elliot climbed up the dirt and rocks, he said, "How did you know they can't follow us?"

"They can, but they won't. When I was scavenging stones to build the golem, I noticed that nothing was coming outside. And I never saw the one creature that left Sister Susan's body roaming the grounds. I assumed it came back in here."

"Assumed? So you didn't really know?"

Sully shrugged. "I made an educated guess."

With gravelly impatience, Gram said, "The two of you can bicker later. We need to find some place to regroup. And my leg is killing me."

"Agreed," Sully said. "We can take the cars and drive off, but I don't like the idea of leaving this rift unattended. Especially now."

"You're right. The time it would take us to drive to a nearby town might be the time it takes for this rift to decimate all of Ireland."

Roni gestured with her chin. "What about the dorm?"

Sully stepped forward, turned around, and eyed the various

buildings. "Presumably, at some point, those creatures will come out of that church. Since they appear to have some type of telepathy between each other, we have to assume all the new creatures will have learned what the older ones know — I would not want to go to the dorm or the library. They would be too familiar with those areas already."

"Where then?" Elliot said, resting against the bumper of the car.

Roni said, "If you follow the path beyond the dorms, there's a barn on the hill. Can all of Ireland survive long enough for that?"

"It'll have to." Sully headed off with the others following behind. "We can rest up and figure out our next move."

Raising her voice, Gram said, "And somebody can tell me, by all that's holy, what is going on around here."

The barn turned out to be smaller than expected but still serviceable. A tractor that could not have been used in nearly five years took up much of the center aisle. Old stalls with rotting wood had been filled with rusted tools, weathered boxes, and whatever else the nuns wanted to discard. A hayloft overlooked them, and Roni's quick search up there suggested they had a good view of the church, if they didn't mind stepping on rat droppings.

As Elliot ran his healing across Gram's leg, Sully found a stack of folding chairs and formed a small circle with them. "I know there's a lot going on between you two ladies," Sully said. "We're out of time. That rift is spewing out living relics. We've got to find a way to put them back in. So, set aside your differences and start talking with each other."

"Roni and I are fine." Gram crossed her arms over her chest.

"Yeah," Roni said. "You didn't see but we hugged it all out."

Sully raised an eyebrow. "One hug and all is well? That must've been one powerful hug."

"It's enough for now," Gram said.

Roni added, "We know how to put our disagreement on hold. Besides, we did have a hug. It happened right before your golem broke down the wall."

Sully had set the golem on sentry duty outside. "Fine. Sister Rachel is tied up underneath the library. I fear what might happen when she gets out and joins the others in the church."

"You left her down there?"

"You'd rather I carry her around or bring her up here?"

"No, but —"

"I wasn't going to kill her. We're not that kind of people."

"I only meant —"

"This is what I'm talking about. Stop criticizing each other, stop questioning each other, and start dealing with the situation as it is. We're running out of time."

Rubbing his forehead, Elliot said, "Perhaps the two of you could explain to Gram and I what is going on, what happened to Sister Rachel, or even Sister Susan, everything. I went to get Gram in the church and found Sister Mary had taken her down to the rift. When I got down there, everything went bad. I barely had enough time to create that protection field."

Pushing his glasses up his nose, Sully said, "It's a bit complicated."

"No, it's not," Roni said. She stood and stretched her arms. After a deep breath, she said, "This is all my fault. It's mine to explain."

"Roni," Sully said, the warning unmistakable.

"Just because you're the leader, doesn't give you the right to withhold from the group."

Gram snickered. "Not so easy, huh?"

Suddenly taking interest in the barn's wood framing, Sully declined to answer.

Before the Old Gang could launch into another bout of bickering, Roni delved in and covered all the details from the moment she and Gram had arrived at the Abbey. Much of it Gram and Elliot had already heard, but Roni wanted to make sure that all members of the team had the same information. When she got to the point where she woke up after releasing Maria, she had the thirst for a strong whiskey. Pressing on, she described the sensations she felt and the voices she heard. And she watched Gram closely. The old woman's face shifted from one emotion to another as if someone controlled her muscles by remote and kept randomly pressing buttons. Roni worried Gram might have a stroke.

Once she finished, Roni perched on the edge of the chair next to Gram. "I don't know if you can believe me, but I didn't do any of this to hurt you. I'm trying to do the right thing. I guess I blew it. I'm sorry."

The barn grew quiet as the team digested Roni's tale. At length, Gram lifted a shaking, wrinkled hand and placed it on Roni's cheek. She looked over Roni's face as if seeing her granddaughter for the first time. Her shallow eyes welled up and her jowls quivered.

In a shaking voice, Gram said, "My baby? Are you in there?"

The attack came stronger than ever before. All the hairs on Roni's body stood as her skin prickled. The smell of molding hay and damp earth faded — replaced with enough sugar in the air to fill a candy factory. The high-pitched whine became a wolf's howl next to Roni's ear.

She doubled over to the ground, pressing the palms of her hands against her ears. Tears streamed from her eyes, and when she gazed up at Gram, her blurred vision knocked forty years off the woman. She saw a young mother reaching down towards her.

Her jaw acted involuntarily. It locked open as her throat convulsed out a voice that did not belong to her. "Mommy?"

"Baby? Maria? Is that really you?" The hope in Gram's voice rose above the horror in her trembling tone.

"I love you, Mommy. Love you. Miss you."

Gram dropped to her knees. Blubbering through her words, she said, "Oh, my sweet baby, I'm so sorry. I should never have brought you here. I was so cocky back then and look what it caused. The Lord has punished me."

"Please. This time. Let me go."

"I know, I know. I'm so sorry. I should never have let you go with me."

"I have to go. You need me. Stop this."

Roni's throat burned as if she had spent the day throwing up acrid bile. Her jaw closed and she collapsed in a fetal position. She could feel Elliot's large hands resting on her head as he performed his regular miracles — checking over for any internal injuries and healing her, if necessary. But she did not feel injured — mostly. Used. She felt used. As when she woke in a stranger's bed, her body spent, her regret growing.

She did not regret bringing Maria out of that hell. Despite the pain it had caused them both, she knew she had done the right thing. She had to have.

With Elliot's help, she sat up and eventually made it to one of the folding chairs. Sully returned from outside — checking on his golem and the church, no doubt.

"How long have I been out?" she asked.

"Only a few minutes," Elliot said.

Gram paced the length of the barn, her fingers rolling over the beads of her rosary — she always had one in her pocket at hand — as she mouthed one prayer after another. Sully slouched on one of the folding chairs, leaned his head back, and stared at the ceiling. He looked like a younger man, though Roni worried he might have trouble getting out of that position.

Elliot shifted over to Sully and patted his forehead with a handkerchief. "You must be careful not to exhaust yourself. We cannot afford to lose you. Ever."

Sully reached up and clasped Elliot's hand between his own. "You are the best friend a man could ask for. But you worry too much. I'm not exhausted at all."

"Lying to me will not help."

Sully sat forward, took off his glasses, and rubbed the bridge of his nose. "I said I'm okay."

"I know that look on you. It's not a good one."

Feeling a little stronger, Roni said, "You said it yourself — we don't have time for these kinds of things. Out with it."

Sully's head snapped up. "I think I have an idea for how we might close the rift."

"I thought it couldn't be closed."

"That was before you came along and pulled out Maria. That was before these nuns found a way to call all those creatures loose. Things are different now, more different than any time ever before when concerned with this rift. We can use that to our advantage."

Gram rejoined the group, opting to stand behind her chair. "She has to go back. Doesn't she?"

"I'm afraid so," Sully said, gazing at his hands to avoid looking at anyone else. "I've been thinking about all that we've learned. I believe that back when you were young and Maria was split — back then, the creatures within the rift had found a way to reach out. We know Sister Mary had already been taken over, but the creature inside her had not been able to pull out any others."

"You think they stole my Maria in a failed attempt to break free?"

"And then all these years since, the piece of her trapped in that rift acted like a stopper on a vial. Once Roni broke her free, the vial was open. The way for the others to come out became clearer. They merely needed a guide, and the nuns provided that."

Roni stood too fast and fell back to her chair. "We can't do this. We can't send Maria back into that awful place."

"We don't have a choice. It's our duty to protect this universe — no matter what."

"But if she's only a stopper, then all we'll have succeeded in doing is preventing more of those creatures from coming in. The rift will still be open and there will still be hundreds of those creatures around."

Gram shared a grim look with Elliot. "I'll have to make a special book. One that can vacuum up all those things."

Elliot said, "And I will have to build a dome around the entire church to contain them until your book is ready."

Lifting his head, Sully gazed at his team, and Roni could feel the regret seeping out of each one. "Then it is possible," he said. "We don't have time to do the proper research. Do you think this'll work?"

"I won't do it," Roni said. "This is all that's left of my mother. Of Gram's daughter. We can't just let her go. And after all I've done to get her back."

"It won't be so easy as letting her go." Sully brushed his hands against his pants and stood. "You will have to go, too. As near to the rift as it takes for Maria to be pulled out of you."

Tossing the chair aside, Gram stepped forward, putting herself between Roni and Sully. "Absolutely not."

"They're connected. But if you chain her —"

"She'll still be at risk."

"There will always be risk."

"Then no. Lord knows I am not going to lose the both of them."

Sully gazed off toward the church. "Then we've already lost."

CHAPTER 20

Rain pattered against the roof of the barn. Roni stood in the hayloft, feeling the occasional raindrop splat upon her nose, as she watched the church in the distance. If not for the intensifying purple glow of the rift, she would have had difficulty seeing the church at all. Like picking out the nuns in the night, the dark stone of the church blended in with the stormy sky.

Soon, they would have to do something. Even in the few minutes Roni had spent watching the church, the pulsing glow of the creatures worsened. The rift kept shooting them out, and by morning at the latest, they would be ready to break free. In fact, the only thing stopping the Parallel Society from fighting those creatures right away was that they had no idea what to do.

No, that's not true. Sully had an idea, but Gram refused to let it happen. Roni did, too, for that matter.

Below her, Elliot sat ramrod straight on a folding chair and meditated. Gram had resumed her pacing of the barn and her praying with the rosary. And Sully — he puttered with his golem.

Not only did they lack a viable option of what to do, but it seemed to Roni that none of them worked hard enough to secure an answer. Until she heard Gram approach Sully with a hushed tone that piqued her interest.

"There must be a better way," she said. "We have no reason to believe your plan will work."

"I'm taking the best educated guess that I can."

"It's still just a guess."

The rain strengthened creating an incessant drumroll on the barn roof. Forced to speak louder than he had intended, Sully said, "I'm in charge around here. I don't take this lightly. But we do have a responsibility to the universe — sacrifice comes with that."

Roni stepped back from the lip of the hayloft and plopped down on a bale that looked reasonably unused by rats.

Maybe Sully was right. Maybe she would have to accept that sacrificing her life was part of her duty. After all, if she refused to help, she sentenced so many others to a horrible fate — perhaps the entire world. Was her puny life worth more than all the billions of the world? Besides, all this trouble existed because of her mistake. If she had listened to Gram and left the rift alone, none of this would have happened. The nuns would still be wishing for somebody to come along who could use the book Sister Agnes had stolen long ago. The rift would still be a stabilized anomaly. And Maria would have remained locked away.

"I don't know if you can hear me," she whispered to the empty air. "I don't even know if I want you to hear me. No, that's not true. I do want that. Part of me wants to call you Mom and feel your arms around me. Part of me thinks I'm like your big sister and that I should have my arms around you. I don't know what to think about any of this. But I want you to know why I did it. Even if the Old Gang never understands, even if you don't, I think I should at least try to give you that much."

The skin on the back of her neck prickled which she took to be the closest thing she could get for communication.

"I don't have a lot of memories of you — that is, the you that grew up into an adult and gave birth to me. There was the car accident. That I remember — but really only the aftermath. The moment when Gram told me what had happened and what would become of me. That sort of thing. Even that is a fuzzy haze. I don't know how many weeks I walked around like a zombie waiting for it all not to be true. But it was. You had died and my father went a bit nuts and I lost a lot of what I knew. But I do have a few rare, precious memories of you. Growing up, when it came to talking about you, Gram tended to focus on all the trouble you got into, but you weren't all bad. In fact, you could be sweet and lovely."

Roni closed her eyes and swam through the dark emptiness of her memories. What she summoned up, she could see as clearly as if it had happened only minutes ago — not too difficult considering the few memories of her mother that she had. With such a limited library at her disposal, she had visited this memory an inordinate amount of times.

She was a girl, around ten, and she had woken from a nightmare. The clock read 3:24 am, and she knew her father would not be around. He had been stuck working the graveyard shift at a twenty-four hour diner. He was the one she preferred to go to when upset, but she needed some comfort regardless. Roni no longer recalled the nightmare itself, but she could still feel how unsettling the dream had been for her, the way it left her skin sensitive to the rub of the sheets, the way the night's quiet caused her heart to beat faster, the way she could taste the danger lurking in her sub-conscious — waiting for her to sleep again so that it could take over.

They were living in a two-bedroom apartment more suited for college students than a young family. From her bedroom doorway, she spotted the light on in the kitchen. As she approached, she heard her mother sniffle and whimper.

Roni never found out what had upset her mother, or if she had, that part of the memory was lost, too. The instant Maria spotted little Roni approaching, she wiped away her tears, blew her nose, and wriggled out a smile for her daughter.

"Did I wake you?" she asked.

The sound of her voice echoed in Roni's head. She had heard those four words so many times that they began to lose all meaning. Whenever in her life she felt the need for her mother's love, she turned to this memory. The fact that her mother could have been so upset about something yet drop it simply to offer concern for her daughter's nightmare always left adult-Roni in a state of awe.

"I wish I could show you more," she said to the hayloft. "That's the best one I have. I just wanted you to not think so terribly of your other half."

Roni's skin flushed with warmth, and she thought it would end there. A simple, straightforward response — she needed no more. But the warmth continued and the temperature increased. It did not become painful, but Roni broke out into a sweat. Her eyes closed. And Maria shared her own memory.

Transported into the rift, Roni swam in a thick soup of orange and red and yellow smoke. No surfaces around her. No up or down. As if she hovered in the middle of the ocean, unsure which way led to the surface.

Most sounds had diminished to the point of being inaudible. Movement slowed, too. Not as bad as when the rift had sent pulses through Roni, but bad enough.

She wanted to move her hand, but of course, this was not her hand to move. It belonged to Maria. This was the girl's memory.

And in that memory, Maria showed a moment when she managed to jerk her body fast to the side. The bright fog of orange reacted equally fast — as if she and the smoke sat upon a seesaw. If she moved one way, the smoke mirrored in the opposite direction. Always matching her speed. It took a long time — possibly years, Maria could not be sure how time progressed in there — but she came to see that her presence in the rift let her control it ... to an extent.

"You really do stabilize that thing," Roni whispered.

Maria offered one last touch — not an image but a sensation. A vengeful wrath overcame Roni, a desire to protect through destruction, to tear down the object of Maria's trauma, of her torture.

She jolted to her feet. Her pulse pounded hard enough to move the skin on her chest. Leaping for the ladder, she hurried down to the barn floor. Gasping, she said, "I know what we have to do."

The Old Gang snapped their attention towards her, each one moving in close to listen.

"We were right that Maria had stabilized the rift. But we don't want her to go back there to stabilize it again. That would not solve any of our current problems, and it would be cruel to her. But she's made it known to me what to do."

Gram braced herself on Sully's arm. "She's going to sacrifice herself. Isn't she?"

"It's painful in there. She doesn't want to go back to that. And she knows she can't stay with us here."

Sully said, "But if we don't send her back, how can she stabilize the rift?"

"She's not going to stabilize it. She's going to overload it. She's going to destroy it." To Elliot, Roni asked, "Can you do anything to help with that?"

Elliot picked up his cane. "I can amplify her energy, but it'll go off in all directions like a bomb. We've had books around that thing for centuries — each one pushing its energy into the rift and that's barely contained the thing. If we can't focus Maria's power right into the rift, it won't have a serious impact."

"Roni is still connected to Maria," Sully said. "She could direct the energy — then that would not be a problem."

"Like what we did in that little town in France about thirty years ago."

"Exactly. Although back then, you sent your energy through the town square like a magnifying glass. We won't have that for Maria's energy."

Straightening, Gram clutched her crucifix. "We have something better. We have the Lord's church itself."

The men paused to share a look with her.

Clearing her throat, Roni said, "The only problem I see in this is how do we get her in a position so that her energy can be amplified into the church and then into the rift?"

Sully's face took an ominous turn. "You forget — the two of you are connected."

"Trust me, I haven't forgotten."

"Then, you do understand what that means, yes? Using the church like you suggest?"

"If we use the church itself, I'm guessing that means from somewhere in the building?"

Gram approached Roni and pulled her in for a hug. "Oh dear, it's worse than that. You have to go into the center of the rift."

Roni pictured the rift tearing apart Sister Ashley, Sister Claudia, and Sister Mary. "Oh."

Waving his hands, Sully shook his head and mumbled as he walked the length of the barn. He chuckled and clicked his tongue. Then he pointed at his golem. "Don't worry. I know exactly what to do." Gram raised an eyebrow, and Sully shrunk a bit. "Well, almost exactly. I got a good idea. Trust me."

CHAPTER 21

Roni leaned against the open barn doors and watched the rain soaking the ground. Behind her, Sully had dismantled his stone golem. With Elliot's help, the two men made preparations for Sully's plan.

"It's going to be okay," Gram said as she sidled up.

"Sure." Roni kept her eyes on puddles forming on the ground. "You almost sound convincing."

Gram stayed silent for a moment. When she leaned against the other side of the barn door, she said, "There's always danger when you come out into the field. Always risks."

"Not so much in the library, huh?"

"There's eyestrain."

Roni laughed. "I'll be okay. I mean I'm scared shitless, but —"

"Watch the language."

"But I'll do the job."

Gram pressed the tips of her fingers together. "If there were another way."

"I know. I agree. We don't have time to hit the books."

"Be sure. You've seen me all over the map with this. It's hard to know what's right. This isn't even my first time in a terrible situation and it's still hard. It's okay if you've changed your mind."

Roni breathed in the fresh, wet air. "I appreciate that, but it's not necessary. An hour ago, I would've thought different. But I had a conversation — of sorts — with Maria." She frowned as the words to articulate her thoughts evaded her. At length, she said, "It's time I move forward. The past won't go anywhere. I'll figure it out when I need to. But the world needs the Parallel Society now. Right?"

Gram gazed down at her hands. "Very brave." She pulled out her rosary and wrapped it around her hand. "I wonder if you might do me a favor before you go over to the boys."

"Of course."

"Maybe I could talk with Maria?"

Roni choked back the crack in her voice. "She doesn't really talk."

"She did before. She used your voice."

"And that hurt like … heck. I'm not sure she could do that again, anyway. I got the sense that it took a lot of effort. But she can hear you. Say what you want to say. I'll let you know how she responds."

Holding her rosary so tight that her fingers turned white, Gram stepped over towards Roni. She inclined her head close enough that she would not have to raise her voice to be heard. "I don't know what you are. My daughter? Part of her? Maybe just an echo of her being used by some creature in another universe. So many nights I prayed for the Lord to give me the means with which to help you. I always thought that meant bringing you home, making you whole.

"Earlier, I was in the church praying, and I saw how hard I had been on you. Not this side of you, but the other you — the one I raised into a young woman. So much of her rebellion came because of how hard I was. I think now I blamed her partially for surviving. I think I also blamed myself for taking you here to begin with, taking you to die.

"And now, I'm sending you to die again.

"I don't know if this matters to you, but I want you to know that I've done all I could for Roni. I've tried to make up for my failings. I've tried to make her into a woman that you could be proud of. I've tried…"

Gram lifted her head, and her glistening eyes held with Roni's. A soft utterance escaped her throat before she hurried off to one of the horse stalls. She crouched down, and though Roni tried to give the woman her privacy, there was no mistaking the sound of weeping.

Elliot walked up and put his arm on Roni's shoulder. "Come on. We are ready. Let your grandmother have a moment alone."

He escorted Roni back into the center of the barn. There she saw the rocks had been laid out according to size. Several small rocks had been placed shoulder-width apart on the ground, roughly in the shape of footprints.

Sully gestured to these footprint rocks. "Stand on them, and we can get started."

With all her concentration devoted to keep from shaking, Roni placed one foot on each of the stone forms. Sully and Elliot immediately got to work. With expert care, Sully chose specific rocks and placed them around Roni's feet. Elliot did the same, following Sully's instructions, while periodically giving Roni a reassuring nod.

As the rocks piled higher up the legs, Sully said to Elliot, "Don't worry about the exact shape. When we're ready, it'll work."

Roni did not share his confidence but kept silent. Every rock further up her body brought with it the weight of what they planned to do. Every extra pound pressing against her skin added to her fear.

When they reached her waist and prepared to lock down her arms, Gram rushed forward. "Hold on."

"We've already talked about this," Sully said, putting out his hands like a crossing guard. "We don't have another choice. There just isn't the time."

Pushing him aside, Gram stepped up towards Roni. She grabbed Roni's right hand and wrapped her rosary around the wrist. "I don't care that you are a non-believer. I have faith enough for the both of us. And if that thing in you is really Maria, then she has faith, too."

Roni clenched the rosary beads. Before she could respond, before she could even say a simple *I love you,* Gram turned away. Sully returned with a piece of paper. He placed the paper in her left hand.

"As long as that paper stays together, the golem will stay together. Strong. You can trust me."

As Sully returned to stacking rocks, Elliot paused. He stepped before Roni. "If you wish, I can create a little something that might ease you."

She shook her head. She needed to stay clear and focused. But she could not say those words — she did not trust her voice to hold steady. Elliot kissed her cheek before returning to help Sully.

By the time they reached her neck, she could no longer hold back the tears. Her body wanted to shake, but the tightly packed stones prevented it. She gazed upward, hoping to dry out her eyes — she didn't even have the movement to reach up and rub them. Lightning flashed and thunder crackled above them, and Roni pictured herself as Frankenstein's monster. The tears flowed faster.

"What is this?" A voice scraped as a nun lurched into the barn, her lame foot dragging behind. "Another abomination?" Stepping out of the rain, Sister Rachel wiped her bleeding mouth with the dark sleeve of her torn habit. "The Angels keep coming. You can't stop them. Soon, the world will become a vessel for them all. And I will gladly be the first to cast you demons back to Hell."

From the side, out of the shadows, Gram stepped forth wielding a shovel. She swung hard and slapped the nun in the back of the head. The young woman folded to the floor.

"Poser," Gram said and spit on the ground.

Standing with rocks in his hands, Sully said, "You're a Catholic. You can't go around striking nuns. We could've done that for you."

"You said she was tied up below the library. Does this look tied up to you?"

"I did my best. I didn't have a lot of good rope. I was using rags from over a hundred years ago." Sully slammed two rocks onto Roni's shoulders. "You think it's so easy? Next time, you find a way out of the crypt filled with bones and rats."

"Next time it might be a Rabbi instead of a nun. You saying you'll fight a rabbi?"

"It depends. Is he Orthodox or Reform?"

Roni laughed — a hardy, full-throated laugh. Tears streamed down, her face reddened, and she laughed more. Though Gram and Sully failed to find the humor, Elliot leaned back his head and roared alongside Roni.

At length, Gram said, "Fine, fine. I will tie up this excuse for a nun properly. You boys finish with the rocks. If that's okay, my leader?"

Waving his hand as he returned to work, Sully said, "Tie her up, don't tie her up, do what you think is right. We've got serious work to do."

He stepped back and passed an appraising eye up and down the thick pile of stones that encased Roni. "You ready?"

Roni nodded.

"Elliot and I are going to cover your head now. It might feel tight in there for a while. But once I whisper my commands, you'll be able to breathe fine. Okay?"

With a strong, steady voice, Roni said, "Let's go save the universe."

CHAPTER 22

Sully's whisper could not come fast enough. From the moment he placed the final stone, the one that covered her face, Roni fought back claustrophobic panic. She had never suffered from such a thing before, but then she had never been entombed in a rock pile before. The feeling of being buried alive did not sit well with her. Yet when Sully finally whispered his incantation into the golem's ear, the stones muffled his voice too much for her to catch what he said. Not that she would have understood the Hebrew.

Regardless, the golem came to life. She could feel it breaking out of the stone mound, feel it moving on its own. Though she formed its skeleton, she had no control over its actions. Two small stones rolled off the face so that she could see. A third stone popped out providing her a much-needed breathing hole.

"Relax your muscles," Sully said. "The less resistance you provide, the easier the golem will move, and the less chance of you being injured."

"Injured? You didn't say anything about this thing injuring me."

"I'm saying it now. Relax, and you'll be fine."

Gram watched from several steps back, both fascinated and horrified with what Roni was expected to do. "Good luck," she managed.

As the golem stepped out into the rain, Roni caught a glimpse of Elliot up in the hayloft. He had his cane held above his head, nearly vertical, and his free hand repeating several complex motions. She knew from past experience that much of the magic Elliot created took time. If she reached the church before he was ready, if she enacted her part of the plan too early, she didn't think she would survive. But he promised it would be okay, and she believed him. She had to.

She squeezed both her hands tight — the golem paper in her left, Gram's rosary beads in her right. The golem proceeded down the hill and the rain soaked through its stone crevices fast. Trickles of water fell down Roni's back, chilling her spine and drenching her pants.

Steady footsteps brought the golem closer to the church. Roni tried to follow Sully's instructions, tried to relax her body, but the excruciatingly slow pace only amped up her tension. She closed her eyes — the golem did not need for her to see in order to move — and she attempted to contact Maria.

This failed. Either Maria could no longer communicate or she refused to communicate. Probably the latter. Probably she needed to put her attention into the final moments ahead. They would be, after all, her actual, final moments — if all went as expected.

After fifteen minutes of a walk that should have taken three, Roni and the golem trudged by the dorms. A rich, purple color pulsed through the windows of the church ahead. The building had become so thick with rifters that the stone walls glowed as well. It was as if Prince had come back from the dead to put on his greatest private concert ever — but Roni knew that inside awaited no great music. Inside, awaited death. Hopefully not her own.

Once the golem set its stone foot upon the first stairs leading into the church, two rifters slipped outside and hovered in front of the entranceway. They made no noise. Simply hovered there, dripping smoke onto the ground. The golem halted. This would be the first crucial moment.

Sully had said that the living golem form would cover up any sense of Roni — any sense of her presence. Of course, he had no way to know for sure. He based his guess on the fact that they never noticed the golem when he broke through the stone wall. As the rifters descended around her head and drifted up and down the golem's stone body, she made sure not to move. She closed her eyes. She waited and hoped Sully had been right.

Her nervous breaths bounced off the rock around her. Between her heartbeats they sounded like a howling wind in a heavy storm. Lightning flashed again, brightening her closed eyelids red, and thunder split the sky.

Roni kept expecting a strange sensation from the touch of the rifters. Perhaps an electric tingle or a static rise or even something as simple as pressure like a hand placed on her back. She felt nothing. The only indication that she had succeeded — the golem moved once again.

She fluttered her eyes open as the golem entered the narthex. The doors leading into the nave were wide open, and a weird, blasphemous service took place. Purple-black balls of smoke filled the pews, the walls, the air, all the way to the vaulted ceiling. A curved tunnel cut through the mass of creatures, leading from the nave straight down to the apse like some twisted wedding pathway formed from friends reaching out to each other.

Roni thought that if the nuns had been around to see this, they would have certainly believed it to be the hand of their Lord. To her, she saw the results of the rift beneath the floor. Like magnets moving metal shavings into odd shapes, the energy from the rift forced these creatures into this strange configuration.

Their faceless bodies pivoted and turned, and with each movement, she thought that surely, they would see her now. They would attack full force, rip apart the stone golem protecting her, and then tear her skin from her bones. She could see it as if it had already happened.

Tightening her hand around Gram's rosary, she fought the urge to scream. Her bladder suddenly decided to put pressure on her abdomen. At least that provided her with something else to focus on. No way would she allow her bladder to let loose.

The golem turned to the right and headed for the spiral staircase leading below. Sully believed it would have little problem navigating the narrow stairs — its body was only slightly larger than Roni's. If it could not succeed at the task, it would back up, leave the church, and enter through the hole in the wall made by the previous golem.

"I'd rather use the stairs," Sully had said. "If the creatures do not react to you being inside the stone, I don't want to give any indication of what we are up to. Coming in through the hole which was the site of the previous attack might tip them off. That is, if they think in any logical way."

That was the thing. They had no idea how these creatures thought. The things lacked eyes yet sensed the world around them to some extent. They lacked mouths, they lacked arms, they lacked anything of substance yet had caused devastating harm already.

But Sully's golem-building skills proved their excellence. The golem navigated the spiral staircase with ease, and in moments, Roni found herself standing before the rift.

The orange-red swirls continued in their mesmerizing fashion, and rifters popped out sporadically. But the rapid-fire force which Roni had witnessed earlier had ceased. Those rifters that did emerge quickly floated upward, seeping through the cracks in the ceiling, to join their brethren in the nave.

For the most part, the basement was empty. Roni knew that would not last for long. Soon, Elliot's magic would take hold and she would have to make her move. But all indications suggested Elliot had yet to accomplish his task. She had to wait — again.

Speaking through shivering breaths, keeping her voice barely audible, she said, "Maria?"

She counted to ten, hoping to feel an answer. Nothing came.

"I know you can hear me. I know you haven't left yet. It's okay if you don't want to talk to me. I understand. I am not really part of your life. In some strange way, I'm from your future — a possible future. Except that even that's not it really. But we are connected — we are blood.

"I don't know what to think of you. But if I'm going to die today, then you need to know a few things. Mostly, I forgive you. Not you, of course, but the other you — the one that lived on to become my mother. I forgive you for leaving me and leaving me so empty. I forgive you for hiding this world from me. I forgive you for everything.

"As kids we see our parents as figures — not quite human. But you are. You have your faults and your desires and you made so many mistakes. I spent too much time wishing things were different, wanting to find my lost time as if that might fill the lost things within me. But that's not true. Here I stand, with part of you filling me right now, yet I'm every bit as scared as I would've been without you. I'm every bit as empty.

"If I survive this, then you should know that I love you, I forgive you, and I will figure out how to move on.

"My lost time — I'll still find it. But if a part of you could not fulfill me, then no memory will either. I'm going to find that lost time because Dad is still alive. He needs me. And I need to understand who he is.

"I'm going to find that lost time not to fill my past but to help forge my future."

Roni waited for the physical reaction from Maria but none came. That was okay. Saying those words, articulating those thoughts and feelings — that was what mattered.

"Besides, I give myself a twenty-percent chance of surviving this."

Part of her thought her odds were even worse.

The colors in the rift faded. Subtle at first, and Roni could not quite believe it. But Elliot had told her that would be the sign. That his power to amplify Maria's force would drain from the rift — and in that way, they would overload it. Simple enough.

Now for the hard part.

"Maria, please tell me, are you ready?"

Roni expected no answer, but the familiar warm flush invaded her skin. She started at the sensation, then settled into a comforting grin.

"Okay." She thought she should say more but the words did not come.

With a few awkward motions, she pulled her left arm free from the rock surrounding it like removing her arm from the sleeve of a heavy sweater. She then performed the same series of motions with her right arm. Against her belly, she brought her hands together.

Here we go. One… Two… Three…

Roni ripped the golem paper in two. And the rocks tumbled away. The weight lifted from her body and the rain-soaked air breezing in through the hole in the wall cooled her skin. She had to step over the small pile of rubble surrounding her but she managed.

As she approached the rift, as she felt its energy pulling from her even as Elliot pulled from it, the rifters seeped through the ceiling. They sensed her presence now.

"You're too late," she said, and without giving herself time to alter course, stepped into the rift.

CHAPTER 23

At the age of eleven, Roni and her friends found great amusement in going to the mall and walking up the down escalator at the correct pace so that they never changed position. Being inside the rift felt the same way. The rift tried to pull her down but Elliot's power kept her in the same spot. She felt motion yet remained motionless. And this struggle of energy thinned the rift walls so that she could see the rifters amassing in the basement.

A few of the daring purple-black smoke balls attempted to attack her. They barreled through only to be disintegrated the moment they touched her skin. She watched as the dark curls of smoke dissipated around her, and she wondered if it was her presence in the rift or that of Maria's which caused such destructive power. Another attacked her and died for the effort.

But this did not stop them. Like ants or locusts, these creatures understood the power that came from attrition. They continued to shove through the rift and slammed into her body. It did not hurt her, not much worse than a mosquito bite, but it most certainly killed them. Yet they continued to come.

Over time, like a water drip cutting through a stone, they would rip into her. The protection Elliot provided would not last forever. Neither would Maria. When those energies left, Roni knew what would happen to her — she had seen these creatures shred Sister Mary and Sister Claudia.

The air heated up around her, becoming like a bad sunburn. Still more rifters bulleted towards her. The bright orange air darkened with their purple corpses.

"Maria! Now!" The words scratched Roni's throat but she repeated them — louder each time.

All the noise and stress spun Roni's head in throbbing pain. She turned in a circle, and in every direction, she saw a greater number of rifters than before. They filled every location upon which her eye fell. They surrounded the rift and consumed all available space in the basement.

"Maria," she called again though slightly weaker.

When she thought to call out a third time, her feet lifted off the floor. The floor? Because she did not expect the floor within the rift. Because there wasn't one. The only floor around her was that of the church basement.

Roni watched as the basement ceiling came closer. She felt as if a coarse rope had been wrapped around her chest, lifting her up and forcing her arms out like wings. She was in the rift and the church simultaneously, fragmented between worlds, held in place by the same forces that threatened her.

Glancing down, the floor filled in beneath her with purple and black. It bubbled like a dark cauldron.

Please, Roni thought, *please Maria. Leave my body. Do what we came here to do.*

She would never understand why those thoughts worked when all her pleading and calling out had failed before. When she would think back upon this day, Roni always came to the same conclusion — that she had never understood Maria nor could she have. The trauma that girl had suffered, the oddities she had experienced, the frozen time and splitting from within herself — these were not experiences another human being could relate to. Whatever spurred Maria into action at that moment, Roni knew that she could never duplicate it.

Like tearing a hundred bandages off simultaneously, Maria stripped free. Roni shrieked. With both the speed of a bomb blast and the stillness of the rift's pulse, Roni experienced Maria's energy pouring out and amplified by Elliot.

A golden sunburst spread across the church. Wherever it touched a rifter, only wisps of gray smoke remained. Thousands of the creatures incinerated in seconds. Roni watched them slowly fall apart.

The distortion of time twisted her stomach even as it hypnotized her mind. The ceiling above her cracked apart, the wood floor of the nave giving way to the energy blast that had been Roni and Maria.

As time reconnected with itself to flow normally, Roni's body rose higher in the air. She slipped through the opening and lifted into the main part of the church.

The rifters soared away from her, the energy pulsing from her body repelling them. They pressed against the church walls like rats abandoning a sinking ship. But they could no longer slide through the stone. The walls glowed golden. They were stuck.

Roni's stomach clenched and her mouth opened. She expected to throw up but instead another blast of golden light erupted from her. It spread out in all directions, decimating the creatures that remained.

The sunburnt feeling on her skin worsened. She smelled burning flesh. Further in the distance, further than she could imagine, she heard a tinny voice. Almost like a coyote howling through a radio on a mountain miles away. But she heard it nonetheless. Calling her name.

... *roni* ...

The orange and red of the rift had gone. The purple and black had disappeared. All that remained was golden light.

And that distant voice. Calling her name.

... *roni* ...

A thin line of dark swiped across her field of vision. Again, she heard her name and again she saw the line. She tried to move her hand but it refused to obey her.

Roni felt as if she were once again surrounded by the stone golem — except this time it was golden light not gray rocks. This time, it was Maria. And the pressure upon her skin hurt. Burned.

Let go of me, she pleaded, but suspected Maria would never listen to her again.

Once more she heard that distant call and saw that gray line appear. This time she understood — *Gram.*

Thinking the name cleared her eyes. Roni saw Gram standing down on the nave floor, twirling a chain at her side. The walls of the church crumbled around her. Bits of stained-glass cracked and fell. Gram remained standing in place throwing her chain at Roni, all of her being focused on trying to lasso her granddaughter.

As the chain soared through the air once more, Roni watched it head directly for her. Except it diverted at the last moment as if it had been swatted aside by an invisible hand. It passed before her eyes like it had each time previously.

Gram gazed up at Roni, the desperation consumed the air between them. Roni tried to call out, try to tell Gram to give it another go. No words would leave her mouth.

Calling her name again, Gram twirled her chain once more. But she sounded so far away — *roni.*

Roni closed her eyes. She focused all of her mind and energy into her right arm. And she felt it — that sickly-sweet energy. Maria. The last vestiges of her existence, the part of her that had kept her alive all those years in the rift, the will that refused to end.

Maria did not mean to harm her — at least, Roni did not think so — but she also intended to keep Roni. Perhaps Maria did not want to let go of her connection to her past, even if that meant hurting Roni. Perhaps she only wanted to go on existing, no matter the consequences, no matter what the rest of her desired.

With every fiber of mental strength she possessed, Roni pushed Maria away and reached toward Gram. And she listened. And she waited.

When she heard Gram call her name once more — *roni* — she snapped her eyes open. The chain sailed towards her, and as it had each time before, it curved away. Except this time Roni thrust all of her thoughts into her right hand. The fingers flipped open and the rosary beads stretched out — far enough to make contact with the chain.

Gram paused, astonished at her success as the chain snapped onto the beads. But she was a professional of the Parallel Society. She wouldn't waste time. Within the next second, she pulled Roni as she backed up towards the exit.

Time threatened to rip apart again. Roni sensed it splitting down her mind. This would be the last time. If Maria held too tight, Roni did not think she would ever get free.

Please, Roni thought with all the firm compassion she could summon. *We love you. But it's time for you to leave. It's time for you to rest.*

Still, Maria held on.

Let me go! Let yourself go! You … you're not my mother. You're not even Gram's daughter. You need to find your own life, your own future, your own peace.

Words continued to tumble out of Roni like a riffing poet. She did not think her pleading would amount to anything, but then she felt a cold chill slip out of her spine. It did not hurt — it was like having an icy hand slowly remove itself.

And she was free.

Two arms, two thick arms Roni knew so well, wrapped around her. Gram kissed her face as she lugged Roni out of the church. Raindrops pelted them, and Roni's legs refused to help, but Gram kept dragging her to safety.

Sitting on the ground with her back against the rental car, Roni watched as Sully and Elliot and Gram eased next to her. Three loud cracks like dynamite signaled the end of the church. In a plume of stone and debris, the old building crumbled to the ground.

As the sound quieted and only the patter of rain remained, Sully returned to his feet and set his hands on his hips. "Well, this is going to take some explaining. Governments can be a real pain in the tush." He turned toward the group. "Is everyone okay?"

All eyes rested on Roni. She gazed back at them. "Me? I feel fine. Absolutely —"

Her head grew heavy and rolled toward the ground as her eyes closed.

CHAPTER 24

Despite her exhaustion, Roni knew sleep would not be coming anytime during the flight home. The boys had no trouble, though. Elliot's serene face across the aisle exuded peacefulness while Sully's deep snores could be heard from several rows back. Gram sat next to Roni, reading her Bible while taking surreptitious glances in Roni's direction.

For the first few hours, Roni buried her attentions in her journal. She detailed the events at the Abbey as best as memory served her, recording all the names, creatures, experiences, everything. She made sure to include that after the collapse of the church, Elliot spent over an hour casting for any sign of Maria, the creatures, or the rift itself. They were all gone. Maria had been set free, the creatures had all been consumed by the rift, and the rift — well, the rift had been closed. Not contained in a book, not stabilized in a state of half-existence, but actually closed. To the best of Roni's limited knowledge, no rift had ever been closed before.

She wrote on about her thoughts and feelings concerning the work they did and how close she had come to losing her life. Not only was it her duty as the researcher and librarian of the Parallel Society to record this information for future Society members to use, but she found it therapeutic. If she did not spew these thoughts onto the page now, she would spend many years ahead of her in expensive therapy.

Later, after a bland and overpriced sandwich, Roni shifted in her narrow seat to face Gram. They had spoken little about Maria since leaving the Abbey, and she had no intention of starting now. However, thinking through all that had transpired so she could write it down, several questions poked at her mind.

Gram leaned her head towards Roni. "Out with it. Whatever's got you thinking, you're going to burst if you don't ask."

With an embarrassed chuckle, Roni said, "I want to ask you about my dad. I've always thought he ended up in a mental hospital because of the car accident, because of losing her. But that isn't true, is it?"

"Oh, I don't know. Your father was always tight-lipped about the thoughts in his head. I do know that he lost touch with reality when your mother died. That was the timing of it, and that was the easiest answer for you to understand at such a young age."

"But he knew about the Parallel Society."

"No, he didn't." Gram spoke as if the very idea fouled the food in her stomach.

Roni wanted to argue, wanted to point out that she had spoken with him at length, and that he had indicated knowledge of the real world, of the Parallel Society, of everything. Perhaps Mom had told him. Perhaps he knew about Roni's past and therefore what the future held for her.

But she held back. Gram had not experienced the same things she had at the Abbey. While Roni had little problem letting go of the past and her lost time — at least, in terms of solving that mystery and filling the void — Gram would not see it the same way. To her, the past had been a secret she carefully guarded. Whether to protect Roni or to protect the Parallel Society or to protect herself, Roni did not know.

And, Roni thought, *she really does care.* The past was only important in how it affected the future. That was why she needed answers about her dad.

"I don't mean to speak ill," Gram said, "but have you ever considered the possibility that your father's mental illness does not come from any trauma caused by your mother, me, or any of this? Perhaps, his mental illness is no different than anybody else's. Perhaps his brain's wires simply are not functioning properly."

"I'll have to think about that." Roni said it to appease Gram, but neither of them appeared to believe the words much.

She returned to her journal, reading over all she had written in the last few months. Her father had warned her over a year ago that something dark and dangerous had begun. She did not give it too much credence back then, but after the Abbey, she wondered.

The rift had been stabilized for centuries, yet it suddenly changed its behavior. Of course, her mishandling of the situation and using the old book caused much of it — but what if there were other forces also at work?

When she got home, she would have to hit the books. Research was her skill for the Parallel Society and she needed to use it now more than ever. But that awaited her at home. And while she had made the choice not to dwell on her past, she saw no harm in spending a few moments basking in the warmth of her success.

They had saved the Earth from an invasion, released Maria from her prison, and closed a rift. Not bad for a couple days work.

About the Author

Stuart Jaffe is the madman behind *The Max Porter Paranormal Mysteries,* the *Nathan K* thrillers, *The Ridnight Mysteries,* the *Parallel Society* novels, *The Malja Chronicles, The Bluesman, Founders, Real Magic,* and much more. He trained in martial arts for over a decade until a knee injury ended that practice. Now, he plays lead guitar in a local blues band, *The Bootleggers*, and enjoys life on a small farm in rural North Carolina. For those who have kept count in the past, I'm no longer listing the animals. As we've gotten older, we don't keep the zoo we once did, and it seems silly to list a more normal grouping of pets. So, yeah, we got dogs and cats and chickens (and a couple other things). Still, the chickens will not be permitted in the house.

For more information about Stuart and his books, please visit *www.stuartjaffe.com*